I0634798

See No Evil

MICHAEL RIDPATH

COUNTY
LIBRARY

F/2039440

MICHAEL JOSEPH
an imprint of
PENGUIN BOOKS

MICHAEL JOSEPH

Published by the Penguin Group
Penguin Books Ltd, 80 Strand, London WC2R ORL, England
Penguin Group (USA) Inc., 375 Hudson Street, New York, New York 10014, USA
Penguin Group (Canada), 90 Eglinton Avenue East, Suite 700, Toronto, Ontario, Canada M4P 2Y3
(a division of Pearson Penguin Canada Inc.)
Penguin Ireland, 25 St Stephen's Green, Dublin 2, Ireland (a division of Penguin Books Ltd)
Penguin Group (Australia), 250 Camberwell Road,
Camberwell, Victoria 3124, Australia (a division of Pearson Australia Group Pty Ltd)
Penguin Books India Pvt Ltd, 11 Community Centre,
Panchsheel Park, New Delhi – 110 017, India
Penguin Group (NZ), cnr Airborne and Rosedale Roads, Albany,
Auckland 1310, New Zealand (a division of Pearson New Zealand Ltd)
Penguin Books (South Africa) (Pty) Ltd, 24 Sturdee Avenue,
Rosebank, Johannesburg 2196, South Africa

Penguin Books Ltd, Registered Offices: 80 Strand, London WC2R ORL, England

www.penguin.com

First published 2006

2

Copyright © Michael Ridpath, 2006

The moral right of the author has been asserted

All rights reserved
Without limiting the rights under copyright
reserved above, no part of this publication may be
reproduced, stored in or introduced into a retrieval system,
or transmitted, in any form or by any means (electronic, mechanical,
photocopying, recording or otherwise), without the prior
written permission of both the copyright owner and
the above publisher of this book

Set in 13.5/16 pt Monotype Garamond
Typeset by Rowland Phototypesetting Ltd, Bury St Edmunds, Suffolk
Printed in Great Britain by Clays Ltd, St Ives plc

A CIP catalogue record for this book is available from the British Library

ISBN-13: 978–0–718–14677–1
ISBN-10: 0–718–14677–8

For Barbara

I

June 18, 1988

I'm scared. There, I've written it. After twenty minutes staring at the empty page trying to think of a way to begin this diary, I've realized I can't start until I get this down.

I'm scared.

Of whom? Of what? Of Neels, for sure. When he lost his temper last night and clenched those meaty fists, for a moment I thought he was going to strike me, more than that, beat the life out of me. But what scares me most about Neels is that I'm losing him. Losing him and I don't know why.

I'm scared of South Africa, or maybe for South Africa. I'm scared of what white is doing to black and black is doing to white. Like Neels, I'm scared the whole place will go up in flames at any moment. And I'm scared of myself, of what's happening to me.

I feel all alone, alone in the middle of my family. Neels spends so much time in the States now. Caroline is sweet, but she's just twelve and such a quiet little thing. I only realized how much I wanted Todd back home when I got that letter from him today telling me he wasn't coming. He's planning to stay in Hampshire with some friends from school over the summer vacation. What is my son doing thousands of miles away in a boarding school in England? And why do I need him so much?

I thought it would help to write it all down. Somehow I need to figure out who I am, what I'm going to do. I bought this fancy notebook in Paris last year. It's black moleskin, the kind of notebook Bruce Chatwin carried across Africa and Australia. It's begging to be filled with great thoughts and insights, but I don't have any of those. I don't know what I think. I didn't want to use a journalist's spiral notebook. I'm not a journalist anymore. So what am I? Wife? Mother? Stepmother? Prisoner? Prisoner of my ideals? Prisoner of my fears?

All questions, no answers.

Goddammit to hell.

2

It was quiet at Langthorpe Aerodrome. There was no roar of aircraft engines running up twenty yards outside the flying school, nor whine of those same engines in the circuit a thousand feet above. The only sound was the gentle plink of recently deposited rain water as it fell in fat irregular drops from the gutters and trees. The air was damp, cold and still. The lurid orange windsock hung limp by the fire truck. A grey mass of cloud, scarcely able to hold its many tons of tiny water droplets, pressed its great weight down on to the runway and the line of poplars on the far side. The sea, seven miles to the north, was invisible. So too was the round church tower of the village of Langthorpe, barely half a mile distant.

Alex Calder peered vainly at the cloud for any sign of sun. According to the weather forecast the slow-moving cold front was supposed to clear at any moment, leaving behind the newly washed brilliant blue skies and tufts of cloud through which it was such a joy to fly. But that wasn't going to happen, at least not for the next couple of hours, so Calder sent home the student who had been hovering around the reception area hoping that part of his scheduled lesson on 'recovery from unusual attitudes' could be salvaged.

There was a pile of recent 'Notices to Airmen' from the Civil Aviation Authority to be gone through, but Calder couldn't resist bringing up the Spreadfinex page on his computer. Numbers flashed up blue and red, familiar numbers, representing the bond markets of the United States, Britain, Japan and the euro zone. There was a time when Calder had been immersed in these numbers ten hours a day, buying and selling millions of dollars of bonds on behalf of his employer, Bloomfield Weiss, a large American investment bank. But two years previously he had quit that world in disgust and together with a partner had bought the aerodrome and its attached flying school. He still missed it: the thrill of pitting his wits against the market, of watching those winking figures as they indicated losses transformed to profit. Throwing his little red Pitts Special aerobatic biplane around the sky went some distance towards slaking his thirst for risk, but not far enough. So in the last few months he had begun to bet on the direction of the bond markets, using an internet spread-betting service. It was almost like the real thing, except he no longer had an edge over the market, he knew he was more likely to lose than to win and the sums he was playing with were thousands of pounds of his own money rather than millions of dollars of someone else's.

That morning he was down fifteen hundred quid on a bet he had made that US bond prices would rise. They hadn't. Yet. He was confident that they would. Perhaps he should bet a little more?

He glanced up as he heard footsteps along the path outside his window. A man and a woman strolled by. The man was young, tall and confident. And the woman . . .

Calder grinned and leaped to his feet. He met them as they entered the reception area. When the woman saw Calder her face lit up and she unhooked her arm from her companion's and embraced him.

'Kim, I can't believe it,' Calder said. 'I haven't seen you for –'

'Ten years,' the woman said.

Calder looked at her. She had changed very little. Kim O'Connell's Irish ancestry had always been obvious, with her white skin, jet-black hair and grey eyes. The hair was cut shorter and the unruly curls had been tamed, faint lines etched the edges of her mouth and eyes, but the smile was there, that warm, generous, flirtatious smile that she bestowed on everyone and anyone.

'You're staring,' she said. 'Do I pass?'

'Sorry,' Calder said. 'It was just so unexpected. But it's good to see you!'

'This is my husband, Todd.'

'Hi, Alex, how are you?' The man thrust out a hand and shook Calder's firmly. He was a couple of inches taller than Calder, with a square jaw, blond hair brushed back from his forehead and bright blue eyes. He was dressed in a turtle-neck, chinos and an expensive suede jacket. Handsome. Definitely handsome. But Calder would have expected nothing less from Kim.

'I'd heard you got married,' he said.

'Of course you had. We invited you to the wedding!'

'Yeah. Sorry I couldn't come. I think I was working in New York at the time.'

'The wedding was in Philadelphia! Pathetic, Alex.'

Calder smiled and shrugged. 'Well, I'm sorry I missed it.'

'What about you? Is there a girlfriend? A wife? Little flying Calders?'

Calder tried not to wince as he thought about Sandy. The row that they had had on the phone following his disastrous trip to New York to see her was still raw. 'No,' he said flatly.

Kim's eyes narrowed. Calder could see her curiosity was piqued, but she decided not to pursue it.

'Look, are you hungry?' he said. 'It's just about lunchtime and there's a nice pub in the village I live in. It's not far.'

He glanced at the sky; if anything it was pressing lower on the airfield. 'Not much is going to happen here for a while.'

There wasn't room for them all to fit into Calder's Maserati so they hopped into Todd and Kim's hired car and Calder directed them through the village of Langthorpe and north towards the sea and Hanham Staithe. Kim rattled on about their drive to Norfolk from her parents' house in Liverpool. He had forgotten how much she talked, but he noticed that the Liverpudlian tinge to her accent he remembered from university had been replaced with a hint of American.

Ten minutes later they were all installed in the Admiral Nelson, an ancient white stone pub, mostly empty on a weekday lunchtime. It overlooked the pot-holed hard, newly inundated with rainwater from above and seawater from below. A variety of vessels, sailing dinghies, small fishing boats and even a couple of thirty-foot yachts strained against their moorings in the creek as they were thrust upstream by the flooding tide. The marsh beyond brooded under the dark clouds. Calder ordered drinks at the bar, a pint of local bitter for Todd, a half of cider for Kim and a ginger beer for himself: there was still a possibility he might be able to fly that afternoon.

Of course he knew Kim had got married. And whom she had married, even if he hadn't recalled her husband's first name. Todd was the son of Cornelius van Zyl, a newspaper tycoon originally from South Africa who owned the *Herald,* a British mid-market tabloid, and other newspapers in America and elsewhere. The wedding had caused a stir among the group of friends from Cambridge which Calder kept up with, and although some of them had seen Kim since then, Calder hadn't. Which was a shame. They had been good friends at university, sharing an overcrowded student house in the Kite in their second year.

'So what brings you to Norfolk?' Calder asked as he returned to their table with the drinks.

'We were over in England visiting with Kim's folks,' Todd said, 'and we figured we would drop in and see you on the way back down to London.' His accent was odd, almost standard English, but with traces of American and South African. Of course, Norfolk was nowhere near a straight line from Liverpool to London, but no doubt Calder would find out what they wanted later.

'So you left the City?' Kim asked. 'Last time I saw you you'd just joined Bloomfield Weiss.'

'Yes,' said Calder. 'I stuck it out until a couple of years ago. I enjoyed the bond trading, and I was pretty good at it too, but the office politics got a bit much for me.'

'We read about that business with the hedge fund,' Todd said. 'Kim got all excited that she knew you. It sounded like quite a mess.'

'It was,' Calder said. Calder had uncovered a scandal the previous year involving Bloomfield Weiss and a large hedge fund that had connived with the investment bank to hide losses of hundreds of millions of dollars. A woman who worked for Calder had been killed as a result. When the scandal eventually saw the light of day Calder had received his fifteen minutes of fame. People still occasionally spoke to him about it.

'And now you're running this flying school?' Kim said.

'With my business partner, Jerry. It's going quite well, we're building up a nice reputation. But it's a struggle just to break even.'

'Did you think about going back to the RAF? I loved the idea of you whizzing about the sky dropping bombs and things. It was so you.'

'They wouldn't let me fly fast jets any more. I injured my

spine ejecting, which is why I left. I suppose I could try and join an airline or something, but I like running my own show.'

'You've got some nice airplanes there,' Todd said. 'What was that big single-engined plane with the red star on the side?'

'Oh, that. It's a Yak. A Yak-11, made in 1956. The insignia is from the old Russian air force. It's great to fly.'

'Looks cool.'

'I'd take you up if the weather wasn't so bad.'

Todd's interest perked up. Kim frowned. Calder was amused to see Kim cast in the role of worried wife.

'What about you?' he said to her. 'You were off to Harvard to do an MBA.'

'That's where I met Todd. Then I worked for a management consultancy in Philadelphia. I usually don't admit it but I rather enjoyed myself. Lots of telling people what to do and then waltzing off before you see the damage you've caused. But now we live in a little town in New Hampshire. Todd teaches English at a boys' school there. And I work in the local hospital administering things.'

There was the tiniest tinge of resentment as Kim said this. Not enough to be rude or disloyal, but just enough for Calder to pick up. And for Todd, of course, who stiffened slightly.

'We decided to get out of the race,' Todd said. 'I was working for my father –'

'Todd just couldn't stand it,' Kim interrupted. 'He realized the newspaper business just wasn't what he wanted to do. Somerford is a beautiful little town and we love it there.'

Calder couldn't quite see Kim getting out of the rat race. She was more the type to elbow herself to the front. She glanced at him quickly, seemed to read his thoughts, then moved a hand on to her husband's as if to reaffirm her loyalty. It was funny how he could still tell what she was thinking all these years later.

Calder picked up the menu. 'Shall we order something? The fish here is usually delicious. It's all caught locally.'

They ordered, then Calder leaned back in his chair. 'So, what's up?'

Kim and Todd exchanged glances. 'Actually, we wondered if you could help us with something,' she began.

'I hope so,' Calder smiled.

'It's to do with Bloomfield Weiss.'

Calder's smile disappeared.

Kim noticed, but ploughed on. 'You probably remember who Todd's father is?'

'Yes, I do,' Calder admitted.

'Right. Well, Todd's mother, Martha, was American. They lived in South Africa, near Cape Town. When Todd was about sixteen she was killed in a game reserve near the Kruger Park in the north of the country. The authorities said she was murdered by guerrillas but Todd has never believed that, have you, darling?' Kim touched her husband's sleeve.

'How long ago was this?' Calder asked.

'In 1988,' Todd said. 'When South Africa was still under apartheid rule.' He hesitated, glanced at Calder, and then went on. 'I was at boarding school in England at the time. My mom and dad were going through a difficult patch, the worst I'd seen by a long way. Things had been really tense the last time I was home and that was the main reason I arranged to spend part of that summer holiday staying with a friend in England. Mom was unhappy about that.

'The fights got worse and Mom decided to go off by herself to a private game farm near the Kruger Park for the weekend. It's a bit of a mystery why she chose that particular reserve; it was a place called Kupugani and she'd never been there before.'

Todd swallowed. Kim's hand tightened on her husband's arm. Todd was staring into his beer, seemingly unaware of her or Calder. 'I pestered my father until he told me what happened. They put her up in a cottage a few hundred yards away from the main camp. It was the morning, she was alone in bed and the other guests had gone off on the morning game drive.' He swallowed again.

'You don't have to tell Alex if you don't want to,' Kim said.

'No, that's OK, unless you don't want to hear it.' Todd glanced up at Calder. Calder could tell he wanted to talk.

'Go on.'

'The cottage was next to a dried-out river bed. Apparently, guerrillas used to come through the area after entering South Africa from Mozambique. If they were picked up they would claim they were refugees. The police said a group of them passed through Kupugani that day. They saw the cottage and Mom inside, and one of them fired through the window from the far side of the river bed. Mom was hit by three rounds in the chest. She was killed instantly.' His voice quivered and he paused to compose himself. 'I'm sorry. It's a long time ago and you'd think I was over it by now, but I don't see why anyone would want to do that to my mother. She was a wonderful woman. She believed in the struggle, in the abolition of apartheid; she always said that was one of the main reasons she married Dad and moved to South Africa.'

'But you don't think the guerrillas shot her?'

'No,' Todd said. 'It's too convenient. It wasn't just a random killing.'

'Martha knew someone was going to kill her,' Kim said.

'Or at least she had a strong suspicion someone was going to try.'

'How do you know this?' Calder asked.

'Martha's mother, Todd's grandmother, died a couple of months ago,' Kim said. 'Todd was looking through her papers when he found a letter to her from Martha. In it she says that she has discovered some information about Zyl News which if it came to light would destroy everything. She seems very frightened. She also mentions a diary which she wants her mother to find and keep safe. We . . .' Kim paused and glanced at her husband. 'We think that this information might give us a better idea of why she was killed and who killed her.'

'Can't you just ask Cornelius van Zyl?'

'We have. Or at least Todd has. And other members of his family. But none of them seems to know anything. And if they do, they aren't saying.'

'I think my dad has tried to erase that whole period from his memory,' Todd said. 'I'm sure he feels guilty about all the fights they had. But I can't do that. I need to know what happened to her.'

'So you have no idea what the information referred to in this letter is?' Calder asked.

'No,' said Kim. 'But Martha did mention a man she had discussed it with. He's a banker. A banker who works for Bloomfield Weiss.'

'I see,' said Calder. 'You want me to talk to this person?'

'Todd's tried,' said Kim. 'But he won't agree to meet him and he doesn't even return his phone calls.'

'Can't your father pull strings?'

'Dad's not quite comfortable –'

'He could but he won't,' Kim interrupted. 'But I told Todd I was sure you could help us. This banker works in

London. You probably know him, and if you don't, you would know someone who does. Also, I know I can trust you to be careful with whatever you find out.' Kim smiled at Calder in encouragement.

'We read about what you did to uncover the scandal with that hedge fund,' Todd said. 'This is just a case of asking a couple of questions and getting some answers.'

'Who's the banker?' Calder asked.

'Benton Davis,' said Kim.

Calder closed his eyes. When he opened them, Kim was watching his face with concern.

'You do know him?' she said. 'I can tell you know him!'

Calder nodded. 'I do. And I'm afraid I can't help you.'

Kim frowned. She glanced at Todd, who gave the tiniest of shrugs. Calder had the feeling that she had assured her husband of his assistance and he had disappointed her. 'May I ask why?' she said. 'It would just be a question of calling him up and going to London to see him.'

Calder took a deep breath. 'Benton Davis is the head of Bloomfield Weiss's London office. He was in charge when I resigned from there a couple of years ago. Jennifer Tan, a woman who worked for me, had brought a sexual harassment case against the firm. They made her life hell, and so she quit. She died soon after, falling from a sixth-floor window. At first it looked like suicide: I held Benton responsible, amongst others. That's why I left the firm. It turned out she had actually been murdered, but I still blame Benton for the way she was treated, and he knows that. There's no love lost between us; I think the chances of him talking to me are nil. Besides which, I've left all that behind me, and I don't want to go back to it.'

'The poor woman!' Kim said indignantly. 'That's a terrible story. What a bastard.'

'What about just giving him a call and asking him to see us?' Todd said.

Calder shook his head. 'Even if I did, he wouldn't take any notice. Can't you tell all this to the police?'

'This was an unexplained death in South Africa in the 1980s,' Kim said. 'There were hundreds of those. Thousands.'

'Anything you can do would be really appreciated,' Todd said. 'I was very fond of my mother – that's a dumb thing to say, everyone's fond of their mother – but I was away at school in England when she died. I hadn't seen her for four months. I wasn't there. I know it's stupid, but I kind of blame myself for that. And I have no idea why she died. It was obvious at the time that the authorities were covering something up, but what? And why? Perhaps the South African security police killed her. Or somebody else. My family has been desperate to bury it all in the past, but that's not right. We have to know the truth. *I* have to know the truth.'

Calder looked at the couple. Their disappointment was plain. They had come a long way to see him. And he sympathized with Todd. His own mother had died at about the same stage in his life. That was a road accident, a head-on collision with a farm worker who had had too much to drink, but Calder too had in some way felt responsible. She had been rushing to pick him up from school after he had missed the bus. His life had never been the same since. And if his own mother had been murdered he wouldn't have rested until he had found out why. He was tempted to offer to help.

But Benton Davis? The man at the very heart of all the scheming manipulation he so much detested at Bloomfield Weiss. No. No, he couldn't do it. There was no point in even trying.

'I'm sorry,' he said.

The food came, and after a couple of awkward minutes the conversation picked up. Todd was an affable, pleasant guy, seemingly unspoilt by all the advantages with which he had been born. Calder found himself warming to him. And Kim, well Kim was as lively as she always had been, and she had that smile, that you-are-the-most-important-person-in-the-world smile, which she flashed at him every few minutes and which sparked a familiar flicker of excitement every time, just as it had all those years ago. To Calder's disappointment Kim had always been someone else's girlfriend. At university that someone else had invariably turned out to be a good-looking, charming bastard. But from what Calder could see that wasn't the case with Todd. And he was pleased. Kim deserved to have someone who treated her well.

Lunch finished, they stepped outside into the small pub car park. The creek had swollen with the tide; its waters now reached halfway up the hard. The clouds were still low and grey: no chance of any more flying that day.

Calder was still feeling bad about his refusal to help. 'I tell you what, Todd. The weather's supposed to get even worse tomorrow and stay bad until the weekend. But if you're around next week and it's cleared up, I can take you up in the Yak. Show you a bit of Norfolk from the air.'

Todd grinned. 'I'd love to do that,' he said. He glanced at Kim, who looked doubtful. 'We're staying with my father in London for the next few days, flying back to the States next Wednesday. So, next Tuesday, maybe?'

'Great,' Calder said. 'Let's talk early Tuesday morning and see what the weather's doing.'

'Your guests from Bloomfield Weiss have arrived, Mr van Zyl.'

Cornelius looked up from his desk as Nimrod stood at the entrance to his rather grand study. Despite his dashing name, Nimrod was a small, wiry Xhosa with a lined face, watchful eyes and flashes of gold in his teeth, whose suits were always just a little too big for him. He had proved his loyalty over thirty years as driver, fixer and right-hand man, and he was the one relic of Cornelius's South African past that Cornelius was happy to keep around.

'Show them in.'

Cornelius grabbed a pad encased in a leather wallet and placed it at the centre of the long walnut table. Edwin was already sitting there, waiting, peering through his thick lenses at a sheet of paper bearing closely printed figures. Cornelius was in shirtsleeves, but his balding son's flabby body was squeezed into a three-piece suit, as always. Edwin was Cornelius's eldest child, a product of the first and least successful of his three marriages. The boy was diligent, and he worked hard, but he lacked the charisma or vision of his younger half-brother, Todd. Boy? He was in his mid-forties. But no matter how earnestly Edwin acted, and he did act very earnest, Cornelius could never take him seriously.

Cornelius himself was over seventy, but he stood tall and straight and precious little of the muscle he had carried when he had played centre three-quarter for the Western Province rugby team fifty years before had turned to fat. His square jaw, firm cheekbones and shock of white hair gave the impression of a block of granite, all the stronger for its age. In his youth, he had earned the nickname of 'the Dart' for his ability to pierce a defensive line of three-quarters, but it could equally well have been used to describe his mind, which if anything had sharpened over the years. He was good at what he did. And what he did was buy newspapers and make money out of them.

The bankers from Bloomfield Weiss had come to advise him on perhaps his boldest move so far, at least since he had taken over the *Herald* in the late 1980s. *The Times* was for sale. Its owner, Laxton Media, had bought the paper from an Australian group at the turn of the millennium, the only real-world property in a string of internet acquisitions. The canny Australian had taken cash, not shares, and since the dot-com boom had turned to bust, Laxton Media had limped along under the burden of its borrowings, holding out for an unrealistically high price for what had become the crown jewel of its portfolio. But pressure from creditors was building, and there were rumours that Laxton was close to an agreed sale to Beckwith Communications, a private company owned by Sir Evelyn Gill. Gill already owned the tabloid *Mercury,* but he had made no secret of the fact that he wanted to own a world-class property like *The Times*.

But so did Cornelius.

Three men came into the room. The first, and by far the most striking, was a tall, elegant black man of about fifty. He held out his hand to Cornelius.

'Benton, how are you?' Cornelius said, shaking it. 'I hope you don't mind meeting at my house. It's not that I don't trust the *Herald* people, I do completely, but the more secrecy we can preserve, the better.'

'Not at all,' Benton replied in a deep, rich American accent. 'I do love these Nash terraces. And what a wonderful view of the park!' He moved over to the window. From his first-floor study, Cornelius could indeed see over the hedges into Regent's Park, dotted with office workers and tourists enjoying the May sunshine. Benton scanned the room. Computer, printer, telephone and filing cabinets were carefully blended in with the paraphernalia of a gentleman's library: bookshelves holding leather-bound volumes, decanters of liquid in tints of amber and gold, sturdy but comfortable chairs and tables, a globe, some lithe bronzes and, scattered among shelves and alcoves, three or four replicas of old racing Bentleys. 'Is that really a Wyeth?' Benton asked, moving over to a picture of a pair of young boys wading through the long grass towards a wooden farmhouse on the brow of a hill. 'I don't remember that from the last time I was here.'

'I'm glad to see you haven't lost your eye for good art, Benton,' Cornelius said. 'We bought it last year.'

'Does it remind you of where you grew up?'

Cornelius snorted. 'Oudtshoorn is so dry it's almost desert. And they farm ostriches there. This was actually painted near our farm in Pennsylvania.' He paused. 'But there *is* something. The American wagon trains heading west; the Boers trekking over the veld. And the freedom to run around barefoot in the fields. I don't do much of that any more.' He smiled, and then turned to shake hands as Davis introduced the other two bankers, younger, smaller, more intense men. 'Now. Have a seat, gentlemen.'

They took their places opposite Cornelius and Edwin, the sunshine from the large window bouncing off the polished table between them.

Cornelius began, peering over his half-moon reading glasses at the bankers. The spectacles appeared tiny on his broad strong face and he used them more as a prop to look over than an aid to see through. 'We think we have an opportunity to snatch *The Times* from under Evelyn Gill's nose, if we can move quickly enough.' He paused to let the excitement build. He was talking about a deal, and a deal meant fees, and fees were what got these Bloomfield Weiss bankers excited. 'Edwin is pretty sure Gill is offering seven hundred million for *The Times* and the *Sunday Times*.'

'That's a full price,' Benton said.

'Yes. But it's not as unrealistic as the billion plus Laxton were talking about a few months ago. We think they're under pressure to do a clean, quick deal, which is why they are suddenly talking to Gill at the lower price. If we're going to shut him out I suggest we offer eight hundred and fifty. Cash. And we leave the offer open for seven days only. Laxton can take it or leave it.'

'They'll want to take it,' Benton said.

'I think they will,' Cornelius said. 'And I don't think Gill will be able to get hold of an extra hundred and fifty million in a week. But the big question is, can *we* get hold of that much money?'

Benton glanced at his colleagues. Cornelius knew it was they who would run the deal, but none the less it was good to see Benton Davis still around. Cornelius had always liked the man, ever since he had agreed to travel down to South Africa during apartheid to help with the acquisition of the *Herald,* the deal that had moved Cornelius up into the big league. For a black American, that had taken courage and some independence of mind.

The shorter and chubbier of the two, an Englishman called Dower, answered. 'I think we can, just. You have a hundred million of cash in Zyl News. We should be able to raise five hundred million in the bank-loan market fairly comfortably. That leaves three hundred and change we would need to raise from a high-yield bond issue.'

'Three hundred and change?' Cornelius said. 'Don't you mean two hundred and fifty?'

Dower shifted uncomfortably in his seat. Benton smiled. 'Fees, Cornelius, you mustn't forget the fees.'

'That much? That's over fifty million pounds!'

'At least that much,' Benton said. 'It's not just for us, it's for the banks, the lawyers, the printers, the accountants.' He shrugged. 'OK, most of it's for us, but if we can get a deal like this away, we deserve it.'

'Fifty million is outrageous,' said Cornelius, scowling. But he knew and the Bloomfield Weiss bankers knew that if they could pull off this deal Cornelius would be happy to pay. 'Could you get a junk-bond deal that size away?'

'Junk bond' was market slang for 'high-yield bond', a bond that paid a high rate of interest to investors because there was a high risk that the issuer would go bust. Even in its most prosperous moments Zyl News had always been in the high-risk category.

'At the moment, I think so,' Dower said. 'You've been issuing in the junk market for, what, twenty years? You've seen it go through good times and bad during that time. Well, we've been through a bad patch, but it looks like we're coming out the other side. Since we're funding a UK acquisition, we'd probably do a sterling deal. There's demand out there from the European fund managers, and not much product. The forward calendar looks thin: we only know of a couple of deals of any size coming to the sterling market and neither of them is in the media space.'

'I haven't missed an interest payment yet,' Cornelius said with defiant pride.

'That's true. But this is going to be tight.'

Cornelius glanced at Edwin. 'We know,' Edwin said. 'But Laxton have been mismanaging the paper for the last five years. There's plenty of duplication between *The Times* and the *Herald*. We think we can squeeze eleven million a year out of things like pre-press, advertising, newsprint, duplicated editorial services and getting rid of a layer of management. We plan to invest some of those savings in improving the editorial quality of the newspaper. We're sure we can increase circulation and win readers back from the competition. We've got a lot of ideas.'

'Good ideas,' Cornelius said. 'You know there's nothing I like to buy better than a badly managed paper. I've done this before.'

'You'll need to convince the banks and the investors,' Dower said. Then he smiled. 'But I'm sure you can manage that.'

Cornelius grinned. Investors loved him. So did bankers. No matter how high the targets he set himself, often written down in black and white in bond documentation and loan agreements, he met them. Always. It was true that at the price they were planning to pay, *The Times* would be a challenge. But it was one of the few truly classy newspaper properties in the world: there was the *New York Times*, of course, the *Washington Post,* the *Los Angeles Times* perhaps, *Le Monde, Le Figaro*, not many more. At seventy-two, Cornelius was nearing his last deal. Zyl News already owned over eighty newspapers in America, Britain and Australia, the two largest being the *Philadelphia Intelligencer*, which he had bought in the early eighties, and the *Herald*, but it lacked a flagship title. If he could snatch *The Times* from Evelyn Gill then Zyl News would be one of the two or three leading players in the world. He glanced at the petulant face of his son and heir, who was glaring belligerently at the investment bankers, and the warm glow of anticipation cooled. Then what would happen? That was another problem he would have to deal with.

'So,' he said. 'How long will it take to put the bid together?'

'The bank loan shouldn't be a problem, the banks will be falling over themselves to lend to you. Obviously it will take several weeks to put the bond issue together, but Bloomfield Weiss can underwrite a bridge loan to provide you with the funds until then. Under the takeover code you will need a letter from us saying we are committed to the funding.' Dower paused. 'We should be able to get all that together in seven days if we push it.'

'Excellent.'

'Subject to internal credit approval,' Dower added.

'What?' Cornelius glared at Dower.

'I'm sure you understand that a bridge loan of this size is a big risk for Bloomfield Weiss; we need to have it signed off at the highest level.'

'Harrison Brothers have been knocking at my door for the last couple of years desperate to deal with me. They say they can sign letters like that on the spot.'

'And that's exactly what I tell my competitors' clients,' Benton said with a grin. 'Don't worry, the approvals are only a formality. You'll have your letter in a week.'

Cornelius glanced at Benton. 'All right. But let me make one thing clear. I demand total commitment from my bankers. Once we're in a deal, we're in it together. No dithering, no waiting for conditions to improve, no delays while you bring one of your other clients to market. I want *The Times*, and what I want, I get. I will need one hundred per cent effort from you, is that understood?' Cornelius switched his stare back to Dower as he said this. Surprised and intimidated, the banker dithered.

'Of course we understand that, Cornelius,' Benton said with a smile. 'When has Bloomfield Weiss given you any-thing less?'

'Hmm,' Cornelius said. 'OK. Let's do it. If you need any more detailed information, ask Edwin. He's had our accountants prepare some initial due diligence for you. Don't go to anyone else in Zyl News. I want the surprise to be total.'

F/2039 440

COUNTY LIBRARY

Cornelius grinned as he thought of Evelyn Gill's reaction to his bid being topped. Cornelius had never liked the man. He posed as a hard-nosed Yorkshire businessman impatient with the egos and vanities of his editors. But Cornelius knew his rival. Evelyn Gill wanted *The Times* more than anything else in the world. And he wasn't going to get it.

Edwin saw the investment bankers out of the house, and came back upstairs to Cornelius's study.

Cornelius rubbed his hands. 'This is going to work. I can feel this is going to work.'

'I hope so,' said Edwin. 'But I don't see how we can make the numbers stack up.'

'Of course we can make them stack up,' Cornelius said impatiently. 'As long as we get the business right, the numbers will come out right as well. And there is so much we could do with *The Times*.'

'Pa?'

'Yes?'

'You know we spoke yesterday about Todd coming back into the business?'

'Yes.'

'I'm not sure he'll do it. And I'm not sure it's such a good idea if he does.'

Cornelius glared at his eldest son. 'He'll do it,' he said. 'And I'm going to tell him that tonight.' He sat down at his desk, placed his reading glasses on his nose and picked up a report. 'Haven't you got some numbers to crunch?'

Edwin was dismissed.

'Ah, there you are, Todd, it's so good to see you!' Cornelius strode into his expensively furnished drawing room and clapped his son on the shoulder. 'And you, Kim.' He turned to his daughter-in-law and embraced her. 'I'm sorry to leave you alone down here, but Edwin and I were working on something upstairs. Edwin has to go on to a dinner shortly, but he wanted to stop and say hello.'

Edwin was hovering behind his father at the doorway. He gave his half-brother a thin smile.

'I see Nimrod found you both a drink,' Cornelius went on. 'Is that the Meerlust?' Cornelius moved over to the sideboard and picked up the wine bottle to check the label. 'Not bad, is it, Todd?'

'It's very good,' said Todd.

'It's absolutely delicious,' added Kim with more enthusiasm. Despite the damp weather, she was wearing a blue summer dress in honour of her father-in-law and had even applied some lipstick and eye shadow, which had the effect of making her face seem even paler under her dark curls.

'If you don't mind, I'll have something stronger,' Cornelius said. He poured himself a brandy and Coke and Edwin a tomato juice with a squirt of Worcester sauce. 'Sit, please.' They all found armchairs and sofas to perch on. Despite the quality of the furniture and the paintings, the room had a cosy feel to it. Outside, dusk was falling over Regent's Park and Nimrod had drawn the heavy gold drapes. 'So you've just come from your parents, Kim? I hope they are well?'

'Oh, they're both in wonderful form, thanks,' Kim replied. 'Liverpool are through to the FA Cup final, which makes Dad very happy, and there seems to have been a complete breakdown in marital fidelity up and down our road, which has given my mother countless hours of amusement.'

'I must come and watch a game with your father sometime,' Cornelius said.

'He'd love that,' said Kim. 'And how's Jessica?'

Jessica Montgomery was Cornelius's third wife, the

daughter of a prominent Philadelphia family. They had been married twelve years. 'Oh, she's excited. She's just bought a new horse and she's at the farm schooling him now. I would have brought her with me to London, but this is very much a working trip, isn't it, Edwin?'

Edwin grunted. They all sipped their drinks.

'We drove down here via Norfolk,' Kim said. 'We dropped in on an old friend of mine who has bought an airfield up there.'

'Oh, yes? Did he take you up in anything?'

'It was too cloudy,' Todd said. 'But he promised to give me a ride in an old Yak provided the weather clears up before we go back to the States.'

'Sounds fun,' said Cornelius.

'I'm dubious,' Kim said. 'It's a very old plane. It looked to me like something out of a museum.'

'He knows Benton Davis,' Todd said.

Cornelius frowned. 'I hope that wasn't why you were seeing him.'

'I've been trying to see Davis ever since I arrived in England but he's refused to meet me. We thought perhaps Kim's friend might have better luck.'

'Who is this man?' Cornelius demanded.

'His name's Alex Calder,' Kim said. 'We were at university together. He used to be a bond trader at Bloomfield Weiss. Which is where Benton Davis still works, as I'm sure you know.'

'Did he say he would help?'

'Er . . .' Todd hesitated.

'We're working on him,' Kim said firmly.

Cornelius frowned into his drink.

'Do you still have contact with Benton Davis, Dad?' Todd asked.

Cornelius slammed his drink down on to the little table beside his chair. 'Yes, I do. But I've told you before, I'm not going to talk to him about that damned letter. Martha was killed nearly twenty years ago. That's all in the past, in a different world, and it's going to stay that way.'

'She was my mother, Dad,' Todd said quietly. 'I have a right to know how she died.'

'How she died? We all know how she died. She was shot, man!' Cornelius's voice was rising.

'Yes, but who shot her? And why?'

'Guerrillas. Guerrillas shot her.'

'You don't really believe that, do you, Dad?'

Cornelius was about to spit out an angry response when he controlled himself. 'I don't know who killed her, Todd. It could have been guerrillas, it could have been poachers, it might even have been the security police for all I know. But the thing is she's dead and there's nothing we can do to bring her back to life. You won't remember, but South Africa was a nightmare in the 1980s, hundreds of people dying every year, blacks and whites. I lost my brother. I lost my wife. You lost your mother. That's why I took you and Edwin and Caroline to America, to put all that behind us, to start again.'

'I need to know,' said Todd.

Cornelius stared at his son. Todd stared back.

Edwin coughed. 'I really must be going,' he said, carefully placing his half-drunk tomato juice on a side table. 'I'll be late.' He murmured goodbyes to Todd and Kim and left.

There was silence for a moment or two. They all sipped their drinks. Kim and Todd could distinctly hear Edwin go back up the stairs to Cornelius's study. The dinner engagement was an excuse, but one they were quite happy to accept.

Cornelius could hear his eldest son too. 'Edwin and I have been working on an interesting deal,' he said.

'Uh huh,' said Todd, with the barest hint of polite curiosity.

'It's still very much at the confidential stage, but I can talk to you about it since you are family.'

'No, please,' Todd said. 'I know how careful you have to be about that kind of thing these days.'

Cornelius forced a smile. 'I'd like to tell you about it. Tell both of you. It's important to all of us.' Todd didn't demur. Cornelius could see that he had awakened his son's attention. 'It's *The Times*.'

'You're going to buy *The Times*?'

'That's the idea. I was talking to Bloomfield Weiss just now about the financing.' Cornelius leaned back in his armchair watching his son's reaction.

'That will be quite a coup if you get it.'

'Oh, we'll get it,' Cornelius said. 'And you're right, it's just what Zyl News needs.'

Todd smiled grudgingly at his father and raised his glass. 'Well, good luck. I'll watch what happens with interest.'

'I was hoping you would do rather more than watch.'

'You mean . . .'

'I'd like you to come back. It's five years since you worked for me. We miss you.'

Todd shook his head. 'I'm sorry, Dad. I enjoy teaching, I like the school, I've made my career choice and I want to stick with it.'

'Todd, I'm a realist, I know this is likely to be my last big deal. But it will be a good one. Zyl News will become one of the top newspaper groups in the world. And when I retire I want a van Zyl to run it.'

'What about Edwin? He has much more experience than me.'

'It's not experience that's needed,' Cornelius said. 'You can hire that. It's imagination. Vision. I had it. You have it. I saw you when you were working for me. You definitely have it. But I'm afraid Edwin doesn't.'

'I'm flattered, Dad, but really. I don't want to work in newspapers. I want to teach kids.'

Cornelius tensed. He leaned forward in his chair. Todd was still. There was a hint of fear in his face. It took a lot of courage to stand up to Cornelius van Zyl.

'Can you leave us for a moment, Kim?' Cornelius said, his voice barely above a whisper.

Kim glanced at her husband. 'Stay,' he said. 'Please stay.'

'I'd like to speak to you in private,' Cornelius said.

'You're going to talk to me about what I do with my life,' Todd said. 'Kim's part of my life. I want her to hear it.'

'Very well,' said Cornelius, glancing at Kim. Kim stared back, politeness replaced by defiance. 'A teacher's salary can't be very high these days.'

'It isn't,' said Todd.

'And I understand you've given up your management consulting?'

'For the time being,' Kim said, with steel in her voice.

'So you will have to rely on your trust fund to provide for you and Kim and your children in the future –'

'Stop right there,' Kim said.

'I'm talking to my son.'

'You're not talking to him, you're bribing him. You're trying to buy him!'

Cornelius glared at his daughter-in-law. 'I'm merely pointing out the harsh economic realities of the world.'

'No, you're not. You're trying to make him do what you want him to do, rather than what he wants to do. Well, you can't. His life, *our* life, isn't for sale.'

'Kim . . .' Todd said.

'This is between Todd and me,' Cornelius said.

'You asked Todd whether he wanted to work for you. That was a very generous offer, but he said no, as you knew he would. End of story. There's nothing more to be said.'

'Young lady, *I* will decide what needs to be said. This is the family business we're talking about, something I have spent most of my life building up. If I want my son to take it over then that's my prerogative.'

'No, don't you see?' said Kim, her voice rising in frustration. 'That's the whole point. It's *his* prerogative, not yours.'

Cornelius turned to his son. 'Tell your wife to shut the fuck up.'

A hostile silence snapped shut on the room. Todd looked from his wife to his father. The agitation left him as he came to a decision. Slowly he drew himself to his feet. 'I think we won't be staying for dinner. In fact we won't be staying here at all.'

His father stood up and faced him. Even at seventy-two, father was about an inch taller than son. 'You will stay here,' he growled.

Todd blinked. For a moment it seemed as if he would crack, but the moment passed. 'Come on, Kim,' he said, and turned for the door.

'I was serious about the trust fund,' Cornelius said. 'If you walk out of that door you will regret it. Believe me.'

'Goodnight, Dad,' Todd said, and he and Kim were gone.

Cornelius picked up his crystal glass of brandy and Coke and flung it at the fireplace, where it shattered into a hundred fragments. It was a long, long time since he had been so angry.

3

The following Tuesday the weather was good, a small high-pressure system dallying over East Anglia for a couple of days. Todd and Kim drove up from London and arrived at the airfield before twelve, Todd excited, Kim apprehensive.

Calder left them sitting on a bench in the sunshine as he ran through a thorough 'A' check on the Yak, examining the wings and fuselage, checking the oil and fuel levels, the instruments, the controls and the tyres and making sure the maintenance log was up to date. The aircraft belonged to a retired advertising executive who lived in Burnham Market. He had spent tens of thousands restoring it, and despite its age it was in very good nick. He was happy for Calder to fly it, for a hirer's fee of course, and Calder had logged about twelve hours. It was fun, but there were only two seats, one in front, one behind. There was no room for Kim.

She looked concerned. 'Are you sure this thing is safe?' she asked Calder. 'It looks like it's made of Meccano. And it was manufactured in Russia, wasn't it? Won't it just fall apart?'

'It hasn't yet, and it's been flying for fifty years. Of course it's safe. All these aircraft are thoroughly maintained and checked. It'll be fine.'

'I don't know.' She glanced at her husband, who was untangling his headset.

'You told me you trusted Alex,' he said.

Kim turned to Calder. 'I did. You promise you'll be all right?' She looked him straight in the eye.

For a second Calder hesitated. Then he smiled. 'Of course we'll be safe. No stunts, I promise.'

He installed Todd in the rear seat and in a few minutes they were up in the sky, washed clear by the previous few days' rain. The mighty 700-horsepower radial engine growled. The Yak felt to Calder like a giant locomotive as it powered through the air.

'Have you ever flown a small plane before?' Calder called over the intercom to Todd.

'Yeah, back in South Africa. My sister has a pilot's licence and she used to take me up. But I've never been in anything like this.'

Calder opened the throttle and increased speed to 220 knots. He called up RAF Marham, his old station, for a flight information service. Although the Yak was fast for a general aviation aircraft, it was nothing like the Tornados he had flown over this same stretch of land twelve years before when he was in the air force. He often saw aircraft from his old squadron, No. 13, speeding along the coast, sometimes alone, sometimes in twos or fours. At first the sight had been almost painful, bringing back memories of the kind of flying he could no longer do, skimming at 600 miles an hour fifty feet above the North Sea, ducking and weaving through the Welsh mountains, spinning and twisting 30,000 feet above the English countryside. But now he had become accustomed to it and admired the stout war machines as they went about their business.

They reached the sea at Hanham Staithe and turned right, passing over his own isolated cottage and powering on towards Blakeney and Cromer. Calder glanced down at the familiar coastline, with its ever-shifting spits of sand, the band of rough marshland and the clusters of houses at regular intervals. He was keeping to 1,000 feet so that his passenger could get a good view.

'I know I told Kim we wouldn't do any stunts, but we can do a loop if you're up for it?'

'I'm up for it.'

Calder could hear the grin in his passenger's voice. 'OK. We'll have to gain some altitude.' He opened the throttle for full power and raised the nose for a climb.

The engine growl turned to a roar, the sea slipped down beneath the nose and the altimeter began to turn. Then it happened. Something in the massive old engine a few feet in front of Calder gave way. There was a bang and then the whole aircraft began to shake violently. The engine cowling bucked and buckled, the aircraft instruments blurred, and the wingtips vibrated to their own chaotic rhythm.

'Jesus Christ!' Calder heard from the passenger behind him, but he had no time to speak to Todd. Instantly he closed the throttle and slammed the propeller pitch to full coarse in an attempt to lower the speed and the strain on the engine. It was as though there were an angry giant in there desperate to get out, and willing to wreck the aeroplane in the process.

Calder tried to focus on the instruments but the shaking was so intense it was impossible to read them. He estimated they were at about 1,000 feet, facing out to sea. He pulled the stick to the right to begin a gentle turn back towards land. The speed was beginning to tail off but the engine was still leaping about like a mad thing. At any moment it might wrench itself free from the rest of the fuselage.

Calder hit the mic button and fired off a rapid Mayday in the hope that he wasn't yet too low for Marham to hear him. He guessed a position somewhere to the west of Blakeney and then focused on fighting the aeroplane.

Oil was now leaking from the cowling in front of him, and worse than that, black smoke. The engine was on fire.

Calder cut off the fuel to the engine and switched off the magnetos. He had to get down to the ground, and quickly. But somehow they had drifted a couple of miles out from the shoreline.

The power was going from the engine and they were sinking. They were probably 400 feet up with a mile and a half to go, cold grey water beneath them.

'Brace yourself, Todd,' Calder called. No reply. 'Todd?'

He turned to see Todd slumped back in his seat. Why? Despite the adrenaline flooding his system he felt suddenly tired himself. Carbon monoxide! Part of the drill for an engine fire was to open the cockpit to prevent carbon monoxide from the engine poisoning the pilot. With arms that were suddenly heavy, he reached forward and fumbled with the knob to release the canopy. He slid it open a few inches and the fresh air rushed by his face.

The sea was very close now. So was the shore, but they weren't quite going to make it. To his left he saw a narrow bar of exposed sand half a mile out from the beach. He could just reach that. But with the engine on fire perhaps it would be safer to ditch into the water rather than risk a hard landing and an explosion. The trouble was that behind him Todd was unconscious; they were not wearing life jackets and if they ditched, Todd would be unable to climb out and swim to safety. Calder would have to pull him out.

Calder had been taught to make decisions under pressure; any decision was better than no decision. He chose the sandbar. He pulled the stick to the left and heaved the sluggish Yak towards the bank. He selected full flap and gear down and then the aircraft slammed into the sand. Had it been a smooth firm runway, all might have been well, but the sand was wet and uneven, the aircraft was bucking like a wild thing, and it slewed round to the left. For a couple of seconds sky, sea and sand whirled in bewildering disorder; there was a jarring impact and then everything was still.

Still, and inverted. Calder was held in his seat by the pressure of the harness on his shoulders. The aircraft was on its back. For a moment the stillness was a relief after the desperate thrashing of the stricken aircraft, but only for a moment. Calder could hear the drip of oil and the crackle of flames, and he could smell fuel. He knew he had only seconds.

Quickly but carefully, so that he didn't fall downwards on to his neck, he unbuckled his harness and pulled himself out of there. He turned, released Todd and dragged him out too. Todd had a serious gash on the side of his head and was out cold. Calder slung him over his shoulder and staggered as far away from the Yak as he could. He was about thirty yards along the sandbank when the aircraft behind him exploded.

He turned to watch a ball of black and orange engulf the fuselage, and staggered backwards away from the heat. It seemed extraordinary that the old Yak could be transformed from perfect flying machine to twisted metal in less than three minutes. He felt himself shaking. They had been extremely lucky to get out.

He lay Todd down on the damp sand in the recovery position and examined his wound. Blood was seeping from the gash. Todd's face was pale, a grey shade of white, but he was breathing shallowly. Calder felt for his pulse; it took him a few seconds of frantic fumbling to find it, but there it was. Faint, irregular, but beating.

There was nothing more Calder could do for him. He looked around. On all sides was the grey sea, calm in the faint breeze, breaking in small wavelets over the edge of the sand. At sea level the bar seemed further from the shore than he had thought, closer to a mile than half a mile. Along the coast was marsh and then a road which ran beside a couple of isolated houses. Black smoke was pouring out of the Yak, it would be easy to spot. Calder could probably swim the distance to the shore by himself, but not while encumbered with an unconscious Todd. Besides which a tidal current seemed to be moving rapidly from right to left. Swimming would be a struggle.

They would wait.

Calder had just decided this when he glanced again at Todd. What he saw made his blood run cold. Todd was still motionless, but whereas the sea had been several feet away from them a moment before, a wave was now lapping against the prone man's feet. The tide was coming in!

Calder had flown over this stretch of coastline many times before. He knew that at high tide this spit of sand was under water. He also knew how rapidly the tide on the north Norfolk coast could cover the miles of exposed sand and mud.

He examined the sandbar, shrinking before his eyes. The Yak, still burning, now rested in a few inches of water. At the centre of the bar he noticed a hump of sand, perhaps a foot above the rest. That would have to do. He picked up Todd, slung him over his shoulder and staggered over towards it. Water began to lap at his feet. He reached the hump and lay Todd on the bare sand.

He looked about him. Where was the help? It had been a few minutes since he had crash landed the Yak so help should be on the way. Assuming Marham had received his Mayday call, or someone on the road had spotted the burning aeroplane and done something about it.

The water ate into the sandbar. A wave stole over the summit of the hump, seeping under Todd's prone body. There was nothing for it. Calder picked up the dead weight of his passenger and slung it over his shoulder once again. He stood there, legs apart, water around his ankles, and waited.

Todd grew heavier. The water rose. Calder's shoulder and back ached under their burden. His spine had suffered a compression fracture many years before when he had ejected from his Tornado after a mid-air collision, and it was complaining loudly. The water was up to his thighs and he could feel the pull of the current along the shoreline. It would be very hard to swim ashore in that. But he was going to have to try.

Up to his waist. It was still only May, and the sea was numbingly cold, especially once it passed his groin. Todd's weight had become unbearable, and Calder slung him off his shoulder, lay his body in the water and cradled his head above the gentle waves. The man was still unconscious.

Up to his chest. This was hopeless. Perhaps he should strike out for the shore with Todd. Or without him. Without him, Calder would survive. It was pointless them both drowning. At some point it would be reasonable for Calder to abandon Todd and save himself, wouldn't it? Calder looked down at Todd's slack, pale features. He thought of Kim. He thought of what it would be like living with the knowledge that he had abandoned her husband to his death. He could never explain that away to her or to himself. When it came to the time, he would try to swim off with Todd and see what happened.

Then he heard it, a roar to the east. Within seconds a Tornado appeared, flying along the coastline. Calder could tell it was moving slowly, for a fast jet. Although Calder would be virtually invisible, the upended tail of the Yak was still just above the waves. The Tornado flew low overhead and waggled its wings. It had seen them. As the aircraft disappeared over the land to the south-east, Calder heard another sound, the rapid beat of a helicopter to the west. The Tornado would have called in their precise position.

The sea was up to his neck, and the current was tugging at him, but he managed to keep Todd's face out of the water. Within a minute the yellow Sea King was overhead and a crewman was swinging down towards them.

4

Well, I'll try again after that junk I wrote a couple of days ago. It did make me feel slightly better: I'm calmer now. Still angry, but definitely calmer.

They say that a diary shows a future you the person you used to be. I wish I had written one nearly twenty years ago when I first came to South Africa. Then I was an idealist prepared to be appalled by this country. Somehow I fell in love with it, and with Neels. Together I thought we could play our own part in changing it. Instead, it seems to have changed us.

So maybe writing this will help me figure out who I am. Why I'm here. What I'm going to do next.

It's been three days since we had that fight. It was the worst of our marriage so far, shouting, screaming, swearing at each other: at one point I thought Neels was going to hit me. He's seemed so much more violent recently, since Hennie was killed. It scares me. He got in a fistfight last week with a stranger in the street, some drunken Boer who recognized him and called him a Kaffir lover. Neels hit him so hard he knocked him out. Three months ago he would have smiled and walked away.

Somehow I think there are going to be many more arguments. He told me he plans to close down the *Cape Daily Mail* and sell the rest of his South African properties. By "properties" he means newspapers. Apparently American investors are uncomfortable dealing with someone who has South African business interests. So Cornelius van Zyl plans to reinvent himself as a non-South African so that he can buy companies in the States and Britain and all over the rest of the world.

I asked him why he couldn't just sell the *Mail* to a friendly proprietor. There are more and more businessmen who are critical of the regime these days. He says the paper is losing money hand over fist and no one would buy it. Although the readership is high, an increasing number of those readers are blacks and the advertisers don't like that. Blacks don't have any money to spend. He says he can't go on subsidizing it for ever.

He's even selling the family paper, the *Oudtshoorn Rekord*, that his father started sixty years ago. However many English-language newspapers he bought in South Africa he always said he would hold on to that Afrikaans one, in memory of his father. He clearly didn't mean it.

Actually, he did mean it then. The point is he doesn't mean it now. Why? What has changed?

I can't help thinking that if he abandons the *Mail* and the other papers, and if he abandons South Africa, then he is abandoning me. I know I'm American, but he's running away from me, not toward me. He spends more and more time in Philadelphia at the *Intelligencer*'s offices. He never asks me to come with him. Why not?

I'm losing him.

June 21

It's a wonderful morning. After I got back from taking Caroline to school I went out for a walk, up to the picnic spot above our house. That's where I'm sitting now as I write this. Above me is the Hondekop, the craggy outcrop of rock in the shape of the head of a great hound that gave its name to our house. To the right I can see the white cluster of buildings that is the town of Stellenbosch, and beyond that, thirty miles away, is a corner of Table Mountain. The narrow valley stretches up to the left, into the Hottentots Holland mountains. It's cold this morning, cold and clear, with no wind. The vines are heavy with dew, and the morning sun is touching the tops of the crags on the other side of the valley, turning the gray rock yellow and gold.

Hondehoek is half a mile down into the valley. I love it. It is a classic Cape Dutch farmhouse built of white stone with a thatched roof, a single gable in the center, and the figures 1815 painted in black above the window. Inside, beautiful yellowwood beams frame the high-ceilinged rooms; the floorboards are also made of well-worn yellowwood, except in the kitchen where the floor tiles are from Batavia. Actually, the original farm was built much earlier than the present building, by a Huguenot called François de Villiers who arrived from Lille in 1694. When Simon van der Stel ventured out of the confines of Cape Town to found Stel-en-bosch, he granted this land to de Villiers, who planted the first vines here, and the oak tree that still stands beside the front door. At about the same time, the first van Zyl arrived in South Africa on a boat from Amsterdam and established his own farm just on the other side of the mountain.

I'm so glad we bought this place. Neels wanted somewhere bigger. He and Penelope lived in a very grand house in Constantia; in fact Penelope still rattles around in there. But when I saw Hondehoek, I fell in love with it. We don't need somewhere huge, and Neels has to admit that the sheer beauty of the place impresses his guests as much as a mansion would. It also means we don't need a domestic army to look after it, just Doris and the new maid Tuesday for the house, and Finneas and some casual labor for the garden. I much prefer it that way, I would hate to be the mistress of a huge domestic establishment. We don't manage the vines either; our neighbor down the valley does that, and does a very good job of it too. But we have retained the Hondehoek label, its Pinotage is renowned. Neels loves to show it off and actually I kind of like it too.

Doris must have lit a fire; a twist of wood smoke is winding its way up into the cold air of the valley.

The winters here are lovely. It's the equivalent of December in the northern hemisphere: at home in Minnesota the ground would already be under a foot of snow, but here the leaves are not even off the trees. The vines are russet and brown, and the leaves on the oaks which line the drive up to our house are still a golden yellow. There is a good view of the garden from up here. A small lawn slopes down to a pond in front of the house, and beside it lies a formal rose garden. Most of the roses are blooming, as are the magnolia trees. I've planted a bed of fynbos, the strange indigenous plants of the Cape, on the other side of the lawn, next to the twin white pillars which hold the bell that used to call the slaves in from the fields. Most of them won't bloom until the spring, but when they do, they'll be gorgeous bulbous flowers of yellow, blue and red, nestling in those spiky green leaves. I have to admit, Finneas and I have done a good job.

They call South Africa God's own country, and sitting here I can see why. No, I can *feel* why. We've lived here seventeen years now, I think. I'm not sure how I fit into the great teeming mass of contradictions that is South Africa, but I do know this about Hondehoek. It's home.

June 22

Todd called. He hasn't called for a couple of weeks now, he knew I'd be angry with him because of his letter, and I was. It turns out that he has a new girlfriend, Francesca, and the boy he wants to stay with over the summer vacation lives near her.

I'm glad he talks to me about his girlfriends and there's absolutely nothing wrong with wanting to see her. But spending the whole summer away from his family? He's only sixteen, for Christ's sake, he's going to be spending the next ten years at least running around after women.

Pathetic, really, isn't it? A mother jealous of her son's girl. But I really need him around here, especially now Neels is behaving so strangely.

Todd did tell me about the "Free Nelson Mandela" Concert he went to last weekend at Wembley Stadium. He said it was amazing; it lasted ten hours and a billion people watched it on TV around the world. He saw Eric Clapton and Dire Straits and some girl called Tracy Chapman who he said was "brilliant." There was no coverage here, of course.

But he's so far away! Caroline's going to high school next year, but I want to keep her near me. Especially if Neels leaves.

Neels and I made love last night. It was nice. I was a little drunk, and relieved not to be fighting. He was very affectionate, I think he feels badly about our fight the other day, and so he should.

Afterwards he asked me whether the family should move to Philadelphia. We could buy a house, send Caroline to school there. We could keep Hondehoek and still spend some time here during vacations and so on. He said that he really thinks the regime is going to collapse sometime in the next five to ten years, and when it does it's going to be ugly. He says he wants to make sure his family is safe.

We talked about Hennie. It's two months ago today that he was murdered. We read about deaths all the time in the papers, but when the ANC blow up your brother with a landmine on his own farm, it really brings things home to you. He admitted that it was what had made him question whether South Africa could survive the fall of apartheid. He says he can't get it out of his mind.

I started talking about not wanting to run away from this country, but he kissed me. "Be quiet, *liefie*," he said gently. "Don't answer me yet. Let's go to sleep now and we can talk about it later, when you've had a chance to think about it."

So what about it? What about moving to America? My knee-jerk reaction is "no," of course. It would mean abandoning all that our marriage has stood for, all our history together. It would imply that I have wasted the last twenty years of my life stuck down here hoping and praying for the collapse of the system. We can't leave just when it's about to happen!

But America is my country, after all. Maybe I should just forget South Africa; it was a phase in my life that has come to an end. There will be other things to do in Philadelphia. Neels is very ambitious, I've always known that. He wants to build up a truly international newspaper empire. He'll have the *Philadelphia Intelligencer* and the *Herald*, and all those local US papers. Then he'll buy more. And I'll be a media tycoon's wife. I suppose I am that here, but I don't feel like it, I feel as if I'm helping Neels right a terrible wrong. I know a lot of people would like the glitter and the glamour of all those parties in Philadelphia and New York and London. But not me. Really not me.

It might save our marriage, though. That is important to me. Maybe that should be more important than what happens in this screwed-up country.

Neels was clever to tell me not to say anything and just think about it.

I love him. I miss the old Neels, but what I need to figure out is if I can love the new Neels just as much. Or maybe there is no difference between the two. Maybe it's all in my imagination, he hasn't really changed.

June 26

Neels said Zan called him. She's coming to stay with us in a couple of days, for two whole months. She's got a place at the London School of Economics in September, and she wants to spend some time with her father first.

I am really not looking forward to it at all. She's been in Johannesburg the last six years, getting herself into all kinds of trouble with the End Conscription Campaign and the Black Sash. I have no problem with that, in fact I admire her for it, but we've hardly seen her that whole time. Ever since she was fourteen she has been vile to me and to her father, but especially to me. Given how things are between Neels and me I'm not optimistic about her stay.

June 27

I am so angry I could spit. More than spit. I could rip Neels's balls off.

I got a call from George Field this afternoon saying that Neels had summoned him into his office and told him he was going to announce the closure of the *Mail* tomorrow morning. He wants George as editor to stand by him when he makes the announcement to staff. George was in deep shock. He hadn't seen it coming and he wanted to ask me what was going on. I told him about Neels's international ambitions and the demands of American investors that he get rid of his South African interests. We talked about why he didn't sell the paper and George confirmed that there are financial problems. But Neels could have *tried*, for Christ's sake. I like George and I don't like the way Neels is treating him.

I snapped at Caroline who ran off to do her homework. When Neels came home, I gave him hell. He was expecting it, I guess; he didn't fight back. But he looked really angry. He stood still with his fists clenched, kind of shaking. He looked like he was only just managing to control himself. It worried me. Then I told him he wasn't sleeping in my room that night, or any night, and he turned around and left, just walked out of the house.

Probably gone to drown his sorrows.

Asshole!

Later . . . technically it's the morning of June 28.

Cornelius isn't back yet. For a moment I was worried. I thought perhaps he had gone out somewhere, gotten drunk and then crashed the car on the way home.

But now I know what's happened. There's another woman. I know there's another woman. I don't know who she is or where she is, but that's where he's gone. He had this strange expression on his face just before he left this evening. He decided then that if I wouldn't let him sleep with me he'd go and sleep with her.

That would explain this feeling I've been having that I'm losing him, that he's slipping away. I *was* losing him. It's not just about the *Mail*. As I write this he's out there fucking some bimbo.

Well, screw him! The bastard. The absolute total fucking bastard!

5

'Take a seat please. I'll tell Kim you're here.'

The nurse disappeared through the doors marked 'Critical Care Unit'. After the rushing around of the last couple of hours, Calder found it very hard to sit still even for a minute. The helicopter had taken Todd and him directly to a hospital on the edge of King's Lynn. Langthorpe Aerodrome had been contacted and Kim informed about what had happened. Todd had been rushed into intensive care, but Calder was undamaged. He had returned to the airfield by taxi to file the accident report and call the owner of the Yak. The man's dismay at what had happened to his beloved aircraft was overwhelmed by concern for Todd plus a tinge of fear that it could have been him injured in that plane. Then Calder had driven back to King's Lynn to join Kim.

'How is he?' he asked as she came into the small relatives' waiting room.

Her face was even paler than usual and her dark hair fell in bedraggled curls over her red-rimmed eyes. As she sat in a ball in the chair next to him, small and hunched up, she was shaking. 'Oh, Alex. He's still unconscious. They've stitched up the wound, but they think he's fractured his skull.'

'Is he breathing OK?'

'Yes. It's just they don't know how long he will be under. And when he comes round whether there will be any . . . damage. You know. Permanent damage.' She began to sob, and leaned into Calder who put his arm round her and squeezed gently. 'He looks so pale. And his head . . . they had to shave some hair off. It's all bandaged now. I asked them when he'll wake up and they wouldn't answer.'

Calder's face tightened as he stared blindly ahead. Kim seemed to be trying to bury herself into his chest. 'What if he doesn't wake up, Alex?' She looked up at him. 'What if he doesn't wake up?'

'He'll wake up.'

For a second there was a glimmer of confidence in her eyes and then she sat up, pushing him away. 'You don't know that. You're just saying that to make me feel better, like you did with the aeroplane.'

Calder shrugged helplessly. 'We have to believe he'll wake up.'

'You said it was perfectly safe. I was worried that the plane was so old, but you said it didn't matter.' A tear slipped its way into the corner of her mouth and she sniffed. 'You always did take bloody idiotic risks. Like that time you crawled over the roof of South Court to get into the college ball. You were pissed out of your head and I was convinced you were going to kill yourself. You thought it was funny, but it was just so *stupid*.'

Calder knew he couldn't run from this. 'I know what I said, Kim. And it should have been safe, but it wasn't. I'm sorry. I'm very sorry.'

Kim glared at him for a couple of seconds. And then she bit her lip. 'What happened? No one here is absolutely sure. I can't make sense of it.'

Calder gave her an account of the engine fire and the landing on the sandbar.

'What do you think caused it?'

'I don't know, but my first guess is a cracked cylinder.'

'Don't they check for that kind of thing? The maintenance people? You said the plane was thoroughly checked.'

'It was. I had another look at the logs just now. All the maintenance was up to date and signed off. I don't think there's anything else anyone could have done. Engine fires are nasty things, but they are rare. This is the first one I've experienced.'

'So we just have to accept it? Will there be some kind of investigation?'

'Oh, yes. The AAIB, that's the Air Accident Investigation Board, will get involved. They're very thorough. They'll look through all the records, they'll probably drag the aeroplane out of the water and examine it. They'll find the cause, they nearly always do.'

'Are you worried?'

'About an investigation? No. I don't *think* I did anything wrong. I'm worried about Todd.'

Kim gave him a weak smile. She clung on to his arm and more tears leaked from the corners of her eyes.

Had he been at fault? Should he have ditched? No, Todd could just as easily have hit his head on impact with the water, and it would have been hard to fish him out. Flying aeroplanes, especially old aeroplanes, was inherently danger-ous. He should have admitted as much to Kim. She had trusted him, and because she had, Todd had.

'Will the police be involved?'

Calder glanced at her. Pensive traces of a new worry furrowed her brow. 'Probably,' he replied.

'Is there any way that someone could have caused this?'

'You mean deliberately?'

She nodded.

'I don't think so. Unless they tampered with the engine somehow. Weakened the cylinder. But it's pretty unlikely.' Calder looked at Kim. 'Isn't it?'

Kim bit her lip. 'Yes, I'm sure it is. It's just that Todd has been asking all these questions about Martha's death and no one else has shown any interest. That seems strange to me. His whole family seems strange. It's almost as if they didn't want him asking those questions.'

'You don't think . . .'

'I don't know what to think.'

'Should *you* talk to the police about this?'

'God, no.' Kim's voice was firm. 'Todd would hate me to do that. I'm probably just imagining things. But see if you can get them to check that there was nothing funny going on, or at least bear it in mind.'

'I will,' said Calder thoughtfully. He considered her question. Sabotage was technically possible. 'Do you really think Todd's family would do something like that?'

'I don't know,' Kim said. 'I don't really trust them. I don't trust Edwin – that's Todd's half-brother – at all. And Cornelius? Cornelius has been trying to get his claws into Todd all his life, and Cornelius usually gets what he wants. We had a major row with him a few days ago about whether Todd should go back to Zyl News. We walked out of his house and stayed in a hotel.' She raised her wide grey eyes to Calder. 'Would you go and see Benton Davis? Please? Ask him if he knows why Martha was killed.'

Calder nodded. 'All right.' His previous reluctance seemed churlish now. After what had happened that afternoon, he would do anything for Kim.

'Thanks.' She smiled quickly. Then she groaned. 'Oh, God. I should tell Cornelius what's happened.'

'Do you want me to do it?'

'Would you? Here, I'll give you the number.' Kim pulled out a PDA and tapped its screen. 'There. It's the London one.'

Calder pulled out his phone and dialled.

49

'Hello?'

'Can I speak to Mr van Zyl?'

'This is Edwin van Zyl.' The voice was South African, curt, precise. And he pronounced his name 'fan Sail', as opposed to 'van Zill', the way that the name was usually pronounced in England and America.

'Can I speak to Cornelius?'

'Who is this?'

'My name's Alex Calder. It's about Todd.'

'You can speak to me. I'm his brother, man.'

Calder gave up his attempt to get to the father. 'I'm with Kim. We're in a hospital in Norfolk. He's had an accident.'

'One moment.'

A few seconds later another voice came on the phone. Stronger, more authoritative. 'What happened?'

Calder gave a thirty-second description of the afternoon's events.

'I'll come up there right now,' the voice said.

It took him just over two hours. Calder stayed with Kim, sitting next to Todd, watching him lie amongst the tubes and machines, still. A nurse informed them of Cornelius's arrival, and they went out to meet him. Calder was impressed by the man's size and aura of determination. He had Todd's square jaw, but he looked harder, stronger, tougher than his son. He also looked very worried. As soon as he saw Kim he held out his arms. Kim hesitated and then let herself be enveloped by that large embrace.

He held her for several seconds and then glanced at Calder. 'You the pilot?'

'Yes,' he said.

'Was it your fault?'

'No.'

Cornelius's blue eyes stared hard at Calder. Calder held

his gaze. He was sensitive to Cornelius's concern, but he wasn't going to be intimidated by the man.

Kim pushed away from Cornelius's chest, her eyes igniting with anger. 'Alex has told me in detail what happened and it's quite clear that he did nothing wrong. In fact, he saved Todd's life.'

Cornelius ignored her. 'Because if I find you were responsible for my son's injuries, you will pay. You will pay dearly.'

The next day was busy. Kim had stayed the night at Calder's cottage but spent most of the time at the hospital. There was no change in Todd's condition. The brain scan showed no signs of permanent damage, apart from probable memory loss, but the doctors couldn't be sure. They also had no idea how long he would be unconscious. They were keeping him on a ventilator, giving him drugs to try to control the swelling in his brain. Kim just sat there and watched her husband.

Cornelius waited with her in the hospital for a couple of hours the next morning, but then he returned to London, extracting a promise from Kim to let him know if there was any change to Todd's condition, one way or the other. He grilled Calder for twenty minutes on exactly what had happened, but seemed satisfied with his responses. Calder was under no illusions that if the accident report showed that someone had blundered, be it himself as pilot, or Colin, the maintenance engineer at the airfield, or a fitter at the specialist firm in Lithuania which had undertaken the last major overhaul on the engine, that person would pay.

The air accident investigators were soon on the scene. They were working on salvaging the Yak and they had lots of questions for Calder. Calder also talked through everything with his partner, Jerry Tyrell, who was the chief flying instructor at the flying school. Jerry's opinion was that Calder had done everything correctly in very difficult circumstances. Calder was pleased and relieved to hear this: Jerry had never shrunk from criticizing Calder whenever he had caught him doing something that didn't comply with his own strict interpretation of safety procedures.

A uniformed police constable came to ask questions, but this seemed more of a formality. Feeling slightly foolish, Calder did as he had promised, and asked the policeman to let him know if he came across anything that suggested the accident was a result of sabotage. This perked the constable's interest, but faithful to his promise to Kim, Calder denied that he had any concrete reason to think that someone might have wanted to kill him or Todd.

He had a close look over the patch of grass between a Warrior and a Seneca where the Yak had been parked, and asked around to see if anyone had seen anything suspicious at the airfield the day, or more especially the night, before the accident. Jerry and Angie, who manned the radio, had left at about eight o'clock the evening before. Angie thought she had seen a lone man walking along the footpath by the poplars on the far side of the airfield as she was locking up, but there was nothing unusual about that. Otherwise all had been quiet. The aerodrome was really not much more than a field; someone could easily have climbed over a fence in the middle of the night and tampered with the Yak's engine without anyone noticing. But the more Calder considered it the less likely he thought that was. The strain of worrying about her husband was causing Kim to lose her sense of proportion.

Amongst all the activity he did allow himself one quick diversion. When he switched on his computer in his office he couldn't resist checking the Spreadfinex web page. The US bond markets had tumbled over the previous twenty-four hours and he was now sitting on a £5,000 loss. He thought for a moment, clicked a couple of buttons and doubled his bet at the lower price.

He picked up Kim late that evening from the hospital and drove her home. She looked worn out, even though she had done nothing but sit and watch her husband all day.

Calder's house was an old cottage nestling at the edge of a salt marsh about a mile from the village of Hanham Staithe. It was dusk as they arrived and the rooks were kicking up a fuss in the trees behind the house. It was clear Kim had eaten very little all day, so Calder warmed up some soup and threw together a salad.

'Glass of wine?' he asked.

'God, yes please,' Kim replied. 'Suddenly that's exactly what I want.'

Calder opened a bottle, poured two glasses and placed them on the solid oak kitchen table. 'Back tomorrow morning?'

Kim nodded. 'And the next morning, and the one after that.' She was still pale and shaken but there was no mistaking the determination in her voice.

'They still have no idea how long it's going to take?'

'No. It could be days, weeks, months. Half the time I'm relieved he's not getting any worse. But I'm also scared what he'll be like when he does come round. Whether he'll remember who he is, who I am. I sit there looking at him and all kinds of wild thoughts go through my head.'

'We have to take it one step at a time,' Calder said. 'We know he's alive, and it looks like he's going to stay that way. They didn't spot any serious damage on the scan, did they?'

'There's damage,' Kim sighed. 'They really won't know how bad it is until he wakes up. Did you talk to the police and the accident investigators?'

Calder told her about his various interviews and the fact that no one had seen anything suspicious.

'It still worries me,' Kim said. 'The more I think about it the more worried I become.'

'It must have been an accident,' Calder insisted.

Kim sipped her wine thoughtfully. A curl of dark hair fell over her face and she let it rest there for a few moments before pushing it out of her eyes. The gloom gathered around the kitchen as the evening light over the marshes outside slipped away. The rooks were settling themselves. 'I suppose you're right. But I would still be very grateful if you could talk to this man Benton Davis. Todd was sure there was something weird about Martha's death, and he's our best bet for finding out what.'

'I'll go down to London to see him as soon as I can get away. But first you must tell me some more about Todd's mother. The police claimed she was killed by guerrillas?'

'That's right. They said it was a random attack by African National Congress guerrillas from over the border in Mozambique, and the family accepted that. Obviously it was a horrible time for Todd; you saw how it still eats him up. Todd says Cornelius was devastated. He moved the family from South Africa to Philadelphia soon afterwards, he closed the *Cape Daily Mail,* sold his other South African newspapers and bought the *Herald.* Four years later he got married again, to Jessica Montgomery. You might have seen her in the gossip columns.' Kim examined Calder doubtfully. 'Or then again you might not.'

'I think I've seen a photo of the two of them somewhere,' said Calder. 'Was Todd suspicious at the time about his mother's death?'

'Not then. There was a lot of random violence in South Africa, much of it blamed on the ANC. In fact, random

54

violence seems to define the place.' Kim's voice was bitter. 'The only thing that bothered him was when his grandmother, Martha's mother, came to South Africa shortly after the murder. She asked lots of questions that Cornelius wouldn't answer. After the initial grief, the tension between the two of them increased. Todd hadn't heard then what those questions were, but he did have a conversation with her in 1997 when he went to visit her in Minnesota. She lived on the shore of a lake just outside Minneapolis. I went there myself once, right after we were married. It's an absolutely gorgeous place. Anyway, Todd's grandmother said that she had been in touch with Cornelius to suggest he bring a complaint to the Truth and Reconciliation Commission. Have you heard of that?'

'Vaguely.'

'It was set up by the new constitution in South Africa to examine abuses during the apartheid regime. People could come to the Commission to tell them about torture or murder committed by whites or blacks, and the TRC would investigate. The perpetrators would be given amnesty if they promised to tell the truth. It looked at thousands of cases, some of them with high-profile victims, most of them just ordinary people. Todd's grandmother thought this would be the perfect way to find out what had happened to Martha. But Cornelius refused.'

'Did he say why?'

'Todd asked him. Cornelius said it would just bring back all the distress surrounding Martha's death and it was better to leave it. Todd and Cornelius had a major row about it, and Todd threatened to go down to South Africa himself to talk to the Commission, but in the end Cornelius persuaded him not to. Given Cornelius's position, Todd's testimony would cause a major stir in the press and Cornelius felt that would be unfair on those members of the family who wanted to keep their privacy. Besides which, Todd himself had very little to say without the support of Cornelius. So, reluctantly, he let it drop.

'Then last Easter Todd's grandmother died. His grandfather had died shortly after Martha. He had had cancer and her death hadn't helped him fight it. Martha's brother had been killed in a car accident when he was in his twenties, so Todd and his sister Caroline were the only heirs. Todd was sorting through his grandmother's papers when he came across the letter we were telling you about, from Martha to her mother. And that's when he started asking questions again.'

'Can I see it?'

'Hang on. I'll go and fetch it.' Kim left Calder to go out to the entrance hall and rummage in her suitcase. She was back a minute later clutching a small leather photo frame and an airmail envelope. She handed the frame to Calder.

'Todd always takes this with him wherever we go. I thought you'd like to see what she looked like.'

The photograph was of a woman sitting on some steps in a garden, clutching an ancient yellow Labrador. She was slender with frank blue eyes and long blonde hair that rested on her collarbones. She was wearing faded jeans and a simple blue T-shirt, she wore no make-up and she was smiling at the photographer, a warm, relaxed smile.

'She was gorgeous,' Calder said.

'That was taken a couple of years before she died. She must have been over forty.'

'Huh.'

'Her family were originally from Norway, I think. Her maiden name was Olson.'

'You can tell.' Calder studied the photograph more closely. 'Can I see the letter?'

She handed over the envelope and Calder carefully removed a couple of sheets of well-thumbed air-mail paper, covered with small, closely spaced, spiky writing.

'Todd said his mother's writing wasn't usually that bad. He thinks it's a sign of how panicked she felt.'

Calder began to read:

Hondehoek
August 25, 1988
   Dear Mom,
   I know this letter is going to freak you out, and I apologize for writing it. When you get it, read it and keep it somewhere safe. When we next talk on the phone, we shouldn't discuss it. I'll tell you more next time I come over to America, which I hope will be in September.
   You know that things are not going well between Cornelius and me at the moment. I told you that he is planning to sell his South African papers and to close down the Cape Daily Mail, *and how upset this has made me. Well, I have discovered some stuff about all that that worries me. It worries me a lot.*
   If anything should happen to me . . . I hate writing those words and I know how much they will worry you, and I'm sure nothing will *happen, but just in case it does, then there are some things I would like you to know. You should get in touch with a friend of mine, Benton Davis. He works for Bloomfield Weiss, which is the investment bank advising Zyl News, in their New York office. I trust him, and he will be able to tell you what I've found out.*
   There's also some stuff in my diary, at the back, on pages marked "Laagerbond" and "Operation Drommedaris." You can read the rest of the diary if you like, just don't show any of it to

Cornelius. I keep it hidden in my desk at Hondehoek. It's a black moleskin notebook and it's stuffed in a box marked "US tax records 1980–85" which is at the back of the bottom drawer. It seemed to me the kind of box no one would open. But if something does happen to me, please come down here as soon as you can and find it.

When you've found it and read it, and when you've spoken to Benton, talk to Dad and decide what to do. I trust you two, of all people, to do the right thing.

It is impossible to put into words how much I love you and Dad. You have taught me so much and given me so much love. If I can be half as good a parent to Todd and Caroline as you were to me, then I will be very happy. I know I have done some things that you thought were wrong, I know you forgave me when that was hard to do, and I thank you for that.

With all my love,
Martha

'Wow,' said Calder, handing the letter back to Kim. 'I can see why you want to talk to Benton.'

'He obviously knows *something*.'

'You said Todd tried to get in touch with him?'

'Yes. Todd called him from America before we left for England, but he couldn't get past Davis's PA. When we got to England we went to Bloomfield Weiss's offices in person, but once again we were told Mr Davis was unavailable. We tried to talk our way in, but the security guards were absolute pigs and wouldn't listen. We didn't know what he looked like, so we couldn't just wait for him. Cornelius refused to help. That's when I thought we could try you.'

'After what Martha says about him here, it is strange he didn't want to talk to you. But then this isn't the Benton Davis *I* know.'

'What do you mean?'

'I wouldn't trust him as far as I could throw him. But I suppose people change. After twenty years at Bloomfield Weiss, even the most trustworthy people might lose some of their integrity. Which is why I got out.'

'What's he like?'

'Well, for a start, he's black. Which is something in his favour. I would guess he joined Bloomfield Weiss in the early eighties, which was quite an achievement for a black person back then. He must have been pretty smart; there weren't that many black investment bankers on Wall Street.'

'You don't think he's that smart now?'

'No. I always thought he was a bit superficial. Talks a lot about opera, name-drops like crazy, that kind of thing. But he might just be burned out. Once you get to fifty there are all kinds of younger men and women snapping at your heels trying to force you out of the hierarchy. He has a lot of charisma, though. He's a big guy, quite athletic, impressive voice, you listen to him.'

'Somehow or other he became a friend of Martha's.'

'Did Todd ask his father about him?'

'Yes. Apparently Cornelius still does business with him. He said that Benton Davis and Martha met when Bloomfield Weiss were working on the deal to buy the *Herald*, right before Martha died. But Cornelius wasn't willing to talk to him about Martha's letter.'

'Why not?'

'He's adamant that he doesn't want to reopen any discussion of Martha's death. Which is all very well for him to say, but Todd has a *right* to know and Cornelius should recognize that.'

'Does he have any idea what Martha had discovered?'

'No. Or at least he wasn't saying.'

'And the diary?'

'Never saw it. Didn't even know she was writing one. He said he couldn't remember the specific box she mentions, but he is pretty sure that it would have been thrown away unopened when they sold Hondehoek.'

'What about this "Laagerbond"?'

'Never heard of that either.'

'Presumably it has nothing to do with beer?'

'Two "a"s, you idiot. Actually, no one seems to know what it is. *Laager* is the Afrikaans word for a circle of wagons around a camp. It's an image from the Boers' great trek away from the Cape to the interior of the country and it symbolizes a kind of defensive mindset that the Afrikaners have in the face of change. *Bond* just means "band" or "group". Todd has asked around and no one has heard of this particular group. He did find one reference to it on the internet. It was from testimony by a spy to the Truth and Reconciliation Commission in 1997 who said that his handler in the security police was a member. But he only mentioned the word once, and the Commission didn't follow up on it.'

'And Operation Drommedaris?'

'*Drommedaris* is Dutch for dromedary; you know, a camel. One hump not two. It's also the name of the boat Jan van Riebeeck sailed in when he founded the Dutch colony at Cape Town. It must be a codename. But for what, who knows?'

'What about the rest of the family? Has anyone any idea about any of this?'

'No. Edwin was equally unhelpful. Todd called his sister Caroline in California, but she didn't know anything – she was only twelve at the time. He also phoned Zan, his half-sister. She's the only van Zyl who still lives in South Africa. She was staying at Martha and Cornelius's house when it all happened. She couldn't help much either, although she at least seemed more willing to try. She's eight years older than Todd; they were quite close when he was little, although she seems to have disappeared from the scene as he got older. She's fallen out with the rest of the family; she wasn't asked to our wedding, for example. I met her once, when we went on a trip to South Africa soon after we were married. I thought she was quite nice, actually. A bit like the best of Cornelius but without the megalomania.'

'Cornelius is a megalomaniac?'

'Definitely. He loves power. And he likes to control the people around him.'

'Like Todd?'

'Todd has always been Cornelius's blue-eyed boy. It drives Edwin mad. Cornelius wants Todd to take over Zyl News when he retires: he's seventy-two, it's got to happen some time. And much to Todd's credit, he wants to determine his own life.'

'Ah.'

'What do you mean, "Ah"?'

Calder smiled. 'I assume you encourage him in this independence of mind?'

She smiled sheepishly. 'You're right. A year after we were married, he decided . . . OK, with my encouragement . . . to quit working for Cornelius and to do what he really wanted to do. Which was teach. So he did an education degree and then we moved to New Hampshire. Cornelius is trying to force Todd to move back to Zyl News. Todd won't do it, though.'

'And you're happy with that decision? To stay in New Hampshire?'

Kim hesitated. 'In theory, definitely. In practice . . . well, that's another conversation.'

Calder left it. He sipped his wine thoughtfully. 'It sounds as if Martha was quite suspicious of her husband. And it sounds as if Cornelius doesn't want anyone to find out why.'

'Absolutely.' Kim frowned. 'Frankly, I'm worried about his role in all this. But Todd isn't. He's crossed swords with his father many times but he's incapable of thinking of him as a murderer.'

'And you're not?'

'Obviously, I don't know. Todd and I have spent hours discussing this and I think it's a possibility we should bear in mind.'

'Are you suggesting Cornelius had something to do with the accident?'

Kim shrugged. 'It might sound far-fetched but . . .' She tailed off, not quite willing to put her thoughts into words.

'But would he kill his own son? Especially one he's so fond of?'

'I'm not so sure he's that fond of him now. He was seriously angry with Todd the other day when he refused to go back to work for him, he was quite scary. Cornelius is planning something at the moment . . .' Kim hesitated '. . . a big deal, something that will transform Zyl News. But I think he's asking himself what's the point of building up an empire if he has to abandon it to Edwin in a few years – he has a very low opinion of Edwin, quite rightly as far as I'm concerned, the man is a worm. We're talking about Cornelius's life's work here, and Todd walking away from it. No one likes being rejected, especially not someone as used to getting his own way as Cornelius. I'm not saying he sabotaged the plane himself, but he's a powerful man, he can organize things. Which is why I was worried about the accident, whether it really was an accident.'

Calder took a deep breath. 'I can see that now. Although

I still don't see how that engine fire could have been anything else.'

Kim shrugged. 'Maybe. But I want to find out what's going on here. Not just for Todd's sake, but for my own. And I'd like you to help me. I trust you more than any of Todd's family.' Her bottom lip trembled, and she began to cry. 'I'm scared, Alex. Just like Martha was when she wrote that letter. I'm scared.'

6

June 28, 1988

I was in a foul mood all morning. Neels didn't come home. I called George, who said that he and Neels had made the announcement. It was one of the hardest things George has ever had to do. The journalists were in uproar. And not just the journalists, a lot of people are going to lose their jobs, including George himself, of course. Neels has given them three months until closure, September 30. George says it's going to be a nightmare keeping things going until then.

What will I say to Neels? Last night I was all set to confront him and throw him out on his ear. But now I'm not so sure. It would be demeaning, degrading, to ask him where he was last night. It's going to be hard to talk sensibly to him, and dangerous to scream at him. I'll ignore him. He can manufacture a little business trip out of somewhere, he's done that before.

Caroline looked scared out of her wits this morning before she went to school. How's she going to take all this? And Todd?

And on top of all that, Zan's coming this afternoon. I wonder how she'll be. Polite and surly? Or awkward and bloody-minded? It's going to be a disaster, I just know it, and I'm not sure I have the strength to deal with it.

Later . . .

Well, Zan came and it was fine. She's gone all African. Her blonde hair is braided with beads, her arms are jangling with bracelets and she was wearing a yellow Hotstix Mabuse T-shirt, car-tire sandals and an East African skirt. She still swims, you can see that from her shoulders which are broad and strong. She looks extremely healthy and she still has Neels's familiar blue eyes. She seemed genuinely pleased to see me when she arrived just after lunch. She was very friendly to Doris; one of the problems we had with her was the way she treated the maids as she got older. You could see Doris was thrilled. I think she was as upset as I was by the way Zan changed as she grew up.

She asked all about Todd and Caroline and my parents. She asked about Neels, and I was positive, I really was. She's staying in the room she always used to sleep in when she came to Hondehoek, and she started to reminisce about how Doris and I used to help her make clothes for her Barbie dolls. She says she wants to dig them out again. I'm pretty sure they weren't thrown away; Caroline used to play with them sometimes. Doris promises she will look for them tomorrow. Four years ago Zan would have been mortified at the suggestion that she ever played with dolls. The Barbie stuff is a tad embarrassing, but it was fun at the time.

In fact we had a lot of fun when she was a little kid. She was only five when Penelope and Neels divorced. After we got married she and Edwin came to stay with us for the odd weekend. I felt sorry for her; her mother was an alcoholic with men around all the time. I was trying to get used to this weird country and she became my ally. I probably spoiled her a bit: we got her the pony, and Matt, who started off life as a cute little puppy before turning into that boisterous bruiser of a Labrador. Poor fellow; I miss him. Anyway, she was my little shadow at weekends, prattling away about this and that. When she took up swimming and began to win races, I used to take her to the meets, I cheered her on.

And then . . . and then it all changed.

But I think it's going to be okay now. In fact in my current frame of mind, it will be nice to have the company. Of course, she doesn't know that Neels and I are not getting on. That's going to be difficult. Because when he comes home tonight she's certainly going to notice it.

June 29

As I write this, Zan is thrashing up and down in the pool outside despite the temperature – it's only about sixty. I don't want her to see me writing in this diary.

She was overjoyed to see Neels last night, and he her. He embraced her so tightly I'm amazed she managed to breathe. Despite myself, I was touched.

But I'm still furious with him, although I did my best to hide it. It worked, I don't think Zan noticed anything was wrong, but I'm not sure how long I can keep it up. If it hadn't been for the fact that my husband is a cheating sonofabitch, it might have been a nice evening.

I made coquilles Saint Jacques. Doris and I are a good team, I do like cooking with her. Zan told us a little of what she has been getting up to in Johannesburg. Apparently she shared an apartment with Tammy Mackie, the daughter of Don and Heather Mackie who were both members of the South African Communist Party and are now in exile. Tammy is banned, which means that she can't go to any meetings of more than a certain number of people, but Zan can and does. I'm sure she didn't tell us the half of what she's up to, but it sounded quite exciting. Neels asked her to promise to be careful while she was staying with us. This she agreed to do, to my surprise.

We didn't mention the newspaper business once, although Neels said he wants to invite the Pellings over to dinner in a couple of days. We know them a little, but we're hardly best friends. Graham Pelling is loaded, so there's got to be some business motive behind that, I'm sure. Perhaps Neels can get him to buy the *Mail*. That would be good.

I let Neels into my bed last night, but I didn't talk to him. He tried to touch me but I shook him off.

Bastard.

June 30

It's been raining. The Hondekop is wreathed in wisps of cloud and a couple of miles upstream the valley has disappeared into a ceiling of thick gray. Everything is dripping wet. There's no wind. The fynbos smells wonderful in the damp air. I was standing by the slave bell, trying to decide how to protect the tulip bulbs from the moles, when I heard a complicated whoop, followed by an answering call. It was a bokmakierie and his mate, flitting about somewhere in the branches of the white stinkwood tree. They are a kind of bush shrike, small with a yellow breast, black collar and loud voice, but the Afrikaans word captures the cadence of the call. The cock sings out "ka-weet, ka-weet, bokmakierie," and the hen answers. There is something wonderfully domestic about them; I feel as if this is their garden as much as mine.

Suddenly I found myself standing there, in the damp lush garden, with tears streaming down my face. I'm jealous of the married bliss of two dumb birds. I really need to get a grip.

July 1

Zan went to an End Conscription Campaign meeting in Cape Town this morning. I considered asking whether I could come with her, but I don't quite have the courage.

I've seen very little of Neels this past couple of days, although whenever I have seen him he looks in a nasty mood. There's some heavy criticism of him in the news-papers today. He's gone from benevolent dictator to evil tyrant in one day. Serves him right. I hope it hurts!

It's Caroline's last day at school before the winter holiday. She seems more subdued than she usually does at the end of term. I'm sure she feels the tension between me and Neels. Poor girl!

July 2

Saturday, and Neels is taking the day off. The newspaper editorials, the letter pages and the journalists are all outraged over the closure of the *Mail*. They hate Neels, and it's really getting to him. George and his journalists are demanding that Neels allow them to buy the *Mail* themselves, or find another friendly buyer. Neels told them that if they could find a buyer he would happily sell. He's certain they won't and I fear he is right.

He spoke to me and Zan about it this morning over breakfast. He is very bitter: disillusioned. He says he has sunk millions of rand into the *Mail* over the years and no one is giving him any credit for that. He is a businessman first and always has been and no one can hide from the fact that the *Mail*'s numbers don't add up. When P. W. Botha first came to power ten years ago saying he would change things, Neels was optimistic. But now he says he is pretty sure that the country is going to go up in flames in a couple of years and there's nothing he can do about it. The police are getting ever more brutal, but so are the blacks. Bombs, necklacings, schoolchildren rioting, the Zulus and the UDF killing each other, his brother's murder. The spiral of violence that he had hoped to avoid has started and it's going to end in the most God-awful bloodshed. It's time to quit.

He directed most of this to Zan, and she listened sympathetically, although I could see she wasn't convinced. For a moment I almost felt sorry for him. But he deserves all this blame! He's right, things do look bad with the State of Emergency and the rioting, but this is when his country needs people like him the most.

And there's the bimbo. I know I don't have any evidence, but I know she exists. I just *know* it. It explains everything.

After breakfast Zan and Neels decided they would go for a long walk up into the mountains. I watched them go, two tall energetic figures cutting through the thin layer of mist hovering a couple of feet above the ground among the golden vine leaves. They left their footsteps in the dew glistening on the lawn. It's three o'clock now and they are still out. Part of me feels a little jealous of Zan; she is taking on the role that I should have, supporting my husband in his hour of difficulty.

Neels has announced that he is going to Durban and then on to Philadelphia next week, to work on the *Herald* deal. I'll be glad to have him gone, believe me. One of his bankers is coming to dinner with the Pellings tonight. I will do my wifely duty.

July 3

Had the Pellings over to dinner last night with Neels's banker. Zan was there and behaved herself well: she looks stunning with her tan and her beaded hair and she impressed Graham Pelling. I played the perfect hostess.

Actually, I'm not bad at entertaining, especially for small groups. Neels does it a lot, and we get an interesting bunch of people, most of whom are very friendly. When we were first married in the seventies we used to invite some of the leading radicals, white and black, but nowadays they are all in prison or banned from meeting other people or just too suspicious. Then there are the academics from Stellenbosch University who are quite amusing and *so* gossipy. There's one of them I particularly like, a professor of journalism of all things, called Daniel Havenga. He's a funny-looking man: he's probably only forty-five but he has a shock of prematurely white hair, a little round face with a beard, wicked brown eyes and little ears that stick out at right-angles from his head. He refers to Stellenbosch as "hanky-panky town," and if half of what he tells us over the dinner table is true, the name is justified. Although none of them talk to us about their support for apartheid, I think several are members of the Broederbond, including Daniel.

I asked Neels once whether he was a brother, and he assured me he wasn't. I believe him, but then the whole point of a secret society is that you're not supposed to admit to being a member. I remember when my friend Nancy discovered her father was a freemason when she was twelve it freaked her out. From what I can make out it is the Broederbond who come up with all the apartheid regime's bright ideas, so it is highly unlikely that Neels would be part of that. I bet they'd love to have him, though.

We all talked about how important the press is, even in these days of ever more draconian restrictions on what newspapers can report, and then Neels mentioned in confidence that he might be forced to sell his South African papers. He did it very well: Graham seemed interested. They talked by themselves after dinner and Neels thinks that Graham might bite. He would make a good owner and with all those gold mines he's got the cash. Perhaps he'd take the *Mail* as well?

The banker was black! Oh, my God, can you stand it? We were, I hope, able to treat the man like a normal human being. The poor guy's name is Benton, and he has to do some kind of work on Neels's South African newspapers. He's stuck in an "integrated" hotel in Cape Town but Neels has assigned him a driver to take him wherever he wants. In practice that's just going to be back and forth to the office.

It was *so* good to talk to another American, especially just before Independence Day. He seems like a really nice guy, more widely read than most of the investment bankers I've come across, and smart too. He's read all the Latin American literature I like – he said the new Isabel Allende is really good, and he's just read Nadine Gordimer. He lives in Greenwich Village. Apparently, it's been hit hard by AIDS; it's like a ghost town. At least that's one problem South Africa doesn't have to worry about.

I feel sorry for the poor man, beavering away at work on the Fourth of July. Maybe I'll bake some of my chocolate-chip cookies and leave him a care package at his hotel.

But what will I use for the chocolate chips? I've still got some Toll House left, but they are made by Nestlé, and I've started boycotting them again. I read the other day that they are still trying to sell baby formula to African mothers who can easily use breast milk instead. You would have thought with all the fuss over the years they would have stopped that by now. I might have to slice the chocolate by hand. Perhaps Zan will help me, just like she used to when she was a little girl.

July 4

Independence Day. How I wish I was in America today, without Neels. I delivered the cookies to Benton's hotel. I hope he likes them.

Zan announced that she's going back to Jo'burg today for a couple of days. I think it's got something to do with the End Conscription Campaign, but she wasn't very forthcoming. I didn't ask. I've asked her about the Black Sash movement, but she won't tell me anything about it other than it's an organization for white women opposed to apartheid. I think she still doesn't trust me. Which is understandable, I guess.

There was a massive bomb blast on Saturday, outside Ellis Park rugby stadium. There was a match going on inside; the papers are amazed that only two people died. It does kind of underline Neels's point about how the country is falling apart. But I'm not sure we should run away.

Just got back from dinner with Benton Davis. He sent me a sweet note about the cookies Zan and I baked for him, so I called him and suggested we meet. Benton didn't want to leave his hotel, so we ate in the dining room. Neels is in Durban tonight, trying to figure out what to do with the *Durban Age*. Alone, I hope, but of course I have no way of knowing.

Unsurprisingly, Benton can't stand this country. He says the worst thing isn't just all the little rules discriminating against blacks, the separate toilets and so on. Those are vile, but he was expecting that. It is the way the white people look at him, a tall black man dressed in an expensive suit. He says the reactions vary: there's fear, there's hatred, there's shock and there's contempt on their faces. The one response that he can handle is astonishment. That's what makes it worthwhile.

He was walking through the lobby of the hotel on his first morning in the country when he heard a shout: "Boy!" He ignored it, not for a moment thinking it was meant for him, when it was repeated. "Boy! Wait!" He turned and saw a short gray-haired man with a moustache approaching him.

"Can I help you, sir?" he had said, falling back on politeness in his confusion. He could smell alcohol as the man got closer.

The man's eyes lit up when he heard the accent. "Go back to your own country, boy. We don't want you stirring up trouble with our Kaffirs here."

Benton's first instinct was to hit the man, who was much smaller and older than him. Then he realized that's exactly what the man wanted, and he turned on his heel and walked out of the hotel. But he spent the rest of the day rehearsing to himself all the replies he should have come up with.

He asked me whether they have the term "redneck" in this country. I told him "redneck" is actually a term the Boers use for English-speaking liberals, but there are a couple of near equivalents to the American usage: "rockspider" or "hairyback." He liked rockspider.

I asked him why he had come. After years of ignoring South Africa, America has gotten itself all excited about the place, especially black America. Didn't he think he was consorting with the enemy?

He said it had been difficult. He hates his boss. When it became clear that someone from Bloomfield Weiss had to go to South Africa to check up on Neels's South African newspapers, his boss thought this was a great opportunity to send Benton. Benton objected and his boss called him a coward. I'd have thought that was asking for a racial discrimination suit, but apparently that's this guy's game: he's always trying to force Benton to play the race card. This is something Benton says he has never done and never will do; he's determined to succeed on his own terms, not because of his color. He was unsure whether to go when Neels spoke to him.

Apparently, Neels had anticipated the whole problem. He said that South Africa needed blacks like Benton to travel there, to show the whites that in the outside world blacks could be well-educated men and women in positions of power and authority. Andrew Young, the US ambassador to the UN, and Leon Sullivan, the black board member of General Motors, were both prominent black Americans who had visited South Africa and sent out an important message. Benton could do that too.

Benton was clearly impressed with Neels. He has always

been a fan of Leon Sullivan in particular. He decided to come.

Dinner was fun. But toward the end Benton let slip something about Zyl News that I hadn't suspected. It was a shock, a major shock. I will try to find out more from Neels when we are speaking to each other again. If we speak to each other again.

July 7

Neels came back from Durban yesterday and he's off to the States tomorrow. I'll be glad to see him go. Especially since I know he will be away from his woman, whoever she is. At the moment I don't want to think about her.

With Zan gone, things were strained. I mentioned I'd had dinner with Benton the night before, but didn't ask Neels about what Benton had told me. We went to bed in silence. Just after he turned the light off, Neels began to speak to me.

"*Liefie?*"

"Yes?"

"There's something I want to tell you. I've been meaning to tell you for a couple of days."

I steeled myself, lying on my side in bed, facing away from him. I was the one who was supposed to mention his mistress, not him. I didn't like surrendering the initiative.

"Do you remember that Zan and I went for a long walk on Saturday?"

"Yes," I said, puzzled.

"She told me something then. Something she heard while she was in London."

"I didn't know she'd been to London."

"Neither did I," said Neels. "Maybe she had to interview

for her place at the LSE. I don't know. I didn't want to ask her."

"Okay."

"Well. She bumped into a South African. A member of the South African Communist Party."

"Who?"

"She wouldn't say. But remember she lives with the Mackie girl. Maybe it was her parents. Or friends of her parents. Who knows? But this South African told her something quite disturbing."

I waited. Cornelius was lying on his back, staring at the ceiling.

"He said there was a list. A list with my name on it."

"What sort of list?"

"A come-the-revolution-who-are-we-going-to-line-up-against-the-wall list."

"No!" I turned toward him.

"Yes."

"Do you believe it?"

"I don't know. I think so. The SACP's headquarters is in London, everyone knows that."

"Who else is on the list?"

"It's a long one, apparently. The man didn't give her any more names. Apart from one."

"Whose is that?"

He raised himself on to his elbow and looked me in the eyes for the first time that evening.

"Yours."

7

Cornelius's study was a mess. Every surface of the expensive furniture was covered with paper: spreadsheets, financial reports, printouts of news articles, consultants' studies, and even some newspapers. Cornelius tried to make sure he read at least the *Herald* and the *Philadelphia Intelligencer* every day, but the copies were piling up. There were also back issues of *The Times*. These he had been studying closely.

Edwin was looking worn. His three-piece suit was intact, he was wearing a tie and the top button of his shirt was still done up, but he was frayed around the edges. Cornelius's insistence that no one else from Zyl News be involved meant that Edwin had had to do a lot of the work he would normally have farmed out to his MBA grunts. He had done it diligently and well, but he hadn't slept much.

Cornelius, on the other hand, was a volcano of energy. He found it difficult to sit still for more than a minute or two without darting from one problem to another. He threw himself into the transaction and drove Edwin into the ground.

The Bloomfield Weiss bankers filed into the study. Benton led the way, followed by Dower, but now they had a real deal for which they would be paid fees, the team had grown to six. There was probably a battalion of Bloomfield Weiss's own grunts back at their office in Broadgate also working on the transaction out of sight.

'Sorry about the mess, gentlemen,' Cornelius began. 'How's it going with the banks?'

Dower opened his mouth, but before he could say anything Benton spoke. 'Very well. I think they had some trouble at first, the numbers are a bit tight, there's no getting around that, but we've got National Bank of Scotland interested in taking on the role of lead manager. They're a good institution, I think they'll do a fine job for you.'

'What kind of covenants will they want?'

'Andy?' Benton turned to Dower, who was obviously seething. Cornelius could see Dower had been upstaged by Benton and was angry about it. He found investment bankers' grandstanding tiresome, but after twenty years he had become used to it. For all Bloomfield Weiss's faults, and there were many, they had stuck with him through good times and bad, and that was worth a lot. Cornelius would never totally trust them, though. They were investment bankers, after all.

Dower went into details of the financial covenants the banks would demand be included in the legal agreements, and the presentation Edwin and Cornelius would have to make to them the next day. Then discussion moved on again to the price they were planning to pay for *The Times*.

'We've had our analysts take a look at Evelyn Gill's Beckwith Communications,' Dower said. 'Of course it's totally private, and the accounts are a tangle of holding companies. When they borrow, they tend to go to a tight group of banks in Switzerland. But we don't think Gill has access to more funding. A cash offer from you of eight hundred and fifty million would be hard to match. He won't be willing to go to the bond markets for it, and his corporate structure is too messy to be able to get an equity offering away in a hurry.'

Cornelius wasn't going to fall into the trap of underestimating his opponent. Sir Evelyn Gill was a stout man with a defiant stare and a heavy lower jaw thrusting aggressively forward. He had worked in his father's business trading steel in Sheffield, but had seen the writing on the wall for the industry and diversified into ever more precious metals, until he had transformed the family firm into an international commodity speculation outfit. He had invested some of his profits in the purchase of Beckwith Communications, a magazine publisher, in the 1980s, before using this vehicle to launch his failed bid for the *Herald* in 1988 and bagging the tabloid *New York Globe* the following year. Since then he had bought the London tabloid *Mercury* and a series of other newspapers and magazines throughout Europe, Australia and South Africa as well as a book publisher in London. Although Beckwith didn't publish figures, his newspapers were rumoured to be extremely profitable. They all took a populist right-wing stance – anti-immigration, patriotic, anti-bureaucratic – that seemed to strike a chord wherever they were published. Even his more serious political weeklies in France and Sweden subtly followed that line, and circulation had increased. His contribution to the national media was recognized when he was knighted by the Conservative government in 1996, the year before their election defeat.

'Gill has been trying to talk the price down,' Cornelius said. 'You know the game: bait and switch. Agree a price in principle and then negotiate it down because of problems you supposedly discover during due diligence. In this case it's accounting discrepancies and under-funded pensions.'

'Those could be real issues for us as well,' Dower said.

'Laxton Media think it's all bullshit. They are pissed off. Even better for us if we come in with a higher offer.'

'How do we know this?' Benton asked.

'Edwin has a source.'

There was a brief uncomfortable silence. Edwin stared at the papers in front of him while the minds of everyone around the table flitted over the possibilities of what Edwin's source might be. Cornelius knew that Edwin had a reputation for the occasional use of underhand methods to get things done. Cornelius also knew this reputation was justified. He hadn't asked Edwin about his source; he hadn't wanted to know the answer. Perhaps he should have done. Cornelius realized that whenever he did retire, his reputation for integrity would retire with him . . .

'Excellent,' Benton said, to break the silence. 'Now perhaps we can talk about the junk-bond issue.'

'Are you sure I can't tempt you back, Zero?' The Saudi smiled as he sipped his orange juice. The dining room in Claridge's was quiet this early in the morning. He and Calder were the only two people there, bar a lone businessman in the far corner. Their table was set for three. One chair was empty.

'I'm quite sure you can't,' Calder replied, responding to the old nickname from his bond-trading days. 'But I do appreciate you asking.'

'Actually, I will always ask,' the other man said. 'Until one day you say yes.'

Tarek al-Seesi had been Calder's partner and immediate boss at Bloomfield Weiss. He was a small man, with a thick moustache, thinning hair, and large brown thoughtful eyes. He was no more than a couple of years Calder's senior but he looked and acted much older and wiser. He combined the street-trading talents of the bazaar with a profound understanding of human psychology and good grasp of macroeconomics, backed up with a PhD. He was also a canny political operator, something that Calder emphatically wasn't. Most importantly he was someone whom Calder not only respected but trusted. When Calder had phoned him the day before with his request, Tarek had been happy to oblige. So Calder had flown his Cessna down to Elstree the previous afternoon, and spent the evening with his sister in Highgate so that he could get up early to meet Tarek at ten to seven.

'You can't tell me you don't miss the markets,' Tarek said.

'I suppose I do,' Calder replied. He was just about to tell Tarek about the little bits of spread-betting he did, but something stopped him. When they had worked together as bond traders they had laughed at 'dumb retail', their name for ill-informed individual speculators. Calder didn't want to admit that that was what he had become. It was only a bit of dabbling anyway. A bit of fun. 'Thanks for setting this up.'

'No problem. I'm curious to see what happens. Ah, here's the man now.'

Tarek stood up and waved, extending his hand. Calder was sitting with his back to the entrance to the dining room. He waited a few seconds and then turned to see Benton Davis striding towards them. The polite smile on Benton's face froze as he saw Calder.

Tarek shook his hand. 'Have a seat, Benton. You remember Alex, of course.'

'Of course,' Benton said, the smile now gone. He curtly shook Calder's hand and hesitated. Clearly he had no desire to have breakfast with his former colleague. But although Benton was nominally head of the London office, that was essentially a bureaucratic and ambassadorial role. Tarek was in charge of Fixed Income in Europe, and his group made lots of money. Hundreds of millions of dollars. Tarek's star was in the ascendant. Benton sat down.

'I congratulate you on your choice of venue, Tarek,' he said, looking around the ornate dining room.

Tarek smiled. He raised an eyebrow and the head waiter came over. He ordered his usual complicated mozzarella cheese, bread and olive-oil concoction, Calder went for a full breakfast, and Benton just a bowl of muesli and some fruit. Calder had forgotten how impressive a figure Benton cut, with his tall trim frame, his perfectly tailored suit and his deep authoritative voice. Outside Bloomfield Weiss he didn't look like the lightweight glad-hander he had appeared to be from the trading floor.

Benton and Tarek made small talk for a few minutes, ignoring Calder, before Benton turned to him. 'Well, Alex, I wasn't expecting to see you here.' He was polite and he kept the exasperation he must surely have felt over Tarek setting him up out of his voice. But his eyes were wary.

'Alex wants to ask you a question,' Tarek said.

Calder thought he noticed a flicker of relief in Benton's eyes. He suddenly realized that Benton's first assumption was probably that Tarek wanted to offer him his old job back, and this breakfast meeting was actually an interview. But a mere question couldn't be that difficult.

'Sure,' Benton said, with a quick smile. 'Shoot.'

'Do you remember Martha van Zyl?'

Benton hesitated, taken aback by the course Calder was taking. 'Yes, I do. She was Cornelius van Zyl's wife. She was murdered, wasn't she? In South Africa. Horrible business.' He shook his head. His concern seemed genuine.

'Martha's son, Todd, has some questions that he wants to ask you about the death. I'm a very old friend of his wife, Kim. She asked me to talk to you.'

'Ah,' Benton said. 'I was aware that Todd was trying to speak with me about that.'

'And you avoided him?'

Benton smiled. 'Cornelius van Zyl is an important client of the firm. It seemed inappropriate for me to be speaking with his relatives about his wife's death.'

'Did you check with him whether you could talk to Todd?'

'No, I didn't,' Benton said. 'Successful men often have complicated families. Martha was Cornelius's second wife, I believe. He has a third now. And Edwin, the son from his first marriage, works for him. I have no idea what the tensions are in that family, but I know I don't want to find out. And if I'm not going to discuss these things with Todd van Zyl, I'm certainly not going to discuss them with you.'

Calder had been expecting this. 'Todd's in hospital in a coma at the moment. He was involved in an aircraft accident a few days ago. We both were.'

Benton frowned. 'I'm sorry to hear that. I hope he's going to be OK.'

'So do I,' said Calder. 'But his wife is anxious to get an answer to his questions. Which is why I'm here.'

'It must be a very trying time for her. But I'm afraid I can't help.'

Calder took a deep breath. 'You remember Jennifer Tan?'

Benton sighed. 'I wondered when this would come up. I've discussed the whole business with Sidney. It's over now. It's in the past.'

Sidney Stahl was Bloomfield Weiss's chairman. To Calder's disappointment, he hadn't fired Benton after Jen's death.

'It's not in the past though, is it, Benton? There isn't a week goes by that I don't think about her.'

Benton glanced at Calder quickly. Calder knew he had hit a nerve. Benton might have been misguided, callous even, in the way he had treated Jen, but Calder didn't believe he had intentionally driven her to her death. Whatever his protestations, however well he covered his arse, Benton knew he shouldn't have suspended her when she brought the sexual harassment suit against her previous boss. The boss in question was a jerk, everyone knew that, he was just a jerk who made the firm a hundred million dollars a year. So when one of them had to go, Benton had made damn sure it was Jen.

'The answer to my question is important to me, and it's important to people I care for. I really would appreciate a reply.'

Benton shifted in his chair. Calder waited. 'All right,' he said. 'As long as this doesn't get back to Cornelius. What's the question?'

Calder described the letter that was found in Todd's grandmother's papers, and its mention of Benton. Benton listened intently. 'So. What was it that Martha wanted you to tell her mother?' Calder asked.

'I don't know,' said Benton. 'I really don't know. The old woman came to see me right after Martha died. It was a shock, Martha's death. I didn't know her well, I'd only met her once or twice, but to die like that. Ugh.' He scowled. 'South Africa was a sick, sick country. Still is, probably. I won't go back there.'

'What did you tell her?'

'I told her I didn't know what Martha meant. I wracked my brains. My only guess was it was something I let slip when we were having dinner in Cape Town. I was sent down there shortly before she died to do some due diligence on Zyl News's South African newspapers. The plan was to sell them off or close them. I found South Africa a loathsome place and she took pity on me. I guess I implied, probably not much more than that, that Zyl News was running out of cash. I think Martha assumed Cornelius's businesses were worth tens of millions. Well, they were, of course, but then so was his debt. He was finding it tight meeting the interest payments. The acquisition of the *Herald*, bringing with it yet more debt, was a brave move. I guess when a rich man's wife discovers that her husband's net worth is close to negative, it comes as a bit of a shock.'

Calder stared hard at Benton. 'Was that all?'

Benton shrugged. 'It's all that I could think of.'

'What was Martha's mother's reaction?'

'She was disappointed. I think she expected more.'

'Did she ask about a diary?'

Benton frowned. 'It was a while ago. She might have done. I really don't remember.'

'You didn't see a diary anywhere? Martha didn't give you a diary to look after?'

Benton snorted. 'I really didn't know her that well. I liked her, but I have no idea if she kept a diary and she certainly wouldn't have shown it to me if she did.'

'And finally, does the word "Laagerbond" mean anything to you?'

Benton shook his head. He drained his coffee and put his napkin on the table. 'If that's all, I need to get on to the office.'

'Thank you, Benton,' Calder said.

'That's OK. Just make sure Todd or his wife don't tell Cornelius that I spoke with you. And I hope Todd recovers soon.'

Calder and Tarek watched Benton stride out of the dining room. 'Did you get what you wanted?' Tarek asked.

'I asked the question. He answered it,' Calder said.

'Do you believe him?'

Calder glanced at his friend. 'Don't know. Do you?'

Tarek shrugged. 'Actually, I'm not sure. But I think that's the best answer you are going to get.'

'Was Zyl News in trouble back in 1988?' Calder asked. 'This was all way before my time.'

'And mine,' said Tarek. 'If you've got a moment we could talk to Cash Callaghan. I'm pretty sure he was selling junk bonds back then.'

The two years since Calder had left Bloomfield Weiss was long enough for him to feel a sense of nostalgia as he followed Tarek into the familiar dealing room on the second floor of their Broadgate offices. There were many faces he knew who smiled and nodded to him, but there were just as many he didn't. Young, fresh-faced, intense-looking men and women, sucked into the Bloomfield Weiss machine to replace those that had been spat out or tempted away by six-figure guaranteed bonuses from other firms. As he caught glimpses of the screens crammed with rows and columns of figures, Calder couldn't repress a surge of excitement, a tingle of curiosity. What was going up? What was going down? What was happening out there in the markets? And in here in the Bloomfield Weiss trading room? Who was making money, who was losing it, who was riding the big positions, who was sitting on the big losses? And the biggest question: was it really possible for him to walk away from all this for ever?

They threaded their way through the maze of desks, computer equipment, chairs and bodies to the Fixed Income sales desk and paused next to an overweight American in his fifties leaning back and talking. Talking fast.

'OK, Josie, you've got close to five hundred million in asset-backeds, right?' The man was in full spiel. 'You switch those into five hundred million Treasuries. You give up yield but you get *convexity*, right? Oodles of convexity. The markets bounce the way you're telling me they're gonna and you got yourself a rocket-fuelled portfolio. I mean you're going to the moon, Josie. Top-quartile performance, investment manager of the year, promotion, big bonus, new car, new Jimmy Choos. Think of the Jimmy Choos, Josie.'

Calder and Tarek could hear the female laughter on the other end of the line.

'OK, you think about it,' the man said. 'But think fast. 'Cos if you think about it for a week, that's not thinking, that's sleeping, know what I mean?'

He put down the phone and turned to Calder. 'Hey, Zero, my man! How are you doing?' He leaped to his feet and held out his hand. Calder took it.

'I'm very well, Mr Callaghan. What was all that about convexity?'

'It's Josie's new word for the week. Every now and then your clients learn a new word and you gotta pay attention. She's a nice kid, but I doubt she's seen her first bond mature. You still out in the boonies playing with model airplanes?'

'More or less.'

'You getting him back to work for us, Tarek?'

'I tried,' Tarek said. 'He's a tough nut to crack.'

'Come on, Zero. We need you here. We need a guy with balls.' He looked contemptuously towards the parallel row of desks where the traders were seated. Cash Callaghan was a salesman, the most successful in Bloomfield Weiss's London office. He had been around a long time, but he hadn't lost any of his energy. Despite appearances, he was well known for his memory. Bonds might come and go, but Cash would remember them all, who issued them, who bought them, who sold them, what happened to them.

'Actually, he wanted to ask you about one of our favourite junk-bond issuers,' Tarek said. 'Zyl News.'

'Ah, yes. So is there something in the rumours they're taking a run at *The Times*?'

'I don't know anything about that,' Calder said. 'I want to ask you about 1988.'

'Hmm . . . 1988.' Cash thought a moment. 'I remember. The *Herald* takeover. Two hundred million dollar issue, thirteen and a half per cent coupon, maturity two thousand, boy was that difficult to get away. It was less than a year after the October '87 crash and the junk market was just opening up again to good issuers. Zyl News was not a good issuer.'

'What was the problem?'

'There were rumours they were in trouble. Their cash flow was barely covering their interest costs. We'd backed Cornelius van Zyl all through the eighties. He bought all kinds of papers in the states – the *Philadelphia Intelligencer* was the biggest, but there were many more, including a couple of major metros in Indiana and Ohio. And he did a great job turning them around, cutting costs, jacking up advertising rates, that kind of thing. But he kept paying up to make these acquisitions and borrowing from the banks and the junk market to do it. It was all great as long as we could keep lending him the money to feed the machine. In '86 he tried a start-up in the Los Angeles market against the *LA Times* – that was an expensive disaster. Then in October '87 the stock market melted down and it looked like the junk-bond market was history. Guys like van Zyl were in big trouble. Without the junk market they couldn't do any more deals, and without new deals they were left struggling to meet the interest payments on the old ones. The only way out of the bind was to buy a larger company and use its cash flow to service the debt. So the *Herald* acquisition was an important one. Make or break.'

'Was anyone else interested in the *Herald*?'

'Yeah. Evelyn Gill. No one had heard of him back then. He'd made his money in commodities and he owned a small magazine publisher. Then he suddenly decided he wanted to use his cash to buy a newspaper. It was his first deal. He ended up offering a higher price than Zyl News, but the *Herald* went to Zyl anyway. Gill was pissed. He and van Zyl have been big enemies ever since. Of course, Gill has bought a whole bunch of other titles since then, including the *New York Globe* and the *Mercury*.'

'But you say it was difficult to get the Zyl deal away?'

'Oh yeah. They had to jack the coupon up, I think they started at twelve per cent and had to raise it to thirteen and a half. I was worried about it, to be honest. You hate to sell something to your customers that's gonna blow up in their face.'

'So you didn't sell any yourself?'

Cash grinned. 'They doubled the sales credit, I had to rethink my priorities. I sold forty million in Europe. The guys in New York loved me.'

Calder rolled his eyes.

'Hey!' Cash said. 'I've dug you out of a hole on more than one occasion.'

'That's true.' Calder had made use of Cash's sales skills to get rid of troublesome positions that the rest of the market didn't want. Calder had had to put up with a certain amount of stick from him, but Cash had been able to sell the bonds. Cash was always able to sell the bonds. 'How's Zyl News been since then?'

'Well, they did a good job. They turned the *Herald* around and met all their interest payments, and although they've done more deals — some regional papers in this country, a couple in Australia and Canada, some more in the US — they've learned their lesson. They've only got one bond issue outstanding at the moment and that's trading well.'

'Thanks, Cash.'

'No problem,' he said. 'Now I've got to figure out what I'm gonna do with those five hundred million asset-backeds if Josie does sell them.'

As Calder left the Bloomfield Weiss building his mobile phone rang. It was Kim. She sounded agitated.

'What is it?' Calder asked.

'When are you getting back?'

'I was planning to fly up this afternoon. Why? What's up?'

'Well, hurry up. I've just been talking to the police. I was right, I knew I was right. The plane crash wasn't an accident. It was sabotage.'

8

July 11, 1988

Went to a board meeting of the Project today, the Guguletu Literacy Project. Nimrod drove me: I don't like driving there by myself since the riots of a couple of years ago. In fact, we've only gone back to holding the board meetings in the township in the last few months; until recently the place was a no-go area for whites. Guguletu doesn't exist in the mind of white South Africa. It isn't even on the map, despite the fact that a couple of hundred thousand people must live there. It's a sprawling warren of single-room shacks made of wood and corrugated iron, each one crammed with people taking up every inch of floor space to sleep on. For some reason the dominant color seems to be pistachio green. But the township is teeming with life: children running around everywhere, chickens scratching about, even the odd cow, which still retains its importance as a symbol of wealth. There are smells of cooking and of filth, sounds of chatter, children's laughter and everywhere the beat of "location music," the same stuff that Finneas picks out on his harmonica at home.

Miriam Masote founded the Project ten years ago to try to teach adults to read and write. Her father has been in jail on Robben Island for nearly thirty years now. Her view is that when enough black South Africans can read they will develop a voice that the rest of the world will have to hear. I hope she is right. There are hundreds, maybe thousands of inhabitants of the township who can now read thanks to her. She does an amazing amount with very little money. That's where I can help, not just by giving them some of our money, but by raising funds from the States. Mom does a good job with the churches in Minnesota.

Libby Wiseman was on excellent form. That woman is a hoot. God knows, you need a sense of humor in a place like Guguletu. She is pretty outspoken about the regime, and I think she's been arrested a couple of times, but she seems to have avoided a banning order somehow. She gets very upset about greedy capitalists in South Africa, without ever actually mentioning Neels by name. Perhaps she's a communist? I wonder if there are any of the SACP left in South Africa, or whether they are all in jail or in exile. She and I get on well, though: she's one of the few South African women who I can call a friend. I can't imagine her putting Neels and me on any execution list, although presumably that's decided by the leaders in exile.

After the meeting she asked me back to her house for a drink, but I said no. I just feel like curling myself up into a ball and hiding away at Hondehoek.

I've been thinking about Neels a lot these past couple of days, thinking about when we first met. It was the moment that defined my life. It was the late sixties, I was a year out of graduate school and I was fired up about all the injustices of the world, foremost among them apartheid. I'd written a couple of successful freelance articles for *Life* magazine on student protest movements, and I planned to try to sell them an article on the press and apartheid in South Africa. I had a friend whose father was the *Time* correspondent and I managed to arrange to stay with him in Johannesburg. He helped me get interviews with some of the editors and owners of the South African newspapers.

With the exception of a couple of the Afrikaners whose support for apartheid was clear, all the newspaper men I met were blind, blind to what was going on in their country. Their political outlook as far as I was concerned was "See no evil." And then I met Neels.

I flew to Cape Town for the meeting, which was at the *Cape Daily Mail*'s offices. I was curious, but not hopeful. I knew of the *Mail*'s reputation for uncovering scandals, but then Neels had an Afrikaans last name, and by that stage I had low expectations of newspaper owners.

He attracted me the moment I saw him. He had power over women. He had it then, when he was in his late thirties, and he still has it now even though he is over fifty. It was, or is, a kind of strength, strength that can protect rather than threaten, a self-assurance that falls short of vanity. Broad shoulders, square jaw and those piercing, honest eyes. I was smitten.

He wasn't, or not at first. Oh, he paid attention to me, men did in those days. He explained how he, an Afrikaner, came to be the owner of the second largest English-speaking newspaper group in South Africa. He told me about his father's little paper in Oudtshoorn. How he was one of five children, how he got a scholarship to the University of Stellenbosch and with his father's encouragement a Rhodes Scholarship to Oxford. How he met Penelope there, and how she had forced him to focus on what he always knew to be the case: the injustice of apartheid. They were married. Her family were English-speakers, wealthy investors in gold mines with a mansion in Parktown in Johannesburg, and suspicious of the Afrikaner from the Karoo. But they soon warmed to Cornelius, and her father funded him to buy a bankrupt newspaper group that included the *Durban Age*, the *Johannesburg Post* and the *Week in Business*. He turned all three papers around and a couple of years later bought the *Cape Daily Mail*. He was just thirty at the time.

He answered my questions with passion and in detail. His view was that the most effective opposition to apartheid was the press, in particular the English-language press. His role as owner was the guardian of that voice of opposition and sanity.

I came back at him. How could the press in a country like South Africa ever be truly free? And if it wasn't, if his journalists were locked up for telling the truth, wasn't he merely supporting the system by working within it?

Neels told me I was suffering from the same lack of understanding as all the English-speaking liberals. This was the fourth time I had been told this, and I just lost it. I was fed up of being patronized by white Nazi racists. I railed on. Then I suddenly noticed that Neels was trying to suppress a smile. Not only that, but he was interested in me. Not as a twenty-something blonde with long legs, but as a woman. As a person. This angered me more, but also disconcerted me and so I shut up.

"I'm sorry," he said. "I didn't mean to insult you. Let me tell you what I did mean." He fixed me with those piercing blue eyes of his. "The fatal flaw of the apartheid regime, what will ultimately bring about its downfall, is its certainty that it's morally right."

"How can apartheid ever be morally right?" I interrupted.

"It's a twisted morality, backed by a twisted understanding of Christianity. But if the regime is to continue to believe that it is legitimate it needs to maintain some semblance of justice, of right and wrong. There has to be an independent judiciary, a parliament where opposition is allowed to speak, and a free press."

"But that's incompatible with a government that's elected

by a small minority of the country, that locks people up and tortures them without trial!"

"Precisely. As time goes on that incompatibility will become more and more apparent until the majority of the National Party can't hide from it anymore. Then they will hand over power. Voluntarily."

"So you're just playing a part in the charade of a fair government?"

"No, not at all. It's Afrikaners like me who will bring this regime to a peaceful end. It might take ten years, it might take fifty years, but it will happen. Independent judges, critical politicians, a free press, lawyers who believe in justice, doctors who tell the truth about the injuries they treat. In time we will be able to show our countrymen that they cannot support apartheid and still think of themselves as moral human beings. Blowing up a railway station won't tell them that, quite the reverse. And I don't want to see my country go up in flames in a bloody revolution."

I was silenced. Neels smiled at me. "How long are you in South Africa?"

"A week."

"Well, why don't you spend that week in the *Mail*'s offices? You can write an article or two on America for us. And you'll get a better idea of how the press in South Africa really works."

So I stayed a week. Then extended it for another week. Then a month. He persuaded me. And we fell in love. There was his wife – but I don't want to think about that now.

I am glad I have written about when we met. It's brought back to me not just the ideals which we shared then, but how much I loved him. Still do love him.

Which makes it all so much more painful when he betrays me.

Neels is back from Philadelphia, although it's only for a few days; he'll be going back there on Friday. Which makes me wonder, why does he spend the weekend there and not here? As usual these days he went straight into the office from the airport and didn't get back here until nine at night. He looks exhausted. He's been very distracted these last few weeks. I assumed that it was to do with our marriage or with Hennie's death, but thinking about what Benton told me perhaps there's something else. I decided to find out.

I asked him if I could pour him a drink. He glanced at me quickly, checking for signs of sarcasm I suppose. Not seeing any he gave me a weary smile. "Yes, please," he said.

I poured him a brandy and Coke and myself a glass of wine, and we sat down by the fire. The scent of the blue-gum firewood hung in the air.

"Is the *Herald* deal not going well?" I asked.

Neels checked again for signs of gloating, but he could see my concern was genuine.

He sighed. "No. I thought we had it in the bag. But it looks as if I can't raise the money they're asking. The junk-bond markets are still tough. The crash last October has scared everyone; they all think I'm too big a risk."

"Do you have to use these junk bonds?" I said. "They always sounded pretty awful to me. Can't you just borrow money from a bank?"

Neels shook his head. "The bankers are just as scared as the bond investors."

"Never mind," I said. "There will be other opportunities."

"I'm not so sure Zyl News will be around to see other opportunities, *liefie*."

This is the first time Neels has admitted what Benton hinted to me: that Zyl News is so overstretched it's on the point of bankruptcy. It's also the first time we've spoken about the company since he told me he's planning to close the *Cape Daily Mail*. Before, in the old days of our marriage, we talked about the business all the time. Discussing what was going on with the newspapers was his way of unwinding, and I was always interested. He is an astute businessman and I like to hear about his exploits.

"Could you sell the US papers and keep the South African ones?" I asked.

Neels glanced at me quickly, his eyes betraying a flash of irritation. But he considered the question. "It's a bad time to sell anything in the States. Everything's on hold, no one's making any plans. No. I've got to figure out a way of funding the *Herald* deal. That's all there is to it."

For a moment, I almost felt sorry for him. Then I remembered the night he hadn't come home.

I drank my wine. "I'm sure you'll figure it out, an international media mogul like you." This time, Neels didn't have to look for the sarcasm.

July 14

I'm sitting here, at the picnic place halfway up the Honde-kop, shaking as I write this. I have got to be *so* careful how and where I write in this diary. At least up here I won't be disturbed and I want to get down as much of this as I can before I forget it. There's no point in worrying about what I write in here now – with that list in the back, the book is dynamite if anyone finds it.

Down in the valley, in the house, our house, is Neels.

What's he thinking? I have no idea what's in his mind. I was absolutely right when I wrote at the beginning of this diary that I had lost him. He's betrayed everything, his beliefs, me. I don't know who he is anymore.

And I'm afraid of this new Neels.

He said he wanted to spend the morning working from home, which struck me as a little odd, given how he likes to escape to the office whenever he can these days. I was getting ready to drive Caroline into Stellenbosch. Neels bought a new compact-disc player last month and the result, which we should have anticipated, is that Caroline wants to buy a whole bunch of new compact discs to replicate her record collection, such as it is. As will Todd, no doubt, when he gets home. Anyway, just as we were leaving, Daniel Havenga drove up with another man, a neat little fellow with a limp. Daniel was his usual cheery self, and was telling his companion how wonderful our garden was, when Neels appeared. It was clear that the visit had been arranged, although I knew nothing about it. This wasn't necessarily surprising since Neels and I say precious little to each other these days, although he had mumbled something about working from home this morning. Daniel introduced his friend as Andries Visser and Neels took them off to the study.

My curiosity was aroused. All our dealings with Daniel have been social, but this was business. Visser was wearing a gray suit and he was carrying one of those slim black businessman briefcases. He looked like a man about to enter an important meeting rather than someone dropping in on a friend in the country.

So, I told Caroline I just wanted to finish something off in the garden, and I strolled around the side of the house. Neels's study is by the slave bell, and I rooted around in the tulip beds there to try to catch their conversation. The window, which he usually likes to keep open unless it is very cold, was shut. I could hear murmuring inside, but I couldn't make out what they were saying, especially since the bokmakieries decided to take that moment to start yelling to each other.

I was desperate to find out what it was they were discussing. I even considered standing outside the room with my ear to the door, but that would have been too obvious. I went around to the front of the house, where Daniel's Renault was parked. I looked inside. The car was a mess, wine-gum wrappers all over the place and a load of books slung on the back seat with Daniel's raincoat. The books were university textbooks on media and journalism. I wondered if there was anything in the trunk. I glanced around. No sign of Caroline or Doris or Finneas or anyone else. I quickly opened it up and peeked in. Inside was a mess of plastic bags, some boots and a small bag of rose fertilizer. I snapped the trunk shut.

I had a last look into the car through the rear window, and caught a glimpse of brown leather poking out from under the coat. Another quick look around to see if anyone was watching and I checked the car door. Unlocked. I opened it. Pushed back the coat to reveal a battered brown briefcase. Opened the briefcase.

Like the car, it was a mess, full of loose crinkled papers, some of which bore the University of Stellenbosch crest. In the back was a plastic folder with a thick sheaf of papers. I glanced at the top sheet. It was a survey of the British newspaper market. I was about to shove it back in the briefcase, when I noticed the words "Zyl News."

I flicked through the report. Lots of figures, lots of analysis of the media markets in South Africa, Europe and the US.

Behind that was a two-page memo. It was headed "Cornelius van Zyl."

I hesitated. I had no idea how long the meeting with Neels would take. But curiosity overcame caution and I read on. It was in Afrikaans, of course, which was a blow, but not an insurmountable one. I made an effort to learn the language once I realized I was in South Africa for the long haul, and I can read an Afrikaans newspaper quite comfortably. With a little care and imagination I could work out the gist of most of the memo.

It was addressed to A. Visser and F. Steenkamp from D. Havenga. As its title suggested, it was about Neels. And this is what it said – this is a paraphrasing rather than a translation, and from memory.

I believe that the time has come for the Laagerbond to approach Cornelius van Zyl. As I have been saying for a while he is becoming increasingly disillusioned with the ANC and the threat of a violent revolution. As we expected, the death of his brother has had a significant impact. For most of his adult life van Zyl has focused on what he perceives as the need to undermine the apartheid state without thinking through the consequences that this will have for the Afrikaner nation. Now he realizes what the future holds for his people if the ANC get their way. These doubts are beginning to affect his actions. In particular his decision to close the Cape Daily Mail *has far-reaching political consequences that van Zyl is fully aware of, despite his insistence that it is economically motivated.*

Impala confirms this. She says that van Zyl's disillusionment runs deep. His relationship with his wife has deteriorated to the point where they barely speak. She confirms my impression that van Zyl's Afrikaner heritage is very important to him and that he feels he has neglected it over the last thirty years. He is not, and never will be, a supporter of apartheid, but he can be recruited as a supporter of the Afrikaner nation . . . (There was some other stuff about Impala but my Afrikaans wasn't quite up to deciphering it.)

All this is confirmed by Eland.

Van Zyl is in a unique position. He is the only Afrikaner who has influence on the world's media. He is a well-respected businessman and newspaper owner who has support in the United States as well as here. He is also a man of honor, and in the role we envisage for him in Operation Drommedaris I would prefer a man motivated by honor and history than one purely in it for the money.

As we have discussed before, there were many reasons why Muldergate was a disaster and very few, if any, apply now. But I firmly believe that Cornelius van Zyl is of a much higher caliber than any of the individuals that were backed then.

I think that's the gist of it. There was some other stuff I couldn't quite understand.

I leafed through the folder. A selection of press cuttings about Neels and then a single sheet of paper: a list of members, of this mysterious Laagerbond, presumably. I counted them; there were twenty-four. Daniel Havenga was there, and Andries Visser and a Frederick Steenkamp. I recognized some of the other names: generals and politicians, very senior politicians; another professor.

I didn't know what the hell this Laagerbond was, but it had an extremely select membership. The list was dynamite. I couldn't simply take it, because it would be missed. I considered briefly removing it and copying it down, but I thought it would be safer to sit in the car. That way, if the worst came to the worst and the meeting finished, I might have time to close up the briefcase and invent some story. So I rushed inside and grabbed a pen and this diary, and copied the names down in the back.

I had just about finished when Caroline interrupted me. I'm afraid I snapped at her, poor girl, and she ran off, but it scared me and I decided to put everything back in the briefcase, which I replaced under the raincoat on the back seat.

Then I set off up here and took the diary with me.

So what the hell is going on? Who are Impala and Eland and what is the Laagerbond? And why are they approaching Neels?

9

Calder hurried back to his sister's house in Highgate to pick up his stuff. Anne had offered to give him a lift from there to Elstree Aerodrome. They climbed into Anne's new luxurious black Mercedes 4x4 and set off on to the thoroughfares of north London.

Calder's thoughts were fixed on the phone call he had received from Kim. He had been wrong not to take her suspicions seriously. Someone had tried to murder Todd and hadn't cared that they might have killed him as well. He recalled those frantic couple of minutes when he had fought for control of the Yak and brought it down on to the sandbar. He remembered the explosion, Todd's pale face, his head wound. They hadn't been victims of bad luck or faulty workmanship, but of a cold-blooded killer. For the last few days he had experienced the intense relief of the survivor. The relief was turning to anger.

'What's wrong, Alex?'

Calder glanced at his sister and smiled. Anne was very small for such a big car. She had spiky black hair and was wearing a purple top and flower-patterned jeans. She and Calder had always been close, but since their mother's death when he was fifteen and she twelve, they had become even closer. They looked after each other. 'Oh, nothing. Just thinking about the flight back.'

'Aren't you nervous, getting into an aeroplane again after that dreadful crash?'

'I was fine coming down from Norfolk,' Calder said. 'It

won't be a problem. It's like riding a bicycle. You have to get back on.'

Anne looked at him doubtfully. 'A bit worse than falling off a bicycle, don't you think?'

Calder grinned. Although he had told her all about the Yak's engine failure, he had no intention of telling her about the police's discovery of sabotage. He knew from long experience that Anne would worry.

'Heard anything from Father?' he asked, to change the subject. Their father was a doctor in the town of Kelso in the Borders of Scotland.

'Yeah. I phoned him last week. He sounded quite chirpy. They're allowing him to stay on at the surgery for another year, part time. Apparently there's a national shortage of GPs.'

'That will keep him happy. The concept of Father in retirement worries me a little.'

'Has he sent you any more cheques?'

'I think so. I got an envelope in March in his handwriting. I returned it unopened.'

'So you've no idea how much it was?'

'No. Nor where he got the money from.'

Anne pulled out on to the A1 in front of an old lady in a small car. The old lady hooted. Anne ignored her. 'I went up to Kelso with the kids three weeks ago. We had a nice weekend. Everything seemed OK.'

'No sign he'd sold anything?'

'Nothing I could see. I did look around. The furniture, the paintings, the silver: it was all still there as far as I could tell.'

'And no copies of the *Racing Post*?'

'Not lying around. I didn't go through his drawers.'

'No, of course not.' Calder stared out of the window at the traffic.

'How much was it?' Anne asked. 'That you bailed him out for?'

'A lot.' The year before Calder had discovered that his father had run up massive gambling debts. Calder had paid them off, £143,000 of them. But he had never told his sister the full amount. To discover that their father, an upright Calvinist who had always disapproved of his son's speculative career in the City, gambled regularly on the horses had been quite a shock to both his children.

'I'd be happy to pay my half,' Anne said.

Calder smiled. 'Thanks. But I'd rather that it was all forgotten. It's not a debt that either you or he owes me.'

They drove on in silence.

'How's Sandy?' Anne asked. 'You haven't mentioned her.'

'Not good,' Calder said. 'We've only managed to see each other three or four times over the last year. When we *do* see each other, everything's great, we get on really well. We had a wonderful week together in Italy last September. But it's been impossible to pin her down.'

'Because of her work?'

Calder nodded. 'Yeah. It's appalling the way these US law firms treat their staff. I mean, I went over to New York to see her last month, just for a long weekend. She wasn't there when I arrived, she'd had to fly off to Dallas or somewhere. I only saw her for an hour before I got my own flight back on the Sunday night. I'm afraid I had a sense-of-humour failure. I said some pretty unpleasant things. We haven't spoken since.'

'I'm sorry,' Anne said. 'I know how much you like her. Is there any chance you can sort something out?'

'I doubt it. She says she would have to change her job, and I don't want to ask her to do that. I can't help thinking it ought to be possible for her to manage things slightly better. I suppose it's just not going to work.'

'Shame.'

'Yeah. Shame.' Calder stared glumly out of the window. 'Clever of you to find William.' William was Anne's husband of eight years. At first Calder had thought him a little stuffy and boring, but he had grown to appreciate the man's consideration for his sister, and the way he put up with her chaotic existence.

There was no reply.

Calder glanced at Anne. She was biting her lip.

'Are things OK with you two?'

'I don't know,' she said. 'We've grown apart these last few months. Like Sandy he works *so* hard. Never home before nine, often working over weekends. It's a funny thing but when I was running around like a lunatic after the children all day, I didn't mind. Oh, I complained, but I could put up with it. But since both the children are at school now, I get the odd minute to think about it and it rankles.'

William worked for a venture-capital company. Anne had been a barrister until a year after Phoebe was born, when she had given up. William's firm had struck gold in the dot-com boom, and weathered the bust, and he had made some good money. But he was nowhere near as bright as Anne. This was something that was obvious to Calder, and presumably was to Anne herself. Calder had always suspected that this bothered his sister, but he had never seen any sign of it.

Anne glanced at her brother. 'Don't worry. It's just a bad patch. All marriages have them, don't they?'

'I suppose they do,' said Calder.

*

It was a pleasant flight back to Langthorpe from Elstree. Anne was right, Calder's experience in the Yak was slightly more serious than falling off a bicycle, but he was pleased that he hadn't found it difficult to climb back into an aeroplane. The cloud cover at 2,000 feet over Hertfordshire broke as he flew north and the Southern drawl of the USAF controller guided him through blue skies above the airbases of Lakenheath and Mildenhall. He descended to 1,500 feet over Thetford Forest and within a little over an hour from his departure from Elstree he spotted the familiar patch of green that was Langthorpe Aerodrome, with the poplars to the right, the village church with its round tower set on a small hill to the left, and the North Sea shimmering ahead. He joined the circuit a safe distance behind Jerry and an erratic student in a Piper Warrior and landed smoothly on the grass runway.

Kim was waiting for him outside the flying school, the wind blowing her dark curls into her face. She was dancing from foot to foot in her agitation. They moved into Calder's tiny office and closed the door. Kim sat in the chair in front of Calder's desk.

'So it was sabotage?' Calder said.

'Definitely,' Kim said. 'They found fragments from some kind of bomb.'

'And presumably they have no idea yet who planted it?'

'No idea at all. Did you find out anything from Benton?'

'Not really,' Calder said. He described his breakfast at Claridge's.

She listened to him with disappointment. 'Do you believe that's all there was to it?'

'Don't know. Tarek didn't know either. Benton seemed to be telling the truth. But the cynic in me thinks that he lies for a living. There's no doubt that Zyl News was right on the brink of bankruptcy back then, and I suspect that would have been a shock to Martha.'

'Yes, but enough for her to insist that her mother fly to New York if she died? And why would that information scare her? Because she *was* scared. All that stuff about "if something happens to me". There's something else, there must be.'

Calder nodded. 'You're right. Maybe that's only half the story. Maybe the diary holds the other half.'

'Or perhaps Benton Davis is lying?'

'Possibly. But I know for sure he won't tell me more. Perhaps the police can get him to talk.'

'That's what I wanted to speak to you about,' Kim said. 'They're going to want to interview you, I know they are. They asked me where you were, and I said you'd be flying back here this afternoon. They'll be here any minute.'

'Good,' said Calder. 'I'll be happy to talk to them.'

Kim looked down at her hands. 'Well . . .'

'Kim?' He looked at her suspiciously. 'You don't expect me not to tell them about seeing Benton?'

'Er . . . I'd rather you didn't. Or at least only if you have to. And if you *do* have to, don't link it to the bomb in the Yak.'

'But you said –'

'I know what I said, but I can't be sure,' said Kim. She was staring hard at Calder now. 'You see Todd and I talked about this a lot before the crash. He was adamant that he didn't want to get the police involved in his family's business. That's why we came to see you.'

'Yes, but things are different now, surely? He was nearly killed.'

'I'm not saying that we shouldn't try to help the police find who planted the bomb; of course we should. But I don't think we should encourage them to ask too many questions about Martha's death.'

'But we can't hide it from them,' Calder said. 'That's probably against the law. Conspiring to pervert the course of justice or something.'

'Please,' said Kim. She said it with her voice and she said it with her eyes. 'If it was just me, I'd be happy to tell the police all they wanted to know. But I *know* that Todd would want us to keep them out of Zyl News. And with him lying in that bed in hospital in a coma, I'd feel terrible going against his wishes.'

'So what do we do?' Calder said. 'Sit back and let the police faff around without telling them the most likely motive?'

'We don't sit back. We find out what Benton knows, what the Laagerbond is, why Martha went to that game reserve, who she was scared of, and then we find out who killed her and why. And *then* we tell the police.'

'We?'

'Me and you. Well, OK, mostly you. But *please*, Alex.'

Calder sat back and thought about it. Then he shook his head. 'I'm sorry, we have to tell them that Todd was asking awkward questions about Martha's death. And I'll have to mention the letter and my visit to Benton.'

Kim's pale cheeks reddened. 'Oh, Alex —'

Calder held up his hand. 'Hold on. We'll give them the bare minimum. We won't tell them what you suspect or what Todd suspects. We let them investigate Cornelius and anyone else they want to investigate. Who knows? Maybe they'll find the guy who planted the bomb. Maybe it had nothing to do with any of this. Maybe Todd had some enemies we know nothing about —'

'That's ridiculous!'

'We don't know, we can't be sure. In the meantime I *will*

help you try to find out what happened to Martha. And if we discover there is a direct link to the bomb in the Yak we tell the police. OK?'

Kim smiled. 'OK.' To Calder's surprise she ran round the desk and kissed his cheek. 'Uh-oh,' she said looking out of the window. A man and a woman were making their way along the footpath to the entrance to the flying school. 'That's them.'

Two minutes later Kim was on her way back to the hospital and Calder was talking to two detectives. The woman was thin, with a pale face and short red hair. The man was slightly younger and much chubbier, with a brush of fair hair sticking straight up. The woman introduced herself as Detective Inspector Banks, and the man as Detective Constable Wardle.

They had lots of questions that Calder answered. He went over again how he had offered Todd a flight in the Yak and everything that had happened on the day of the crash. The police had already examined the ground around where the Yak was parked, and interviewed Angie, the radio operator, about the man walking on the footpath that ran along the boundary of the airfield the evening before the crash. Then Calder mentioned that Todd had some suspicions about his mother's death and had wanted Calder to speak to Benton Davis.

Their interest was immediately piqued, and they asked lots more questions, during which Calder described the contents of Martha's last letter to her parents. DI Banks was asking most of the questions, and watching Calder closely as he answered them. He was glad that he had decided not to lie.

'Why do you think Mrs van Zyl didn't tell us any of this?' she asked.

'I was talking to her just now about it,' Calder said. 'I don't think she thought it was necessarily relevant.'

'Oh, come on, Mr Calder,' the inspector said.

'The van Zyls are a private family, her instinct was to maintain that privacy,' Calder said. 'I did discuss it with her and I'm sure she'll tell you anything you want to know. She has the letter, I'm sure she'll let you see it.'

'So am I. Has she gone back to the hospital?'

'I think so,' said Calder. The detectives stood up to leave. 'Do you have any idea how the bomb was set off?' Calder asked.

'They recovered some fragments from part of an explosive device and what look like the remains of an altimeter.'

'An altimeter?' Calder thought it through. 'I see. It detonates the bomb as soon as the aircraft reaches a certain altitude?'

'That's the idea. You told the accident investigators that the aeroplane was climbing when the bomb exploded?'

'That's right.'

'They said that if it had been any other light aircraft the engine would have been blown right away from the fuselage. That Yak had such a big sturdy engine that it remained intact after the explosion. You were very lucky, Mr Calder.'

He returned home at about eight to find Kim already there cooking supper for the two of them.

'How's Todd?' he asked, taking a bottle of wine from the fridge and pouring two glasses.

'No change.'

'I'm sorry.'

Kim gave the tiniest of shrugs as she stirred a sauce in the pan. 'Cornelius called three times today. And Todd received some flowers from his sister, Zan.'

'The one who lives in South Africa?'

'That's right. It was quite sweet of her. Edwin told her about the crash.'

'What kind of name is Zan, anyway?'

'Short for Xanthe. Her mother was a little on the pretentious side, apparently. She sounds a dreadful woman. She died ten years ago: her liver gave out.'

'Didn't you say Todd has a younger sister as well?'

'Caroline, Martha's daughter. Her husband is Herbert Hafer IV, of Hafer Beer. The Hafers are one of the wealthiest families in Pennsylvania. She's the only one of the van Zyl children who married well; Jessica, Cornelius's current wife, saw to that. Actually, he's a pretty down-to-earth guy for a billionaire, calls himself "H" and invests the family fortune. They moved out to San Diego soon after they were married. It's a long way from New Hampshire so we don't see her much.'

'That smells good,' Calder said.

'It should taste good. We'll see. Fish is a bit tricky with a grill you don't know.' She checked the two fillets of plaice. 'Looks OK so far.' She stirred the mushroom sauce bubbling gently in the pan on the hob and took the glass of wine Calder handed to her. 'I see you spoke to the police.'

'Did they come and see you again?'

'You bet they did. They weren't very happy that I hadn't told them about Martha's murder and Todd's suspicions. I showed them the letter.'

'I'm sure it was the best thing to do.'

'We'll see,' said Kim. 'At least it means they'll check Cornelius out pretty thoroughly, but I still feel bad about it. Like I've betrayed Todd.'

'Someone tried to kill him!' Calder said. 'And me, for that matter.'

'I know, I'm sorry.' Kim touched Calder's hand. 'I do appreciate you going to see Benton Davis. Thank you.'

'Oh, no, it's . . . um . . . it's the least I could do.' Calder was disconcerted by Kim's touch. 'But we still have to figure out what happened to Martha.'

'Now we've drawn a blank with Benton, I'm not sure what to do next.' Kim checked the grill again. 'It's ready. Give me a hand, will you?'

They took their supper outside, to the small garden behind the cottage, where there was a teak table, chairs and a bench.

'We need to get Cornelius to talk,' Calder said.

'Todd tried,' Kim said. 'And got nowhere.'

'That's true, but things are a little different now that we know someone tried to kill his son. Perhaps next time he comes up to see Todd you could try to speak to him. Be a bit more subtle about it than Todd was.'

'He said he's coming tomorrow afternoon. It's difficult to talk when we're all sitting around in Todd's room staring at him. Perhaps I'll suggest we go out for a meal.'

'It's worth a try,' Calder said, biting into the plaice. 'This is delicious.'

'Thank you. My cooking has come on a bit since university.' She took a bite herself. 'Mm, not bad. Pretty garden,' she said, surveying the apple tree, the small patch of lawn, the roses, the wisteria and the crowded border. 'I would never have thought of you as a gardener.'

Calder grinned. 'Neither would I. You should have seen this place when I bought it. It was beautiful. All I do is try to stop things dying. But I'm getting into it, it's quite therapeutic. I don't know what half the plants are called. As soon as I learn the name of something it dies.'

'It's peaceful here.'

'It is.' The garden was southerly facing, away from the

sea and towards a wood rising up to a low ridge. To the right was a field of inquisitive bullocks, to the left, along the ridge, an old windmill, its sails fixed. Evening sunlight streamed into the garden from the west, although the sun itself had crept round behind the house.

'I can't imagine you in a place like this,' said Kim.

'And I can't imagine you in a small town in New Hampshire.'

'No.'

'Do you like it there?'

Kim hesitated. 'No. No, I don't. I can admit that to you, but I could never admit it to Todd.'

'Why not?'

'He loves Somerford. He loves teaching. He teaches English and he's very good at it – inspiring, or at least that's what he tells me. He's started up a rugby team at the school. But I think what really turns him on is the role of schoolboy hero. He's very popular with the boys and the principal loves him. That kind of thing is important to Todd. I made such a big deal to him that he shouldn't be ruled by his father, that he should do what *he* wants to do, so when he goes off and does it I can hardly complain, can I?'

'Your life is important too, isn't it?'

Kim looked at Calder. 'Yes,' she said, steel in her voice. 'Yes.' She took another bite of her fish. 'Everyone always laughs at management consultants, but I was bloody good at it. I earned good money and if I'd stuck at it I would have been a partner pretty soon. I didn't *need* to marry a rich man.'

'What about the hospital? Aren't you doing some good there?'

'Oh, yes. I'm sorting that place out: they don't know what's hit them. Of course working in a hospital is a worthwhile thing to do and everyone's so damned nice all the time. Sometimes I find it unbearable. I get gripped by these insane ideas, like firing everyone on their birthday, or making a charitable contribution to the Association of Tobacco Manufacturers. I don't think they'd notice. It would still be a big smile and a "how are you today, Kimmy?" from everyone.'

Calder winced. 'You sound dangerous.'

'I've kept myself under control so far. But it is frustrating. We've been trying for a baby. *He* wants one, so I have to produce it.'

'Don't you want a child?'

'Yes. Yes, I do. Especially if we're going to be stuck in Somerford. But the point is I don't think Todd even notices what I want. He's a nice guy, a really kind man, but he's used to everyone doing everything for him, to being the centre of attention. He just assumes that I will do what's best for him, that our marriage is a partnership whose aim is to do what makes *him* happy.'

'You've obviously been thinking about it a lot.'

'Yes. I'm sorry to moan at you, and it's terrible when he's lying there unconscious, but yes, I have been stewing over it more than is healthy. Do you remember Dom?'

'Your boyfriend at Cambridge? The cricketer?' Calder could recall a tall, dashing cricket blue that Kim had gone out with for a couple of terms in their second year.

'Yes. Todd's a bit like him. Totally self-centred.'

'Didn't you catch him having it off with Emma?' Emma was one of the three other students who had shared a place with Kim and Calder.

'Yes,' muttered Kim. 'The bitch. In our house too! At least Todd doesn't do that kind of thing.'

'He seems like a pretty straight guy.'

'Oh, he is. God, I'd forgotten how awful Dom was at the end. But I do remember how head-over-heels in love with him I was. I was young and innocent then.'

'Well, young.' Calder smiled. Kim had looked delectable at nineteen. She still looked pretty attractive fifteen years later, he couldn't help noticing.

'Yes, young. You were very good to me after all that.'

'Probably just trying to get you into bed,' Calder said.

'Alex! And I thought you were such a kind, sympathetic man.' Kim smiled that smile that Calder remembered so clearly from all those years ago.

'And so I was. A kind, sympathetic man who wanted to get you into bed. Didn't work, though, did it? Should have gone for the selfish bastard approach.'

'Nah,' said Kim. 'You would have been really bad at that. Trust me. I know a lot about that technique.'

The level of the wine slipped down the bottle.

'What about you?' she said. 'When I asked you about the existence of a girlfriend you came over all grumpy. What's up?'

Calder told her all about Sandy. Kim was generally sympathetic, although when Calder described the bust-up following his weekend alone in New York, she gently took Sandy's side.

'You know she probably felt just as badly about it as you did?'

'If she did, she could have done something about it.'

'Maybe she couldn't.'

'I know. But it's still not going to work.'

'What if you moved to New York?'

'I'm not sure the relationship has progressed that far. Besides, the only job I could get over there would be in investment banking, and there's no way I'm going back to that.'

'Why not? I'd have thought you'd make a good trader. In fact I thought that was the perfect job for you after the RAF.'

'I *was* a good trader,' Calder admitted. 'Very good. And I got a buzz out of it. But it's not the real world. After a few years of flinging millions of dollars of other people's money around you lose touch with reality. Everything has a monetary value. Your salary, obviously, your profit and loss, your bonus, your trading positions, your house, your car, before you know it, even your relationships. You begin to think that poor people are stupid people. Then you think that someone who won't do what it takes to get a deal is a wimp. Not just a wimp, but a stupid wimp. It changes you.'

'Oh, come on, Alex. Not everyone in investment banking is evil. There are plenty of ordinary decent people who work there.'

'Yes, but there are fewer of them than there should be, and those few change. Look at Benton Davis! Martha said she trusted him: well maybe she could have done eighteen years ago, but she certainly wouldn't now. The same thing was happening to me.

'Remember I told you about my assistant, Jen, the one who everyone thought committed suicide? Her former boss had bullied her the whole time she was working for him, totally destroyed her self-esteem. That's why she joined my group. Then in a bar after work one evening he suggested that she and I were sleeping together. Taken in isolation, that might not sound too bad, but for her it was the last straw. She decided to sue Bloomfield Weiss. Benton Davis and all the others made her life hell. And you know what I did? I tried to talk her out of it. I told her her career would benefit and she would make more money if she put up with those kinds of insults. Well, she was a brave woman, she stood up to them, stood up to them all. In the end she died. And only then did I really try to help her, when it was way to late.'

'Wow,' said Kim.

'That's why I'm here, tootling around with aeroplanes.'

'Rather you than me,' Kim said. She yawned. 'It's amazing how sitting around doing nothing all day can make you tired. I'm off to bed.'

'Good night.'

As Kim disappeared inside, Calder sat alone in the garden, watching the night creep up around him.

Andries Visser pulled his Land Rover Discovery off the road and along the poplar-lined drive to his farm. The veld stretched brown and yellow in the distance to his left and right. He saw the large frame of his older brother Gideon sitting on an open tractor pulling winter feed for the cattle, a prize herd of Limousins. Gideon was a strong, hard-working, if unimaginative farmer. He lived in the cottage behind the main farmhouse, but he did most of the work. Andries and his family lived in the main house even though Andries's physical contribution to the farm was negligible. He had provided the money to invest in the farm, and the ideas. If the place had been left to Gideon, the Vissers would still be scratching around in the dirt.

There was another reason Andries lived in the main house and his elder brother and his family in the cottage. Twenty years earlier, when their father was still alive and Gideon was in his late thirties, Gideon had got himself involved in a spot of legal trouble. Gideon and his wife and five children had gone to a *braai* at a neighbour's farm. True to tradition it was an all-day affair, *boerewors* on the fire and Castle beer in the cool box. The weather was glorious, the kids were playing, the women were gossiping and Gideon and the neighbour were getting pleasantly drunk. Then there was a commotion from the sheds at the back. One of the farm hands had discovered a thief. He was a runt of a man, a black of course, and he had been caught stealing a can of red paint. Why he wanted to steal the paint wasn't entirely clear, but Gideon and the neighbour were indignant, especially when Gideon, wrongly as it turned out, identified the man as a suspected thief of a cow from another neighbour's farm the month before. The two Boers decided to teach the man a lesson, and in order not to scare the children they slung him in the rear of the *bakkie* and drove off. He was found the following day in a ditch, beaten to death.

The law took its course and several months later Gideon and the neighbour found themselves in the dock accused of murder. The thief, whose name was Moses Nkose, was incontrovertibly dead, but hard evidence of murder was difficult to pin down. Andries discussed the matter with his father and with Gideon, and the three of them came to an arrangement. Andries had a word with the right people and Gideon ended up with only two years for manslaughter. Andries, the son who was happiest wearing a suit and carrying a briefcase, inherited the farm. Over time Gideon's resentment had faded, and the arrangement worked well.

Andries could easily have arranged his brother's acquittal, but he had chosen not to. After all, he still walked with a slight limp from where his big brother had belted him with the flat of a pick axe when he was twelve.

Andries drove up to the house itself, surrounded by an inner fence of twelve-foot-high barbed wire, topped off with three electrified strands. Yellow signs warned of an armed response to intruders. Cattle rustlers these days carried guns. Inside the fence, a modern-day kraal, was an oasis of green irrigated wealth. There were tall trees, poplar and cypress, there was a lush green lawn, there was a swimming pool, and the house itself, a simple low white one-storey affair to which Andries had added two extensions. To one side stood the water tower, a windmill, the labourers' shacks and, most importantly, the cow sheds. The fences were there to protect the cattle as much as the humans.

Andries was no farmer, but he was immensely proud of his farm. It had been in the family for 160 years. The Visser family had set off from Graaff-Reinet in the Karoo on the Great Trek in the 1830s, had crossed the Drakensberg mountains into Zululand, and then a few years later been ejected by the British and re-crossed the mountains to this spot, forty kilometres from Pretoria. Here they had scratched a living, a God-fearing, hard-working, honest family, struggling against the depredations of poor weather, poor soil and vindictive British colonial administrators. A small, physically weak man with a limp, Andries had found his talents more suited to the needs of government administration in Pretoria, but he never forgot the physical labour and suffering of his ancestors, and now he had retired from government service he was proud to be occupying the same land they had farmed through the generations.

He parked next to a car he recognized, an unprepossessing blue Toyota Corolla. He stubbed out his cigarette in the pot by the stoep. His wife, Hannah, had banned him from smoking indoors a couple of years before. He swung open the security gate guarding the front door and entered the house.

His wife was in the kitchen drinking a cup of coffee with a big, square man with a thick neck, a moustache and close-cropped hair.

'Kobus! Good to see you,' Visser said in Afrikaans with a thin smile. 'Why don't you bring that through to my study? We need to talk.'

Colonel Kobus Moolman sat stiffly in the chair next to Visser's desk and sipped his coffee. He was now in his early sixties but he still looked hard. Rock hard. His reputation in the security police had as much to do with his cunning as his ruthlessness. He had served his country in South West Africa, and had been a senior member of the notorious death squad that had tortured and killed dozens if not hundreds of people at Vlakplaas. Visser had had serious doubts when Freddie Steenkamp had suggested him for the Laagerbond, but Freddie had been right. There were times when the *bond* needed a man like Moolman.

Once away from his wife, Visser's smile disappeared. 'What went wrong?' he said.

'I must be getting rusty,' Moolman answered. 'It was a simple question of not enough explosive. It must have been a stronger aeroplane than I gave it credit for. But the guy's in a coma, isn't he? He's stopped asking questions.'

'He could snap out of it at any time.'

'Do you want me to finish him off?' Moolman asked.

'In the hospital?'

'It would be tricky, but if it was necessary . . .'

Visser stared out of the window, over the veld towards the ravine where the Elands River, almost dry now, wound its way towards the Limpopo and the Indian Ocean 500 kilometres away. His chest was wracked by a cough, and he felt a pain in his shoulder. The cough was getting worse, he really ought to see a doctor about it. 'No,' he said. 'Not while he's still unconscious. It might just stir up more trouble. The British police know it wasn't an accident and they have started an investigation. I hope they won't turn up anything. But I would like you to fly back to London to be on hand in case we need you.'

Moolman nodded. The truth was he much preferred operating on his home turf, even if these days the number of old friends in authority he could rely upon to provide him with assistance was dwindling. But he prided himself on his abilities, he had always been a loyal member of the Laagerbond and he was not about to let them down now.

'Very well, Andries. You can count on me.'

10

July 18, 1988

I had lunch with George today in Greenmarket Square. It was raining. On the way I saw a copy of the *Financial Times* on a newsstand: the front-page story was blacked out. This country is pathetic.

George is really down about the *Mail* closing. He has been trying to find a buyer without any luck, its losses are just too big. I suggested he approach Graham Pelling to see if he will take the *Mail* along with the other newspapers. George said he will try, but he doesn't hold out much hope.

I asked George about Muldergate. It's ten years since it happened and I'm a bit fuzzy about the details. The *Mail* was one of the papers that broke the scandal, and George remembered it well. I asked him whether he has heard of the Laagerbond. He hasn't. He was clearly curious about my questions, and I promised I would tell him more when I could. But not yet. Not until I've figured out what's going on with Neels.

July 20

I am crying as I write this. I have just had a huge fight with Neels. It wasn't about his woman, I chickened out of talking to him about that. It was about the Laagerbond.

All I did was ask him who they were and he exploded.

He demanded to know how I had found out about them. When I told him I had looked in Daniel's briefcase he was furious. He said I was the lowest of the low, I was scum for spying on him. He said I had no right to pry into his business, he said I wouldn't understand it anyway, he said I had betrayed him, and I had been disloyal. I fell apart. I burst into tears and ran out of the room into the bedroom.

It's all so wrong, *he's* the one whose being disloyal, *he's* carrying on an affair, *he's* dealing with these weirdo Boers.

For the first time in our marriage I couldn't stand up to him, I ran away.

He actually called me "scum." His own wife. I can't forgive him for that. Never.

July 21

Neels slept in Todd's room last night. He got up early to go to work, I heard him. At least he didn't sneak off in the middle of the night.

Zan and Caroline were very quiet at breakfast. They must have heard the shouting and the tears last night. Poor Caroline! It's her second day back at school and it's obvious she's pleased to be out of the house.

July 22

Spoke to Todd on the phone this evening. I suggested that he come out here for a week at the end of his summer vacation and bring Francesca with him. He seemed to like the idea, but he said he'd have to check with her. I hope he does come.

Neels is working so hard on the *Herald* deal I scarcely see him. Thank God. He's going to London tomorrow and then Philadelphia. He says he might be away for three weeks. My feelings toward him are so confused. I'm angry, *so* angry, about the way he treats me these days and about what he's done with the *Mail*. And I'm still sure he's got another woman hidden away somewhere. I haven't seen any more signs of it, but I just *know* it.

But I'm also afraid. The violence that I have always known exists in this country seems to be closing in on me, stealing into my own family. First there was Hennie, then the SACP list, then there are these Laagerbond people. Men that high up in the Afrikaner establishment can only be dangerous. And then there's Neels. He hasn't threatened me again directly, but he always looks angry, as if he's about to explode at any second. I fear that he has changed, but more than that I fear that it is this creeping, all-pervasive violence that is changing him.

July 23

I drove into Cape Town to have lunch with Libby Wiseman. She lives in Tamboerskloof in a blue-painted little house on the slopes of Signal Hill opposite Table Mountain. She lectures in English literature at the University of Cape Town, and her husband Dennis is an attorney who specializes in political prisoners. He does a good job too. Although he fails to keep most of them out of jail, he inflicts maximum embarrassment on the authorities every time, which is what his clients really want. It's Saturday and Dennis was out playing golf. Libby suggested we go to a restaurant in the Bo-Kaap.

We walked down the hill and then along toward Bo-Kaap. I love the area with its steep cobbled streets, its rows of old brightly painted houses, car-repair shops, mosques with dainty cream-colored minarets, and the smells of Africa mixing with the Orient. It's segregated: only coloreds live there. "Colored" is a typical South African euphemism: it means people of mixed ancestry, people who don't fit into neat racial categories. Bo-Kaap is a wonderful celebration of what that word can represent: the genes of Malays, Indians, Europeans, slaves from Guinea and the East Indies, even the original Hottentot inhabitants of the Cape are all jumbled together in a melange of brown skin, high cheekbones and broad smiles. And the food is delicious.

Libby led me to an orange-and-yellow restaurant on the corner of Wale Street with a terrific view of the city and Table Mountain opposite. The morning fog had disappeared and the sun was out, illuminating the gray crenelated battlements of the mountain in a soft winter glow. We exchanged gossip about the other members of the Guguletu Project Committee and she told me a story about one of her first-year students who has somehow gotten George Eliot and Charles Dickens confused and is convinced that Dickens was a woman.

I mentioned the SACP hit list Zan told Neels about. Without giving any hint that she had links to the Communist Party, Libby did say it sounded unlikely to her. Apparently Joe Slovo proclaimed last year that change will come through negotiation, not revolution. But Libby admitted that not all party members would necessarily agree with their leader. Frankly, it still worries me.

I decided to tell her about my suspicions about Neels and another woman. She was sympathetic. She confided that she and Dennis are having their problems too. I told her Daniel

Havenga's description of Stellenbosch as hanky-panky town: it's full of forty-something women washed up on the shores of failed marriages. What's so strange about Libby and me joining them? It was good to talk to her, to feel that I have an ally in this goddamned country.

July 25

I went into Stellenbosch with Zan this afternoon. It was a clear sunny day, the old buildings gleamed white, and the few leaves remaining on the oak trees along the sidewalks sparkled gold. We went to Oom Samie's like we used to when she was a girl. That place is still full of the same old junk, it hasn't changed. She bought a couple of useless knickknacks and some sticky toffee, I bought some spices and we had a cup of coffee.

We talked about the End Conscription Campaign. Zan said that 150 men have refused the call up so far. I told Zan about the friends of mine who dodged the draft during the Vietnam war and the articles I wrote for *Life* magazine about the student protest movements in the sixties. She was clearly surprised, and interested. But when I started to ask her about the Black Sash, she clammed up. And when I suggested I could join her on one of her ECC demos, she just shook her head. It bugged me.

"Why didn't you tell me about the SACP hit list?" I asked her.

Zan looked down into her cup. "I wondered when you'd get around to that."

"Don't you trust me?"

Zan shrugged, still avoiding my eyes.

She didn't trust me. I could understand that, given our

past, but I felt, or hoped, that since she had come to stay at Hondehoek we had rebuilt our relationship. I felt like she was my ally, and boy do I need allies. I took a deep breath. "I want to apologize for something."

Zan's eyes flicked up.

"What happened with that creep Bernie Tunstall. Perhaps I shouldn't have told Neels. I know you asked me not to, but I was furious and I wanted him to stop it. You were only fourteen, for Christ's sake!"

Zan stared back into her coffee.

"Can you forgive me?"

Zan mumbled something.

"Excuse me?"

"I said, I can forget. That's all I can do. Not forgive. Forget. It's forgotten." She looked at me, her eyes angry, confused, sad. "Don't bring it back. Please."

"Okay," I said. "I'm sorry I mentioned it. It's just that you can trust me, you know."

She smiled quickly, although I could see she wasn't convinced.

"Can you at least tell me a little more about the list?"

"I told Pa all I know."

"But does it really exist? I thought the SACP leadership is talking about peaceful revolution."

"Oh, it exists, all right. The leaders say one thing for the international press and another for the comrades. There's a list. Pa's on it. So are you."

"And you?"

Zan shook her head. "No."

"Who told you?"

"Someone . . ." She hesitated. "Someone who is very fond of me."

"A man?"

She nodded.

"That you met in London?"

She nodded again.

"And you trust him?"

"Oh, yes," she said. "I trust him." Her eyes met mine, warmer this time, more sympathetic. "It came as a shock to me too. A big shock. That, and Uncle Hennie's death. I mean, in theory I know that the only way this regime is going to change is through violence, and that some people will die, people with the same color skin as me. I can accept that. But when it's my father . . . That's why I want to stay here for a bit. I need to sort all this out in my head."

You mean you want to have a last visit with your father before your "comrades" assassinate him, I thought. But I didn't say it. "When you get to London you're not just going to study at the LSE are you?"

Zan shook her head.

We sat in silence for a while, watching the good burgers of Stellenbosch going about their errands. "Martha?"

"Yes?"

Zan gave me a nervous smile. "When I heard your name was on the list, it didn't really bother me. But now it does: it bothers me a lot."

I've enjoyed having Zan here, I'll definitely miss her when she goes off to London. Perhaps she is right, it is best to forget. I still think it was the right thing to do to talk to Neels about Bernie Tunstall. I know she had told me about him in confidence, but how could I not have done something about it? He had, after all, seduced a fourteen-year-old girl. But it was that that marked the deterioration of our relationship. Bernie Tunstall was rich, well connected and smart enough to put up a convincing show of innocence. Penelope believed him rather than her daughter. Zan refused to make a statement to the police and then she was examined by a doctor who confirmed that she wasn't a virgin. Penelope told the police that she thought Zan had been sleeping with boys, and Zan didn't deny it. This made Neels even angrier. There was a custody battle for a year. Zan didn't want to live with us, and Neels refused to let her go back to Penelope, so she spent the term-time at her boarding school and the vacations with her Uncle Hennie at his sheep farm in the Karoo. In the end she went back to Penelope. She still came to visit us occasionally, but she was always angry and surly, and her visits became increasingly awkward.

She swam fast, and I mean really fast. Then when she was seventeen and she beat the Olympic qualifying time, that was when she got really upset. Of course it wasn't her fault she couldn't go to the LA Olympics, it was just another consequence of apartheid and, as I told her, not the most important. She couldn't swim in an international competition but at least she was treated like a human being in her own country, unlike 80 percent of the population. An obvious point, you would have thought, especially for a daughter of Cornelius van Zyl. But she didn't accept it, she wouldn't accept it. It was all the fault of the ignorant, narrow-minded Americans, of people like *me*. I was so angry. Of course I now realize that she was pushing me away, and this was the perfect way to do it. Well, she succeeded.

At about this time, no doubt egged on by Hennie and his family, she began to develop an interest in her Afrikaner heritage. Hennie always thought that Neels had betrayed his people, and he was anxious to take the opportunity to show Zan how a real God-fearing Afrikaner farming family lived. At first Neels was pleased. This country is split as much between English and Afrikaans speakers as between black and white. Zan was brought up entirely in the English-speaking education system. Neels is very proud of his Afrikaner ancestry, and I think what he regrets most about his skepticism about apartheid is the way it has forced him away from the language, the Church, the community and the rest of his family. He's an outcast now among his own people. So when Zan started taking a serious interest in the language and reading van Wyk Louw and Malherbe for pleasure, he was thrilled. He was even more thrilled when she said she might go to an Afrikaans university. Of course he assumed she would try for a place at Stellenbosch, which is becoming more what the South Africans would call liberal, but I would call normal. But in the end Zan decided to apply to the new Rand Afrikaans University in Johannesburg to study history. Probably just to spite him.

We didn't hear from her for nine months. Then she showed up at our door saying she had made a terrible mistake. She was shocked by the racists she had met at the university, and by the apartheid ideology that she was studying. The last straw was when she was out with a group of rugby-playing students who picked a fight one evening with an old black man, and left him broken and bleeding in the gutter. They all laughed about it. She wanted to get out.

Neels was relieved. She switched to the much more liberal English-speaking University of the Witwatersrand and became a changed woman, organizing demonstrations, writing articles in underground magazines, getting in trouble with the police. After university she stayed in Johannesburg, doing more or less the same thing, bumming around from temporary office job to temporary office job.

And now she's going to London to do Christ-knows-what.

It occurred to me that there was a slight chance that the Laagerbond might be a secret *anti*-apartheid society. I told

Zan about Havenga and Visser seeing Neels, but she has no idea what the Laagerbond is either. I think that was just wishful thinking on my part.

Neels has been in London for a couple of days now. It's good to have him out of the house.

July 27

I've just had a visit from the security police. It hasn't happened to me before. A polite young man came to the door in a coat and tie. When he saw Zan he said he wanted to talk to me in private. Doris made us cups of coffee and we sat and chatted about the garden. He likes the magnolias and the fynbos beds, and he wanted to know how old the oak tree by the front door is. Apparently Finneas and I are doing a good job.

He asked me how well I knew Libby Wiseman. When I told him quite well, he asked me whether I knew she was a member of the Communist Party. I professed shocked disbelief. I asked him whether she was banned, and he answered that she wasn't but they were keeping a watchful eye on her. Then he said it wouldn't be wise for a woman in my position to become too close to her.

"My position?" I said. "By 'my position' do you mean as the wife of a newspaper proprietor or a citizen of the United States."

"Both," the policeman replied. "We believe in the rule of law in this country, and we treat all citizens equally, whatever their nationality or marital status."

I choked on my coffee as he said this. But I knew what he meant. He meant "watch out."

Zan was anxious when he had gone. Naturally, she had

assumed the policeman was here to talk about her. When I told her he hadn't mentioned her she was relieved. She thought a moment and then asked me what he did want to talk to me about. I just smiled.

I started writing this with the smile still on my face. How exciting for my activities to be taken seriously enough for the security police to pay attention! But the more I think about it, the more worried I am becoming. I have never been visited before. That's mostly because of the pact I made with Neels just after we got married, one I've stuck to for the past twenty years. I won't get involved with "the struggle," or "the cause."

Neels always knew I would make my opinions known, but that was one of the reasons he married me. It didn't take me long to get into trouble. It was just after we had gotten married and bought Hondehoek. Doris had been our maid for only a week. I was unfamiliar with the whole concept of domestic servants, especially those that wore uniforms, but Neels was adamant that we needed them to manage the house and garden. It turned out Doris and I hit it off straight away. On her third day I found her crying. Her brother had gotten into some kind of trouble with the police; he'd been found with some beer, and blacks were not allowed to drink alcohol then. She needed twenty rand to bail him out. She wasn't asking me for the money, but I gave it to her, and she was embarrassingly grateful.

I was explaining this at a dinner party Neels and I had been invited to the following Saturday. The host was one of the most important businessmen in Cape Town, a pillar of the English-speaking community and a big advertiser. The hostess, who was a real Kaffir-basher, was shocked by my action. She said I was stupid to trust a maid, especially one I didn't know, and I would be lucky to see that money again.

In fact, Doris would probably disappear that very weekend. She implied that it was people like me that were responsible for the ill discipline and licentiousness among black South Africans.

I said that Doris looked trustworthy, and that even if she wasn't, she and her brother could probably use the twenty rand better than I could. The hostess turned red; she didn't like the fact that I was American and criticizing her country. They get *so* defensive.

"You don't understand," she said. "Your blacks are not like ours."

"I don't have any blacks. Neither do you," I said.

She scowled. "Are you some kind of communist?"

"I would be happy to admit to being a communist if you'll admit to being a Nazi," I replied. Not exactly subtle.

Her jaw dropped. Then she turned to her husband. "Geoffrey! I won't have this woman in my house. Can you see her out, please?"

Our husbands broke us up and we stayed at the table under a frosty truce until the coffee was served. Afterwards Neels gave me a lecture. He said it was quite simple: he couldn't run his newspapers if I talked to people like that. He also said that it would compromise his position if I were seen with known radicals, black or white. I understood what he was saying. I had come totally to believe in his strategy for changing things. The work of the *Mail* and his other papers was too important for me to jeopardize for the sake of gestures which had no benefit beyond salving my conscience. Since then, I've pretty much stuck to the pact. I've been tempted over the years to help the cause; I've received tentative approaches from people, but I've always rebuffed them, and I've always explained why. Most people seem to understand. I guess I've thrown my energies into charities over the years: the literacy projects, the scholarships for black and colored students, and the clinics. I have made some small difference that way.

But now trouble has come looking for me. Is it really a result of my visit to Libby Wiseman, or is it Zan's presence in our house? Perhaps it's something to do with the Laagerbond. I assumed that I had Neels's protection, but has he removed that now? I'm an American citizen. Doesn't that make me untouchable? Or does it make me a spy?

I used to think violence and injustice happened to other people in this country. Perhaps they might happen to me.

I must be careful what I write in here.

The minor crises of the operation of a small airfield are unrelenting. The issue of the morning was body bags. Langthorpe didn't have one, a fact that had somehow been missed during the last Civil Aviation Authority inspection. Jerry had belatedly realized that one was required: technically without it the airfield was unlicensed. When they had first bought the flying school Calder and Jerry would have taken a relaxed attitude towards the problem, but they had swiftly learned that you didn't mess with the CAA over even the tiniest detail. Especially over the tiniest detail. If the CAA felt that it was unsafe to fly unless there was a body bag stowed away somewhere on the airfield, then Calder wouldn't argue. So, where could he get a body bag in a hurry?

Calder's eyes strayed to the window and the runway outside, where a Piper Warrior was making a heavy landing, and then strayed back to his computer. Curiosity got the better of him and he tapped on the Spreadfinex icon. The bond market had gapped down overnight. He had lost £29,000.

He leaned back and stared at the numbers. A cold wave seemed to wash over his body followed by a burning sensation in his cheeks. It wasn't anger, it wasn't frustration, it wasn't even resignation, it was shame. That moment when he had paused and decided not to tell Tarek about his spread-betting had stuck in his mind. He was ashamed of it. And this was why. He knew that the US bond market had been balanced on a knife edge, pulled one way by those who feared global inflation and the other way by those who feared deflation. Over the last twenty-four hours, the fear of inflation had grown more powerful. Calder had completely failed to anticipate this. The reason was obvious: he had given the matter only passing consideration as his mind had been taken up with Todd and Kim and Benton Davis and Sandy and the day-to-day problems of running an airfield. Of course he had no idea which way the bond market was going to go.

He was ashamed that he had kidded himself that he had.

He may as well have bet on the spin of a roulette wheel or the three-thirty at Goodwood. And only the previous morning he had been complaining to his sister about his father's gambling.

He quickly clicked the mouse a few times to take his loss and close out his position. He stared at the screen a moment longer. Maybe he should terminate his account with Spreadfinex? Remove the temptation.

Maybe. Maybe not.

He picked up the phone to call Steve at Little Gransden Airfield to see where they got their body bags from, or indeed if they had a spare one to tide Langthorpe over until Calder could order one.

'So, Alex, have you been speaking to the police?'

Cornelius was wearing his half-moon reading glasses as he held a menu in front of him, and his sharp blue eyes flicked upwards, fixing on Calder. They were in the restaurant of a smart country-house hotel a few miles from the hospital. Todd's sister Caroline had flown over from San Diego, and she and Cornelius had spent the afternoon with his comatose son. Edwin had arrived late that afternoon.

Cornelius had accepted Kim's suggestion that they all have dinner together. It was a sombre gathering.

'Of course,' Calder replied. 'Once they realized the Yak had been sabotaged, they had lots of questions.'

'About?'

'About the Yak, about the engine fire, about the crash landing,' Calder said warily.

'Did they ask about our family?'

Calder carefully put down his own menu. 'If you mean, did I tell them that Todd had been trying to find out about your late wife's death, the answer is yes, I did.'

There was silence around the table.

'I would rather you hadn't mentioned that,' said Cornelius. 'Those are private family matters.'

'And the police are conducting an investigation into attempted murder,' Calder said reasonably. 'Which means they are quite likely to want to know about private family matters.'

'Matters which have nothing to do with you,' Cornelius said.

'I told the police about it as well,' said Kim. 'Not the first time I spoke to them, but once I'd thought it through I realized I had to. Alex is right. Todd could easily have been murdered; we have to tell them everything and trust them to work out what is and isn't relevant.'

Cornelius glared at his daughter-in-law. She shrugged and smiled a small sad smile.

Cornelius's stare softened. 'I'm sorry, Kim. I'm worried sick about Todd, we all are, and I didn't appreciate answering a barrage of intrusive questions from that policewoman. You know how concerned I am about the family's privacy. But it must be hardest on you.'

Kim smiled weakly. 'Alex has been quite a support to me over the last few days.'

Cornelius turned to Calder. 'Thank you for all you are doing,' he said grudgingly. 'I'm sure Todd would appreciate it.'

Caroline, who had said very little, was sitting next to Kim. She moved her hand over to touch her sister-in-law's. Kim grasped it, squeezing so hard that the knuckles went white. She had been doing well, but Caroline's sudden gesture of sympathy seemed to pierce her defences. A tear ran down her cheek as she turned towards Caroline and mouthed, 'Thank you.'

Caroline was a few years younger than Todd. She was thin, with Todd's even features but not his easy self-assurance. She was well dressed in cream trousers and a silk top, but apart from some discreet but expensive earrings, there was no indication that she was married to a billionaire. She had left her nine-month-old daughter at home, and was intending to stay in England for only a couple of days before going back to her. But she had wanted to see Todd and hold his hand, even if Todd couldn't see her.

There was silence as we all stared at Kim with varying degrees of sympathy. The waiter seized his moment and took everyone's order. Kim was a tough woman; she visibly pulled herself together. 'I saw your bid for *The Times* in the papers,' she said to Cornelius. 'The columnist seemed to think you'll get it. That must be very exciting.'

Cornelius paused for a moment, but decided to respect Kim's wish to change the subject back to safer ground. 'There's a long way to go yet,' he said. 'Evelyn Gill is a formidable opponent, it would never do to underestimate him. But it would be very exciting to own *The Times*. I just hope Todd can share in the triumph. I never understood why he walked away from the newspaper business.'

'Different people are suited to different things, Pa,' Edwin said.

Cornelius was taking no notice of his son, and instead was looking intently at Kim.

'Edwin's right,' said Kim. 'Todd is his own man.' She smiled at Cornelius. 'In that I suspect he is like his father. And there's nothing you or I can do to change that.'

'I guess not,' said Cornelius, his disappointment showing.

'I suppose this is your biggest deal since the *Herald*,' Kim said. 'When was that – 1988?'

'That's right,' Cornelius smiled. 'That was the deal that transformed Zyl News from a South African company to an international media group. If we can get *The Times* it will complete the process, give us a real flagship title to be proud of.'

'That must have been a difficult time,' Kim said. 'From what I understand you nearly went under then.'

Cornelius looked at her sharply. 'Did Todd tell you that?'

Kim didn't answer, managing to look coy as though embarrassed by her husband's indiscretion. Calder was impressed at the way she was probing Cornelius.

'There's no point in denying it now, although I don't think the outside world has ever realized just how close we were to bankruptcy. It was the old junk-bond story. We needed to do ever-bigger deals to raise the finance to pay off the debt on the old deals. When the stock market crashed in October '87, the merry-go-round came to an abrupt halt and a lot of guys went flying off the sides. We would have gone too if we hadn't closed the *Herald* deal. Since then we've been much more careful.'

'You don't have any South African papers left in the Zyl News group,' Kim said. 'I've often wondered why that is. I mean, I know you had to sell them in the 1980s to satisfy US investors, but surely there would be no problem in buying one or two now?'

'It's a small fragmented market and it's very competitive,' Edwin answered.

His father ignored him. 'I've left South Africa behind me,' he said. 'I have a US passport, an American wife and I split my time between here and there. But not South Africa.' He glanced at Kim. 'I hope to God that you never have to learn this, but when your spouse dies, you reassess things. You begin to realize what's important to you. In my case it was my family,' he smiled at Caroline and Edwin. 'Not my country.'

Kim struggled to keep a brave face at the reference to Todd's situation. But Calder could see she was determined to find out more. 'Did you consider leaving before Martha died?'

'Yes, yes I did. As you know I was a consistent opponent of apartheid from when I bought my first newspapers in 1962. But during the eighties I became worried about what would happen when the regime did fall. The police were becoming ever more brutal, as were the ANC and the others. There were riots, my brother was blown up by a landmine, and then Martha . . .' He sighed. 'Then they got Martha. If I had only insisted we get out a few months earlier.'

'So you have no regrets about leaving?'

'No, none,' Cornelius's voice was firm. He paused, considering what to say next. 'I am an Afrikaner. Rather, I *was* an Afrikaner. In the couple of years before Martha died that was becoming more and more important to me. During most of my adulthood I had denied my heritage. I criticized apartheid, I knew it was wrong, I passionately disagreed with the National Party and their loathsome ideas, I married an English-speaking South African, and then, God forbid, an American. My brothers and sisters believed I had betrayed

141

my heritage, but I was happy to deny it. Until I saw the end coming.'

He sipped his wine, checking round the table to see if his audience were following him. They were.

'I became convinced that once apartheid fell and a black majority government came to power the Afrikaner people would disappear. As the architects of apartheid, they would be destroyed, either immediately, or slowly over the decades. Take away apartheid, and there's much about Afrikanerdom that seems worth preserving. There's the language. And there's the history. Afrikaners have been in Africa for three hundred years: we are African, we can't go back to the Netherlands, or anywhere else for that matter. We suffered tremendous hardships to establish our way of life, the Great Trek from the Cape to the Transvaal, the battles against the Zulus and against the British. My ancestors suffered in the Boer War – my mother was born in the Bloemfontein concentration camp and my grandmother died there – and afterwards we were treated like second-class citizens. When my father was a boy if you were caught speaking Afrikaans at school you were told to stand in a corner and wear a dunce's cap. Literally, a cap with a big "D" on it.

'My father was a good man. You know he founded an Afrikaans newspaper, the *Oudtshoorn Rekord*? Well, the paper supported South Africa joining Britain in the Second World War and it opposed the National Party when they came to power in 1948 and brought in apartheid. Believe me, those positions weren't popular with all his readers. But he also believed passionately in education. The only way the Afrikaner would ever be the equal of the Briton was if he received an equal education. He encouraged me to get into Stellenbosch and then into Oxford. And what did I do with all that education? Did I do my bit to help him and his kind? No, I turned my back on them.

'I felt guilty about all this. It seems to be the destiny of the white South African to feel guilt in one form or other and that was mine. And then Martha was murdered . . .'

Cornelius hesitated. There was silence around the table. 'She was a truly wonderful woman and we had a great time together. I guess you all know that there were some strains in our marriage for a few months before she died. Strains I've always regretted. When she died everything changed. I didn't care who my ancestors were, what language they spoke, or how many of them had died slaughtering the Zulus at Blood River. I knew I had to get my family out of there as quickly as possible. And I did. We sold Hondehoek, sold or closed the papers, and started afresh in America and England. Caroline and Edwin are married to Americans, Todd married Kim. My grandchildren will have new countries. South Africa is in the past for all of us.'

'Except for Zan,' Edwin said.

Cornelius let slip a hint of mild irritation. 'Except for Zan. But that's her choice.'

'Do you really think Martha was killed by ANC guerrillas?' Kim asked.

Cornelius looked at her. 'Probably.' He held his hand up to stall Kim's next question. 'I know we can't be sure. Perhaps it was poachers. There could have been a cover-up. Perhaps the security police killed her for some twisted reason known only to themselves. Or someone else. Frankly, I don't want to know. Martha's mother suggested that we raise her death with the Truth and Reconciliation Commission, but that's the last thing I wanted. Having to listen to the sordid details of how some twisted thug, be he white or black, took it into his head to murder Martha. And it wouldn't just be me listening, it would be the commissioners, and the press and the public. It would follow me in every newspaper article written about me from now onwards. Follow all of us: Edwin, Caroline, Todd, even you. Really, I'm glad I let it drop.'

'Todd isn't.'

'I know.'

'Alex has been helping me try to find out what really happened.'

'Have you?' Cornelius shot Calder a warning glance.

'I asked him to,' Kim said. 'For example, what happened to the diary?'

'You mean the one that Martha mentioned in her letter to her mother?' Cornelius said. 'The one I wasn't supposed to read?'

'Yes. That one.'

'I've no idea. I didn't even know she was keeping one.'

'I did,' Caroline said.

'*You* did?'

'Yes. Remember I was only twelve, and I was around the house much more than you, Dad. I caught her a couple of times writing in a black book. A really neat black book, kind of small and mysterious. She looked embarrassed each time, she tried to hide what she was doing. She told me once it was private and I should never read it.'

'Did you?' asked Edwin.

'No,' said Caroline. 'Although I was tempted to search for it, I never did.'

'So you never saw her put it into the bottom drawer of her desk?'

'No.' Caroline hesitated, looking around the table. She appeared shy, but determined to say what she had to say.

She was the only one of the van Zyls to have picked up a completely American accent, which made her seem a little bit of an outsider. The others kept quiet, waiting. 'I saw her once doing something that I knew was wrong.' She paused again. Cornelius's brows were furrowed in disapproval, Kim was hanging on every word and so was Calder. Caroline decided to plough on. 'She was sitting in a car outside our house, copying something down into the diary. It was from a sheaf of papers which were lying on top of a briefcase.'

'Whose briefcase?' Kim asked.

Caroline glanced at her father, who was glaring at her. 'He was a man with a beard and sticking-out ears; I think he was a friend of yours and Mom's. He came to Hondehoek with another man to see you. A stranger, I'd never seen him before. Do you remember? It was only a week or so before Mom died.'

'I've no idea who that could be,' said Cornelius.

'When Mom saw me she was really angry,' Caroline said, 'but she was scared at the same time. Almost manic. She told me to forget what I had seen and never tell anyone.'

'But now you have,' said Cornelius.

'She was my mother too,' said Caroline. 'I want to know what really happened.'

'I wonder where the diary is now,' said Kim.

'It never turned up at Hondehoek,' said Cornelius. 'I'm sure of that.'

'Could it have been found at the game reserve where she was murdered?' Calder asked.

'If it was, I didn't hear about it.'

'But if the police found it they wouldn't necessarily have told you,' Calder said.

'They should have.'

'Unless they were covering something up,' Kim said.

'In which case we have no chance of uncovering it now.' Cornelius spoke this last statement with an air of finality.

'I'm going to try,' said Kim. 'For Todd's sake as much as my own. And Alex will help me.'

Cornelius glared at Calder and then at Kim. 'I said, there's no point. Drop it. Do I make myself clear?'

Kim glanced at Calder. 'Perfectly,' she said mildly, with a conciliatory smile. 'Could you pour me some more water, Edwin?'

Calder guided the Maserati through the dark Norfolk lanes back towards Hanham Staithe.

'You did an expert job of pumping Cornelius,' he said.

'It was like he wanted to talk. At least about why he left South Africa.'

'But not about Martha's death. It's as if he'd rather not know what happened to her.'

'See no evil,' Kim said. 'But that's tough. He may be a powerful man, but he doesn't have a right to decide what Todd should or shouldn't know about his mother. Or Caroline for that matter.'

'I liked her,' Calder said.

'Yeah. She's a nice woman. She's quite like Todd but not so self-centred.' She glanced quickly at Calder. 'Sorry, I didn't mean to say that. I didn't mean to say that at all.'

They drove on in an uncomfortable silence for a minute or so.

'Do you think Cornelius is genuine?' Calder said.

'You mean, is he hiding something?'

'Yeah.'

Kim considered the question. 'I don't know. That's the infuriating thing. Obviously he's still upset about that period in his life, I'm sure that's genuine. But I don't believe he's told us why, or at least not all of the reason why. You will help me, won't you, Alex? Find out what's going on. What he's hiding.'

'Absolutely,' said Calder. 'I don't like people destroying lovely old aeroplanes like that Yak. Especially when I'm flying them.'

When they got back to Calder's cottage, Kim went straight upstairs to bed. The emotional strain of the previous few days had worn her out. Calder had not drunk much at dinner because he was driving, but now he was home he poured himself a stiff malt whisky from the decanter his father had given him as a twenty-first birthday present. He sat down in an armchair and put on some music, with the volume turned well down. Tom Waits.

He reflected on his answer to Kim's request for help. It was true that he and Todd had almost been killed, and for that very reason the prudent thing to do would be to back off and demonstrate that he was no threat to anybody. He knew that was what his sister would want him to do. But backing down wasn't in his nature. There was clearly something fishy about Martha van Zyl's death. Todd and Kim were asking difficult questions bravely and they needed his help, now more than ever. It would be wrong, cowardly, to walk away from them. Besides, he was confident he could look after himself.

He was impressed by Kim. Those qualities that he had admired in her when she was a student had matured. She had stood up well to Cornelius, and had pumped him skilfully, despite her own fragile emotional state. She was determined to see through what her husband had started. She clearly loved Todd very much, although there was that comment in the car about him being self-centred. And she was obviously unhappy playing second fiddle to him in small-town New Hampshire. She looked better too; her bony frame had grown into the fullness of womanhood. And that smile. He had always thought that her you-are-the-most-important-person-in-the-world smile had been freely bestowed on everyone, but now she seemed to be keeping it for him. Her new smile, the smile she showed the van Zyl family, was more restrained, more mature, still friendly but with a hint of reserve. He represented the certainty of the past in the uncertain present. It was clear that she trusted him completely, and that she needed him. He liked that.

He remembered the night he had crashed the college ball so many years ago, scaling walls and climbing over roofs. Kim's concern for his safety had been written all over her face, much to the annoyance of her escort who had after all paid for her ticket. Much later, after dawn, after the ball was over and the man, whoever he was – Calder couldn't remember his name – had retired to his own college, Kim and Calder had walked along the river towards Grantchester. It was a still, peaceful morning, swans gliding silently in the water, mist hovering a few feet above the fields. Kim was wearing a simple green dress that made her look delectable. It was cold, so Calder had placed his dinner jacket bought that week at Oxfam over her shoulders, and shivered in his shirtsleeves. They were both drunk, they were both tired. Magic seemed to hang in the morning air with the mist.

He wanted to kiss her. It was one of those brief periods when Kim was without a boyfriend: the man who had taken her to the ball was never really in with a chance. He wanted to kiss her desperately, but he hadn't. Just in case she had pulled away from him. Or perhaps what scared him more was that she wouldn't pull away, that he would become another one of her boyfriends, here today, gone tomorrow.

So he hadn't kissed her. They had remained friends. And he had always wondered what might have happened.

He glanced up at the ceiling: she was sleeping in the bedroom directly above where he was sitting. He banished the thought before it had been fully formed, with a flash of shame. Her husband was in hospital in a coma, for God's sake! He gulped his whisky.

His thoughts turned to Sandy. They had met the year before. She was a close friend of Jennifer Tan and had helped him find out who had killed her. A relationship of sorts had blossomed between them. She was a tall, slim woman with short blonde hair and tiny freckles on the end of her nose. She had worked as an associate at a major New York law firm on secondment to their London office. After she was transferred back to New York she and Calder had made sporadic attempts to stay in touch. When they were together, everything was fantastic. They had spent an idyllic week the previous September driving around Tuscany, wandering from hill town to tiny village, totally relaxed in each other's company. They had carried on a week-long conversation, rambling over everything and nothing. Afterwards, Calder had flown over to New York to snatch a day or two with her, but she was always preoccupied with work, an urgent deadline, documents that had to be on the client's desk by Monday morning. She had visited London and Norfolk on a similar two-day basis. Plans to spend Christmas together had fallen through. She was entitled to only two weeks' vacation a year, and many of her colleagues didn't even take that. It was hard for Calder, too, to get away at weekends: that was prime flying time, and the flying school needed all the instructors it could get. Then in April when he had finally managed to escape for three days to New

York, it had all ended in disaster. The relationship wasn't going to work.

Perhaps he should make it work? Extricate himself from the airfield somehow and move over to America for a few months. Perhaps even consider working on Wall Street for a bit.

But that was a level of commitment he wasn't ready for. An emotional risk that he, the risk-taker, wasn't willing to assume. He poured himself some more whisky.

Sandy was history.

The neat spirit was having its effect. Feeling slightly woozy he glanced upwards at the ceiling again.

It was only ten o'clock on a Monday morning and already Benton's week was not going well. He had spent an hour with Linda Stubbes, his head of Human Resources, and Jack Grote from Finance in New York about how to allocate expenditure on training between the different departments. As head of the London office it should have been easy for him to decree what should happen, but in the real world he didn't have the power. He would have to negotiate between the different prima donnas who ran each group in London protected by their respective patrons in New York. He couldn't wait to get back into the *Times* deal, real business with the prospect of a real fee.

As the two bankers left his office his personal assistant, Stella, came in. 'There are two people to see you,' she said. 'Police. They say they are from Norfolk CID.' Stella was generally discreet, but it was clear that these visitors had aroused her interest. Her eyebrows were raised in a silent demand for information.

Benton wasn't going to tell her anything. 'Norfolk, you say? Where are they?'

'Downstairs in the lobby. They arrived fifteen minutes ago. I said you were in a meeting. They said they would wait.'

Benton knitted his brows. 'Give me ten minutes and then send them up.'

'All right,' said Stella as she headed for his door. Then she paused. 'Oh, yes, and there was a call from a Mr Moolman.'

'Moolman?' Benton said. 'Do I know him? I'm sure I've heard the name before.'

'He had a South African accent. Strong, very strong. He said he was calling to say how sorry he was to hear about Todd van Zyl's accident. He said you needn't call him back and he didn't leave a number.' She stared at her boss. 'Benton? Are you all right? You look as though you've seen a ghost.' Her boss didn't answer, but stared at her with a mixture of shock and fear. 'OK,' she said. 'I'll, um, I'll tell the police to wait a few more minutes.' She left the room as quickly as she could, shutting the door behind her.

Two miles east of the City, on the executive floor of the *Herald*'s building at Madeira Quay, Edwin was listening to a grey-haired, hyperactive journalist called Jeff Hull. Jeff was a South African, a former employee of the *Cape Daily Mail*, who had recognized early on that it made sense to make friends with the boss's son. Their relationship had been cemented during the takeover of the *Herald*, when Jeff had discovered some fascinating information about the *Herald*'s proprietor Lord Scotton and a visit he had made to a public lavatory in Piccadilly, that had persuaded Scotton to sell out to Zyl News rather than Evelyn Gill. Jeff had left Cape Town for London when Edwin took over the management of the *Herald*. Jeff thought of himself as a hard-nosed invest-igative journalist; some of his colleagues, and indeed his editor, saw him more as a ruthless muckraker. But whatever his editor's opinion of him, he was untouchable. And he did have the ability to come up with sensational stories on a regular basis, some of which the *Herald* deemed fit to print.

'That was quick,' Edwin said. 'What have you got?'

Jeff handed over a single sheet of paper. He bit his thumbnail as Edwin read it. 'Do you really think this will do the job?' Edwin asked doubtfully.

'You bet,' Jeff answered.

'Let me get this straight. The superintendent's brother was arrested for downloading child pornography from the internet, but no charges were ever brought?'

'That's right,' Jeff was grinning as he gnawed at his thumb.

'Was the superintendent downloading porn?'

'No.'

'Do we even know the last time the superintendent saw his brother?'

'No.'

'So?'

'So we have a headline with the words "policeman" and "paedophile" in it. That will go down nicely with the readers, and with the Norfolk Constabulary. There will be questions about whether the superintendent leaned on someone to have his brother's charges dropped.'

'Can we prove that he did that?'

Jeff grinned. 'Can he prove that he didn't? And if he did, why did he? Is he a member of the paedophile ring himself? He worked on the vice squad in the Met twenty years ago, I can go digging there. Plus I've got a mate that's on the paedophile register. I'll get him to apply for every temporary job in Norfolk that's involved with children. Someone will give him a job. Then all hell will break loose. Plus, and this is the really important point,' Jeff leaned forward, grinning, 'our superintendent friend will know we're digging. And if he's got something to hide, and let's face it, everyone has, he'll want us to stop.'

'I was hoping for something a bit more substantial than this.'

'Believe me, there's nothing the cops of today are more afraid of than a paedophile scandal. I'll call him tonight. I'll ask him to confirm that he is aware that his brother was arrested for downloading kiddie porn, and I'll ask him a couple of innocuous questions about his time on the vice squad. And we just leave it at that. No need to be specific, no need to push it, no need even to print anything. Just so he knows who he's dealing with. All he has to do is go a little softly, right?'

'Right.' Edwin thought a moment. There was a lot in what Jeff was saying. A veiled threat was probably more effective than out-and-out blackmail anyway. 'OK, do it.'

I 2

July 28, 1988

Poor Doris! She got a phone call this afternoon. For her to have a phone call at the house, I knew it must be something pretty serious. I overheard her talking in Xhosa on the phone, then she screamed, a heart-rending wail. It was an awful sound, especially from Doris who is always so cheerful. She wouldn't stop. I tried to comfort her but she wanted to finish the phone call. Then she just let the receiver drop and sobbed.

It was Thando. He was killed with three other boys by some unknown thugs last night. Some white men broke into their shack and shot them. Thando lives in a township outside Port Elizabeth; I think he works in one of the car factories there. He's only seventeen. He's Doris's only son, only child. Finneas came in from the garden. He and I did what we could to comfort Doris but she was inconsolable, and why not? I would be if it were Todd.

Doris doesn't know any of the details. Her son will be branded a criminal, of course. But I know him well: as Doris says, "He was a good boy."

I told Finneas to take the Renault and drive Doris to P. E. tonight.

What a day! I went to the funeral. I thought, why not? Doris and I have been together for eighteen years, since just before Thando was born, and I'm damned if I won't be allowed to support her just because of my color or her color. Zan offered to come with me, but with Doris away I said I'd prefer to have her stay at home with Caroline. I got the first flight of the morning to Port Elizabeth and took a taxi. The funeral was held in a soccer stadium in a township on the outskirts of Uitenhage, an auto-manufacturing town a few miles from P. E. itself. A cordon of police surrounded the township: young men in camouflage uniforms brandishing guns, some of them perched on "Hippos," the nickname for those creepy armored cars they use.

I had to talk my way through the cordon; they didn't seem to understand that a white woman, and an American at that, could be a friend of one of the victims. I pleaded, and in the end a sergeant gave in with a shrug that suggested that if I was that crazy I deserved what was coming to me.

Passing through that cordon was like passing into another country, a country run by blacks for blacks. A marshal directed me to where I should sit in the sports stadium. There must have been 40,000 people there. The whole place was a riot of warmth and color and passion. I've never experienced an atmosphere like it. There were banners everywhere in the bright colors of the trade unions, the black and yellow of the UDF, and the black, green and gold of the ANC. I even glimpsed, briefly, the red flag and hammer and sickle of the Communist Party. The speakers sat on a raised platform, beside which were rows of seats for relatives. I could make out the plump figure of Doris, but there was no way she could see me. My idea of joining her to express my sympathy was clearly unrealistic.

Lying in the field in front of the speakers were four coffins, three in dark brown wood and one smaller white one. One of them was Thando. Another must have been a small child.

I asked the woman next to me if she knew what had happened. She said that they had been killed by the police.

"Didn't it happen in the middle of the night?"

"That's when they do these things," she said. "Then no one sees. They don't have to go through the bother of arrests and lawyers and courts, they just kill them," and she put two fingers to her temple like a gun.

"But why them?"

"The policemen, they never liked Joshua. They think he is a troublemaker. The people say he knew he was going to die some time. But he was a brave comrade."

"And Thando? Was he a troublemaker too?"

"No," said the woman thoughtfully. "But he was also a brave comrade. And Joshua's little brother, he never done anyone any harm."

I thought of Thando, the shy trusting boy with his mother's generosity of spirit. Neels and I offered to pay for his education at high school and on to university, but he didn't want to go. He wanted to earn money, he said, good money in a car factory. I'm sure he wasn't a troublemaker. I'm not convinced he was a "brave comrade" either. I guess he was in the wrong place at the wrong time. I wondered what impression the hero's burial would make on Doris: whether it gave her comfort to have so many people joining her in her grief, or whether she would be happier alone with her son at the graveside. I didn't know. The whole idea of losing Todd like that is too awful to contemplate.

And what about the child in the little white coffin? Just how much a threat to anyone could he be?

The funeral took hours, but I didn't care. Very little time was spent on the actual funeral service, but there were speeches, shouting of slogans, preaching, the toyi-toyi dancing of the young men, and singing, beautiful singing. The whole crowd sang "Hambe kahle Umkhonto", the song praising the Umkhonto we Sizwe guerrillas, the song that strikes fear into white South Africans' hearts. At that moment, it lifted mine.

Then a group of young men raised the coffins on to their shoulders and carried them out of the stadium. I followed. Although there were very few white faces in the crowd, just some press men and photographers, I felt part of it, swept along by the heady mixture of grief, pride, passion and joy, opposing emotions that combined to create a kind of mass elation.

My seat was close to the front of the crowd as it left the stadium. I could see the men carrying the coffins, and in front of them a couple of small boys swooping back and forth on their bicycles. The police watched. They weren't like riot police in other countries, dressed for protection. They had no shields or body armor, not even helmets. But they did have guns and batons and dogs. I stared into their faces: they looked like members of a street gang spoiling for a fight. I caught the eyes of a couple of them, who glanced away as if embarrassed to see a white woman.

Cameras flashed. Not from press photographers, but from the police lines. One of them was pointing straight at me. The photographer saw me staring at him, and gave me the thumbs up.

I wanted to get out of there. The chants of the crowd were becoming more aggressive. Hippos shunted about, taking up better positions. I could see the boys on the crest of the hill ahead pedaling in circles in front of the police lines, wobbling unsteadily as they raised their arms in the black-power salute.

Suddenly a dog, a German shepherd, tore out of the police lines and launched itself into the air at one of the boys, bowling him off his bike. I didn't see what the dog did to the boy once he was on the ground, but after a second of stunned silence, the crowd howled.

There was movement everywhere, shouts, screams, barks and then shots. Some in the crowd surged forward, some, myself included, scrambled back toward the stadium. More shots, and then the whole lot of us, thousands of people, were running, scattering. A young man with long dreadlocks saw my fear, and grabbed me by the arm. He dragged and pulled me through the crowd and up a side street. We ducked to left and right through the shacks of the township until we emerged on an open road behind the line of Hippos.

I slumped to the ground and gasped my thanks, gulping air into my lungs. The man didn't seem tired at all. He smiled quickly and left me.

I'm writing this on the plane back to Cape Town. Neels will be worried about the photographs. He will say I shouldn't have gone. He'll remind me of my promise not to make trouble. But now Neels is closing the *Mail* down, who cares about me being seen at a black funeral? I sure as hell don't.

August 1

Well, I'm feeling kind of mellow and I rather like it.

I was beginning to wonder about Zan's social life. She disappears into Cape Town quite regularly to do God knows what, and she's been to Jo'burg, but there's no mention of a boyfriend, or indeed any other kind of friend. Then today she called me from Cape Town to ask if she could bring two people over to stay the night.

They arrived this afternoon. The man is called Bjorn, and he's some kind of Scandinavian. He is over six feet tall, with a dark beard and calm blue eyes. Quite cute, really. And then there was his girlfriend Miranda who is almost as tall, with an Afro hairstyle and gorgeous golden-brown skin. They look like a pair of hippies straight out of the seventies, and make Zan look positively Establishment by comparison. After a minimum of small talk with me, they disappeared to Zan's room.

I was out working in the garden. The window was open, and I could hear music, I think it was Dollar Brand, and then I smelled that familiar smell of my college days. Grass. Marijuana. Dagga, they call it here. I didn't know what to do. I wasn't too happy about having someone smoking dope in my house, but I didn't want to come across as the heavy authority figure with Zan, especially in front of the first friends she has brought back to Hondehoek. I know Neels will be absolutely furious if he finds out and so I decided I really had to stop them, or Zan might think she could smoke dope any time she liked.

I went indoors, steeled myself outside her room, knocked and walked in. The sweet smell hit me. Zan and Miranda were sitting cross-legged in the middle of the floor, and Bjorn was lying back against the bed, holding a long joint, while Dollar Brand played his heart out on the piano.

Zan looked up at me guiltily. I paused, grasping for the right words that would be firm but not too dictatorial.

Then Bjorn spoke. "Hey, Martha," he said quietly, and held the joint up to me. I looked at him as though he was crazy.

He smiled a small smile, shrugged but didn't retract the joint. There was something amazingly calm, almost wise about him.

What the fuck, I thought. Screw Neels. I took the joint.

It's the first time I've smoked marijuana in over twenty years, and probably the last, but it was good to do just once more. I did tell Zan later that I didn't expect to see dagga in my house again. She apologized with a smile.

I tell you what, though. If my sixteen-year-old son so much as tries to smoke a cigarette here he's in big trouble. And he and his girlfriend are having separate rooms. I'm 100 percent certain about that.

August 2

Oh, God, Neels was right all along. This is a horrible, evil country and I wish I had never set foot in it. I have been stupid when I should have been careful. I *hate* this place.

Yesterday. Yesterday I was a different person.

Yesterday I went to a board meeting at the Project. Finneas drove me, poor broken Finneas. If it had been Nimrod things might have been better. Despite his small size, Nimrod is quite capable of looking after his master. And his master's wife.

After my experiences at Thando's funeral I was enthusiastic about going to the Project and I actually felt safe as we drove through Guguletu. The meeting lasted a couple of hours and then we took our usual look around the school. It was about four o'clock when Finneas and I set off for home. We had barely gone a quarter of a mile when two *bakkie* pulled up, one in front and one behind us, and men leaped out with guns. They were black, but they didn't look like locals, they were bigger and stronger and better dressed and they had an air of disciplined purpose. They definitely knew how to use the guns they were waving.

Finneas started sobbing and chattering and I was too stunned to know what to do. They dragged me out of the car and I began to scream. I can remember seeing three small boys standing by the roadside staring at me and then some foul-tasting cloth was shoved in my mouth. I tried to kick out but there was no point, these men were strong. Then they thrust a sack over my head, yanked my hands behind my back and bound them. I was lifted up and dumped on to hard metal. The rear of the *bakkie*. A sheet of some kind was thrown over me and someone heavy sat on me. Then they drove off.

God knows how long they drove for, I lost all track of time. Maybe twenty minutes. Maybe an hour. But eventually the *bakkie* came to a halt. I could hear the sounds of traffic in the distance, but not the constant hum of township music and chatter. I was carried off the *bakkie* and into a building, through a couple of doors and dumped on to a hard cold floor. A moment later the hood was lifted.

I was in some kind of store room. There was a small window which was boarded up. A single electric bulb hung from the ceiling. A rickety table stood in the center of the room, on either side of which were two upended Castrol oil drums. The two men who had dumped me on the floor left the room, locking the door behind them. I stood up and began to yell for help. Instantly one of the men was back. He stepped rapidly over to me and struck me once in the stomach. It didn't seem a particularly hard blow, but it winded me and left me doubled up on the floor again, gasping for breath.

"Quiet!" he snapped, glaring at me. Then he left the room again.

I decided not to scream anymore. I stood up and paced about the room, my hands still tied behind my back. I wondered who these men were. If they were kidnapping me for money, would Neels pay? A couple of months ago, I wouldn't have had to ask that question. But now? Would he view this as a simple means of getting me out of the way?

The men were tough and professional. I assumed they wanted money.

I was very scared.

After about ten minutes the door opened and another man appeared. He was white, which surprised me. He was short and bulky, muscular rather than fat. He had a thick neck, a small moustache and hard little eyes. I noticed his hands were very large. I realized my first instincts had been wrong: this man was a policeman, a "rockspider," as Zan would no doubt call him. He looked mean, but my spirits rose. I was in the hands of the authorities. I should be safe.

"Sit down, Mrs van Zyl." Although the accent was harsh, the voice was surprisingly soft. Soft and confident.

I did as he asked, perching on the oil drum. He sat on the other one.

"I'm sorry we had to bring you here," he said, pulling out a packet of cigarettes. He offered me one, and when I had shaken my head, lit one up himself. "I'm afraid we don't have any coffee. But we do have some water. How about that?"

I shook my head again.

The man smiled. "I think you'll need some water before we have finished." He went over to the door and shouted out to someone called Elijah.

Then he sat down on the oil drum and examined me across the table.

"Why have you brought me here?" I asked.

"To talk to you."

"But why did you kidnap me like that? Who are you, anyway?"

A man came in with a plastic cup of water, the man who had pulled the hood off my face and hit me in the stomach. The white man waited until the other had left.

"I'm a member of the Laagerbond."

"And what are you holding me for?" I said. "You can't do this. I'm an American citizen. I demand to speak to someone from the US consulate. Do you know who my husband is?"

The *Laagerbonder* smiled. "I know very well who your husband is, Mrs van Zyl. In fact, that's why you are here. And as for the consulate, well you can demand what you want, but although my friends and I are employed by the government, we are acting in an unofficial capacity."

"Well, in that case let me go."

"I want you to tell me everything you know about the Laagerbond."

"I don't know anything about the Laagerbond. I've never even heard of it."

"Now, I know that's not true. Please answer my question."

"I have answered it. I've never heard of the Laagerbond."

"I can make you tell me."

"No you can't," I said, stupidly.

This made the rockspider smile. "I can't think how many dozens of people, hundreds of people, have told me what I want to know over the years. You will tell me."

It was the certainty of his last comment that shook me. Until then I had been doing well with the bravado, buoying myself up with it.

"You won't torture me," I said. I meant it as a brave

statement, but it came out of my mouth more as a half question.

"I won't have to," the man said, leaning forward. "There's really no need. I will, of course, if necessary, but you and I both know that what you are hiding from me isn't that important, at least not to you. I could make you betray your own mother, your husband, even," he paused and smiled quickly, "your daughter. It wouldn't take me long, less than an hour. But I don't want that. All I want is for you to tell me something that really has nothing to do with you. You don't care, or you shouldn't."

"You dare not torture me," I said. "My husband is an important person. There would be all kinds of diplomatic consequences."

"I'm going to show you some photographs," the man said. "You'll probably recognize Elijah, he's the man who showed you in. And although you won't see my face, you might recognize these hands." He held out his meaty fists and opened and closed his fingers. "And you might recognize someone else."

He opened the brown envelope and withdrew about twenty prints which he placed face down on the table in front of him. He turned the first one over. It was a black and white photograph of the terrified face of a black man, or kid really. Eyes wide, teeth bared, I had never seen such fear.

Another photograph. This time a black woman of about twenty. Fear again, but not just fear, dread. "Remember this face, you'll see it later on," the rockspider said.

I should have shut my eyes, but I stared at the photographs, I couldn't help it.

The next was of the torn back of a child of about ten. The man called Elijah was standing next to him, a rhino-hide whip in his hands. Then more photos. Men, women, children; naked, bloodied, bruised, broken. Then the face of the first woman I had been shown, pressed against the floor, her eyes staring sightless. "I told you to remember that face," the rockspider said.

Then, I think I started to sob. But I couldn't tear my eyes away from the photos. A white man being hit with chains. The chains were held by the same meaty fists that were clutching the photo. The white man naked on the ground. The man's face, dead.

"Isn't that . . . ?" I said.

"Yes," the rockspider said. "I thought you would recognize him."

It was the face of the Reverend Tom Kettering, an activist in the UDF who had been found murdered in Soweto two years ago. The authorities had said it was one of the township gangs. Except it wasn't.

"Was that you?" I asked.

"You thought you recognized the hands?" the man said. "Mr Kettering had important friends in the US, didn't he? I'd say he was more important than you, wouldn't you agree?"

"You're not going to do that to me, are you?"

The man smiled. "It's entirely your choice. I can if you want. Oh, I've got one more photograph for you to look at." He pulled out one final print. It was Caroline! She was chattering with her friends in the school playground. The man reached into his pile of prints and picked out the one of the ten-year-old boy with the torn back and placed it next to the photograph of Caroline.

That was it. I broke down. The tears came. It was true I was afraid for myself and for Caroline, but it wasn't just that, I was crying for the people in those photos, for all the victims of the evil regime and the monster sitting in front of me.

He waited, until my sobbing had abated. "All right. Back to my questions. How much do you know about the Laagerbond?"

I told him, of course. It wasn't as if I knew that much. I told him about stealing into Daniel Havenga's car, I told him about the memo about Neels and I admitted I had seen the list of Laagerbond members. This last information caused him some concern. He asked me several times whether I had removed the list, but each time I said I hadn't. Then he asked me which names I could remember. I couldn't remember all of them, but I recounted the famous ones, the generals and the politicians I had recognized. Then I mentioned Visser and Havenga and a couple of others on the list. His eyes flickered when I said Moolman, a funny name that had stuck in my mind. I bet that's him.

He never asked me whether I had copied the names down so I didn't tell him.

He asked me who I had spoken to about the Laagerbond. I mentioned George Field, Neels and Zan, but swore that I hadn't told any of them any of the details, although I assumed Neels knew them all already.

At last, the questions stopped.

"Thank you, Mrs van Zyl. Now that wasn't so hard, was it?" the rockspider said. "I knew there wouldn't be any need for physical force."

I didn't answer. I hung my head, ashamed that I had given in so easily, when those other brave people I had seen in the photographs had held out.

The rockspider seemed to read my mind. "Oh, don't be ashamed. I'm certain you would be a much more difficult case if you were protecting someone you loved."

"What do you mean?"

"Like your daughter."

"You won't harm Caroline!"

The man sighed with impatience. "Of course we won't harm Caroline. Because you will never mention the Laagerbond to anyone ever again. Not even to your husband. Will you?"

I didn't answer.

"Will you?" His voice, which had been unnaturally soft throughout the whole interview, hardened.

"No," I whispered.

He examined me, trying to make sure I meant what I had said. I did.

"Excellent. I can see you have no need to fear for your daughter's safety. Now, time you went home. Elijah will take you. But it will involve putting that hood back on."

An hour later I found myself by the side of the road half a mile up the valley from Hondehoek.

Finneas came home a couple of hours later. He had two broken ribs and had lost a tooth.

I've talked a lot over the years about fighting the regime. Only now do I have any inkling what that really means.

13

Sandy Waterhouse stood in the 'All Other Passports' queue at Heathrow's Terminal Three. Her flight from New York had arrived at the same time as one from Pakistan and another from Jamaica, and the line was moving slowly. She was tired – she hadn't done more than doze on the plane – but her brain was buzzing.

She knew that this was an important trip, but now, standing on British soil, she was beginning to *feel* it. She was scared and excited and impatient. The dice were thrown and she wanted to see how they would land.

Officially she was in London for three days working with a client, a large American insurance company, on the acquisition of a British investment-management firm. But she had an appointment to see the senior partner of her own firm's London office that morning at eleven o'clock. She checked her watch. It was barely seven. She had plenty of time to go to her hotel and have a shower before seeing him at Trelawney Stewart's office in the City.

The firm, medium sized by New York standards but with a strong reputation, was doing well in London and was expanding. They were recruiting locally, and planning to send over two more partners from New York. They also needed experienced, capable associates who understood both the American and the British way of doing things. That, Sandy hoped, was a good description of herself.

She had spent two years in London and had hated most of it. She had no friends there and because of the ridiculous hours she had been forced to work she had found it virtually impossible to make any. There had only been Jen, whose death had deeply shocked her. And Alex. Alex Calder.

Jen's death had brought them together as she had supported him in his single-minded attempts to find out what had really happened to his assistant. She liked Alex, she liked him very much. It wasn't just that she found him physically attractive, with his strong, well-toned body and those thoughtful blue-grey eyes that seemed to assess and understand her, his kind smile and his gentle voice with that soft Scottish intonation. She admired him too. He had been willing to take on great risks to do what he, and she, thought was right. Many of the men she met every day on Wall Street took few risks in doing what they knew was wrong.

She hadn't encouraged the relationship, if it could be called that; she knew that her eighty-hour weeks weren't really conducive to it. But they had had a great time together in Italy. Since then their encounters had been characterized by frustration and the occasional snatched jet-lagged day. Then there had been the awful weekend when he had come to New York to see her and she had been whisked off to Dallas. All right, he had blamed her for that, but he didn't seem to understand that there was nothing that she could do about it, that a deal was closing and there was no other lawyer who knew the documents, and that she couldn't have refused to go and still keep her job at Trelawney Stewart. She had been looking forward to the weekend too! It hadn't been exactly fun to spend Friday and Saturday night awake until four a.m. arguing over warranties in legal agreements. He hadn't understood that.

The conclusion was obvious to both of them: there was no future in this relationship. Sandy was angry about this. Angry with herself, and angry with Alex. But as the weeks went by she was sad about it too. It wasn't often that someone like Alex came along. Couldn't she do *something* to make things easier? It would be difficult. She knew what Trelawney Stewart's partners would think. That she was a soft-headed woman who was willing to put her career second to her love life. Before long she'd be married and having babies. They'd never say it, probably not even to each other, but they'd think it.

Why should it be she who made the compromise? Why couldn't Alex move to New York? She understood very well his reasons for stepping away from the financial world, but perhaps he could do something with airfields or flying. He could at least try; he could at least discuss it with her. The anger and frustration that had been simmering since that disastrous weekend flared up again.

Then she had flown up to Martha's Vineyard to spend the long Memorial Day weekend at the end of May at her folks' place. Over dinner her father asked her about Alex. She explained the problem, why the relationship wasn't really going to work. She expected him to leave it at that, her father never usually seemed to take more than a polite interest in her boyfriends, whether because he wasn't interested or he respected her privacy, she wasn't quite sure. But this time it was different.

'Do you like this man?' he had asked.

'Yes. Yes, I do.'

'A lot?'

She had reddened at this untypical question from her father. 'Yeah, I guess. A lot.'

'Then why don't you talk to Trelawney Stewart? See what they can do.'

'You know how these firms work, Dad,' she said. 'They'll

just view it as a sign of weakness. I'm doing really well at the moment and I don't want to screw it all up.'

Her father exchanged glances with her mother. Sandy detected a conspiracy. They ate in silence. Sandy was wary.

'Stanhope Moore asked me to go to Sydney once,' her father said at last. 'They wanted to make a big push in Australasia. They wanted me to head it up. It was a great opportunity. I guess I was about thirty-five. You were three.'

'I don't remember going to Sydney,' Sandy said.

'No. Grandmother Peabody was very sick. She had cancer and Mom was spending a lot of time with her. I told them we couldn't go. They suggested I leave the family in the States and spend one month there and two weeks here. They were very persuasive. But your mother needed me here with her.'

'OK, but that didn't hurt your career, did it?'

'Sure it did. I got passed over for promotion that year and the next. It took me three or four years to get back on to the fast track.'

'That was different,' Sandy protested. 'You're a man, they understand that kind of thing. I'm a woman. I'm not supposed to put my personal feelings ahead of the job.'

Sandy's father shrugged. 'I don't know where you get that idea from. I *nearly* went to Sydney. I guess all I'm telling you is that I'm glad I didn't.'

Sandy looked at her father, countless arguments running through her head. Her father's point was, of course, that his career had recovered. Until the bank had been swallowed up in a merger a few years earlier, he had been chairman of Stanhope Moore, one of the most prestigious and conservative commercial banks in the country.

But Sandy couldn't agree with her father. It just wasn't

allowed. She loved him of course, and he loved her, but ever since she was eighteen he had been the enemy. At college she had stumbled into a student debate on whether the United States' big banks should forgive the billions of dollars of debt owed to them by the world's poorest nations. The argument that they should seemed to Sandy incontrovertible. She also realized that her father was one of the few men in the country who could really make it happen. And so, unlike the other fifty or so students in the room, Sandy could actually influence the fate of the Third World.

That running war with her father was still being waged, if on a much lower level than it had been in her early twenties. Cornered by him on her attitude to Alex and to her work, Sandy's instinct was to summon the plight of the starving in Africa and Latin America to her aid, but she didn't. She did, however, exercise her right to behave grumpily for the remainder of the weekend.

But her father's point had sunk in. And now, now she was willing to give it a go.

Her passport stamped, she strode through baggage reclaim and customs, her carry-on sized suitcase trundling along behind her. She decided to take the train to Paddington rather than a taxi. She didn't know what it was about her, but whenever she took a cab in London, invariably the driver began a conversation. Usually she didn't mind, but this time she wanted some peace and privacy. She bought an *International Herald Tribune* to hide behind and sought out the platform.

She had been wary of discussing her plan with Alex. This was partly because there was always a chance it might not work, but also to give herself the opportunity to back out if she changed her mind. Although, as she found herself drawing nearer and nearer to Trelawney Stewart's London office, she realized she was becoming surer of what she was doing. She'd call him after the meeting, perhaps arrange to see him that night or the next.

She had no idea how the relationship would develop. But she smiled to herself. She was looking forward to finding out.

Calder spent the day at the airfield. It was a perfect morning for flying, and he had taken the opportunity to put his little red Pitts biplane through its paces, performing a series of barrel rolls, outside loops, Cuban eights and Immelmann turns over the Norfolk sky. But a stiff crosswind picked up in the afternoon, making take-off and landing impossible. He decided to meet Kim at the hospital. After his stray thoughts of the previous evening, he wanted to see Todd again, remind himself as forcefully as possible that Kim had a husband and he was in a coma.

As he pulled the Maserati into a parking space, he saw Kim unlocking her rented car on the other side of the car park. He got out of his own car and waved to her. She saw him, and came over to him, smiling.

'Are you here to see Todd?'

'Yes,' said Calder.

Kim looked at him strangely. She couldn't really ask why, but she could think it. 'I'll come back in with you.'

'Any change?'

'None. I spent the whole day with him, though. I got some reading done.' She lifted the thick paperback she was carrying.

'Any sign of the other van Zyls?'

'Cornelius took a helicopter down to London first thing. Caroline was here this morning, but she's on her way back to California now. We talked a lot. I like her.'

They walked through the familiar corridors to the private

room where Todd had been transferred. By the head of his bed was the figure of a woman crouching on a chair, bent over towards his face. Calder saw her straight away, but Kim didn't notice her at first. As they moved closer, the woman turned. She was young and strikingly pretty, with yellow hair in a bob, white teeth and an upturned nose. Her big blue eyes were red and brimming with tears. When she saw Kim her jaw dropped and her face, red from crying, lost its colour.

'Donna?' Kim said.

'Oh, my God,' the girl said in an American accent, and put her hand to her mouth. She stumbled to her feet, pushed past Kim, and headed for the exit.

'Donna!' Kim shouted after her. 'Donna!'

Kim's face was pale. Her lips were trembling. A nurse appeared to see what the fuss was about. 'Has that woman been in here before?' Kim asked the nurse. 'Have you seen her before?'

'Here, have a seat, Kim,' the nurse said. She was a solid woman with a strong Norfolk accent.

'She has been here before,' Kim said. 'Hasn't she?' She glared at the nurse, demanding an answer.

The nurse nodded.

Kim's cheeks, so pale a moment before, reddened. She switched her glare to her unconscious husband, entangled in tubes, oblivious to the drama around him. Then she stared at Calder, her face a mixture of anger and bewilderment.

'Let's go,' Calder said, putting an arm round Kim and leading her from the room. A tear ran down her cheek and then another. They walked in silence down to the hospital café, and Calder got them both a cup of tea.

'Who is she?' he asked.

'Donna Snyder. Art teacher at the school.'

Calder nodded. There was no need to ask what she was doing in England, or why Kim was so upset. For a moment he considered suggesting that there was a misunderstanding, but one look at Kim convinced him that that was pointless.

'She must have waited until she saw me leave,' she said. 'I wonder how long she's been here, skulking in the car park, watching.'

'I'm sorry,' Calder said. 'I'm so sorry. What a terrible way to find out.'

'I should have realized,' Kim said. 'I knew they liked each other. They would always talk to each other at school functions, joke together and so forth. I suppose I was mildly jealous, Donna does have those big baby-blue eyes after all, but you can't go through life being jealous of every attractive woman your husband is friends with.' She sighed. 'Or maybe you can. Maybe that was my mistake. Anyway, I noticed about a month ago at a dinner party given by the principal that they were avoiding each other. Stupidly I was relieved. I thought they'd fallen out, had one of those staff-room squabbles, something like that. But that's what happens when flirtation turns into an affair, isn't it? Ignore each other in public, but in private . . .' She broke down in sobs. Calder leaned over the table to touch her arm. There were a few other visitors in the café, and they looked on in sympathy. Grief is what you expect to see in hospitals.

Calder drove her home, promising to bring her back the next day to pick up her own car. He cooked some supper. Kim went out for a long walk through the marshes alone. When she returned, there was a little colour in her cheeks but her dark hair was a mess. Calder had a bottle of white wine open. She took a glass thankfully.

'I don't know, Alex, I don't know what to think. I mean, I love him, I love him so much. And I see him lying there every day, so helpless, not knowing when he's going to recover, *if* he's going to recover. And all the time she's outside, tearing herself up with her own grief. I feel like such a bloody idiot. I want him to get better but I also want to strangle him. And the terrible thing is, if he doesn't get better, then I'll know that at the end he was in love with *her*, not me. I couldn't face that, I just couldn't face that.' She buried her face in her hands.

Her agony was painful to watch. Calder would not wish Todd's condition on anyone, but his anger was building too. It had turned out that Todd was like all those other good-looking charmers after all. He had used Kim and he had hurt her. Except that this time Kim looked as if she had been hurt so badly it would be difficult to recover.

They ate supper and moved outside to the bench in the garden. Calder opened another bottle of wine. It was a warm evening, despite the clouds overhead, but to the west there was a band of clear sky into which the sun was dipping, throwing its long shadows across the garden. The rooks kicked up their evening fuss. Kim talked and drank. Calder listened and drank.

They talked about university, the other schmucks. Calder spoke about an old girlfriend who had dumped him. They opened a third bottle of wine. He put his arm round her and she buried her head in his shoulder. The sun sank beneath the horizon and the windmill on the ridge retreated into the darkness. The rooks settled down. He kissed her, or did she kiss him? They broke away. She rested her head on his shoulder again. Then she turned her head up to his and they kissed again.

They made angry, passionate, drunken love, there, on the grass, under the apple tree.

*

Calder heard the car draw up outside the front of the house. Then he heard the engine splutter and stop. Then he heard the door knocker. It took him several moments to react. He looked frantically around for his clothes. Kim was lying semi-naked on the grass, her mouth open, asleep. Calder grabbed a shirt and some trousers and pulled them on. Who the hell was that?

'Hello?'

Christ! He recognized the voice. It was coming closer, around the side of the house, checking the garden.

'Hello?'

'Sandy!' he shouted, frantically zipping up his trousers. 'Sandy. Wait there! I'm in the garden. I'll be right round.'

Kim stirred, and raised herself on one arm. 'Huh?'

'Alex?' The voice was nearer. The little side gate to the back garden squeaked open. 'Alex? What the hell . . . ?'

Calder stood barefoot, shirt hanging out of his trousers. Sandy stopped by the side of the house, speechless. Kim was sitting on the grass, blinking, her top half still clothed, but her jeans and panties in a ball at her feet.

'Oh, my God!' Sandy put her hand to her mouth and turned and ran. Calder ran after her. 'Sandy, stop! Wait!'

'Didn't you get my message?' Sandy said as she opened her car door.

'What message?'

'I left you a message. That I was coming up to see you. Oh, God.' She jumped into the car.

'Sandy, stop!'

But Sandy slammed the car into gear, spun it round and drove off back to the village and the road to London.

Calder stood there, watching the tail lights disappear round the first bend.

'Alex?'

It was Kim, still blinking, but now wearing her jeans. 'Who was that?'

'Sandy,' Calder replied.

'Jesus,' Kim said. 'I'm sorry.'

Calder looked at her, his alcohol-sodden brain torn between confusion and a rising surge of panic.

Kim pulled her arms around herself. 'Alex? What have we done?'

14

'Can I have some of that?'

Kim motioned towards the pot half-full of coffee. Calder poured her a mug. She sat down. It was eight o'clock. He had been up since six, stewing.

Kim sipped at her mug and stared straight at Calder. 'We've messed everything up, haven't we?'

Calder had been running over in his mind all the things he would say to Kim, the explanations, the excuses, the self-recrimination. In the end, she had made it easy for him.

'Yes,' he said.

A tear ran down her cheek. She took a deep breath. 'I can't believe I did that. With Todd in the hospital.'

'You were drunk. And I led you on,' Calder said. 'It was my fault.'

'It was both of us,' Kim said. 'We created this mess together. But I can't use the drink as an excuse. I *wanted* to get drunk. I was angry and I wanted to get back at Todd. I used you to do it.'

Calder didn't answer, but stared into his coffee.

'So that was Sandy?'

'"Was" is the right word.'

'I'm sorry.'

'So am I.'

They sat in silence. All night Calder's brain had shifted between two images: Todd, lying prone in his hospital bed for days, and Sandy standing staring at him. He had listened to the messages on his mobile. There were three. The first was from her, saying she had some good news and she wanted to tell him in person. She'd rent a car and drive up to Norfolk to see him. She should be there by nine. Could he call her at her hotel to say he had got the message? Then there was a message from his sister asking if she could bring the kids up for the weekend. And finally there was a second message from Sandy saying she hadn't heard from him, but she was coming up anyway, she had been delayed and she might not get there till ten.

He wished he had checked his mobile the night before, but he had been too wrapped up in the shock of seeing Donna Snyder and Kim's despair.

What was Sandy's news? It must have been something dramatic, something that would allow them to rekindle their relationship. Maybe she had decided to give up the law. Or she had got another job. Or a transfer back to England. Something that was good news for her, good news for both of them.

And then there was Todd. Calder had never had sex with a married woman before. It was wrong. Perhaps there might be special circumstances when it was OK: when the couple were irrevocably separated, for example. But the husband being in a coma was definitely not one of those, no matter if he had cheated on her.

Calder's father was a strict Presbyterian; his grandfather had been a minister, and his English mother had had her own strong sense of right and wrong that she had inculcated in her children. What Calder had done was wrong. Incontro-vertibly, irrefutably wrong.

He glanced at the married woman in question. She didn't seem very pleased with herself, either.

'I should find a hotel,' she said.

Calder was about to protest, to feign hospitality, but he

simply nodded. 'The pub in the village will have some rooms. I'll take you there this morning. When we've fetched your car from the hospital.'

'I'm not sure I can face seeing Todd today,' Kim said. 'I know we did wrong, but I'm still furious about Donna. What if she's there, lurking in the car park? And what will I say to Todd? I talk to him, you know. Even though he's unconscious.'

Calder took a deep breath. In some ways it was easier to deal with Kim's problems than his own. 'How about this? Don't see Todd today. Spend the day alone. Try to sort yourself out a little bit and then tomorrow go and see him. I'll find Donna and get her to go away.'

'How will you do that?'

'I'll do it,' Calder said. 'Don't worry. That's my problem.'

His mobile phone rang. Calder picked it up. 'Hello?' His voice was hoarse. At first there was silence down the line. But Calder knew who was there. 'Sandy?'

'Alex. I just want to say it's quite OK that you have another girlfriend now, it's been, what, two months since we last saw each other, and I don't own you –'

'Sandy –'

But she had her speech prepared and she was getting it out as fast as possible. 'I guess I made a mistake. A big mistake. We were communicating badly and I guess that was my fault. But I've realized my mistake now and I know where we stand, and I'm sorry if I caused you some embarrassment last night –'

Her voice was speeding up, breathless and beginning to crack.

'Sandy, you haven't made a mistake –'

'As I say, I know where we stand, and I won't embarrass you again, I can assure you of that.'

'Look, can we talk about this —'

'So, goodbye, Alex.' The phone went dead.

Calder stared at it for a second, and then called the number of the hotel Sandy had left him in her message of the day before. It was the Swissotel Howard in London. He asked to be put through to her room. The phone rang once before it was snatched up.

'Yes?'

'Sandy?'

The phone went dead again.

Calder slumped back into his chair. 'Well, I'd say that was the end of that.'

'Are you sorry?' Kim asked.

'Yes,' Calder said. 'I'm very sorry.'

'Shall I talk to her? Call her up and explain the situation?'

Calder's anger flared up. 'What, that I was shagging someone else's wife, that it didn't matter, the husband was in a coma and may never wake up? That will explain it all.'

Kim's mouth dropped open and then she burst into tears.

Calder reached over to touch her hand. 'Oh, God, I'm sorry, Kim. I've just fucked up so badly.'

Kim removed her hand. 'I'm going upstairs to pack.'

Calder poured himself another cup of coffee as she left the room. But however many cups of coffee he poured, this wasn't going to get any better.

'Thank you for coming,' Andries Visser said to his two guests. His voice was unusually hoarse. The three men were sitting in armchairs around his living room cradling glasses of brandy and Coke. Logs burned in the grate. Outside, beyond the burglar bars and the high fence, the night air whispered in the long yellow grass of the veld.

His guests were fellow members of the Laagerbond, both

in their sixties, men who had been brought up in a different South Africa. Daniel Havenga had recently retired as professor of journalism at the University of Stellenbosch. Freddie Steenkamp had been deputy director of the feared Military Intelligence and was the current deputy chairman of the Laagerbond. Despite the fact that Steenkamp had operated at the brutal end of the apartheid regime, he had continued to serve his country's security services until the late 1990s, when he had retired with a generous pension.

Neither man was relaxed. They knew that if their chairman had dragged them out to his farm at such short notice, something must be up. 'What's the problem, Andries?' Professor Havenga asked.

'I think there's a real threat to Drommedaris,' Visser said.

'To the current plan or to the whole operation?'

'The whole operation.'

'But isn't Todd van Zyl still in a coma?'

'He is, but his wife has persisted in asking more questions about his mother's death. She has recruited a friend in Britain to help, an ex-banker with Bloomfield Weiss. Evidently they are quite determined.'

'But it's too long ago, surely?' Havenga said. 'If the TRC couldn't find anything, will they?'

'I think they might,' Visser said. 'I fear we might be losing control of the situation.'

'That's something we cannot allow,' Steenkamp said. He was a tall imposing man, balding, who sat upright even in the most comfortable of Visser's armchairs. 'As you know, I sometimes wish that we did not commit quite so much of our resources to Drommedaris. But it is now such an important part of the Laagerbond's activities that we cannot allow it to be compromised.'

'What do you think, Daniel?'

The professor sipped his brandy. His sharp brown eyes set deep in his round face assessed the others. He tugged at his beard. 'As a general rule, I think the lower the profile we can maintain, the better. I'd rather not do anything that will draw attention to the Laagerbond. We know the British police are already investigating Todd van Zyl's . . . accident.'

'If we don't act, and act quickly, then others will draw attention to us,' Steenkamp said.

The professor sighed. 'I have never liked this aspect of our activities.'

'In my experience,' said Steenkamp, 'the sooner one acts in cases like this, the less messy the outcome is in the end.'

'You should know,' said the professor. 'So what do we do?'

'That, gentlemen, is what I brought you here to discuss,' Visser said. He paused to allow a violent cough to convulse his lungs. 'Kobus is back in England, awaiting our instructions.'

15

August 3, 1988

I had a horrible night last night. As soon as I went to sleep, the images came back to me, the images from those photographs. The boy's back, the young woman's lifeless eyes. At one point I scrambled to the bathroom and threw up. It didn't make me feel any better.

I'll do what the man said, of course. I won't mention the Laagerbond to anyone ever again. I can't risk what that monster might do to Caroline. I wish I'd never opened Daniel's briefcase, never laid eyes on those papers. What is Neels doing with people like that?

I've got to get out of here. I want to go home. I want to *be* home. I'm going to book a flight to Minneapolis right now.

Later . . .

I've got the ticket, leaving tomorrow night. Doris is back from Port Elizabeth, so Caroline will be all right with her, especially now Zan's around as well.

August 5

I've caught him. And I feel terrible.

It happened like this. At the last minute I decided to stop off in Philadelphia on the way to Minneapolis. I don't know why I did this. I told myself that it would be good to spend a couple of days there with Neels, see how Philadelphia was for us together, make some attempt at conciliation. I hadn't figured out what I would say to him about the *Laagerbonder*, Moolman, or whatever his name is. On the one hand I desperately needed the comfort of Neels's strong arms around me, on the other I didn't know whether I could trust him. And if Moolman ever found out I had spoken to him . . .

But there was something else. I didn't warn him I was coming. I wanted to surprise him, to see what this American life he's leading all the time now is like without him having the chance to cover anything up. I wanted to catch him out, get things out into the open, find some resolution to the way I am feeling.

I took a taxi from the airport downtown. Philadelphia was hot: thick, sticky heat, the kind of heat that feels more like syrup than air as you walk through it. The *Intelligencer*'s building is a solid nineteenth-century edifice on Chestnut Street, with columns and Latin mottos scraped into the stone. Neels has the top floor. I announced myself at the lobby and an attractive black secretary met me and ushered me upstairs. She was very friendly, showed me into Neels's office and gave me a cup of coffee. His office looks much the same as it did last time I was in there a year ago. That old photo of me is still on his desk, I was glad to see, although that's pretty sad, isn't it? A wife checking up to see if her photo is still on her husband's desk. There is one new photograph there, of Todd playing rugby, taken last year. Neels is proud of Todd's rugby playing, and he's pretty good, although he's never going to be as good as his father was.

I sat there, on his sofa, watching the saturated air build

into afternoon storm clouds over the city. The pressure was falling, I could feel it in my ears.

Then I heard Neels's loud voice approaching. He was speaking in Afrikaans. A woman was answering him, a young woman. As they approached the doorway to his office, she said, "Oh, Neels!" He laughed and said something I couldn't catch, except he ended it with the word "*liefie.*" *Liefie* means "darling." But it means more than that, so much more than that. It's what Neels calls me. It's the one Afrikaans word he uses with me, the only one. He says it's mine. He never used it on any of the children, not on Zan or Caroline; he once told me that he never used it for Penelope. Just me. And her. This woman whom I hadn't even seen yet.

They came into the room. She was beautiful, of course. Blonde hair scraped back from her forehead, pale skin, strong angular face, smart business suit, perfect make-up. Only about twenty-five, maybe twenty-eight. And cool, oh so cool. Neels looked shocked to see me, but the woman smiled politely and held out her hand. "You must be Martha," she said with a distinct South African accent. "I'm Beatrice Pienaar. Cornelius has kindly allowed me to work here for a couple of months."

I took her hand and looked into her eyes. Blue, intelligent, calm, calculating. Her control was perfect, almost. But, as I watched, two tiny blushes of pink appeared on those fine alabaster cheekbones. She was betrayed by a dozen capillaries.

I'm not quite sure what happened next. Neels stumbled and stuttered before regaining his self-control. The Beatrice woman made her excuses and left. Neels got into his stride and talked heartily about his plan to buy the *Herald*. A rival buyer has popped up with a higher offer, but Neels thinks he will win. No mention of impending bankruptcy. No mention of the Laagerbond. He said how pleased he was that I had come to see him, how we'd have a great couple of days together. I smiled and nodded, still dazed, although I remember thinking that if I had interrupted him in a business meeting instead of flirting with his lover he would have been much less friendly.

Neels had lunch booked with the editor of one of his Ohio papers, and so he suggested Edwin take me out. We agreed I'd see Neels at the apartment at seven. I really don't like Edwin. He's only twenty-eight, but he's *so* pompous in his little three-piece suit despite the ninety-degree heat. He acts like he's forty-five, and the way he's gaining flab and losing his hair he'll soon look like it too. He's so unlike Neels. But he's not stupid, he's a devious little creep. He doesn't like me much either; I did steal his father from his mother, after all. But we've always been polite to each other. I think Edwin has a much bigger problem with Neels, but that's another story.

I couldn't face lunch with him, so once we were out on the sidewalk I shooed him away, and stood outside the *Intelligencer* offices with my suitcase, waiting for a cab. It had started to rain, one of those summer torrents that sends giant pebbles of water hopping all over the streets. I watched the rain for a quarter of an hour before a cab stopped.

I told it to take me to the airport.

I'm writing this on the plane to Minneapolis. There's quite a bit of turbulence, the pilot said something about more thunderstorms, so it's difficult to keep my pen on the page.

I feel terrible. I feel as if a giant hand has worked its way into my stomach, grabbed my guts and started twisting. And it won't stop. That last sentence is blotted by a tear, not the vodka and tonic I've just spilled. That landed on my knee, staining my white pants. But I don't regret going to Philadelphia. I had to know. And I didn't want to find out by snooping around Neels's stuff, or hiring a private detective, or asking our friends about the gossip. I'm also glad I saw her.

Glad? As I was standing in the rain waiting for a cab, I realized the obvious. She's just like me, or like I was. I met Neels in exactly that way. I was her age when he suggested I work in his offices for a while. He was married then and I was tall, blonde, attractive, although I was never a cold-hearted bitch like her. But there's a pattern.

I knew I was wrong to take Neels from Penelope, but I didn't regret it. I told myself I had no choice: I was in love, and Neels loved me. She was an awful woman, already on the way to becoming an alcoholic. Mom and Dad didn't approve. At first I think they thought I had gone off my head, marrying some apartheid-loving Afrikaner, but when they met Neels they recognized at least that he was a decent man, decent, but older, ten years older, and married.

My parents are good people. They forgave me. I think they even grew to like Neels. What am I going to tell them now? That he is the cheating philanderer they always assumed he was?

I need another vodka.

August 6

How I love my parents! My mother was *so* good. She knew something was wrong, of course, when I showed up at the door, half-drunk, my face dark with misery. Apparently Neels had called all agitated wanting to know where I was, why I wasn't at the apartment in Philadelphia. Mom didn't ask questions, she didn't pressure me, she just welcomed

189

me home. She called Neels back to tell him I was with them and I was okay, but I was too tired to talk to him.

This morning I'm sitting on the swing seat out on the porch looking out over the lake. I've called Caroline, she's just gotten back from school and she's fine. I feel bad about leaving her, but I know she'll be okay with Zan and Doris for a few days.

I'm going sailing with Dad this afternoon. I hope he's up to it. He looks a lot more frail than he did last time I saw him, which was when they came out to South Africa at Christmas. He's over seventy now, seventy-two, and for the first time he looks it. Although Mom's sixty-nine, she doesn't act anything like an old lady yet.

I think I will talk to her about Neels. She's the only person I really can talk to.

Later . . .

I went sailing with Dad. He could scarcely manage it. I'm sure he couldn't go out by himself now. It's a horrible feeling to see him getting old.

But it was nice out on the water, darting around the little islands I know so well. And I could see that he loved being out there with me. It's hot here, in the mid-eighties, but not nearly as humid as it was in Philadelphia. Too hot for Dad, though. I was glad to get him back indoors in the air conditioning.

I spoke to Mom about Neels. She was really good about it, as I knew she would be. She wasn't at all judgmental, she never said she knew he was a bastard all along. She didn't give me any answers; there aren't any easy answers and I know her – she would say that it's up to me to decide what to do. But I needed to talk about it, and to receive such love in return, simple, unqualified love. I know she can't kiss me and make it all better, but it doesn't do any harm to live under the illusion for a couple of days that she can.

I didn't tell her about the Laagerbond and my experience in Guguletu, though. That would scare her silly. It still scares *me* silly.

I called Monica to see if we can get together. She said that Nancy is over from California with the kids visiting her folks. She said she'd try and get hold of Arlene and fix something up for tomorrow night.

August 7

Just got back from an evening out with the girls. I'm a little drunk and a little worked up. But I've got to write it down. Just for a moment it all seems clear to me. America, South Africa, Neels, that fucking Afrikaner bitch Beatrice. I know what I should do. What I should do about Neels that selfish creep. He thinks he can do what he likes with that Beatrice bitch and forget about me just because I'm forty-four. I still look good, I know I look good, he's the one who's old, and what about his children, what does he think he's doing to his children, and what about his country, he's abandoning his country, what a goddamn coward, what a goddamn fucking old old coward.

August 8

It's eleven o'clock and I've just got up and had a cup of coffee. Actually I'm on my third cup. Hangover. Big time. And what a lot of embarrassing drivel I wrote last night.

Did everything really "all seem clear to me"? If I really did have the answer to all my problems, I can't remember a thing about it. It's pretty sad when the world seems to make more sense when you are drunk than when you are sober.

We went to a place called TGI Fridays in Minnetonka. They're big on cocktails at TGI Fridays. It was great to see the others, at least at first. Monica, Arlene and I have all been friends since Elementary School, and Nancy joined us at Junior High. We were all a hit with the boys, but we were all smarter than them too. I think we scared them. We probably scared the teachers as well, we were so full of ourselves. But we all went on to good colleges, Monica and Arlene went to St. Olaf in Minnesota, I went east to Smith and Nancy went out west to Berkeley.

The drink flowed, and the stories came thick and fast. They've all had a tough time with jobs, children, husbands. Especially husbands.

I told them about Neels and the Beatrice woman. I didn't intend to, but after they had told me so much about their lives I felt I had to do the same. They were sympathetic, but all three of them seemed to think that men were like that. I tried to explain about South Africa, about how I still believed in the need to end apartheid and in the rights of black people there to be treated like normal human beings.

On the way out of the restaurant, Monica touched my arm. "If you feel like you have to stay there, stay," she said. "See it through. Don't run away." I *think* she was talking about South Africa, not Neels. I wonder if it will come to that choice.

Actually, I think I remember what I was thinking about last night. I'm not sure it's such a good idea now I'm sober. But . . . we'll see.

We land in Cape Town in a couple of hours. The sun is rising over the continent of Africa to the east, and I am happy.

It's so long since I have felt like this. I couldn't sleep last night for thinking about it.

But I can't write it down. I'd like to, I've gotten so used to confiding in my diary. I'm careful to keep it hidden. I'm positive Neels doesn't even know it exists, let alone what I've written. I think Doris and Caroline might have seen me scribbling in it once or twice, but neither of them has said anything. The trouble is you can never be 100 percent sure that no one else will read it in the future. So you can't tell the whole truth. I want to, but I shouldn't.

No doubt once I am back at Hondehoek, Neels and the *Cape Daily Mail* and everything will grind me down again, but for now I shall put this away, stretch out my legs, watch the sun rise, and smile.

16

It was early summer in Zurich and the Swiss had taken note of the fact: the people strolling around the Paradeplatz were in shirtsleeves, jackets slung over shoulders, and summer dresses were getting their first airing. The sun streamed through the plate glass windows of the *konditorei* and warmed Andries Visser's sallow, sagging face. He sipped his coffee and stared out over the square at the blue trams trundling backwards and forwards and behind them the solid grey stone buildings which housed the private banking headquarters of the large Swiss banks. No gleaming skyscrapers in this city: here, power was discretion. It was only an hour and a half since their plane had touched down after the long flight from Johannesburg, and his cough had kept him awake. He had done his best to smother it so as not to disturb the other passengers in business class, but from the expressions on their faces in the morning he hadn't succeeded.

He coughed again.

'Are you all right, Andries?' asked his companion, Dirk du Toit, as he polished off the last crumbs of his *torte*. Dirk was a strapping man of about forty with a shock of red hair, which these days he slicked back in a bankerly way. He was, in fact, a banker, and a very smart one, for the United Farmers Bank, the third biggest in South Africa. His father, Martin, had been chairman of the bank until five years before, but there was no suggestion that du Toit's rise had anything to do with nepotism. Neither had his induction into the Laagerbond at the age of thirty nor his recent assumption of the role of treasurer from his father. Given the scale of the Laagerbond's assets, treasurer was no small responsibility and du Toit handled the position admirably.

Visser coughed again and shook his head. 'Just a smoker's cough. My doctor has convinced me to give up. I hope it will go away. We'll see.'

His doctor had indeed convinced him to give up when he had seen him earlier that week, by the simple expedient of telling him he had lung cancer. He was booked for an appointment the following week for further tests and scans, but the doctor was quite confident of his diagnosis. Lung cancer was bad. A low chance of survival, lots of chemo and radiotherapy, lots of pain. Visser was still trying to grasp the enormity of the news. He hadn't told anyone yet, not even his wife, and certainly not other members of the Laagerbond. His mind constantly returned to the idea of his own mortality, what it would mean to have only a few months left to live, what he would do with the time, how he would find the courage to put up with the pain. He hadn't come to any conclusions yet, but he was beginning to feel that the Laagerbond would play an important part in whatever time was left to him.

He touched his shrunken bicep where he had placed a nicotine patch that morning in the toilets at the airport. It was hard dealing with this kind of problem without a cigarette. Especially sitting in the sun with a cup of coffee. Maybe he should just go back to fifty a day and be done with it.

Du Toit's face was full of concern as he examined his colleague. Visser summoned a smile. He had always thought that du Toit was a good kid. Perhaps he would take over as chairman one day, after Visser had gone. That would be good. The Laagerbond needed to be run by a new generation, not the dinosaurs from the apartheid years. The Afrikaner nation was finished if it defined itself by the glory days of Verwoerd and Vorster.

'Dirk, you know we have an opening for two new members now that Jan and Dawid have died.' General Johannes Lessing had played a leading role in the invasion of Angola in 1987, and had just died at the age of eighty-one. Dawid Roux had held a senior position in the Foreign Ministry. Like many of the other *Laagerbonders* they had both been key members of the State Security Council, the body that coordinated South Africa's counter-revolutionary activities throughout the 1980s. The Laagerbond was limited to a complement of twenty-four members; when one member died another had to be elected.

'I thought Freddie Steenkamp had a candidate?'

'He does, he does. Paul Strydom. He's a sound man and well connected, and we are going to initiate him next week, but do you know anyone for the other position? Anyone more ... forward-looking? Maybe someone in his thirties who's heading for the top.'

Du Toit nodded. 'I understand. I'll see what I can do.'

Visser smiled. 'Good. I am worried. I want to keep the Laagerbond intact so it can influence South Africa long into the future. If we succumb to funding lunatics like Eugene Terre'Blanche, with his pseudo swastikas and his stiff-arm salute, or any of those other nutcases who want to start a Third Boer War, we'll be finished. Oh, the money will last a long time, but we'll be exposed, discredited, maybe even destroyed. But if we can use our funds to promote those who will leave us alone and discredit those who will do us harm, then we will achieve something. The Afrikaner nation will live on in Africa, where it should be.'

'But there's no chance we'll do anything as stupid as that again, is there?' du Toit asked.

'Not while I'm around,' said Visser. 'But much as I like Freddie, and admire his cunning, he does have an old-fashioned view of the world. He would like to see an Afrikaner country somewhere, be it a corner of the Free State, or Perth, or Argentina, some little patch of the southern hemisphere that we can fence off and declare white in perpetuity. But that's not practical, it's a dangerous dream. Don't you think, Dirk?'

Du Toit nodded his agreement. 'We might win a battle against the blacks, but in a war we'll always lose: they out-number us eight to one.'

'We've done quite well so far,' Visser said. 'Twelve years on and they haven't turned on us yet. But we have to be ever vigilant; use our funds to manipulate and influence. That's why Drommedaris is so important. And this phase of the operation is the culmination of all I have been work-ing for since I became chairman of the Laagerbond.'

'Speaking of which,' du Toit said, glancing at his watch, 'I think it's time to see a man about some money to buy a newspaper.'

'Here, let me dry.'

'Be my guest.'

Anne picked up a dish cloth and began working on the breakfast plates. It was Saturday morning, and she had arrived with her family late the night before. They had all had a leisurely breakfast and then William had driven the two chil-dren off to take them swimming in the pool at Hunstanton.

'I didn't know William was coming up,' Calder said. 'He's very welcome, of course, but from your message it sounded as if it was just you and the kids.'

'It was originally,' Anne said. 'William told me he would be working all this weekend. I was pretty pissed off and that's when I decided to take the kids up here. You know how they love it and I needed to get away. But, to be fair to William, he got the message. He dumped all his work on his associate and said he'd come too. I couldn't really say no.'

'I'm glad you didn't,' Calder said. 'Are you OK?' His sister was looking tired. The lines in her thin face had deepened.

She sighed, and ran her hand through her short black spiky hair. 'I don't know. Not really, but then what do you expect when you've got two small kids and a husband who has to work all the hours God gives him? There are lots of other couples who are suffering just as badly. Or worse. If I were still working the whole thing would be a nightmare.'

'Do you regret giving up?'

'Yes, frankly. But there was no choice. Other women who are super organized might have managed it, but you know me. The family is in permanent chaos as it is. Which William doesn't like.'

'You must have been organized as a barrister.'

'I suppose,' Anne grinned. 'Actually, not really. The clerk of chambers hated me. I was never in the right place at the right time.' She rubbed away furiously at a coffee cup. 'I dunno. We'll be OK. I do appreciate him coming with us this weekend. As long as we're able to make gestures to each other like that, we'll make it.'

'Heard anything from Father?'

'I spoke to him on Thursday. And no, he didn't say whether he had just come back from the horse races.'

'Sorry. You know I'm worried.'

'Yeah. But there's nothing much we can do. He did talk about Mrs Palmer again.'

'Mrs Palmer? Didn't she teach at the high school?'

'She still does. Her husband died a couple of years ago. It suddenly struck me he seems to mention her name rather a lot.'

'You don't think . . .' Calder looked at his sister.

She smiled slyly and shrugged.

'That would be weird,' Calder said.

'Seriously weird,' Anne agreed. 'But it's just speculation. We'll wait and see.'

'Huh.' It had never occurred to Calder that his father might remarry. It was nearly twenty years since his wife had died, and although he was constantly being invited to dinner parties as a spare man, he had never shown any indication that the matchmaking was having any effect. But why shouldn't things change? He was a popular doctor in Kelso and his twinkling eye and reassuring smile were famous.

'How's Todd van Zyl doing?' Anne asked.

'Still in a coma, I'm afraid.'

'Has his wife gone back to the States? I thought she was staying with you.'

'She's still here in Norfolk. She's taken a room at the pub. That seemed to work better,' Calder said.

'I hope we didn't kick her out?'

'Oh, no. When she realized she was going to be here for a while, she decided she would prefer somewhere private.'

Calder was tempted to tell his sister about the mess with Kim and Sandy, but couldn't bring himself to admit to what they had done. His sister was forgiving, but not that forgiving. *He* wasn't that forgiving. If only it was as easy to hide what had happened from himself.

He had driven Kim to the car park at the hospital in silence, and transferred her stuff into the boot of her car. She had returned to the pub in the village, while he had waited for Donna.

The art teacher arrived eventually, in her own hired vehicle, and parked facing the hospital entrance. Calder had walked over to her car. He had asked her quietly but firmly to leave, to go back to the US. She had argued at first, then she had pleaded and then she had burst into tears, but he had been firm. He told her that Kim could insist that the hospital forbid her from seeing Todd. He took her phone number and promised her that he would call if there was any change in Todd's circumstances one way or another. He found his own anger with her had subsided. How could he be angry with her after what he and Kim had done?

'I can't imagine what it would feel like if something like that happened to William,' Anne went on. 'It must be simply awful for her. Have you had any luck finding out what happened to the mother? The one who was killed all those years ago?'

'Not yet,' Calder said. 'But we haven't given up.'

'I wish you would.'

'What?'

'Give up.'

'Why?'

'All that kind of stuff is dangerous.'

'It's just asking questions.'

Anne snorted. 'That's what you said last time and you nearly got yourself killed. If the van Zyls do have enemies, they are probably powerful ones, and you're better off staying well clear.'

'Well, it's nice to know my little sister is looking after me,' Calder said.

Anne flicked the dish cloth in his face. 'Someone's got to.'

Calder grabbed another towel and flicked her back. She pushed him back against the wall and raised her knee towards his groin.

'Now that's a mean trick,' Calder said. 'I can remember you getting in big trouble for doing that before.'

'That's only because you went crying to Mum. Wimp.'

'Hey, look out!' Calder pushed past her to turn off the hot water, which was flowing out of the washing-up bowl.

They finished the washing up in companionable silence, and then Anne started opening cupboard doors.

'What are you looking for?' Calder asked.

'Butter. Sugar. Eggs. Self-raising flour. Cranberry juice. Phoebe is determined to make you a cake when she gets back.'

'Cranberry juice?'

'I know. Phoebe swears it makes the cake taste better.'

'Well, we've got eggs, sugar and a little butter. Probably not enough. No cranberry juice and no flour. They might have some in the shop in the village.'

Anne banged the cupboard doors shut. 'I'll go and see. Damn. William's got the car.'

'You can borrow mine,' Calder said.

'What, your Maserati?' Anne's eyes sparkled.

'Sure,' said Calder.

'Will the insurance be OK?'

Calder shrugged. 'It's only to the village and back. Just watch how hard you put your foot down. It can be a bit quick.'

'I'll be careful,' Anne said, grinning.

Calder tossed her the keys, and she grabbed her bag from where she had slung it on the chair, and went out the front door.

Calder put the last of the breakfast things away. Could he trust Anne in his Maserati? How much damage could she come to on the road to Hanham Staithe?

He heard the familiar sound of the car door opening just outside the kitchen by the side of the house.

Then silence.

Then a huge explosion ripped through the kitchen window, tearing his life apart.

At that moment Colonel Kobus Moolman buckled his seatbelt as the captain on the easyJet flight from Stansted announced that it would be ten minutes to landing at Amsterdam's Schiphol Airport.

17

She wasn't dead. Somehow, by some miracle, she wasn't dead.

Calder ran outside to find the mangled wreckage of his car in flames, shards of metal scattered all over the road and garden. At first he thought his sister was in there. He considered diving into the flames to try to drag her out, but there was no point. He looked around him quickly. The car door was lying on top of the hedge at the side of the road. And in the field next to the house, about twenty yards away, was a bundle.

He leaped the fence and ran over to it. It was Anne, and she was alive. Her eyes were flickering. The bottom half of her body was a mangled mess, her legs were splayed at an odd angle, her face was splashed with blood and her clothes were badly ripped, but she was alive.

Her eyes focused on him and her lips moved. 'Alex?'

'Yes? Yes, Annie, it's me.'

'What happened?'

'I don't know,' he said, although in truth he did.

'My legs . . . they hurt.'

'Be still. I'll call an ambulance. I'll be back in a moment.'

'Wait!' It was scarcely more than a whisper, but it was an urgent one. Calder waited. 'Phoebe. Robbie. Look after them. William will need help.'

'You'll be able to look after them yourself once we've got you to hospital,' Calder said stupidly.

Anne frowned. She tried to speak, but she couldn't. She

shook her head. Calder realized his mistake. 'Of course I'll look after them, Annie. Of course I will.'

His sister relaxed and closed her eyes.

Calder ran inside the house to phone an ambulance and to grab a couple of towels to try to staunch the flow of blood. He sat by his sister in the field, cradling her head on his lap, waiting for the ambulance, willing her to live, praying for her to live, her warm blood soaking his clothes and seeping through to his own skin.

The next few hours were a blur. He followed the ambulance in a taxi from the village and called William on his mobile to tell him to meet them at the hospital. The hospital itself was emotional bedlam. Anne went straight into the operating theatre.

They were in the same small relatives' room that Calder and Kim had waited in when Todd had been admitted. William was distraught, as were the children. No one could say whether Anne was going to live or die. Then William started laying into Calder. He was a balding, thickening man in his middle thirties, prematurely middle-aged, and normally mild mannered, friendly and slightly dull. But not now.

'You know that bomb was meant for you?' he demanded.

Calder nodded.

'Well, why weren't you in the fucking car then?'

'She wanted to fetch some baking stuff from the village,' Calder replied.

'Why didn't you go?'

'I let her borrow the car.'

'You should have taken it yourself.'

'I didn't know what was going to happen, William,' Calder said gently.

William had begun pacing in a tight little pattern up and down, running his fingers through the remnants of his hair.

The two children watched their father, wide-eyed with fear. Calder sat slumped in a chair next to them. A television babbled on low volume in a corner. Calder got up and switched it off.

'This wasn't a random event, you know, Alex,' William said. 'There was a reason someone planted the bomb, wasn't there?'

Calder took a deep breath. 'I suppose so.'

'What was it? Eh? Was it something to do with this van Zyl business?'

'Probably,' Calder admitted.

'Probably? Probably! Of course it fucking well was!' William lowered his face to Calder's level, spittle on his lips. 'Do you know that your sister spends half her life worried sick that you're going to kill yourself? Either in a bloody little aeroplane, or messing around with gangsters where you're not wanted. Well, it looks like she was right to be worried, wasn't she? Except it wasn't you who was blown up as a result of your little games. It was her.' He straightened up and tears began to run down his cheeks. Phoebe took her cue from her father and began to cry quietly. Robbie, aged four, stuck out his chin, his stare shifting from his uncle to his father. Neither of them really comprehended yet what had happened to their mother.

'I didn't know she was in any danger,' Calder said quietly. 'If I had known –'

'You'd have carried on anyway!' William shouted. 'You make me sick!'

Someone touched William's elbow. It was Kim, together with an anxious-looking nurse who must have fetched her from Todd's room.

'William?' she said softly.

William turned to her, blinking.

'William. I'm Kim van Zyl. I'm a friend of Alex's. My husband's in this hospital too. I'm very sorry about what happened to your wife.'

William opened his mouth as if about to berate her as well, but Kim's smile, warm, sympathetic, reassuring, stopped him.

'Do you want Alex and me to take the children down to the café for a drink?' she said. 'Perhaps it would be good to be alone for a moment. I'll bring them back in half an hour.'

William looked at Phoebe and Robbie and at Kim, and nodded.

'Are you OK?' Kim said as she and Calder led the two children through the corridors by the hand.

'Physically, yes,' Calder said. 'But William's right. He's bloody well right. It was my fault. First Todd and now Annie.'

'Hey, I know Todd wasn't your fault,' Kim said sternly. 'And you had no way of knowing there was a bomb in that car. If anyone should feel guilty, it's me for getting you involved in the first place.'

'It should have been me,' Calder said. 'It should bloody well have been me. I wish it had been me.'

With her free hand, the one that wasn't gripped tightly by Phoebe, Kim touched Calder's arm.

They bought the children a cup of hot chocolate each, and then a man and a woman approached them: DI Banks and DC Wardle. They ushered Calder to another table away from Phoebe and Robbie to ask some questions.

At first Calder answered them dully. He explained where the car was parked, how he was the usual driver, how he had suggested his sister drive it to the village. Then DI Banks asked the obvious question. Had he any idea who had planted the bomb?

'It has to be the same person who planted the bomb in the Yak, doesn't it?' Calder said.

'We can't be sure of that,' Banks said. 'At least not until our forensic people have had a chance to look at the evidence.'

Calder stared at her. 'Yes,' he said. 'Yes, I do know who blew up my sister. Or at least I know who arranged it, even if I don't know if they planted the bomb themselves.'

Inspector Banks's hazel eyes studied his face carefully. 'Yes?'

Calder paused to think it all through. But there wasn't really very much to figure out. 'Cornelius van Zyl. Or his son, Edwin van Zyl. Or both of them.'

Banks's eyes narrowed. 'Do you have any evidence?'

'You find the evidence,' Calder said. 'It's your job. And do it before anyone else gets blown up.'

Banks smiled sympathetically. 'It is our job, and we will. But it would help us do that if you could tell us what makes you so sure Cornelius van Zyl is responsible.'

So Calder told her all about the dinner with the van Zyl family and how vehemently Cornelius had opposed Kim's desire to find out what had happened to Martha van Zyl all those years ago.

Banks listened. Wardle took notes. When they had finished they moved over to where Kim was talking gently to Calder's nephew and niece. As they asked Kim questions, Calder did his best to chat to Phoebe and Robbie, but all the time his thoughts were with their mother, in the operating theatre fighting for her life.

Calder barely held it together over that long day. Mid-afternoon they transferred Anne from the operating theatre to intensive care. The doctors spoke to William rather than

Calder, so Calder didn't get the details, but two things were clear: firstly, Anne would live; secondly, they had amputated her left leg above the knee. They weren't sure whether they would have to remove the right one as well.

Calder found the atmosphere in the hospital intolerable. Part of it was the hostility from William, part of it was the feeling of total powerlessness, of being unable to do anything but ask the medical staff stupid questions. Most of it was the guilt.

He decided to leave. Kim offered to come with him, but Calder said that would make things worse. She looked offended and Calder knew that she had made the offer from the best of motives, but he also knew that spending time with her would pile on the guilt. He had called his father, he had had no choice. He had explained that Anne's injuries were a result of a bomb, not an accident. And his father said he would be down the next morning. *That* would be very difficult to face.

He took a taxi from the hospital straight home. Police tape surrounded his house and men and women in white forensic overalls were peering at the wreckage of the blackened Maserati. It brought home to Calder how lucky Anne was to have been thrown clear. It appeared that she had left the door open when she had turned on the ignition, presumably in case she needed to summon him to explain how something worked. Whatever the reason, it was a miracle. Had she strapped herself in and shut the door, she would have burned alive. If she hadn't been killed instantly, of course.

A policeman ushered him along a marked path to his front door and another asked for his permission to pick over all his possessions inside and out. He wanted to get away from all the people. He also needed a drink. The decanter was empty, but he found a bottle of whisky in a cupboard; twelve-year-old Laphroaig his father had given him for his last birthday. A fine single malt meant to be sipped, not gulped. Tough. He met the sympathetic smile of the policeman guarding the crime scene with a curt nod and headed out into the marshes in front of the house, clutching the bottle in his right hand.

He walked fast. Although it was May, and the sun had been shining, there had been a breeze blowing from the east all day that had kept the air cool. Calder strode rapidly along the path towards the sea, ignoring the stares of other walkers. He headed for a quiet hollow in the sand near a creek, out of sight of the footpaths. He sat down, opened the bottle and took a long pull. The liquid burned the back of his throat and a moment later the lining of his empty stomach. The pain felt good. He took another swig.

He stared out over the creek and the sea and heaved a couple of deep breaths. He had to empty his mind, get a grip, control the screams inside his head. He focused on a solitary sailing boat half a mile away that had just rounded a headland and was aiming for the main creek to Hanham Staithe. The breeze had dropped and the boat, a ketch with a tan sail, was making slow progress. The sand in front of Calder was alive with small birds scurrying this way and that among the shells. All around was urgent twittering and chattering, and also the occasional clear cry of a curlew which he could hear but not see. A few feet from the water's edge was a band of clear white scum. As he stared harder he realized that it was in fact a pile of tiny white baby crabs, thousands of them, maybe millions, all dead. No wonder the birds were having such a great time.

Anne with no legs. No. Another pull of whisky. Look at the headland, actually an island of sand and grass cut off from the mainland at high tide. The boat was now making better progress, but would have to tack once more to make the creek. He felt air on his cheeks, the breeze had got up again. He could see the sailing boat accelerate.

Anne with no legs. Anne's face, scarred and bloody and in pain. William's face, full of hostility, more than that, hate.

More whisky.

Would Anne hate him too? Would she ever forgive him? Could William cope with two boisterous children and an invalid wife? He would have to give up his job. Had they enough money to get by? Would their marriage stand it?

Phoebe crying. Robbie being brave. More whisky.

William blaming him. Rationally, Calder knew his brother-in-law was talking crap. It was pure bad luck that Anne had got into the Maserati, rather than him. But that wasn't really William's point. William's point was that Calder took stupid risks. That even when he hurt himself he hurt his family as well. But this time he had hurt his sister directly, and to William that was unforgivable. Calder had taken risks all his life: be it rock climbing when he was a boy, diving head first into trouble on the rugby field, flying Tornados in the RAF, staking millions in the City, or . . . or what? Asking the van Zyls difficult questions.

Could Calder forgive himself? He didn't know. More whisky.

A few days ago everything had been fine. Of course the accident in the Yak had been a harrowing experience, but it was one that he could cope with. Todd's injury was bad, but he had been able to reassure himself that it wasn't his fault. He was good in tough situations.

But now, now it was all too much. Suddenly, he knew it was all too much.

He couldn't justify what he had done with Kim. There

might be explanations, but no justification. It made him angry that he had been so weak. That he had turned himself into the kind of sex-crazed, selfish, callous bastard who would sleep with another man's wife when the man was in a coma. Really, what kind of person would do that? And it couldn't be changed: he couldn't undo it, he couldn't apologize, he couldn't make it better or make it go away. Todd would almost certainly never find out, but Calder would know. He'd know for the rest of his life.

More whisky. A big gulp that hurt his raw throat. That pain was good.

It was that act, sleeping with Kim, that had undermined his defences, made him less able to cope with what had happened to Anne.

He wished he had someone to talk to about it. Sandy. Kim. Anne. None of those would do. He had grown away from his old friends in the City and although he had made some new friends in Norfolk, none was close enough for him to fall apart on. He missed his mother. She would be, what, sixty-four by now, if she had survived. She would be there for him, for Annie and him.

He struck the sand with his fist. But of course his mother had died, hadn't she? Died because he had missed the bus from school and she had driven too fast along country lanes to pick him up, and met a farm worker driving too fast the other way. He had picked over his role in that tragedy so many times in the past, surely he didn't need to do it again. Not now.

But that was the point. He had this image of himself as a tough guy, someone who could take difficult decisions quickly, who could take risks and win, who was in control of his own destiny. But that wasn't him at all; he was a reckless idiot who ruined the lives of the people around him.

His father would be coming tomorrow. Of all the people he could conceivably speak to to try to straighten himself out, his father was bottom of the list. Since his mother had died the relationship between father and son had frozen over. The doctor never missed an opportunity to criticize his son's choices, be it on what to study at which university, his activities in the City, or even his choice of girlfriends. Calder's discovery that the old man was a compulsive gambler had hardly helped things. His father's criticisms always stung, but tomorrow . . . tomorrow he wasn't sure whether he could face them. In fact, he wasn't sure whether he could face tomorrow at all.

More whisky. The pain was dulled now. The crabs were blurred. It took him several seconds to locate the sailing boat, now entering the creek.

At least the police would get Cornelius.

The key to the whole thing was Martha van Zyl's death in 1988. Todd had been asking difficult questions about it and he had nearly been killed. Then Kim and Calder had started asking difficult questions and there had been an attempt to kill them. It was obvious who was behind these deaths: Cornelius, perhaps with some help from his weasel son Edwin. Calder knew very little about South Africa or South Africans, but he did know that it was a brutal country and that Afrikaners like Cornelius had been responsible for much of that brutality.

He smiled. He'd enjoy attending Cornelius's trial.

Then a thought struck him. Would the police be able to bring a case against Cornelius? He was a wealthy, powerful, intelligent man, well capable of paying people to do his dirty work for him, professionals who would keep their distance from him and from their own handiwork. It would be tough for the police to gather the necessary proof to connect him to the two crimes. They would have to link the explosions to an unknown assassin, and the assassin to Cornelius or Edwin. The assassin could be anyone: an American, a South African, a London criminal. DI Banks looked clever, but she wasn't that clever. The police would question Cornelius who would hire an excellent lawyer to advise him to say very little. Calder's smile disappeared as he realized the man would walk free.

The anger welled up inside him. Here he was beating himself up for the injuries that had been done to Todd and Anne, when actually he knew who was responsible for them, and that man was going to get away with it. OK, he could hardly blame Cornelius for what he had done with Kim, that was something he was just going to have to live with, but everything else . . . that was down to Cornelius. And he, Alex Calder, was going to take the shit for it for the rest of his life. And not just him: Anne and William and Phoebe and Robbie and Todd and Kim.

More whisky.

The sun was drifting down towards the horizon. Tomorrow beckoned. A horrible day, the first of many vile, unimaginably ghastly days stretching into the future, days in which Calder could do nothing, days in which Cornelius plotted his takeovers and counted his millions. Calder couldn't face tomorrow. He couldn't face the inaction.

He hauled himself to his feet. Marsh and sea spun about him. He took an unsteady step forward and focused on the ridge above his house, willing it to stay in one place. He pulled out his mobile phone and called Alfie, the local one-man taxi firm, telling him to meet him at his cottage and take him to King's Lynn station.

*

Calder bought two litres of bottled water in an attempt to sober himself up on the train. He also tried to keep himself awake, but it didn't work. He remembered the train pulling out of Cambridge station and the next thing he knew it was jolting to a stop at King's Cross.

He ignored the disapproving stares of his fellow passengers and staggered off the train on to the platform. It was dark now. He could feel a headache developing, and worse, his resolve weakening. He still had a small amount of whisky left in the Laphroaig bottle, which was wrapped in a plastic bag, but he lurched into a shop at the station and bought another half-bottle of White Horse. He found a quiet corner and took a swig. The whisky had its effect, warming him up to further action.

He made his way to the taxi rank and slowly and deliberately read out Cornelius's address to the driver. It wasn't far to Regent's Park, and the driver let him out in front of a terrace of fine cream-stuccoed houses with imposing columns beside the doors. He squinted at the numbers, found the right house, and walked carefully up to the door. He blinked as a security light switched itself on, and rang the bell. A moment later, the door opened, and Cornelius stared at him in surprise.

'Alex?'

'Can I come in?'

'All right.' Cornelius stepped back and led Calder through the hall to a sitting room. 'Is something wrong? Is it Todd? Or Kim?'

'No,' said Calder.

'Do you want to sit down?'

'No,' said Calder again.

Cornelius looked at him suspiciously. 'I can tell you've been drinking,' he said.

'My sister was blown up today.'

'My God,' said Cornelius. 'I'm sorry. Was she . . . ?'

'She's alive,' Calder said. 'But she's lost her leg. Maybe both her legs.'

'Christ, man. How awful. Sit down.' Cornelius indicated a chair. Calder ignored him.

'Aren't you going to ask how it happened?' Calder said.

'Yes . . . yes. What on earth happened?'

'Someone put a bomb in my car. They meant to blow *me* up. To stop me asking questions. About your wife.'

'What?'

'Just like they put a bomb in the Yak I was flying with Todd. To stop him asking questions about her.'

'Are you sure about this?'

'Am I sure?' Calder laughed and rocked on his feet. 'Of course I'm sure. Aren't you?'

'Please, sit down,' Cornelius said.

'Because, you see, I know you got someone to plant the bomb in the Yak. And in the Maserati.' Calder could feel himself grinning.

'What! You think I tried to kill my own son?'

'And I've told the police all about it,' Calder went on.

Cornelius pulled himself together, straightened himself up. 'That's probably a good idea, Alex. I'm sure they'll be here to talk to me in the morning. Now I'm very sorry about your sister, but you'd better go.'

Calder noticed him flapping a signal with his left hand. He turned to see a woman in her nightgown standing in the doorway looking scared. Jessica Montgomery, the third Mrs van Zyl: Calder recognized her from newspaper photographs of her with her husband. She seemed to be in her fifties, tall, narrow, blonde, just on the emaciated side of attractive.

'Don't worry, honey,' Cornelius said. 'I'll handle this.'

'Oh, you'll handle it all right,' Calder said. 'The police will come and ask you polite questions and you'll answer them and if the questions get difficult you'll get a lawyer and the police will never arrest you because you're too fucking clever and they won't be able to pin anything on you.'

'I can assure you I'll cooperate fully with the police. I want to find who injured your sister as much as you do.'

'Huh,' Calder snorted. He knew what he wanted to do next, but he knew he was almost too drunk to do it. Cornelius, although in his seventies, was still big and strong and alert. If Calder took a drunken swing, Cornelius would block it and Calder's whole journey would have been in vain. He focused on Cornelius's chin, fixing it still. His feet were well balanced. He would have to be quick.

'Alex . . .' Cornelius took half a step forward and raised his right hand towards Calder's shoulder. Calder was fast and accurate. He hit Cornelius directly on the chin. Cornelius staggered two steps backward. Calder hit him again and again. Cornelius slumped to the ground, and Calder kicked the old man in the ribs once, twice. He heard screaming and someone pulling at his arm. He flung the woman off. Cornelius groaned. Calder kicked again. Then something large and hard hit his head. He staggered and half turned. He saw Jessica Montgomery swing a table lamp towards his head for a second time. He lifted an arm and the table lamp hit his shoulder and struck the top of his skull. He fell to the ground, fighting to retain consciousness.

Cornelius pulled himself to his feet, rubbing his chin. 'Don't do that, honey,' he said to his wife, who had picked up the telephone.

She ignored him.

Cornelius hauled Calder to his feet. The room was spinning. Until it stopped Calder couldn't hit Cornelius again.

'Listen, Alex,' Cornelius said, grabbing him by the shoulders. 'The police will be here in a minute. Now go out of that door and run. Doesn't matter where. Just run.'

'You can't let him go!' Jessica shouted.

Cornelius picked up the plastic bag Calder had been carrying, pushed it into his hand, turned him towards the door, shoved him out into the hallway and out of the front door. 'Run!'

Calder looked back at the house, then at the gate on to the street, and ran.

He heard sirens. He ran faster, round a corner, round another. It felt good to run, to feel his legs pumping up and down, the blood rushing through his system, his heart rattling in his chest. But his stomach suddenly churned and he had to stop to throw up. He wiped his mouth and trotted on, soon finding himself in the warren of back streets behind Euston station. He slowed to a walk, or a stagger. No sirens. No police.

What had he done? Hit Cornelius. That was good. That was very good. But he hadn't solved anything. Tomorrow was still there, lying in wait for him.

He stopped, polished off the last of the Laphroaig and threw the bottle away. Had a swig of the White Horse.

He walked. It was still Saturday. It had been a very, very long Saturday. The streets were full of people, many of them drunk like him. He didn't care where he went.

Sandy. Sandy was staying somewhere in London, he knew it. The Howard Hotel, that was it. The Howard Hotel. Down by the river near the Strand. He'd see Sandy.

He staggered on. He didn't know how long it took

him, or even how he navigated the once familiar streets of London, but eventually he found himself at the steps of the Howard Hotel, which for some reason had acquired a Swiss white cross above its door since he had last been there. It was late. The doorman tried not to let him in. Calder said he had to see a guest, and the doorman reluctantly took him to the reception desk. With a great effort he put on a pretence of sobriety sufficient to persuade the receptionist to check his computer.

'Miss Waterhouse checked out two days ago,' the man said.

'No, you don't understand,' Calder said, lurching forward.

Strong hands grabbed him by the collar. Strong arms pushed him out of the door.

Calder looked around him. Cars flashed by on the Embankment in front of him. Beyond that was the river.

He swayed up to the road. Waited. The cars didn't stop. Waited. A light somewhere went red and there was a gap in the traffic. He lurched across the road. A car hooted. He stumbled along the pavement beside the river. There were lights everywhere – God this city was bright – everywhere but down below where the river pulled and tugged at the light, pulling it down, down into the darkness. Calder watched it, the darkness. He felt himself drawn towards it.

Tomorrow. God, who wanted tomorrow?

He pulled out the bottle for a swig.

'Hey, mate!' He looked down at his feet. A scrawny man with a three-day stubble and wearing a torn denim jacket and jeans was slumped against the wall. Calder hadn't even noticed him. 'Hey, mate. Can I have some of that?'

'Sure,' said Calder, sinking down beside him. 'Here. Take it. Take it all.'

18

The sunlight woke him up, burning red through his closed eyelids. He was slumped on his side on the pavement, dried vomit inches from his nose. He sat up and looked at his watch. Five past five. The sky was the light grey of a summer dawn, there was no one to be seen on the Embankment, although single cars were speeding past even at this time of the morning. His head pounded. He ran his tongue over his teeth: the inside of his mouth felt as if someone had poured vinegar and lighter fluid on to a large ball of cotton wool and then ignited it. The pounding increased in intensity and chemicals in his stomach began to gurgle and churn.

He pulled himself to his feet. There was no sign of his companion of the night before, nor of his bottle of whisky. He felt his trouser pocket for his wallet: still there. He began staggering unsteadily northwards towards King's Cross. There was still enough alcohol in his bloodstream to disrupt his balance, but the walk and the early-morning sunshine did him some good, stirring his feeble circulation.

He reached King's Cross, found an all-night chemist and bought some paracetamol, found an all-night café and grabbed a fried breakfast. There were quite a few people around King's Cross at that time on a Sunday morning as the dregs of the night traders in sex and drugs overlapped with early-morning workers. His head still pounding, he crossed the road into the station in search of the first train to King's Lynn.

It was nine-thirty by the time he got to Norfolk and he

decided to take a taxi straight home. There was no way he could face the hospital in his current state. The cottage was guarded by police tape and a uniformed constable. He introduced himself, climbed upstairs, pulled the curtains and went back to sleep. The phone rang a couple of times and he ignored it.

At one in the afternoon he woke up, had a shower and called Alfie to take him to the hospital. The taxi fares were racking up: he would have to organize himself a car. There was still some activity outside the cottage, where the twisted wreckage of his Maserati was being carefully loaded on to a lorry. A policeman was taking down the scene-of-crime tape. He nodded to Calder and jotted something in his notebook.

In the back of the taxi Calder checked the voicemail on his mobile. Messages from William, Kim, Jerry and his father all asking where the hell he was. The only one he called back was Jerry. He quickly explained about his sister and said he wouldn't be at the airfield for the next couple of days. Jerry's anger changed to shock and sympathy. Calder took a deep breath as he hung up. If only the same could be said for his father and for William.

The throbbing in Calder's head ratcheted up a notch as he approached intensive care. He saw the hunched figure of William sitting in the waiting area. His brother-in-law looked up, recognized Calder, and returned his stare to the floor.

'How is she?' Calder asked.

'What do you care?'

'How is she?' Calder repeated.

William sighed. 'She did well overnight. She's in the operating theatre again this morning. They think she's going to make it, we'll know more when they've finished in there.'

'And the other leg?'

William shrugged. 'They're going to try to save it. No guarantees.'

'I'm sorry,' Calder said.

'Go away,' William said quietly and clearly.

'Where are the children?'

'With Kim and your father. Somewhere. I don't know where.'

Calder left William and wandered around the hospital. Eventually he spotted them outside, squatting on the grass beside a rose bed. Kim was reading to Phoebe and Dr Calder was reading to Robbie.

'Hi,' Kim said when she saw Calder. She finished her sentence and closed the book. Dr Calder ignored his son and read two more pages to his grandson. Calder sat down beside them and watched the quiet concentration on his father's craggy face, the shock of thick white hair on his bent head. Robbie was sucking his thumb, transfixed as he listened to the low Scottish rumble of the story.

'All right now, Robbie. Take your sister and see how many of those wee petals you can collect for me,' he said, pointing towards the bed of yellow roses. The early blooms were past their prime and the soil was scattered with wilting petals. 'Put them in a nice big pile and count them. When you get to twenty, let me know.'

Robbie was proud of his counting abilities and dragged his sister off to do as he was bid.

'You look dreadful, Alex,' Kim said. 'What have you done to your head?'

Calder grunted and touched his temple. There was a large bump where the table lamp had made contact with it the night before.

Dr Calder eyed his son up and down. 'Are you sober?'

'Yes,' Calder said. 'I'm at the hangover stage. It hurts like hell.'

'Stupid bugger,' the doctor said.

Calder couldn't argue. A wave of exhaustion swept over him. He was ready for it. Ready for all the criticism his father wanted to pile on. He had no defence. He would accept it all.

'I'll go and play with the children,' Kim said, and moved off towards the rose bushes.

'She's been a great help, that girl,' Dr Calder said. 'She's really been very good with Robbie and Phoebe. I don't think William could have handled them without her.'

Calder looked at his father. He hadn't meant to say anything, but he couldn't help it. 'I'm sorry, Father. I'm so sorry.'

His father smiled. The eyes twinkled, that sympathetic twinkle that was famous throughout Kelso. He reached out and touched Calder's arm. It was a light touch, but it was strong and reassuring at the same time. Calder began to talk, talk in a confused torrent about Anne, about the van Zyls, about the bomb, about hitting Cornelius, about his mother, about everything but Kim. That he was still too ashamed to mention.

The doctor listened.

'I know how much you love Annie, Father,' Calder said. 'And you know how much I love her. You know I wouldn't have done any of this if I thought there was any risk to her.'

There was a squeal as Robbie impaled his finger on a rose thorn. Calder and his father watched as Kim swiftly examined it and kissed it better. Eventually his father spoke. 'Someone tried to kill my son and ended up nearly killing my daughter. I'm angry about that, very angry about it, but not with you. Getting plastered and hitting an old man in the face doesn't help very much, although I can understand why you did it.'

'Men like that are untouchable. He'll get away with it.'

'We'll see,' said Dr Calder. 'Kim told me how much you've helped her after what happened to her husband. Anne and William and the children will need your help now.'

'William won't talk to me,' Calder said. 'And I can quite understand why.'

'Och, that will change. I've told William I'm going to take the children home to London tomorrow. Maybe even take them back to school. Kim's been a great help here, but William's in no shape to look after them.'

'What can I do?'

Dr Calder looked at his son carefully. 'Let's talk about that later, shall we? In the meantime let me look at that bump on your head.'

It was evening and Calder had been home from the hospital for an hour. There was some straightening up to do: the police had thoroughly searched the outside of the house and had also been over his clothes and shoes. He was beginning to feel a bit better, the headache had subsided, but there was still muzziness around the edges of his brain. He couldn't help thinking about Anne; the operation had been a success, but he tried not to dwell on the explosion and his part in it.

He heard a car draw up outside. It was his father's beaten-up red Volvo, with Kim in the passenger seat.

'We won't stay long,' Dr Calder said as he entered the house. 'But I want a quick word with the both of you before I go down to Highgate with the wee ones tomorrow.'

Calder led them both through to his sitting room. 'Can I get you something to drink?'

'Have you got some of that Laphroaig I gave you?' his father asked.

'How about a glass of wine?'

The doctor frowned. 'Finished it last night, did you?'

'Started it *and* finished it, I'm afraid,' Calder admitted.

'Hmm.' Dr Calder's disapproval of the use of expensive single-malt whisky for binge drinking ran very deep. 'Wine will do fine,' he said grudgingly.

Calder opened a bottle and poured two glasses, giving himself iced water.

'Very wise,' said Calder's father, noticing.

'What do you think about Annie?' Calder asked. 'The doctors are so uncertain at the hospital.'

'She'll pull through,' Dr Calder said with confidence. 'She's a tough girl. With injuries like that, recovery depends on the attitude of the patient. The more stubborn and bloody-minded they are, the better.'

'I hope you're right,' Calder said.

Dr Calder smiled. 'I'm right.' He sipped his wine. 'Now. Someone has severely injured your husband and your sister,' he said looking at Kim and Calder in turn. 'My question is, what are we going to do about it?'

'What do you mean?' Calder asked.

'Well, I've listened to what you've said and what Kim's told me and I've heard about your bloody stupid antics in London, and I'm angry too. There's obviously some link between what happened to Todd and what happened to Annie, and that link must be your inquiries into the death of Martha van Zyl. Alex is right: the most likely person behind it all is Cornelius van Zyl.'

Kim and Calder nodded. Dr Calder continued. 'We should help the police as much as we can, but I share Alex's concern that they won't find the evidence to arrest him. If he got away with it, I would be very angry.' The bushy white eyebrows knitted together and the craggy face set itself in a determined stare. 'Very angry indeed.'

'Me too,' said Kim.

'Alex?'

Calder nodded.

'So. What are we going to do?'

'I can't see what else we can do, except tell the police all we know,' Calder said. 'I can hardly beat a confession out of Cornelius, can I?'

'Come on, Alex,' his father said. 'I'm disappointed in you. You've done this kind of thing before, haven't you? I won't have the bastard who crippled my daughter getting away with it. You were asking what you can do to make up for what happened to Todd and Annie. Well, I'm telling you. Nail him.'

Calder smiled at his father. Suddenly the fuzziness in his brain cleared. 'There *are* things we can do,' he said. 'We can't investigate the bombs in the Yak and the Maserati any better than the police can. But Kim's original instincts are exactly right. Martha van Zyl's death is the key. If we can find out who killed her and why, then what's happening now will make much more sense.'

'There's something there Cornelius doesn't want us to discover,' said Kim. 'And he'll go to great lengths, even to the point of murdering his own son, to stop us.'

'We can't be sure it is Cornelius,' said Dr Calder.

'Fair point,' said Calder. 'But once we find out more about Martha we'll know one way or another.'

The three of them exchanged glances. There was a new sense of purpose in the room.

'It's going to be dangerous,' said Kim. 'Todd and Anne have both been injured. If you persist in asking questions, they'll come after you.'

'She's right,' Dr Calder said.

Calder looked at his friend and his father. 'What do you want me to say?'

'Say what you want to say,' his father said. 'It has to be up to you.'

Calder closed his eyes. The danger was real, he knew it. But so was the opportunity: the opportunity to do something for Todd and Anne, for Kim and his father, but most of all the opportunity to do something for himself. It was a way out, a way for him to face all those tomorrows.

'I'll do it,' he said.

His father smiled.

They heard a loud knock at the front door. Calder noticed a crisp cream envelope lying on the mat. He opened the door to see a small black man in a baggy suit whom he recognized as Cornelius's driver getting into a Mercedes parked a few yards down the lane.

Calder picked up the envelope and took it back into the sitting room to show to the others.

'Did he drive all the way up from London just to deliver that?' said Kim.

'Presumably.'

'I wonder what it is. Probably a threat of some sort.'

'Let's see.' Calder slid his finger along the seal of the envelope and took out a single sheet of paper bearing a bold, forward-sloping scrawl. He scanned it and passed it on to his father and Kim.

Dear Alex

I was very sorry to hear about your sister's injuries. My thoughts are with her and your family.

I can understand the pain and anger you must be feeling now. I can also see how in the heat of the moment you might believe that I was responsible. I hope that now you have had a few hours to reflect, you can see that I would never harm my own son, nor an innocent woman like your sister.

*You can be confident that I will give the police all the assistance
I can in finding whoever it was who committed these appalling
crimes, and also that I won't mention what occurred at my house
last night.*

If I can be of any help to you or your sister, please ask.
Sincerely
Cornelius van Zyl

Dr Calder examined the letter. 'Sanctimonious bastard,'
he said, when he had read it. 'You should have hit him
harder.'

Calder felt a little better at breakfast the next morning.
His father had stayed the night and had gone for a brisk
early-morning walk down to the sea. William and the kids
had checked into a hotel in King's Lynn. Calder scanned
the newspapers over a second cup of coffee. There was a
big article in the *Financial Times* on the bid for *The Times*,
which was now threatening to turn into a full-scale takeover battle. The Laxton Media board were dithering over
Zyl News's offer. In the meantime, three other potential
bidders were said to be looking closely at the situation: a
large German publishing conglomerate, an Irish property
tycoon who owned papers in South Africa, Ireland and the
United States, and Telegraph Newspapers, who published a
rival quality broadsheet. The price was high, but *The Times*
was a unique newspaper. According to the *FT* there was
no clear favourite. The Germans had deep pockets but a
struggling share price, and the Irishman was showing signs
of breaching his own rule never to overpay. Despite the
likelihood of referral to the Competition Commission, Telegraph Newspapers were reported willing to try their luck.
Sir Evelyn Gill and Cornelius van Zyl were well known for

their desperation to own the paper, but both were stretched financially.

Any one of them could emerge as a successful bidder. Anyone but Cornelius, Calder hoped.

Calder realized that inactivity was his enemy. He phoned his insurance company to set in motion a claim for the wrecked Maserati, then he and his father drove to the hospital, where Anne was stable but unconscious. The doctors had saved her leg, reconstructed it almost. They pronounced her 'a fighter' and were now much more confident that she would pull through. There was no change with Todd. Calder avoided William, but exchanged some friendly words with Kim. Dr Calder set off with the children for London, and dropped off Calder at a local garage where he hired an old black Golf to last him until he got around to buying another car. He drove it back to his cottage to find Detective Inspector Banks and her chubby friend waiting for him.

He invited them into the house, and made them a pot of coffee. Banks looked even paler than she had the previous Saturday, except for the dark smudges under her eyes. It had obviously been a long weekend.

'How's it going?' Calder asked.

'Forensics have confirmed that the bomb in the plane was made by the same person who made the bomb in the car.'

'Big surprise,' said Calder. Banks glanced at him sharply. 'Did Benton Davis tell you anything?'

'No more than he told you. We have made inquiries with the police in South Africa about Martha van Zyl's death. We're waiting to hear back from them. In the meantime, we'd like to ask you a few more questions.'

'Please do.'

She pulled a single sheet of paper out of a folder. It was

a sketch of a middle-aged man, beefy with short hair and a moustache. Calder studied it.

'Have you seen anyone like this around here?' Banks asked. 'He's about five foot eight inches tall, and he might have been wearing a black leather jacket.'

Calder shook his head. 'I don't think so. Why?'

'We have a witness who saw this man driving along the lane outside your house on Friday. He stopped and had a good look round. It matches the description of the man walking along the airfield perimeter the night before the Yak bomb went off.'

Calder studied the drawing. 'Sorry. I don't recognize him at all.'

Banks took back the sketch. She showed no sign of disappointment. More questions asked, another blank drawn, it was all part of the process.

'How long have you known Mrs van Zyl?' she asked.

'We were at university together. But I hadn't seen her for ten years until a couple of weeks ago.'

'I see. But you've spent some time with her over these last couple of weeks?'

'Yes, I suppose I have.'

'Have you been able to get a sense of the state of her relationship with her husband?'

'Yes,' said Calder. 'She loves him very much. She's devastated about what happened to him.'

'She hasn't mentioned any strains in their marriage?'

'No. She's a bit frustrated with where they live, I suppose, but that's all. Why? Are you suggesting *she's* responsible for the bombs?'

'She would stand to inherit a fortune if Todd were to die.'

'That's absurd!' Calder said, too loudly.

'Possibly,' Inspector Banks said. Calder was aware that

she was looking at him closely now. 'Are you sure that you know of nothing else that might suggest marital difficulties?'

Two scenes flashed into Calder's mind: Donna Snyder at Todd's bedside, and himself and Kim in his back garden. Just as quickly he tried to banish them. 'Quite sure,' he said slowly.

'What about your relationship with Mrs van Zyl?'

'I know what you are implying and I resent it,' Calder said calmly. Inspector Banks's hazel eyes searched his. He held them.

'All right,' said the detective. 'Just one last question.'

'Yes?'

'Where were you on Saturday night?'

Calder frowned. 'I don't see what relevance that has to this.'

'You were last seen, intoxicated, getting into a taxi to King's Lynn station. You didn't return home until the next morning.'

'I don't have to tell you where I was,' Calder said.

Banks sighed. 'No you don't. But you've been cooperative up to now, and it seems odd to me that you refuse to answer the question. It arouses my suspicion. Makes me curious. If you don't tell me, I *will* find out the answer.'

Calder looked at her. He wanted to help, and she almost certainly would find out anyway. 'I went to see Cornelius van Zyl.'

'Ah. I don't think that was a good idea, Mr Calder.'

'But I'm sure he's responsible for this,' Calder said.

'If he is, and I stress if, the last thing we want you to do is go barging in accusing him. He will need to be treated carefully.'

'Have you seen him yet?'

'I'm going down to London early tomorrow morning, with my superintendent.'

'Superintendent?'

'This is an important investigation.'

'And Cornelius van Zyl is an important man?'

'He certainly is,' said Banks. 'Thank you for your time, Mr Calder.'

Calder saw the two detectives to the door. He was shaken by Banks's questioning, especially about his relationship with Kim. He really didn't want that to come out. He was quite sure that it had no relevance to the attempt on Todd's life: the idea that Kim was in some way responsible was absurd, no matter how much money she stood to inherit. But on the other hand he was encouraged by Banks's persistence and perceptiveness. If she grilled Cornelius like she had grilled him she might get somewhere.

19

It was a fine room, Cornelius thought: a long antique board table, portraits of venerable nineteenth-century bankers and the ships that they had financed, and a partial view of the Thames between the flanks of two new City tower blocks.

They were in the boardroom of Leipziger Gurney Kroheim, the merchant bank that had been swallowed by a German leviathan but was still plying its traditional trade of advising companies how to buy and sell. On the other side of the table were three Gurney Kroheim bankers, led by a smooth Jewish man in a nice striped shirt; Peter Laxton, the deal-doing founder and chairman of Laxton Media; and Tim Rollinson, his recently appointed finance director. With Cornelius were Edwin, Benton Davis, Dower and another Bloomfield Weiss banker whose name Cornelius hadn't registered. The Gurney Kroheim man was talking, asking for more time before accepting the Zyl News bid.

It boiled down to the classic game of chicken. Who would blink first. Zyl News had made an offer for Laxton Media shares that in accordance with Takeover Panel rules had to be open for at least twenty-one days. Peter Laxton owned only 10 per cent of the shares of the company he had founded, most of the rest were held by large investors who were sitting on significant losses and were by now fed up with the company's management. They were waiting before tendering their shares, hoping for a higher bid to emerge. But the company's bankers wanted their money back and they wanted it now.

Laxton Media were playing for time, trying to extend Zyl News's deadline in the hope that they might elicit a higher bid from Evelyn Gill or one of the other potential suitors. Zyl News didn't want to give them more time for exactly the same reason. If Cornelius refused Peter Laxton's request for an extension, he risked Laxton rejecting the Zyl News bid. This would be fine for Laxton if another higher bid materialized, but disastrous if it didn't. Laxton's bankers were impatient. If Peter Laxton and his board dithered and a higher bid failed to appear, the banks could force the company to come back to Zyl News with their tails between their legs and accept any price Cornelius chose to offer them.

So, a game of bluff. Of the key players around the table, three were professionals of the first order: Cornelius himself, the Gurney Kroheim banker and Peter Laxton. One wasn't: Tim Rollinson. He was thin, he was bald, he wore thick glasses and he was mean: he had a reputation as a hard man, a vicious cost-cutter, and he had been put in place by the banks. But he wasn't a player. Cornelius kept his eyes on Rollinson. Rollinson noticed and shifted in his chair. He twisted the top of his Waterman pen to the left and to the right, gripping it so tightly that Cornelius feared he might break it.

When the banker had finished, there was silence, all eyes on Cornelius. Cornelius kept his on Rollinson. He let the silence drift. 'We rather thought that you would want to do a quick deal,' he said eventually.

'We appreciate that,' Laxton replied, 'but you can understand why we might want a couple more weeks to give other interested parties time to put a bid together.'

'I'm just thinking through what will happen if they don't come up with a bid,' Cornelius said, ignoring Laxton and focusing on the finance director. 'It will be tight meeting the payments due to the banks, won't it, Tim?'

Rollinson looked up from his papers at Cornelius. The finance director was staring through his thick lenses, Cornelius was peering over his more delicate half-moons. 'I'm quite certain we will have plenty of time to arrange things satisfactorily with the banks,' Rollinson said. 'They have assured us that they will give us all the time we need to come to the very best deal for Laxton Media shareholders.' He held Cornelius's eyes for a second, two seconds, and then his own eyes flicked sideways towards Peter Laxton for the tiniest instant before returning to Cornelius.

The instant was enough. Rollinson was lying. Cornelius knew it, he couldn't put into words how he knew, but he *knew* it. He smiled at Peter Laxton, just to let him know that he knew. 'I'm sorry, but we can't extend our offer. It expires in, what is it now, eleven days' time. I'm sure your shareholders will see the sense in going with us.'

Laxton cleared his throat. 'We'll have to consider our position,' he said gravely.

'Of course you will,' said Cornelius, smiling. 'That's your prerogative.'

As they left the Gurney Kroheim offices, Benton clapped Cornelius on the back. 'You've hung them out to dry! There's no way the banks will let them delay recommending our offer. You could see it in Rollinson's eyes.'

Dower glowered. 'We'll have to wait to see what Laxton come back with,' he said. 'We can't be sure they were bluffing.'

Benton caught Cornelius's eye and winked. Dower glowered some more.

*

Calder drove over to the hospital to see how Anne was doing. The doctors were pleased with her progress, but she was still unconscious. There was good news from Todd. He was awake: awake but very groggy.

Kim was ecstatic. Todd had no clue where he was or what he was doing there, but he had recognized Kim. They had spoken, though he had made little sense and soon gone back to sleep. But it was a beginning. Cornelius's plan, to which Kim had grudgingly agreed, was to move him down to a private hospital in London sometime during the next couple of days, but until then she was determined to stay at his bedside as long as they would let her in case he woke up again.

Calder had difficulty persuading her to leave him for half an hour. They strolled out of the entrance to the main hospital building and wandered through the grounds, such as they were, ignoring the racks of polysyllabic signs pointing in all directions. Calder recounted his interview with Inspector Banks, although he didn't mention her probing questions about Kim's relationship with Todd.

'Let's hope she gets somewhere with Cornelius,' said Kim.

'I was thinking,' Calder said. 'Whoever planted the bomb in the Yak must have known that Todd and I were going to fly that plane on that day. Now, people at the flying school would have known, and it would have been on the booking sheets there, but it's highly unlikely that an enemy of Todd's would have checked. Which leaves the question –'

'Who did we tell?'

'Yes.'

'Well, I told my parents on the phone, I remember that.'

'They're in Liverpool, aren't they?'

'That's right. And when we saw Cornelius in London, we

had a conversation about it. I said I was worried about the safety of such an old plane. He just said it sounded fun.'

'Very interesting. Did you mention it to anyone else?'

'No.' Kim screwed up her face, thinking. 'Just Cornelius and my parents.'

'I think we can rule your parents out. Your father isn't an international terrorist with a grudge against Todd, is he?'

'No. He's the retired owner of a lighting shop who dotes on him,' Kim said.

'That leaves Cornelius.'

They walked on, passing an elderly lady with a patch over one eye making slow progress towards an outpatients clinic. She paused for breath and to wish them a good evening.

'There's not much more we can do here,' Calder said. 'I think the next step is for me to go down to South Africa. See where Martha died. See where she lived. See if I can find anyone who knows anything about the last few weeks of her life. Perhaps try to find the diary. I was hoping Todd might be of some help.'

'He might be later, but not now,' Kim said. 'What about Caroline?'

'She was only twelve at the time, wasn't she?'

'Yes. But she noticed the diary. And she told Cornelius she wanted to find out more, remember. I could call her, if you like. She and I got on quite well. In fact –' Kim pulled out her mobile '– I could call her now.'

'OK,' Calder said. 'Go for it.'

They sat on a grassy bank outside the orthopaedic out-patients clinic, and Kim rummaged in her bag for a number. It was about six o'clock English time, so morning in San Diego. She punched out the number, and Calder sat with his ear close to Kim's to hear the conversation.

Caroline answered and seemed happy to hear from Kim,

and very happy to hear that Todd had woken up. Then Kim explained what Calder was going to do, and asked Caroline whom he should see.

'That's hard,' Caroline said, her voice sounding noticeably more Californian over the airwaves. 'Mom and Dad were often entertaining people, but I'm not sure which ones were true friends, or whether Mom would have confided in any of them. There's Zan, of course, who was staying there at the time. She lives in Camps Bay now, I think. It's a swish suburb of Cape Town.'

'I've got her address,' Kim said.

'OK, good. And Doris, who was the maid. If Alex sees her, tell him to give her a big hug from me. I really liked her. Wait, there was a newspaper guy who worked for Dad, George something, George Field, I think. Mom and he became quite close. And she used to go off to some kind of project in one of the townships a lot. Guguletu. She had friends there. It's kind of hard to think of anyone else. I remember my friends' parents quite well, but they were important to me rather than Mom.'

'What about the diary?' Kim asked.

'Hondehoek has been sold now, of course. She said it was hidden in a desk with some tax stuff, didn't she? God knows where that is. Perhaps at Dad's house in Philadelphia? Most probably the desk was sold in South Africa and the old tax papers thrown away, like Dad said.'

'Oh,' Kim said, disappointed.

'But there is something else I've remembered about the diary. Actually, I've always known it, it just seemed that Dad was so jumpy at that dinner the other night, I didn't want to mention it then. You remember I said I saw Mom copying something into her diary from a man's briefcase?'

'Yes.'

237

'I don't know the name of the guy with the briefcase, but I do remember the name of the other man. Andries Visser. I remembered it because "Visser" was the last name of my best friend, and it was one of the few other Afrikaner names in our school, so I was curious. I asked her about him, in case it was her father or something, but she didn't know him. He did have a limp, I remember.'

Kim raised her eyebrows to check that Calder was listening. He nodded to show he was. 'Well done, Caroline,' she said.

'I was afraid of mentioning the name at the dinner. Dad was obviously pretty touchy about the whole thing. And Edwin was there.' She paused. 'I don't trust Edwin. In fact I remember he and Mom got on particularly badly.'

'I understand,' said Kim. 'What about Zan?'

'No, she did fine with Mom. We hadn't seen much of her since I was very little, but then she showed up that winter and stayed with us for a couple of months. Mom and she seemed to get on really well. She might be worth speaking to.'

'Thank you, Caroline.'

'Look,' she said. 'If you need any financial help with any of this, please let me know. Perhaps I can help with paying for Alex's trip?'

Kim glanced at Calder, who shook his head. 'I'll ask him. And we'll let you know what happens.'

'Good. And Kim?'

'Yes?'

'Give Todd a kiss from me, will you?'

They walked back towards Todd's room.

'It's funny,' Kim said. 'After I saw that woman Donna here I was scared of Todd waking up, scared of how I would feel about him. But I'm just pleased. Thankful. Happy.'

'I'm glad.'

'This may sound stupid, but I think what you and I did made me less angry with him. I'm more angry with myself perhaps, but it's made it easier to forgive him. Maybe our whole marriage will fall apart when he recovers, but I hope it won't. I'm willing to try again if he is.'

'He'd be a fool not to,' Calder said.

Calder spent the evening preparing himself for his trip to South Africa. He logged on to the internet to buy an air ticket to Cape Town for the following day and to do some preliminary research. He checked out Andries Visser. There were several men of that name mentioned on Google, of course, but the most likely candidate was a bureaucrat in the South African Finance Ministry in the 1980s and 1990s. There wasn't much about him: some speeches he made to conferences, his name among a list of members on dull-sounding committees. It was odd that someone like that would have had a significant meeting with Cornelius. There was no indication of his current job or whereabouts, but at least it was a start.

He also tracked down the reference to the word 'Laagerbond' in the Truth and Reconciliation Commission testimony. It was as scant as Kim had suggested. A man named Ben Dillard was testifying in relation to an amnesty application for his part in the bombing of the ANC offices in London in 1982. He was a spy for the South African security police and during questioning he mentioned that his handler, Colonel Retief, was rumoured to be a member of the Laagerbond. Colonel Retief could not be called on to testify as he had died in 1990.

Calder checked South African news sites for any further mention of Dillard. It turned out he was granted amnesty, but he was murdered in 2000 when his house in Durban was broken into by robbers.

Turning away from his computer, Calder phoned Donna Snyder at the New Hampshire number she had given him. She was nervous when she heard his voice, but overjoyed to learn that Todd had woken up. Calder tried to keep the conversation short, and cut her off when she started talking about how upset she was and whether she should resign from her position at the school. He had done what he had promised to do. He was happy to be leaving that particular problem thousands of miles behind him.

The next morning he set off for Heathrow planning to stop at Langthorpe and the hospital on the way. The airfield was in its usual state of minor turmoil. Jerry was sympathetic about Calder's sister, but not impressed with his travel plans. It would mean more cancelled lessons and frustrated students, but Calder was adamant. Jerry would just have to cope by himself.

There was good news at the hospital: Anne was awake. Calder was just about to follow the nurse into the ward to see her, when William blocked his way.

He looked bad: his face was yellow, his eyes glinted manically from hollow sockets, the little hair he had stuck out in odd directions from his scalp. 'I don't think you should disturb her now, Alex,' he said.

'I won't be long,' Calder said reasonably. 'I'm going to South Africa for a few days. I just want to see her before I go.'

'South Africa, eh?' William laughed, an unpleasant high-pitched bray that Calder hadn't heard before. 'You never learn when to leave things alone, do you?'

'Excuse me,' Calder said, edging past him.

William grabbed hold of his arm and tugged. 'I said you shouldn't go in.'

Calder held his ground but kept his temper. The nurse had gone on into the ward, unaware of the delay. 'I'm her brother. I have a right to see her.'

'She doesn't want to see you,' William said.

'How do you know?' Calder said. 'I heard she can't speak.'

'I'm her husband,' William said. 'I know what she thinks.'

Calder sighed in irritation and broke free of William to meet the nurse who was returning to look for him. He followed her to Anne's bed.

Like Todd, she was hooked up to all sorts of machines and instruments. The first thing Calder noticed was that her left arm was in plaster. The second, after a quick glance at her bed, was that the sheets were flat where her left leg should have been. The third was that her cheek and her forehead were bandaged. Her nose and mouth were covered by an oxygen mask, and her eyes were closed.

He moved over beside her. She opened her eyes. He took her right hand and pressed it. 'Annie, it's Alex,' he whispered.

Her eyes took a moment to focus on him. Then they widened. Her fingers, which had gently clasped his hand, opened. She began to shake her head, gently at first and then more violently.

'Annie! It's only me,' Calder whispered again, more urgently.

Anne turned her head away from him.

The nurse put her hand on his shoulder. 'Come with me, love,' she said. 'We don't want to upset her.'

Calder stared at the back of his sister's head, her short spikes of hair plastered to her skull. Then he let himself be led out of the ward.

'What did I tell you?' William brayed in triumph at the door. 'Now, don't come back!'

Calder ignored him. He reeled down the corridors. He needed to get out of there.

'Alex!'

He turned. It was Kim. 'Alex! What's wrong?'

Calder put his hand to his brow. 'I just saw Anne,' he said.

'What's happened? Has there been some kind of complication?'

'No,' Calder said. 'She . . .' He could hardly bring himself to say it. 'She didn't want to see me. She turned her head away.'

Kim touched his arm in sympathy. 'She's probably a bit groggy. She'll be fine next time she sees you.'

Calder swallowed. 'I'm not sure of that, Kim. I'm not at all sure.'

'Here. Let's get a cup of coffee.'

Calder looked down the corridor towards the café and shook his head. 'I'm sorry, Kim, I've got to get out of here.'

He turned and stumbled out of the hospital.

20

August 12, 1988

Winter is really here now. They had storms while I was away. The vines in the fields are bare and the oaks have lost most of their leaves too. It's noticeably colder and there are flashes of white snow on the peaks at the top of the valley. It's quite a shock after the heat and humidity of America in mid-summer.

I saw George today for lunch. He's still not getting anywhere finding a buyer for the *Mail*.

I asked him about Beatrice Pienaar. Evidently she graduated with a masters from Stellenbosch School of Journalism, where she did extremely well. Her professor suggested she work for Zyl News for a few months in Philadelphia. Her professor would be Daniel Havenga, I realized. She's a bright woman, apparently; Neels will like that.

I told George my suspicion that Daniel is a member of the Broederbond. George said he wouldn't be surprised, a lot of academics are. In fact, George suspects the ice-queen Beatrice of being a spy for the security police. I thought he was joking at first, but he was deadly serious. The newspaper editors believe that the government has been trying to infiltrate their newsrooms for years. The journalists play spot-the-spy in the office. It's done half in jest, but there is a lot of suspicion about. When anyone is working on a scoop George makes sure that only three people know about it: himself, the journalist involved, and one other to add a sense of perspective. He fired a journalist a couple of months ago whom he suspected of leaking an investigation into corruption in defense procurement.

He hasn't told Neels about his suspicions; relations between them are poor at the moment. I urged him to talk to Neels, but I doubt he will.

I asked George whether Beatrice had been in Cape Town at the end of last month, which was when Neels stayed out the whole night, although I didn't tell George about that. Apparently she did spend a few days in the Cape Town office then. In fact, George said Beatrice is accompanying Neels when he flies back tomorrow. I am *so* angry.

August 13

I got a real scare when I went to pick up Caroline from school this afternoon. We were walking along the sidewalk when I saw him. Moolman. He was sitting in a blue car opposite the school entrance watching us. He must have realized I had spotted him, but he gave no indication of it. He was just staring at me. And Caroline.

I *have* to make sure he doesn't touch her. If I do exactly as he says he won't. I must let Neels know that I have given up all interest in the Laagerbond.

Neels is back. He arrived on the flight this morning and went straight into the office. Presumably he has Beatrice shacked up in some hotel on the Foreshore. I haven't confronted him yet about her, but I will.

I wonder if she really is a spy. And if she is, is she "Impala," the woman referred to in Daniel Havenga's memo about Neels? She must be!

Neels didn't get back here until nine last night. He looked exhausted. He poured himself a large brandy and sat by the fire. I joined him.

"I saw George Field yesterday," I began.

"Oh, yes?" Neels replied without interest.

"He says that there have been spies on the *Mail*."

"I know. We've had several conversations about it over the years. He sacked a journalist back in May."

"Has he mentioned Beatrice Pienaar?"

"No he hasn't." Neels's eyes flashed angrily. "Why should he?"

"He told me she seemed suspicious."

"Well, she isn't. Anyway, she's working in Philadelphia, not here. And she was introduced by Daniel Havenga. He's a friend of mine."

"Who's probably a member of the Broederbond."

"Every Afrikaner of any importance is a member of the Broederbond. There are thousands of them."

"Including you?"

"No!" Neels said. "I've told you. I'm not a member."

"Have they ever asked you?"

"No. I'm sure they would have done if they thought I would say yes. But apart from anything else, the *Mail* has written dozens of articles over the years exposing their activities."

"Is the Broederbond anything to do with the Laager-bond?" I asked.

Neels frowned. "I thought I told you not to concern yourself with that subject."

I felt a surge of anger that I did my best to control. The fact that he had called me scum that night still hurt. The fact that we were sitting calmly discussing his mistress as if she were any other employee hurt more. But I had something important I wanted him to know. "You're right. It's forgotten." He glanced at me sharply. I tried to smile. "Who you see is your business," I said. "I don't want to know anything about it."

"Good," he said. "We should be careful who we speak to, what we do. All of us. This country is getting more and more dangerous. I need to have a word with Zan, tell her she must stop going to whatever meetings she goes to while she's staying with us. And you should be careful too."

"Neels, listen to yourself," I said. "Think of all the brave men and women you have supported over the years. People who have been to jail for what they believe in. How can you of all people have a problem with Zan going to an End Conscription meeting? Or with me, well, me . . ."

I had started a sentence I didn't know how to finish. Neels noticed. "You what, Martha?" he said. "What have you done that I might have a problem with?"

"Nothing." I thought of Libby Wiseman, of the police photographers at Thando's funeral. And of Moolman. Especially of Moolman. "I told you, who you deal with is your affair."

He wasn't convinced. "Listen," he said. "We're in the endgame here, and it's being played for high stakes. These days, you're no longer immune, you know, none of us is. You could end up in jail or worse. Remember the promise you made to me just after we were married?"

That did it. Until then I was willing to pretend that Beatrice didn't exist, that she didn't matter, just for an evening. I slammed down my glass. "We both made promises when we got married, Neels. I'll keep mine if you keep yours!" I stormed up to bed.

Neels came up much later. But we didn't speak.

Eventually, Neels fell asleep. But as I lay in bed awake my thoughts drifted from Neels to *him*. In fact, I can't get him out of my mind. I wonder when I will see him again. I can't wait to hear from him.

Later . . .

We've just had a visitor. Penelope. And what a visit! It would have been funny if it wasn't so sad.

She arrived at about three o'clock in the afternoon, with a driver, thank God. I was in the garden pruning the roses with Finneas. We like to do that together, compare strategies. When they bloom the rose garden looks gorgeous, and I think much of that is down to our pruning. The bok-makieries were whooping loudly to each other in the stink-wood tree.

Anyway, I saw a Jaguar roll up the drive and Penelope got out, tottered up to the front door in her ridiculous white heels and rang the bell. I walked up behind her and said hello. She almost jumped out of her skin. She was wearing tight bright yellow pants and a white frilly blouse. I haven't seen her for five years at least. She's gotten a lot heavier and she sags and her hair is dyed an orange color; it really didn't go with the pants. I've seen photographs of her when she married Neels and she was stunning: a terrific figure and flashing eyes under long lashes. Even a few years ago you could see some vestiges of that beauty. But not now. Now she's old, fat, and bitter.

"Hello, Penelope," I said with what I hoped was a polite smile.

"I've come to pick up my daughter."

"I didn't know she was expecting you?"

"She's not. But I've come to take her back."

"What do you mean?"

Penelope drew herself up to her full height. She's not nearly as tall as me, but she was standing on the front doorstep and she was wearing heels, so she looked down on me. "I mean that you have taken my daughter, and I am taking her back. You've been keeping her here and forbidding her to come and see me. Well, I won't have it."

Her accent has always irritated me, the way she affects an upper-class British twang. I noticed a slight slur in her words for the first time, and there was a whiff of alcohol in the air. I wasn't surprised.

"She's twenty-four," I said. "She can come and go as she pleases. You can't take her and I can't keep her."

"You've stolen her from me, haven't you? Just like you stole my husband and you stole my family newspapers."

For a wicked moment I felt like admitting that I had stolen her husband, and I was sorry, and she could have him back now. She and Neels would have a whale of a time together.

"Speaking of the newspapers, I hear they're up for sale. Is that right?"

"I believe so," I said.

"Well, I hope Neels realizes that they are *my* family's papers. If he sells them he should at least have the decency to give *me* what he gets for them."

"I'll pass that on," I said. When Penelope gets going on the subject of the newspapers she can be very tiresome. I understand her anger to some extent. Soon after she and Neels got married, her father staked him to buy the ailing newspaper group that owned the *Johannesburg Post* and the

Durban Age. A couple of years later he provided him with the funds to buy the *Cape Daily Mail*. It was a gift. As Neels tells it, he and Penelope's father got on very well and the old man was quite happy to give the money to him, not invest it, nor insist that the shares were in Penelope's name as well as Neels's. He died in 1967, leaving Penelope a fortune in mining shares, by the way. Then, when she and Neels divorced in 1970, she argued that she deserved at least a 50 percent share in the newspapers. It all got ugly, and Neels spared me the details, but I know he kept ownership of Zyl News. It rankled, it obviously still rankles. She has no need of the money. I think what upsets her is the papers are a continuing reminder of her father's love for Neels. Maybe once they're sold she'll calm down.

"Well, where is she?"

"I'll see if I can find her." I left Penelope on the doorstep – it may have been rude but there was no way I was going to let her into the house – and walked around to the back. Zan was powering up and down our swimming pool. It's really too small for her, she spends most of her energy doing tumble turns, but she craves the exercise, and she swims every day no matter how cold it is. I told her her mother was out front. She grimaced.

"I can tell her you don't want to see her if you like," I said. "Or I can say you're not here."

She stood in the water, panting from her exertions. "I haven't seen her since Christmas," she said. "I just can't bear it. She's always drunk by midday."

"Xanthe!" We both turned to see Penelope tottering over the lawn toward the pool. "Xanthe! My poor darling! I've come to fetch you."

"Hello, Mom," Zan said.

"You can stay with me, dear," Penelope said as she got

to the edge of the water. "You don't have to stay with your father or Martha. We've got a wonderful pool, you know that." She squatted down on her ample haunches. She was wobbling alarmingly. "You can come along with me now. I'll send Jimmy over to bring your things later."

"No, Mom," Zan said. "I want to stay here."

Penelope turned to me. "Can you leave us alone, please?" she demanded haughtily.

I began to withdraw when Zan stopped me. "Wait, Martha. There's no need for you to go anywhere. I'm staying here."

"But Xanthe," Penelope cooed, "I miss you so much, dear."

"Mom. Go home," Zan said. "I'll come and see you next week before I go to London." With that she pulled her goggles down over her eyes and set off at a powerful crawl up the pool.

"Zan!" Penelope tottered after her, but Zan turned and Penelope ran back along the pool the other way. Zan was swimming faster than Penelope could move in her high heels. Penelope eventually figured this out and tottered around to the end of the pool. As Zan touched the edge, Penelope bent down to grab her wrist. I don't know what Penelope was thinking of, but the result was inevitable. Zan tumbled, Penelope lost her balance and fell in with an enormous splash. It was the deep end, and she sank. Zan realized immediately what had happened, swam back and grabbed her mother, dragging her to the steps at the edge of the pool.

I somewhat reluctantly offered her my arm to drag her out. The poor woman was sobbing. Zan and I took her into the house, and Zan got her out of her wet things. There was then the problem of what to put her into, but I had the idea of digging out some of Neels's old clothes. He's a big man, but even his pants were tight around her waist, although his shirt came down to her knees. As quick as we decently could we packed her into her car, and her driver took her back to Constantia.

Poor Zan. Poor Penelope. But it was pretty funny.

Will he call me sometime? I wish we had made some kind of arrangement to see each other again. Discussed our relationship, such as it is. I don't know whether he will want to see me again, and I can't stand the thought that he won't.

August 17

Neels flew off to London today to talk with his bankers about the *Herald* takeover. It's been a really unpleasant few days. We didn't mention Beatrice again, or the Laagerbond. In fact we have barely exchanged a word. But I made damn sure Beatrice isn't going with him to London. She's flying back to the States tomorrow.

And I'm going to Jo'burg tonight. Just for one night.

I'm beginning to lead a secret life; secret even from this diary. I find it strangely thrilling. It is difficult to edit my thoughts when writing this. I'm pretty sure no one has read the diary yet, but I can never guarantee that they won't. It's probably stupid to write it at all. But it has helped me get my life in some kind of perspective, and God knows it needed that. I've just reread the first page; it brings back how desperate I felt then. I still do feel that way a lot of the time. Things are bad, but there's hope. There's always hope.

And there's Jo'burg tonight.

Jo'burg was wonderful. He was wonderful. Even though it was only one night, it was worth it.

We so nearly got caught. I saw Roger Temple, one of those smug guys who work for Anglo-American, get out of an elevator when we were getting into it. Fortunately he was wrapped up in conversation with the businessmen he was with. I'm amazed he didn't recognize me, it's only a couple of months since we sat opposite each other at the Jamesons. We were probably stupid to risk meeting there. But I'm *so* glad we did.

Will we see each other again? We didn't talk about it. I wanted to ask him at the end, when we were saying goodbye. But that would just raise a whole new set of questions about the nature of our relationship, the impossibility of it all, the fact that the whole thing is mad, crazy, stupid and has no future. I didn't want to think about all that. I just wanted to enjoy every moment with him.

Do I feel guilty? Let's not ask that question either.

My heart is singing.

21

Calder could tell the woman sitting opposite was Cornelius van Zyl's daughter. She was tall with his square jaw and his blue piercing eyes surrounded by crows' feet. She also had his broad shoulders, but her body was lean and sinewy, angles rather than curves. She was wearing tight jeans and a light sweater, her blonde hair was cut short, revealing ears that were pierced with three sets of gold earrings. Calder calculated that she must be in her early forties, but apart from the wrinkles around her eyes, she looked younger.

They were in a restaurant on the Victoria and Alfred Waterfront, a large redeveloped area of wharves, shops, restaurants, yachts and fishing boats. The wharf in front of them was heaving with the tourists and citizens of Cape Town, almost all of them white, enjoying the late-autumn sun. A cacophony of music drifted in from the open windows as gospel singers, a saxophonist and a group of four electric guitarists wearing kilts launched a combined assault on the crowd. Behind it all were the glass and steel towers of the city centre, and behind them Table Mountain, a long high wall of grey, pale in the soft sunlight, supporting its mysterious plateau 3,000 feet above the city.

Calder had caught his first glimpse of it that morning, when he had looked up from his airline breakfast to see the great mountain silhouetted black in the gunmetal-blue dawn light, rising like an island out of a broad sea of white cloud which stretched out to the jagged profile of more mountains to the east. As the plane drew nearer he could see the cloud moving and swirling about the summit, like waves hitting a rocky shore. Now, seven hours later, it had all burned away to leave the sky bright blue and the mountain shimmering.

Still feeling muzzy from the broken sleep of his flight, Calder squinted at the menu, trying to decide between springbok pie and ostrich. In the end he went for the springbok. Zan chose pasta.

'So you're the only van Zyl to stay on in South Africa?' Calder said.

'That's right,' Zan replied. She had a much more distinctive South African accent than her siblings or her father. 'I like it here, especially Cape Town. You have to admit, it's a beautiful city.'

'It certainly beats mid-winter in London,' Calder agreed.

'I know. I spent a year there and the long nights got me down. That, and the way everyone wore black; it's the last thing you need in such a grey country. I was supposed to be studying at the LSE but I spent most of my time doing my bit for the struggle. I dropped out after the first year and went to Mozambique for a spell. It was all very exciting, but when we won and Mandela came to power I decided to come home. A free South Africa was what we had all been fighting for, after all.'

'What are you doing now? Something political?'

'Oh, no. After 1994 the political urge sort of left me. It's up to others to figure out what to do with the country now. I came into an inheritance from my mother which I invested in property. That's how I met Piet, my husband. Now I'm a suburban housewife with two kids and I'm very happy with that.'

'Do you think your father was wrong to leave South Africa?'

Zan glanced at him. 'Yes. Yes, I do. He always used to

make such a big deal about how important the country was to him, and then he changed his mind. I know that bugged Martha too.' She sighed. 'I'm afraid I've lost touch with the rest of my family since she died. They say that something like that either pulls a family together or forces it apart. I guess in my case it forced me away. I still talk to Edwin every now and then, and I saw Todd and Kim when they visited here just after they were married, but not my father.'

'Who do *you* think killed Martha?' Calder asked.

'You mean do I think my father killed her?' Zan looked at Calder sharply, her blue eyes, Cornelius's eyes, piercing.

Calder held her gaze and shrugged.

She relaxed a touch. 'It's a question I have asked myself many times over the years. The police story was that it was ANC guerrillas. Obviously you couldn't trust anything the police said in those days, but it is possible, I suppose. The guerrillas would cross the Kruger Park and then the game reserves on its western edge, like Kupugani, before losing themselves in the towns and villages on the other side. Normally they wouldn't make trouble on the way; the whole idea was to infiltrate the country quietly. I asked around when I was in Mozambique the following year, but no one knew anything about Martha's murder. It could have been poachers: there were quite a few of those about then. Todd seems to think it was a cover story. Perhaps he's right. Perhaps the security police killed her. Or, well –' She hesitated '– perhaps it was my father. That's what you've come here to find out, isn't it?'

Calder nodded. 'I'm trying to keep an open mind. Someone tried to kill Todd and me, and someone maimed my sister –'

'I heard about that,' Zan said. 'I'm so sorry.'

Calder smiled quickly. 'Someone is trying to prevent Todd

or me finding out what happened to Martha. And yes, your father is a possibility.'

Zan frowned. 'He and I haven't got along for a long time, but even so it's difficult to think of him actually killing her. Or Todd, for that matter.'

'You were living with them when she was murdered. I understand that their marriage was going through a rocky period?'

'That's right, I stayed at Hondehoek for part of that winter, although I had just left for London a couple of days before Martha was murdered. But to answer your question, yes, the atmosphere in the house was terrible. Some of it was to do with Pa's decision to close down the *Cape Daily Mail*. Martha really didn't like that idea. But there was more to it than that. My guess is that one or other of them was having an affair.'

'Really? Which one?'

'I don't know,' Zan said. 'At the time I didn't want to think about it. I wanted to get on with them both. You see I'd grown away from them when I was at university. My politics had become pretty radical, much more radical than theirs, and I suppose I was rebelling. But then my uncle was killed, I knew my relationship with my mother was irreparable, and they were the only family I had. I was worried for their safety if the revolution came and it was violent. I wanted to build bridges.' She paused, bit her lip and looked away from Calder towards the mountain. When she turned back she was blinking. 'I think I succeeded. I was very fond of Martha. She was a wonderful stepmother to me when I was a kid, more of a mother than my real mother – much more, and I pushed her away when I was a teenager. I'm so glad we spent that winter together before she died.'

'I'm sorry to bring this all back,' Calder said softly.

'No, that's all right,' Zan said. 'Someone has to. My father won't. Todd tried and look what happened to him.'

'Was there anyone else who could have had a reason to kill Martha? Anyone who hated her?'

'My mother hated her,' Zan said. 'Understandably, really. She never forgave her for stealing her husband. And she was angry that Pa kept the newspaper business after they got divorced. Her father had staked him the money to buy it.' Zan saw Calder struggling to ask his next question tactfully, and put him out of his misery. 'But I really doubt she did it. If Martha had been found hit over the head with a gin bottle, maybe, but Mom was drunk most of the time. She certainly wouldn't have been capable of killing her herself, and I doubt she was organized enough to arrange it. She's dead now, anyway, so you can't ask her.'

'I'm sorry.'

Zan shook her head. 'I'm glad in a way. She was getting worse and worse.' She ran her hand quickly through her short blonde hair as if trying to brush the memory of her mother away. 'But to go back to your original question, perhaps it was the security police. Although Martha was always against the apartheid regime, she never did anything political about it. I think she didn't want to embarrass Pa. But towards the end she asked me a couple of times whether she could join me on a protest march. She went to a huge funeral for our maid's son, which at that time was a political statement. And she was a good friend of Libby Wiseman.'

'Libby Wiseman?'

'They were on the board of a charity together, a literacy project in Guguletu. Libby Wiseman was a lecturer at the University of Cape Town and quite a radical. She was prob-ably a member of the Communist Party at that time, she

257

certainly was a member of the Party later on. She became a junior minister in the first post-apartheid government. Martha might have done some things with her, things that the security police disapproved of. In fact I remember a couple of policemen came round to warn her to be careful who she spoke to.'

'Do you know where I could find Libby Wiseman now?'

'No idea,' Zan said. 'But she was relatively well known a few years ago. It should be possible to track her down.'

'Did you ever get in trouble with the security police yourself?' Calder asked.

Zan smiled. 'A few nights in jail when I was a student in Jo'burg. But I didn't get involved in anything heavy until I went to London.'

'And Mozambique?'

'And Mozambique.'

Calder wondered what doing something 'heavy' in Mozambique entailed. Zan looked as if she could handle herself, even now. 'Do you still swim?'

'Yes, I do. What made you ask that?'

'Someone told me you used to be an Olympic-class swimmer. And you look in good condition.'

'I swim. I run. I do the triathlon. In fact I'm training for the Comrades Marathon in Durban in a couple of weeks. Eighty-nine k's.'

'Jesus! And you run all that way?'

Zan smiled. 'Oh, yes. I'm getting older, but I'm not slowing much, especially over long distances.'

Calder, who usually prided himself on his physical fitness, felt like a slug as he mopped up the last of the springbok gravy. The waitress took away their empty plates and brought some coffee. The sun shone brightly on the multitude thronging the wharves. The darkness of apartheid seemed a long way off, although Calder still couldn't see many black faces in the crowd.

'No one seems to know why Martha chose to go to Kupugani that weekend,' he said.

'You're right, it is a bit of a mystery. I remember her telling me she was going. She said she just wanted to get away. We used to stay at a game reserve as a family when I was a kid, a place called Mala Mala. It's quite upscale, quite famous, I know Martha enjoyed going there. But I'd never even heard of Kupugani before. Perhaps a friend recommended it.'

'Just another one of those things that doesn't quite make sense,' Calder said. 'I know Todd asked you this, but did you ever see Martha writing anything in a diary?'

'No, I didn't. Nor have I ever heard of the Laagerbond.'

'Oh, well. Is there anyone you know who I could ask about it?'

Zan fiddled with the row of rings in her ear. 'Actually, I might be able to help you there,' she said. 'The National Intelligence Agency merged the old regime's security forces with those of the ANC. I've never quite figured out how they managed that. A lot of documents relating to the security forces' activities were destroyed in the early nineties, literally tonnes of them. I don't know whether anything about the Laagerbond will have survived. Or the ANC might have some information in their files. I can ask a couple of comrades from my days in the struggle who work there now.'

'Let me know what they say.' Calder scribbled down his mobile phone number. 'If you can get in touch with them in the next few days while I'm still here, that will be a great help.'

'I'll see what I can do.' Zan looked at her watch. 'I must

go. I've got to pick up the kids from school. It's going to be difficult, you know. To find out what happened. There were many crimes committed in those days, and this country has become expert at forgetting them. It's had to to survive.'

'I know. But I'm quite determined. This isn't about history for me, it's about today, about what happened to Todd and my sister. Whoever it was who tried to kill them, I'll find them.'

'I believe you will,' said Zan.

Sandy brushed the breadcrumbs off the documents in front of her. It was three o'clock and she had just finished what was supposed to be lunch, although her body clock was so messed up she didn't really know what meal it was. She had arrived at Heathrow on an overnight flight from New York that morning and she was due to return the following evening after a big meeting with the client.

The clause in front of her blurred as she read it for the third time. It was one of those badly drafted legal sentences where the distance between subject, verb and object could be measured in vertical inches on the page. But the reason she couldn't concentrate was the thought of the meeting she was due to have with the senior London partner that afternoon.

She still wasn't absolutely sure what to do: whether to try to withdraw her request for a transfer to the London office, or whether to leave it and hope that it would be turned down anyway. She was quite sure that there was no future in her relationship with Alex, and she couldn't believe that she had been so stupid as to think that there might have been. But she would look a total loser if she told the partner that, sorry, she had made a mistake, she didn't have an English boyfriend after all. How unprofessional was that?

The anger welled up again. Damn him!

The phone rang a couple of desks away, and a moment later a secretary called over to her. 'There's a Mrs van Zyl downstairs to see you.'

'Van Zyl? As in Cornelius van Zyl?' The *Times* takeover was all over the business press, and Sandy had been following it with passing interest.

The secretary shrugged.

'OK. Tell her I'll be right down.'

Sandy took her jacket off the back of her chair, went to the bathroom to check herself in the mirror and headed for the lifts. The man at reception nodded towards a pair of slim legs beneath an open copy of *The Times*.

'Mrs van Zyl?' Sandy approached, an expectant smile on her face.

The newspaper was lowered. It took her a moment, but Sandy recognized the dark curly hair, the pale face, the lively eyes.

'You!'

Kim smiled nervously and scrambled to her feet. 'Hello, Sandy.'

Sandy's mouth hung open. 'Are you who I think you are?'

'Probably.'

'Then what the hell are you doing here?'

'I want to talk to you. About Alex.'

'You must be crazy.' Sandy turned on her heel.

'Wait! Please. For Alex's sake.'

Sandy stopped. 'For Alex's sake! And just why exactly would I do anything for Alex's sake?'

'OK, for your sake.'

'What can you have to say that could be of any interest to me?'

'Look, I know you must be angry,' Kim said quickly.

'I know I would be in your situation, but listen to what I have to say and then you can walk off. Please.'

Sandy hesitated. The other woman looked sincere, troubled, honest even. She shrugged. 'There's a Costa Coffee around the corner. Let's go.'

They walked quickly out of Trelawney Stewart's offices and on to the pavement.

'Your secretary in New York said you would be over here for a couple of days,' Kim said. 'When are you going back?'

Sandy resolutely ignored the small talk. They walked in rapid silence to the coffee shop, both ordered skinny lattes and sat down.

'OK,' Sandy said. 'Talk to me.'

'Alex was absolutely devastated after you discovered us the other day.'

Sandy shrugged. She was a tall woman with short wispy blonde hair, high cheekbones and clear blue eyes and she could look cold when she wanted to. She looked very cold.

'I've been a friend of Alex's for a long time, since university, a very good friend, but that's the only time we've ever . . .' Kim hesitated searching for the right euphemism.

'Screwed each other?' Sandy suggested.

'Yeah, well. And it hasn't happened since. I know Alex would like nothing more than to see you again. So I've come to ask you to give him another chance.'

'Did he send you?'

'God, no. He'd be too humiliated. I'm humiliated. But I *am* fond of him and I don't want to be responsible for messing up his life as well as my own. We talked about you; he told me how important you are to him. He thought you weren't interested in him any more, but you must have been to appear at his house so suddenly like that.'

'Perhaps I was,' said Sandy. 'But I'm certainly not now.'

'Please give him a chance. He's in South Africa at the moment, but when he gets back, call him.'

Sandy studied Kim, her face impassive. 'Didn't you say your name was *Mrs* van Zyl?'

'Yes,' Kim said, lowering her eyes.

'Are you related to Cornelius van Zyl?'

'He's my father-in-law.'

'I see. And where was your husband when you and Alex were rolling around in the grass?'

Kim looked down at her coffee and mumbled something.

'Sorry, I didn't catch that.'

Kim raised her head and looked straight at Sandy. 'In hospital,' she said, her voice quavering.

'You're not serious?' Sandy said, unable to keep the contempt from her voice.

Kim tried to hold Sandy's gaze, but her chin wobbled and a tear ran down her cheek. Without a word, she dabbed her eyes with her knuckle, sniffed and blundered for the exit.

Sandy watched her go.

Benton glanced around the small conference table. One of the few good things about being head of the London office of Bloomfield Weiss was that he rated a large desk, leather sofas and chairs, a corner view of Broadgate Circle and his own little conference table. He had managed to manoeuvre Dower into coming up there to make the call, rather than traipsing down to Investment Banking. It wasn't a question of convenience, it was much more important than that; it was a question of status, who was leading the deal. They had bad news to deliver to Cornelius van Zyl, and Dower wanted Benton to do it. Coward. And fool. Benton would become more indispensable to the deal. So now Benton,

Dower and two bag-carriers huddled around the speaker phone.

Benton punched out Cornelius's number in his Madeira Quay office. Since the *Times* deal had become public Cornelius had decamped from his home to the *Herald* offices in Docklands.

'Morning, Cornelius,' Benton began. 'How are you today?'

'I'm fine, Benton.' Cornelius's voice was loud, clear and impatient. 'What's up?'

'I've got Chris Dower here and a couple of his colleagues,' Benton said. 'We've just heard from Gurney Kroheim. Laxton Media have received another bid.'

'Shit,' said Cornelius. 'From Gill?'

'That's right. Eight hundred and seventy-five million. Cash.'

'Shit, shit, shit. I thought you said you didn't think Gill could get access to more funds?'

'It looks like we were wrong,' said Benton.

'Will the Laxton board recommend it?'

'According to Gurney Kroheim, "they are minded to".'

'What the hell does that mean?'

'It means if we are going to come up with a higher offer, we'd better do it now,' said Dower.

'Shit. Can you get over here now?'

'We're on our way,' said Benton.

It was a twenty-minute taxi ride. The four of them were squeezed into the back of the cab. Benton's long legs stuck into the thigh of the more junior bag-carrier on the jump seat.

'Can we raise our offer?' Benton said.

'It's going to be tricky,' said Dower. 'The Capital Markets guys were talking to me yesterday. They're not as sure as they were that they can get the three hundred deal away we were talking about originally. A bigger deal at a higher price would be very difficult.'

'What? I thought you said the junk market was improving?'

'It looked like it was. But we had that Matzin Industries default last week. It was a biggie. It's got people scared. And there's several billion of new deals lining up for the summer. Our guys are not convinced the demand is there from investors.'

'I don't understand you people,' Benton said. 'Two weeks ago you told the client that the market is strong. Now you change your minds. You can't tell a client one thing one day and another the next, especially when he's basing all his plans on what you say.'

'Markets change, Benton,' Dower said. 'You've been around long enough to know that.'

'What changes is you people's willingness to take risk,' Benton said. 'One default and you run scared. Junk-bond issuers go belly up all the time, that's why they pay such a high coupon. There are times when Bloomfield Weiss has just got to stand up and be counted, and this is one of those times.'

'Benton, you know that that's not something for you or me to decide, it's for the Underwriting Committee.'

Benton didn't reply but stared out of the window at the Canary Wharf tower, growing ever taller as they approached Docklands.

This was a problem. Approval from the Underwriting Committee was required before Bloomfield Weiss could write Zyl News another letter committing to a larger bridge loan. The committee included managing directors from sales and trading, as well as some of the firm's most senior executives. They wouldn't approve a bridge loan unless they were confident that the loan would be repaid from the successful launch of a junk-bond issue some time in the next few months. The committee was often willing to take big risks, but if the junk market was looking wobbly perhaps they wouldn't this time.

If Cornelius didn't raise his offer, they would lose the deal, it was as simple as that. Benton couldn't afford that. For several years now as head of the London office he had been away from the sharp end of investment banking, away from the big deals and the big bonuses. He was paid a substantial salary, but the lifestyle he and his family had built up in expatriate London required big bonuses to fuel it. During the last few barren years he had borrowed to pay the bills, but that couldn't go on for ever. He *needed* a big bonus, and a high-profile deal like *The Times* could get him one.

In the past he had succeeded through subtlety and contacts, but as the corporate world became ever more aggressive this had not been enough. The sad truth was that a successful investment banker was one who persuaded his client to pay the highest price. Those were the guys who earned the big fees and the big bonuses. Benton was determined to be one of them. Dower could go screw himself.

The taxi pulled up outside the all-glass building which housed the *Herald*'s offices and the investment bankers were whisked up to the executive floor. In a moment they were in the chairman's office, with its expensive modern American artwork and its views of the Thames, the Millennium Dome and the gleaming architectural melange of the new Docklands.

A harried-looking Edwin was sitting in front of a laptop, surrounded by a mess of papers on the long conference table. Cornelius was pacing.

'Sit down, gentlemen,' he said. But as Benton and his colleagues took their places, he stayed on his feet. 'We have to decide whether to come up with a higher offer. Any sign of the other potential bidders?'

'Nothing,' Dower said. 'We know the *Telegraph* people have been talking to Laxton, but their offer would be certain to be referred to the Competition Commission, and Laxton don't have time to wait for that. The price has become too high for the Germans and the Irish. So it's just us and Gill.'

'I'm not going to lose to that bastard,' Cornelius said.

'I assume there is no way you can get your hands on some more cash?' Dower asked.

Cornelius shook his head. 'No. Nothing significant, at any rate.' He scowled. 'I'm not like some other newspaper proprietors I could name. Everything I've got is already in this bid. There are no secret stashes in Switzerland or the Caribbean.'

'I was not suggesting there were,' Dower stuttered.

'If you weren't, you should have been, right, Benton? I know Edwin thinks the family should have a nest egg ready for a rainy day, don't you, Edwin?' Edwin ignored his father. 'But no, if we pay more, we'll have to borrow the money.'

Benton was just about to speak but Dower got in ahead of him. 'There might be a problem –'

'That's what we thought –' said Benton talking over him.

Cornelius raised his hand to silence them both. 'A problem?' He stared at Dower.

Dower swallowed. 'The junk market is not recovering as strongly as we had hoped. There was a big default last week and investors' confidence has been dented.'

'Wait a minute.' Cornelius bent over the table, leaning his large frame on his hands as he stared at the banker, his jaw thrust forward. 'You gave me your assurance that we would have no trouble raising three hundred million pounds only the other day.'

'I said it would be tight.'

'But you gave me a letter.'

'I know we did,' said Dower. Beads of sweat had suddenly bubbled up on his brow, and around his fleshy neck. He was glistening. 'We committed to fund the offer at eight hundred and fifty million. But we can't commit to higher.'

'The cash flow is very tight at eight fifty,' Edwin said, looking up from his papers. 'Much higher and the whole thing falls apart.'

Cornelius glared at Edwin. Although Edwin and Dower avoided each other's eyes the bond between them was almost palpable. The numbers didn't stack up.

There was silence around the table. Cornelius frowned. He looked at Benton. 'What do you think?'

Benton paused. He had to get this just right. He was glad now he hadn't said anything. It meant he had retained some authority, whereas Dower had blown his. He looked Cornelius straight in the eye. 'At nine hundred million can you make the deal work?'

'There just isn't enough cash flow to service that amount of debt,' Edwin said.

Benton raised his eyebrows at Cornelius.

Cornelius sat down. He perched his half-moon spectacles on his nose, picked up one of Edwin's spreadsheets and studied it. Then he tossed it back on to the table. 'I know you've worked hard at the numbers, Edwin, and I know what they say. Normally I hate to overpay. But sometimes . . . sometimes you have to take a leap of faith. *The Times* is a unique property. With us in charge it will be a great one. It's going to be worth more than a billion in a few years, much more. We took a leap before, with the *Herald*, remember? That worked. I have a feeling,' he glanced at his son, 'no, more than a feeling, a *conviction* that this is another one of those times. So, yes, Benton, I can make the deal work.'

'In that case, so can we.'

'Hold on, Benton,' Dower interrupted. 'We need to chat to some people back at the office about this.'

Benton ignored him and returned Cornelius's stare. 'You have my word.'

Edwin stalked back to his own office and slammed the pile of papers down on his desk. His father was overreaching himself. Sure, he could get his MBA grunts to alter the assumptions about circulation, advertising rates, cost cutting: 1 per cent here, 2 per cent there, the numbers could be made to add up on paper, but not in real life. In real life the deal wouldn't work unless Cornelius performed some kind of miracle once he took over the paper. This was possible, Edwin admitted to himself. But it was probable that they just wouldn't generate enough cash from the business to service their interest payments, and that would bring down not just *The Times*, but the whole of Zyl News.

If his sister-in-law and Alex bloody Calder didn't tear the whole thing down anyway.

Edwin didn't want that. He believed that in the last few years he had made himself indispensable to the company. Cornelius couldn't carry on much longer; although he still seemed to have limitless energy, he *was* seventy-two. Todd had practically taken himself out of the picture when he decided to become a teacher, he was certainly out of it now. Zyl News would be Edwin's in a very few years' time.

Unless Cornelius bankrupted it through one last mis-judged leap.

The phone rang. It was Jeff Hull, his pet journalist.

'How was our superintendent friend yesterday?' Hull asked.

'Very polite, very respectful,' Edwin said. 'You could tell his sidekick was itching to ask difficult questions, but he wouldn't let her.'

'What did I tell you? There's nothing that scares a policeman more than a whiff of a paedophile scandal.'

Edwin smiled. 'You were right. I'll get your bonus paid into your account tomorrow.'

'You might want to increase the figure.'

'What do you mean?'

'I've got something else for you, Edwin.' Hull sounded excited. 'I've been doing a little extra snooping up here in Norfolk and I've discovered your brother has a little secret.'

'Go on.'

'Did you know he had a squeeze on the side?'

'No. Talk to me.'

'Apparently a young, very attractive American woman named Donna was hanging around the hospital for a few days. She would creep in to see Todd when his wife wasn't there. She said she was a colleague from work, but the nurses had their doubts that that was all she was, especially when his wife discovered her and went ballistic. They didn't see her around after that.

'I checked with Todd's school in New Hampshire. A Miss Donna Snyder is a member of the faculty there. Teaches art, apparently.'

'Now that's very interesting.'

'I thought you'd like it. I don't know how you want to use that information, but I'm sure you can figure out a way. In the meantime, you can rely on my discretion.'

'Well done, Jeff.'

'No problem. But put a little extra on that bonus, won't you?'

'I will,' said Edwin. 'Good work.'

As he put down the phone, he went through the angles. This kind of knowledge provided leverage. It was a question of where exactly to apply the lever. Edwin knew. He summoned a couple of his strategy grunts into his office to get them to rework the forecasts, and then left the building to grab a taxi across town.

He found Kim where he expected, at Todd's bedside. In the gleaming private hospital to which he had been transferred, Todd had his own room with television, armchairs, flowers and nice curtains, although the bits and pieces plugged into him looked similar to the equipment in the Norfolk hospital. He was asleep. Kim was sitting in a chair next to him, staring into space through reddened eyes.

She looked up as he came in and gave him the barest trace of a polite smile.

'How is he?' Edwin asked.

'Better,' Kim said in little more than a mumble. 'A lot more lucid. But he sleeps a lot.'

'Good. Can we have a word?'

Kim indicated another armchair.

'No, not here.'

'He's asleep,' Kim said.

'I think it would be better to talk somewhere else.'

Kim shrugged and followed him out of the room. They found an unoccupied waiting area down the corridor.

'I know about Donna Snyder,' Edwin said.

Kim shook her head, more resigned than angry. 'Why am I not surprised?'

'I understand that Alex Calder is in South Africa rooting around into Martha's death.'

'So?'

'I don't think that's a good idea.'

'Why not?'

'Zyl News is in a delicate position at the moment. Calder might make the position even more delicate. It wouldn't take much to tip everything over.'

Anger flickered in Kim's eyes. 'What are you afraid he might find?'

'I have nothing to hide,' said Edwin. 'But the timing is not good. I think you should ask him to return to England.'

'I will do no such thing. Someone nearly killed Todd, someone nearly killed Alex's sister. The answer as to who it is lies in South Africa.'

'Do the police know about Donna Snyder?'

'I don't think so. Why would they be interested?'

'Oh, I think they'd be very interested. You see they asked my father and me all kinds of questions about you and how much you stood to inherit if Todd died.'

'They asked me those questions too,' Kim said. 'But it was just routine. I don't think they seriously suspected *me*.'

'Not then,' said Edwin. 'Because then they didn't know that your husband was cheating on you.'

'That wouldn't make any difference,' said Kim with contempt.

'Oh, I think it might,' said Edwin. Then he had a brain-wave. 'And what about you and Alex Calder?'

'What about us?' Kim said, but her face flushed bright red.

Edwin smiled. 'Tut-tut. While your husband was in hospital, too.'

'There is nothing going on between me and Alex Calder,' Kim said, the anger rising in her voice.

Edwin raised his hands. 'All I'm suggesting is that you get hold of Calder and tell him to come home.'

'Piss off,' Kim said.

'It's the easy answer,' Edwin said. 'It will avoid all kinds of unpleasantness.'

'I said, piss off!' Kim was nearly shouting now. 'Get out of here. I'm going back to Todd.'

She turned on her heel and began walking down the long corridor away from her brother-in-law. 'I'll give you a day to think about it!' Edwin called after her. 'One day!'

Kim entered Todd's room and slammed the door behind her.

22

Calder decided to walk from his hotel near the Victoria and Alfred Waterfront to the cigar bar on Long Street where he was due to meet George Field. It was early evening, and getting dark. Away from the Waterfront the city itself was a mixture of totally different architectural styles: towering modern office blocks, elegant British colonial, concrete government brutalist, pristine white Cape Dutch, colourful African and shabby urban dilapidated. The people too were of many different shapes and colours, whites now a definite minority. And above it all was the mountain, always in sight, its summit currently covered by a thin cloth of cloud.

The bar was dark: dark wood, dark leather and rows of whisky and brandy bottles glimmering behind the green-waistcoated barman. It did indeed smell of cigars, a group of businessmen were puffing away at huge samples near the door, but there was also the sweeter aroma of pipe smoke. This came from a man in his sixties with a shock of wiry iron-grey hair and thick white eyebrows, wearing a corduroy jacket that looked too shabby for the establishment. He was drawing contentedly on a briar, a glass of whisky in front of him. When he saw Calder, he pulled himself to his feet and held out his hand.

'Alex? George Field. You found the place all right? I rather like it here, especially at this time of the evening. It's quiet, you know, a good place for a chat. And there are so few places these days where one can actually smoke.'

'Thanks for seeing me at such short notice,' Calder said.

He had tracked down George Field on the internet before he left England, and when he had telephoned him the former newspaper editor had seemed suspicious.

'Not at all. I spoke to Todd van Zyl's wife and to his sister. Both of them urged me to talk to you. I haven't seen Todd or Caroline since they were kids. I remember Caroline especially. Funny to hear her now, a grown woman with an American accent.'

'But you didn't speak to Cornelius?'

'No,' George said, knitting those bushy eyebrows together. 'I haven't spoken to Cornelius for a long time. Certainly not since he reinvented himself as an American newspaper tycoon. But I liked Martha. I owe it to her children to talk to you.'

'Thank you,' Calder said. He interrupted himself to order a whisky from the hovering waiter. No cigar, though. 'I know you and she were friends. I wonder if you could tell me what happened around the time she died.'

'We *were* friends, especially at that time. I was editor of the *Cape Daily Mail*. That winter Cornelius decided to close us down and sell off his other South African papers. I was furious, as you can imagine, and so was Martha. I know she tried to change Cornelius's mind, but she failed.'

'There was a lot of tension between the two of them, wasn't there?'

'Yes, at least at that stage. From what I could tell they had had a pretty good marriage until about a year before Martha died. She was ten years younger than him, but she was much more than a blonde trophy wife. In fact, she didn't really do the trophy-wife thing very well.' George chuckled to himself. 'That's one of the reasons I liked her. Then it all fell apart. Part of it was the row about the *Mail*, but there were other reasons.'

'Such as?'

George sucked at his pipe, his eyes assessing Calder. 'Such as Cornelius's mistress.'

'Mistress?'

'Mistress, lover, call it what you will. A young woman named Beatrice Pienaar. Stunningly beautiful, and intelligent. She was a journalism graduate and the story was she wanted a few months' work experience at Zyl News.'

'The story?'

'She was a spy. I had a strong suspicion of it at the time, but later, in the late 1990s, her name came out during testimony to the Truth and Reconciliation Commission. Oh, she wasn't involved in any violence or torture or anything, but she was working for the security police. She even had a rank: lieutenant. The security police recruited a number of spies among students, put them through liberal universities and encouraged them to work for the newspapers or join radical movements. Some of the names have become public: Joy Harnden, Craig Williamson, Beatrice Pienaar; some we will never hear about.'

'Did Cornelius know?'

'I told him of my suspicions, but he said I was being ridiculous. I also told Martha.'

'Did she know about the affair?'

'She strongly suspected something.'

'What about Martha's death? What do you think happened to her? Do you believe she was killed by ANC guerrillas?'

'No, I'm sure she wasn't. That was a classic security-police cover story.'

'Did you try to find out what really happened? You are a journalist, after all.'

'I never got the chance. The day after Martha was murdered, I was arrested.'

'What for?'

'I never found out.' He smiled wryly. 'In those days you often didn't know why you were arrested. The police were allowed to lock you up for ninety days without charging you. While I was in jail the paper was closed down and Cornelius left the country for America. At the time I assumed that I was locked up to prevent me from finding a rescuer for the *Mail*. But perhaps it had something to do with stopping me asking awkward questions about Martha's death.'

'Were you able to find out anything when you were let out?'

'I didn't bother,' George said, looking uncomfortable. 'I had become disillusioned with being a journalist in South Africa. I decided I could do more good reporting on the country from abroad. So I moved to London and became the South Africa correspondent for a newspaper there. I never did dig into Martha's death. And neither did her husband.'

'Does that surprise you?'

'Yes, frankly,' George said. 'When the TRC was set up I expected Cornelius to ask for Martha's death to be investigated, but he didn't. It would have been a high-profile case. They might well have got to the bottom of it.'

'Cornelius says it's because the case would have been so prominent that he didn't want to stir things up again.'

George shrugged.

'Did Martha mention the Laagerbond to you before she died?'

'Yes, as a matter of fact she did. It was the first time I'd heard the name.'

Calder felt his heartbeat quicken. He was getting somewhere.

'It was the week before she died. She was quite agitated by then, about the *Mail* and about Cornelius. But we had lunch in Greenmarket Square, I can still remember it. She started off by asking me about Muldergate.'

'Muldergate?'

'It was a big scandal here in 1978. You've never heard of it?'

Calder shook his head.

'Too young,' George said. 'It was a big deal. It destroyed the career of Connie Mulder, who had been a shoo-in to succeed Vorster as prime minister, and left the door open for P. W. Botha to take over.'

'What happened?'

'A man called Eschel Rhoodie at the Department of Information diverted lots of government funds to set up newspapers in this country and to acquire media abroad. The idea was to influence the way South Africa was perceived at home and abroad, to put across the government's point of view. They bought a couple of magazines in Europe and tried to buy the *Washington Star*. The money was diverted illegally and the press found out. The *Mail* helped break the story. Connie Mulder, who was then Minister of the Interior, Nico Diederichs the Finance Minister and General van den Bergh, the head of the secret service, were behind the whole thing. Vorster was forced to resign, and P. W. Botha beat Connie Mulder in a leadership election to succeed him. The irony is that during the 1980s Botha diverted much larger sums into a secret nuclear and chemical weapons buying programme. But at the time of the scandal, he seemed like a relative liberal. Even I was fooled for a couple of years.

'Martha knew in general terms what had happened, but she had all kinds of detailed questions about the affair. She was clearly excited about something, and what I was telling her was just making her more excited. Then she asked me if I had heard of the Laagerbond. I told her I hadn't. I asked her what she was up to, and she said she would tell me, possibly very soon. She said it was something big, something I would want to write about. She said she could trust me to get the story out, however difficult it was.'

'You mentioned that that was the first you heard of the Laagerbond. You heard more later?'

'Yes. Not much, just rumours. You know about the Broederbond?'

'Only a little. Tell me.'

'The Broederbond is a secret society set up after the First World War to further the cause of Afrikaner culture in South Africa. Of course, when it was founded the main threat was from the white English-speaking South Africans. But it was the Broederbond that developed the concept of apartheid; all the important members of government were in it and by the 1980s there were at least 10,000 members. It was the Afrikaner establishment. It became a kind of government think-tank; most of the policies of the National Party were dreamed up by Broederbond committees.

'Now, the rumour is that the Laagerbond is some kind of ultra-secret cell within the Broederbond itself. It has a limited membership and it has power. Power over what, no one knows. Conspiracy theorists love it, but no one has been able to turn up any hard evidence. No one is even sure who any of the members are, although there seems to be some agreement on the founder.'

'Who was that?'

'Dr Nico Diederichs. He was Minister of Finance in the seventies and then state president. He was an important *Broederbonder* who studied in Nazi Germany in the thirties. He died in 1977 but apparently the Laagerbond still exists.

A friend of mine tried to write an article on it a couple of years ago, but ran into a brick wall at every turn.'

'Any idea what the purpose of the organization is?'

'None.'

'I read a reference to it from the Truth and Reconciliation Commission records, in which it mentioned that a Colonel Retief was a member.'

'Colonel Retief? That wouldn't surprise me. He was one of South Africa's spymasters during the seventies and eighties. He was probably involved in recruiting Beatrice Pienaar. A useful man to have as a member.'

'What about the Broederbond? Does that still exist?'

'After a fashion.' George smiled. 'It's changed its name to the Afrikanerbond. It's not secret any more, it even has its own website, and it seems pretty harmless. Its aims are to promote Christianity and the Afrikaner way of life.'

'Just before she died, Martha wrote a letter to her mother saying that she had written some notes in a page in her diary marked "Laagerbond". Caroline saw her copying something down from a briefcase belonging to one of two men who visited Cornelius at their house. One of these men was called Andries Visser. He had a limp. Do you know him?'

George sucked on his pipe for a moment. 'There was an Andries Visser who was a senior bureaucrat in the Ministry of Finance. He had a limp.' The eyebrows waggled. 'Actually, he was a protégé of Nico Diederichs, if I'm not mistaken. He was always influential, but kept himself in the background. He's almost certainly retired now, I haven't heard anything about him for years.'

'So he could be a member of the Laagerbond?'

'He could well be,' said George. 'And the other man?'

'Caroline couldn't remember his name. She said he had a

white beard and sticking-out ears. That's not much of a description to go on, I know.'

'It's enough,' said George. 'That will be Professor Daniel Havenga. He was a friend of Cornelius, and Martha for that matter. A professor of journalism at Stellenbosch University. And the man who recommended Beatrice Pienaar to Cornelius.'

'Another member of the Laagerbond?'

'Who knows?' said George. 'You say they were visiting Cornelius at Hondehoek?'

'Yes. Caroline says that her mother was agitated by what she had read, and scared. Martha's letter mentioned a page in her diary marked "Operation Drommedaris". Any idea what that might be?'

George shook his head.

They sat in silence, both of them assessing the new information, making connections. Calder glanced at the older man. 'Were they planning another Muldergate, do you think?'

George drew on his pipe, mulling the idea over. 'It's certainly possible,' he said eventually. 'Visser could have organized the finance. Havenga was an expert on the media. The Laagerbond was set up by Diederichs who was intimately involved in the first scandal. He was long dead by 1988, but his protégé could have carried on his work.'

'Remember Cornelius was in the middle of trying to take over the *Herald* in London.'

'And he was making all those US acquisitions.'

'But if Muldergate was such a disaster, why would the Laagerbond risk another scandal ten years on?' Calder asked.

'South Africa had changed by 1988,' George said. 'Things were more repressive: after three years of a state of emergency the government had much more of a grip of things. During the original scandal Eschel Rhoodie behaved like an international playboy: he charged apartments and boondoggles to the Seychelles to his expenses, and it was that as much as anything else that brought him down. Visser and Havenga could have learned from his mistakes. If the Laagerbond was set up as a secret cell within the establishment but not actually within government, it might be very difficult to find any trace of its actions. When Rhoodie eventually talked, he hinted that there was much more going on that he couldn't disclose. Perhaps there was.'

'But wouldn't the ANC have found out about this when they came to power in 1994?' Calder asked.

'Not necessarily,' George said. 'The security establishment were diligent in destroying evidence. Some of it came out during the TRC a few years later; a whole new government department that no one had heard about called the Directorate of Covert Collection was discovered then, for example. But that was just a glimpse; a lot more is still hidden. There were rumours that Diederichs stashed significant sums from the sale of gold bullion in Switzerland. By the 1980s the defence budget had ballooned to many billions of dollars. Under the Defence Special Account Act this was protected from public scrutiny, so it was the source of funds for the purchase of weapons secrets from the likes of Israel and Pakistan. Why not for buying up foreign media?'

'And the Laagerbond lives on?'

'That's the beauty of it,' George said. 'By then many Afrikaner nationalists realized that apartheid's days were numbered. But because it's not part of the government the Laagerbond can carry on supporting the Afrikaner cause after the fall of the regime.' George puffed hard at his pipe.

He frowned. 'I can see why in many ways Cornelius would be the perfect person for these people to back. He's really South Africa's only international media entrepreneur. But I can't see why they would think he would listen to them. He was always a major thorn in the side of apartheid, not a supporter.'

'I get the impression he was re-evaluating his views on South Africa,' Calder said. 'And if the Beatrice Pienaar woman was planted by the Laagerbond, perhaps she might have persuaded him to go along with them.'

George shook his head. 'You're right, he was changing. But although I didn't like the man he was becoming, I still can't believe he would take their money. Presumably they wanted him to toe the apartheid line once he had bought all these newspapers. I haven't seen much evidence of that.'

'How do his papers cover South Africa?' Calder said.

'Objectively, from what I can tell. I haven't noticed any bias. I don't think he takes much of a personal interest in South African coverage. If he was funded by the Laagerbond, you would expect his papers to be full of anti-ANC propaganda.'

'Did you know that Cornelius is bidding for *The Times* now?' Calder said. 'I wonder if the Laagerbond is still funding him?'

'That would be a real prize for them.'

'And an expensive one,' Calder said. 'I remember reading the price tag was over eight hundred million pounds.'

'Do you know where he gets his funding from?' George asked.

'Historically he's borrowed most of it,' Calder said. 'But I can check. Could you find out where Visser and Havenga are now?'

'No problem, that will be easy.'

'And a woman called Libby Wiseman?'

'Libby Wiseman? What does she have to do with this?'

'Apparently she was on a charity board with Martha. They were friends.'

'I know Libby Wiseman vaguely,' George said. 'She was in government for a brief time, probably less than a year. I think she lives in Johannesburg now, it should be easy to track her down. I'll give you a call at your hotel when I've got the information.'

Calder finished his whisky, preparing to leave. 'Are you still working?' he asked.

'Oh, I still write the odd piece now and then. And I'm helping out on the *Rainbow*. It's a black-owned paper, very well respected, but quite critical of the government. The ANC have achieved a lot over the last ten years, but they now have a monopoly on power. Someone needs to point out the dangers of a one-party state, and that's what the *Rainbow* does. But it's always short of funds. *Plus ça change.*'

Calder liked George Field: he was an intelligent man with a good understanding of South Africa. Calder decided to take a step into the minefield that was racial politics. 'It can't have been easy being a white South African.'

'A lot easier than being a black one,' George said.

'You know what I mean. The apartheid regime was obviously evil, but what could you do about it? Voting for the opposition didn't do much good since the National Party always had a majority. You and Cornelius tried to protest peacefully, but that didn't work, you were both forced out of the country. Cornelius's daughter, Zan, got involved in the armed struggle, but a violent revolution doesn't seem the right answer either.'

'Most white South Africans looked the other way,' George said. 'They say now that they had no idea what was going on in their country, but that's crap. We told them in our newspaper, as did others. OK, sometimes we weren't allowed to report the whole truth, but if you read the *Cape Daily Mail* it was easy to work out what was going on. People refused to see it: it was like a mass denial.'

'Many of the people who perpetrated these crimes have got away with it, haven't they?'

'That's true,' George said. 'A lot of them are still in positions of power, even now. Or they've retired on good pensions. This country has all sorts of problems: unemployment, violence, AIDS, a horrific past. But when South Africans argue about whether things are going well or badly, whether the glass is half full or half empty, they forget the most important thing. The glass wasn't smashed..It took an extraordinary effort by our leaders, not just Nelson Mandela and Archbishop Tutu, but also F. W. de Klerk and his government, to forgive and forget and to try and build a new free country, however flawed it might be.'

'Is Martha's death part of that past? To be forgiven and forgotten?'

'Perhaps not,' George said. 'But digging into the past in South Africa is dangerous. That you have already seen.'

'Are you suggesting I leave it?' Calder asked.

George smiled. 'No. Just be careful.'

As soon as Calder arrived back at his hotel, he called Tarek al-Seesi in London. He was fortunate to catch him in his office, working late. He asked him to check with the Bloomfield Weiss analyst who covered the media industry to see if there were any unexplained holes in where Cornelius got his funds from. Tarek was happy to help.

Then he called Kim on her mobile. To his surprise, she was having supper with his father in Anne's house. Todd was making very good progress, already he seemed much less confused than he had when he had first woken up. After Todd had been transferred down to the private hospital in London, Kim had decided to stay with Dr Calder and the children in Highgate rather than with her father-in-law. Calder told Kim about his discussions with Zan and George Field, and the theory that the Laagerbond might have financed Cornelius in his attempts to buy foreign newspapers. Kim was shocked at first, but she liked the theory. It was clear that her mistrust of Cornelius was growing by the day.

'Will you be able to discuss this with Todd, do you think?' Calder asked. 'If Zyl News was financed by mysterious South Africans, Todd might know something. He worked for the company for several years, didn't he?'

'He did, although from what he has told me Zyl News was funded entirely by bank loans and junk bonds,' said Kim. 'Todd's still pretty groggy. We've talked about the plane crash, but not about who might have caused it. I'll see how he is tomorrow.'

'I'll leave it up to you to decide.'

'Cornelius and Edwin have been to the hospital. Cornelius has spent quite a lot of time with Todd, but I keep out of the way whenever he's around. And as for Edwin . . .'

'Yes?'

Kim whispered, presumably so that Calder's father wouldn't hear. 'He tried to threaten me. He's found out about Donna Snyder and he said he'd tell the police. He seems to think they would view me as a suspect. He wants me to get you to come home. I told him to piss off.'

'Good for you. Call his bluff, the police won't care. They'd never take you seriously as a suspect. Speaking of which, how are they getting on?'

'Pathetically. I've spoken to Inspector Banks and she says they are not pursuing Cornelius as a line of inquiry. It sounded to me as if she wasn't very happy with that, but I couldn't get her to admit it. Oh, and the South African police told her that the records relating to Martha's murder have been mislaid.'

'Destroyed, they mean,' Calder said. 'I can't believe that the police are leaving Cornelius alone. At least I'm making some progress here.'

'Thanks. Keep trying. Do you want to have a word with your father? He's right here.'

'Yes, please.'

He waited a moment and then he heard his father's Borders' brogue. 'Alex? So you're getting somewhere then?'

'I think so. Kim will tell you.'

'Good. I'm relying on you.'

Calder smiled. 'How's Anne?'

'Stable. She'll keep the other leg.'

'Is she conscious?'

'Yes. I spoke to her this afternoon on the telephone.'

'Did she say anything about me?'

'I think William has been getting her agitated. I've told him he really shouldn't, but it's difficult to be firm with him from up here.'

'So she did say something about me.'

'Don't worry about it, Alex. Just concentrate on finding the bastard who did this.'

'I will. How are Phoebe and Robbie?'

'They went to school today. I think it's best to get them into some kind of familiar routine. Robbie is very quiet indeed, but he did have a chance to speak to his mother on the phone.'

'Will they get over it?' Calder asked.

'Aye, they will,' said Dr Calder. 'Especially once we get Annie down here.'

'I hope you're right.'

'Alex, before you go . . .' Calder could hear footsteps as his father walked somewhere more private. Trouble.

'Yes?'

'When I was staying with you in the cottage in Norfolk, I couldn't help noticing some statements from an outfit called Spreadfinex.'

'Couldn't help noticing? You were snooping!'

'You'd know about that.' His father was referring to the year before when Calder had discovered bookmakers' statements amongst the doctor's papers.

'Yes, well. It's a kind of stockbroker. It's to do with my investments.'

'It's a spread-betting firm.'

'That's just an easy way of buying and selling currencies or shares,' Calder said.

'It's gambling.'

'I said, it's just a way of investing,' Calder protested. 'Just drop it, will you? And don't go through my stuff.'

'Alex,' his father said. 'I'm glad you persuaded me to go to Gamblers Anonymous last year. One of the first things they teach you is to recognize you've got a problem.'

Sitting alone in his hotel room in Cape Town, the anger welled up inside Calder. He opened his mouth to swear at his father, but put down the hotel phone instead. The idea that he had a gambling problem was absurd. Typical of his father to somehow ascribe his own flaws to his son.

Now in a foul mood, Calder stalked down to the hotel bar in search of more whisky.

*

The light from two candles flickered feebly in the vast Hall of Heroes, illuminating the gaunt face of Andries Visser and barely picking out the silhouette of Paul Strydom, the latest candidate for induction to the Laagerbond. They were in the heart of the Voortrekker Monument, a massive granite structure squatting on the brow of a wooded hill overlooking Pretoria. The monument had been built in 1938 in Nazi-Gothic style to commemorate the Great Trek of the Boers a hundred years before. Outside was the Laager wall, a stone circle of sixty-four ox carts, and reliefs of black wildebeest symbolizing the Zulu enemy. A frieze of twenty-seven scenes from the Great Trek itself stretched around the inside wall of the building, and right in the centre was a cenotaph, arranged so that at noon on 16 December, the day of the Battle of Blood River, the sun would shine down from a window in the ceiling high above directly on to the inscription 'Ons vir jou Suid Afrika', the last line of the old national anthem 'Die Stem van Suid-Afrika'.

Visser sang the first line of that hymn now, his voice weak and hoarse. The refrain was quickly taken up by the twenty-one men standing in the deep shadows behind the candidate. It was two o'clock in the morning, and the men had gathered in the utmost secrecy, the usual combination of blackmail, bribery and threats ensuring that they would not be disturbed. The Laagerbond's ceremony followed closely the pattern of the Broederbond induction of the old days.When the last verse had been sung, Visser coughed and began in little more than a whisper. 'Paul Gerrit Strydom, your fellow Afrikaners, who are members of the Laagerbond, have after careful consideration, decided to invite you to become a member of this organization.'

He continued, following the prescribed order of ceremony, which revealed steadily more of the nature and aims of the Laagerbond to the candidate, requiring him at each step to accept what he had heard. Strydom stood straight and tall, answering a clear 'Yes' to each question as it was put to him. Most candidates had little knowledge of the identities of the other members of the Laagerbond until the end of the ceremony, but Visser assumed that Strydom, who was number three in the National Intelligence Agency, would have a better idea than most.

His voice nearly failing, Visser eventually came to the climax of the ceremony.

'In the presence of your brothers gathered here as witnesses I accept your promise of faith and declare you a member of the Laagerbond. Be strong in faith if the struggle becomes onerous. Be strong in the love of your nation. Be strong in the service of your nation. Hearty congratulations and welcome.'

With that he shook Strydom's hand, and the other members of the Laagerbond stepped forward out of the darkness to do likewise, one at a time.

More candles were lit. An old general of at least eighty-five approached Visser. 'I hope you know what you are doing with Operation Drommedaris, Andries,' he said gruffly.

'It will be a wise investment, you'll see,' said Visser.

'Humph. I was told *The Times* will cost ten billion rand.'

'At least that,' said Visser.

'Ten billion rand will buy a lot of firepower,' the general said.

'It's political power we want, not guns,' said Visser. 'And I can assure you the money will buy us power.'

The general shuffled off. There were a number of members of the Laagerbond who just didn't understand, Visser reflected. Fortunately they were getting older and dying off. The Laagerbond *was* powerful. It hadn't needed guns to achieve that power. It had money and knowledge. It used manipulation to get its way rather than brute force. Operation Drommedaris influenced public opinion at home and abroad. Dirk du Toit and his father had multiplied the original billions supplied by Nico Diederichs through inspired investments. Some of this money could be used to bribe. If that didn't work, Freddie Steenkamp and now Paul Strydom could use their extensive intelligence files on all of South Africa's important politicians and bureaucrats, both black and white, to persuade and extort. Everyone of any importance in South Africa had a past, and in that past they had done things they were ashamed of. The Laagerbond knew those things. And if all else failed there was Anton van Vuuren, the grey-haired, bespectacled professor of physics who was at that moment talking earnestly to Daniel Havenga, and the sizeable stash of weapons-grade uranium buried deep in a disused diamond mine near Kimberley.

Visser smiled to himself. Under his stewardship as chairman of the Laagerbond, the Afrikaner nation had been safe.

Then he saw Kobus Moolman, and frowned. He moved over to the former policeman. 'I heard that Alex Calder is in South Africa?'

Moolman raised his eyebrows. 'I'm surprised. He obviously doesn't scare easily.'

Visser's frown deepened. 'You seem to have lost your touch.'

Moolman smiled confidently. He wasn't about to be intimidated by a former civil servant, even if he was chairman of the Laagerbond. 'Don't worry, Andries. Now he's on my home territory I won't let him cause trouble.'

'I'm glad to hear it,' said Visser. 'Because if this van Zyl business gets out of hand it could destroy everything.'

'We'll have him on a plane back out of the country in a

couple of days,' said Moolman. He grinned. 'In a coffin if necessary.' Then he moved off to talk to the new initiate.

Visser coughed, the pain wracking his chest and shoulder. He would be lucky if he lived long enough to attend another one of these ceremonies. He surveyed the frieze around the walls of the monument. That tiny group of brave men and women clinging to life and freedom on the edge of such a vast continent. He remembered how when he had studied history at the University of the Orange Free State he had read extracts from *The Times* castigating the ignorant Boer farmers. He smiled again. Soon that mighty mouthpiece of British colonial rule would be under the control of those ignorant Boers. That was a day he was looking forward to.

The next morning George Field called Calder at his hotel with the addresses of Daniel Havenga, Andries Visser and Libby Wiseman. Since Professor Havenga lived in Stellenbosch, less than an hour's drive from Cape Town, Calder decided to start there. But first he wanted to see Hondehoek, Martha's house.

He drove out of the city past Mitchell's Plain and the teeming township of Guguletu towards the Hottentots Holland mountains. His head throbbed vaguely from the whisky he had drunk the night before. He was still angry, angry with his father for accusing him of gambling, angry with his sister for blaming him for what happened to her, angry with Edwin for threatening Kim, and above all angry with himself. He had made mistakes over the last few weeks, but he was going to atone for them. He was sure that he had made real progress with George. There was more to be done, but the anger made him more determined to do it.

He left the highway and soon he was in wine country: rolling hills and acre upon acre of vines, russet and yellow.

Many of these were watched over by low white farmhouses whose central gables proclaimed their Dutch ancestry. He skirted the town of Stellenbosch and followed a winding road up into a valley. The valley floor was lush: oaks, vines, pasture, a river, but on either side rocky mountain crags rose up into black clouds. It had just been raining, water dripped from the trees and glistened on the vines.

He rounded a corner and came to two white gateposts, one of which bore the name Hondehoek. The other had the usual series of badges threatening armed response and vicious dogs. He drove up the driveway, bordered by golden-leaved oak trees, to the farmhouse, proudly bearing the figures 1815 on the gable. In front of it was the garden: moist, luxuriant, mysterious.

He rang the bell. The door was answered by a tall grey-haired man, dressed neatly in Ralph Lauren shirt and chinos. Calder explained that he was a friend of the van Zyl family, and the man smiled broadly and offered to show him round. It turned out that he was a German who had bought the house and land from Cornelius in 1989. The house and garden were in immaculate condition, and the German said he had taken back the management of the vineyards on the estate.

Calder asked about Doris and Finneas. The German knew them, and had kept them on when he had taken over the property. Finneas had left a few years later, weakened by AIDS, and was now dead. Doris too had died, of a stroke three years before. The new owner remembered Martha's desk. It had been left behind by Cornelius, but he had sold it when he had moved in. As far as he could remember the desk had been empty; if there were any papers in it, they would have been thrown away. No diary.

As they wandered round the garden, Calder imagined

Martha van Zyl working there. It was a beautiful place. Although only a few miles from Stellenbosch, the house seemed much more remote, wrapped in the mists and the valley. Everything was pristine, more pristine than Calder imagined it with Martha in charge. He was standing by a bell suspended from two white posts, when he heard a bird whooping loudly in the tree behind him.

His host swore in German.

'What was that?' Calder asked.

'They call it a bokmakierie,' the German replied. 'The South Africans love them, but I think they're a pest, especially in the summer, when they wake up at five o'clock in the morning and start yelling. There are two of them. I thought they'd gone a couple of years ago, but they seem to have returned.'

Calder thanked him and left, the call of the bokmakierie ringing in his ears.

Calder was aware that the theory he and George Field had hatched about the Laagerbond funding Zyl News was just that, a theory. There could be all kinds of innocent explanations for Havenga and Visser's visit to Cornelius that day. If there was an innocent explanation, then Daniel Havenga would probably give it, so Calder decided the direct approach would be the best way to test the hypothesis.

Stellenbosch was a quiet town, where imposing modern university buildings shared the streets with much older residences. Havenga lived on Dorp Street, an oak-lined road of white Cape Dutch houses with black painted railings and window-frames, many of which had been turned into art galleries. Peaceful, wealthy, old, it felt more like New England than Africa. A gap-toothed woman with wild black hair enthusiastically ushered Calder's car into a space outside an ancient-looking general store named Oom Samie's: she would demand a small tip later for watching over it. Calder walked a few yards along the street to Havenga's house and rang the bell. The professor answered the door himself. Calder could see what Caroline meant about the ears. He was a small man with white hair, a beard and a mischievous monkey face. He raised his eyebrows in puzzlement when he saw Calder, but he also smiled in tentative welcome.

'Professor Havenga?'

'Yes?'

'My name's Alex Calder. I'm a friend of Todd van Zyl. I know you knew his parents. He has some questions he would like me to ask you.'

'About what?'

'About his mother.'

'I see. Come in.'

Calder almost tripped over a compact suitcase that was lying in the hallway.

'Sorry about that,' said the professor. 'I've only just got in from Pretoria this morning. Through here.' He showed Calder into a cramped living room, made even more cramped by the floor-to-ceiling bookshelves that covered every wall. An attractive woman of about forty appeared, whom Havenga introduced as his partner and sent off to make coffee.

'Do I detect a Scottish accent?' Havenga said.

'You do,' Calder admitted.

'Well, you've come a long way. How can I help?' The professor's eyes were bright, and his smile was friendly, but he was leaning forward nervously in his armchair.

'I understand you were a friend of Martha's?'

'Oh, yes, a great friend. I thought it was a breath of fresh air to have an American around. It's much better now, but

295

in those days the university was very inward-looking, very insular.'

'Do you have any idea who killed her?'

The professor's eyebrows shot up. 'Wasn't it ANC guerrillas somewhere in the north? Near the Mozambique border?'

'That's what the police said.'

'I see. And Todd doesn't believe them?'

'No.'

Havenga shrugged. 'He may be right. All kinds of awful things were covered up by the authorities in those days. I suppose Martha's death might be one of them. It's very hard to unravel those mysteries now. It was what, fifteen years ago?'

'Eighteen,' Calder said. 'And it is difficult. Which is why I am here.'

The woman arrived with a cafetière of coffee and two mugs. Havenga gave her a meaningful look and she withdrew. Havenga poured the coffee and swore as he spilled some. Definitely nervous.

'I was very fond of Martha,' Havenga said as he passed Calder his mug. 'But I didn't know her that well. If she had personal problems, I wouldn't know about them. There were rumours of some difficulties with her husband, but there are always those kinds of rumours in Stellenbosch. The town is notorious for it.'

'I wonder if you could tell me about a meeting you had with Cornelius van Zyl a short time before Martha was killed.'

Havenga sat up straight. 'Meeting? I don't follow.'

'Yes. With Andries Visser, from the Finance Ministry.'

Havenga looked nonplussed. He didn't say anything.

'You do know Andries Visser?'

'Um . . . We served on some committees together, I think. A long time ago.'

'Right,' Calder said. 'And one day you and he paid a visit to Cornelius.'

'I don't think so.'

'Caroline saw you.'

'Caroline? Martha's daughter? She was only a kid, wasn't she?'

'An observant kid with a good memory.'

'She might have a good memory, but I don't. I don't remember any meeting.'

'Are you sure?'

'Quite sure.' The smile had gone, the eyes were no longer twinkling, but wary.

'Were you a member of the Broederbond, professor?'

Havenga forced a laugh, pleased with the change of subject. 'That's something I couldn't possibly divulge to you. But I am a current member of the Afrikanerbond, which is its successor organization. As you no doubt know, my field is journalism, and so I have a close professional interest in the Afrikaans language and its role in modern-day South Africa.'

'How about the Laagerbond?'

Havenga was just about to take a sip of his coffee. He paused with the rim of the mug millimetres from his lips.

'The Laagerbond,' Calder repeated. 'Are you a member of the Laagerbond?'

Havenga recovered, lowering his coffee and pursing his lips. 'Laagerbond? Interesting name. I can't say that I have heard of it, though.'

'What about Operation Drommedaris?'

Havenga slowly shook his head, his lips tightly shut.

297

'No, of course not,' Calder said. 'Thanks for your time, professor. I think I've found what I was looking for.'

Havenga put down his mug and leaped to his feet. 'I don't see how. I had no idea what you were talking about.'

Calder smiled at the professor. 'Oh, you were very helpful. Believe me, very helpful.'

Daniel Havenga was severely agitated after Calder left. He paced about the tiny living room, playing over the conversation in his head. He hadn't made any slips, had he? Alex Calder had seemed to think he had. He was shocked at how much that man had been able to piece together. Martha's death had devastated him at the time, and even now, eighteen years later, his eyes prickled at the thought of it. The irony was that neither he nor Andries Visser nor the Laagerbond had been responsible. He wished he could just tell Calder that but he couldn't. There was too much else at stake.

He picked up the phone and dialled a number. 'Andries? It's Daniel. I'm worried . . .'

23

As soon as Calder arrived back in Cape Town he booked a flight for that evening to Johannesburg. It was obvious that Havenga had been lying about his meeting with Visser and Cornelius and that he knew very well what the Laagerbond was. Calder decided to track down Andries Visser at the address George Field had given him: a farm near Pretoria.

Before leaving for the airport he called Kim. She had decided to speak to Todd, who had been shocked at the idea that Cornelius might have been financed by the Laagerbond. In fact, he hadn't believed it, and he wanted to confront his father about it. This seemed a very bad idea to Calder and he urged Kim to try to stop him. Kim promised she would do her best.

Todd's proposed action annoyed Calder. While at the outset it had been reasonable that Todd and Kim called the shots, now Calder felt he had just as much right to decide how they approached Cornelius. His sister had lost a leg, and he was risking his neck in South Africa. It seemed to him to be a clear mistake to show their hand now. But there was little he could do about it at this distance.

His flight arrived at Johannesburg at about eight o'clock. He hired a car and drove on to Pretoria, where he checked into a hotel in Arcadia, the diplomatic quarter. The next morning he headed out on to the high veld in search of Visser's farm.

Where Cape Town had been green and mountainous, the

veld was yellow and flat, or at best gently undulating. For miles on all sides stretched grassland dotted with heavily guarded farms, patches of succulent green in the parched landscape. They needed rain.

Visser's farm was set back from a small straight road that led from one tiny dorp to another. It seemed to be bigger than most of its neighbours, the farmhouse itself was substantial, as was the cattle shed next to it. There was a perimeter fence along the road, and then an inner barrier of twelve-foot-high floodlit barbed wire. The metal plates on the gate threatened armed response, dogs and electrocution. Calder almost expected to see a sign telling him to beware of the minefield.

He opened the gate and drove along the track towards the farm. After Professor Havenga he had felt quite confident about meeting a retired civil servant, but this wasn't the quaint rustic farmstead he had expected. It looked more like a military camp. He almost turned back, but he had come this far and he didn't want to waste the trip. Besides, he planned a more subtle approach with Visser, less confrontational, more indirect.

He approached the inner gate to the farm to be met by two Dobermanns barking their heads off. No way was he going to open that gate, so he hooted the hired car's horn.

He waited a minute and then the door to the farmhouse opened, followed by the iron security gate. A thin man emerged. He tried to shout at the dogs, but his voice was hoarse and weak. Despite that, the dogs seemed to hear and slunk towards him. He shut them into a shed next to the house and limped over to the gate to open it.

Calder leaned out of the window of his car. 'Mr Visser? My name's Alex Calder –'

'I know who you are,' wheezed Visser. 'Come in.'

Calder parked his car and followed the man inside. 'A lot of security you have here,' he said.

'We need it. We lose several cattle every year. We have to protect them ourselves, we can't rely on anyone else.'

'I see,' said Calder.

Visser led him into what was clearly a study of the practical sort, cluttered with books, ledgers, box files and computer equipment. He coughed, a rasping affair that shook his whole body.

'Sit down,' he said, indicating a sofa. As Calder lowered himself into it, Visser moved to the corner behind his desk. There Calder noticed a rifle. He leaped to his feet, but Visser had already picked up the gun and was pointing it at him.

'Keep still!' he wheezed.

'OK, OK,' Calder said, raising his hands in a placatory gesture.

'Hands by your sides!'

Calder let his arms drop.

'You should know, Mr Calder, that I am very different from my friend Professor Havenga. Not as friendly. In fact I object to the way you questioned him.'

Calder swallowed. 'I see.'

'This isn't Britain,' Visser said.

'I know.'

'You see, I can shoot you right now. This is my land, my farm, and you are an intruder. I know the local police chief. He might ask a difficult question or two, but he wouldn't argue with my story. My family and his have known each other for generations.'

Calder remained silent.

'You ask too many questions. Turn around.'

Calder remained still.

'I said turn around!' Visser raised his voice, but that

brought on a fit of coughing. Calder stared down the barrel of the rifle and then did as he was asked. He faced a blank wall.

'This isn't the Wild West, either,' Visser continued. 'Here it's OK to shoot an intruder in the back. In fact it's more credible. And I'm going to shoot you on the count of three. Are you ready?'

Calder swallowed again. Jesus! What was this? So much for the subtle approach. Was he going to be shot dead just like that? Visser was bluffing, surely . . .'

'One.'

Maybe he was, maybe he wasn't. But Visser was too far away for Calder to jump him; the second Calder moved he would be dead. Perhaps he could talk him out of it. 'Andries . . .'

'Quiet! Two.'

This was it. Calder closed his eyes. He thought of his father. And from somewhere he thought of Sandy. Odd.

'Three!' There was a sharp crack, the feeling of wind on his cheek and then the plaster on the wall next to him exploded, fragments tearing into his face. He flinched as his ears and chin burned. He touched his face. Blood from the plaster.

He turned to see Visser holding the rifle to his shoulder. 'On second thoughts there would be some tiresome inter-views to deal with,' Visser said. 'But remember, this is my country, not yours. I can have you killed here easily any time I like. And I will do that unless you take a plane out of South Africa tonight. My people will be watching you. Now go.'

Calder hesitated.

'Go!' wheezed Visser. Calder left the room and walked stiffly out to his car. His knees were weak and he had a strong urge to run, but he didn't want to give Visser the pleasure. He slowly climbed in, and drove off down the track. As he reached the small country road, a blue Toyota Corolla appeared behind him. There was a white man inside with a thick neck and a baseball cap. Calder made no attempt to evade the car as it followed him all the way to Pretoria.

There were many Bloomfield Weiss bankers that Benton Davis disliked, but the one he loathed most was the man who was at that moment screaming at him down the telephone. Simon Bibby was an Englishman, but he was based in New York where he was head of Global Fixed Income, and also chairman of the Underwriting Committee. A powerful man. An angry man.

'Are you trying to tell me that you committed the firm to underwriting a junk-bond issue without referring to the Underwriting Committee first?'

'Yes.'

'Jesus fucking Christ! I thought we'd sorted this problem out years ago. Bankers cannot commit the firm to a client on a whim in a meeting. Didn't you know that?'

'I did what I had to do to secure the deal,' Benton said. 'The financing letter went out to Zyl News yesterday.'

'Why couldn't you leave it to Dower?' Bibby said. 'He'd never have done that. It's a rookie's mistake, Benton.'

'There's only another fifty million pounds needed,' said Benton. 'That's less than 10 per cent of the value of the transaction. Surely we can raise that? What happened to that famous Bloomfield Weiss placing power?'

'The point is that it's we who decide how much of the firm's capital we risk, not you. You know that. I do not like being bounced into taking decisions by idiots who will sell the firm to win a deal.'

'If you haven't the balls to stand up for a lousy three hundred and fifty million for one of the bank's best clients don't blame me,' said Benton.

Bibby sputtered. 'You're out of here,' he snarled. 'Once this deal is over, you're history, I'll make sure of that.'

'Great to have your support,' said Benton as he put down the phone.

Bibby wasn't his direct boss, but he could get him fired. Benton knew that he had sinned, he had known it at the time he had given his word that Bloomfield Weiss would come up with the funds. There was a strong likelihood that he would lose his job as a result. But he didn't regret what he had done.

Cornelius van Zyl deserved support from Bloomfield Weiss. This was the key moment in Zyl News's history. The company had been a loyal client for over twenty years, since Bloomfield Weiss had structured the complicated set of parallel loans that had enabled Cornelius to evade South African exchange controls and make his first investment in US newspapers. Since then the firm had done a dozen deals with Cornelius, big and small, profitable and less profitable. At that moment Cornelius had needed Bloomfield Weiss's unequivocal support and Benton was glad he had given it. It had been the right thing to do. And he was sick of cowering before the likes of Simon Bibby.

His phone rang. He picked it up. 'Benton Davis.'

'I've just had Peter Laxton on the phone,' said Cornelius.

'Yes?'

'He's worried that we can't raise nine hundred million.'

'Where did he get that idea from?'

'Gurney Kroheim. They're telling him that the debt markets are getting tougher.'

'That's true, but we can handle it.'

'Did you see the article in the Lex column this morning?'

'Yes, I did,' said Benton. The *Financial Times*'s daily Lex column carried comment on the stock market and recent takeover gossip. That morning it had questioned the reliability of Zyl News's bid, and suggested that shareholders might be safer taking the slightly lower price from Sir Evelyn Gill. 'Gill's PR is working overtime.'

'So you're sure you can raise the funds?'

'Absolutely,' said Benton. 'You've got our letter, haven't you?'

'Good. Because that's what I told Peter Laxton. My reputation's at stake on this one.'

You're not the only one, thought Benton. But he didn't say it. What he did say was, 'You can rely on us, Cornelius.'

'I don't know whether Laxton will go with us,' Cornelius said. 'But I do know we can't bid any higher than nine hundred.'

'That's higher than Gill. Laxton's shareholders will get more cash if they sell to us. That's the important point.'

'Very few of the institutional investors have tendered their shares to us so far,' Cornelius said.

'Don't worry. They're playing a waiting game, hoping for a better offer. When one doesn't materialize they'll accept ours, you'll see.'

'I hope you're right,' said Cornelius and rang off. Benton stared at the phone. He went through the outcomes. If Zyl News won the deal and the junk-bond issue was a success, he would live to fight another day. If they didn't win the deal, he was in trouble. If the bond issue flopped and Bloomfield Weiss were left with a three hundred and fifty million pound bridging loan to a struggling Zyl News, then he was toast. There was nothing more he could do to influence the outcomes one way or the other.

Cornelius was worried too as he replaced the receiver. He appreciated Benton Davis's support, and he himself had sounded supremely confident to Peter Laxton. But he could *feel* the doubt in Laxton's voice. They were going to go for Gill's offer, the safer option.

He looked up from his desk as his assistant came in. 'I've just had a phone call from Todd,' she said. 'He wants to see you. Right away.'

'Is he all right?'

'I think so,' she said. 'He says he has something to ask you.'

Calder took Andries Visser's threat seriously. He was confident that he was on to something and he didn't want to give up. The closer he got to finding out who had really killed Martha van Zyl, the more determined he was becoming, for Todd's sake, for Kim's, for Anne's, for his father's, for his own. But neither did he want to die. He might evade the Toyota, but there could be other people watching him, people he hadn't seen. The Laagerbond was clearly a powerful organization, and at this stage he had no idea how powerful, or how widely its tentacles stretched through South Africa.

If he was to stay alive he had to be seen boarding a flight leaving South Africa that day.

He drove back to his hotel in Pretoria, where there was a message for him to call Tarek in London. He tried, but his friend was in a meeting. So he checked out, drove the fifty kilometres south to Johannesburg airport and bought a one-way ticket to London via Lusaka. Two hours' wait, two hours to Lusaka, and there he bought a one-way ticket back to Johannesburg. He was back in South Africa by ten o'clock, hoping that whoever had watched him leave the country was not hanging around the arrivals hall to see if he returned. He hired a car and drove to Sandton, a northern suburb of the city, where he found a hotel. It was too late to call Tarek, but he did call Kim's mobile. It was switched off, but he left her a message on her voicemail explaining where he was.

Despite the fact that his room was four floors up, that he kept his window firmly closed and locked, that he slid into place the deadbolt and the chain on his door, he didn't sleep well that night. He had only to drift off for a few moments when his eyes would start open to examine the dim outlines of armchair, lamp and curtains and his ears strain in an effort to pick out the sharp sound of an intruder above the muffled din of the night outside. He could tell his conscious self that there was no one there. But his unconscious self didn't believe it.

Libby Wiseman lived in Yeoville, which, according to Calder's map, was a suburb just to the east of the Central Business District of Johannesburg. Sandton in daylight was quite a sight. Opulent hotels, smart new bank headquarters wider than they were tall, vast shopping malls, the place reeked of wealth. Wealth and white people. He drove south through leafy suburbs of well-fortified houses. As he neared the centre of the city things changed. More black people, fewer trees, dilapidated houses, impossibly large bus queues. By the time he reached Yeoville, there wasn't a white person around, apart from two shaven-headed thugs in a police patrol car.

Uneasy, he located Libby Wiseman's street and drove up to her house. It was a large rambling edifice with peeling paintwork, surrounded by similar properties in a worse condition. Fifty years ago it might have been a grand residence;

now it was a dump. The street was busy with hawkers and loafers. A painfully thin, very black man tried to sell him a packet of something. Calder said no without really knowing what it was. He looked about him. He felt like a sitting target for Visser, or anyone else for that matter. He was relieved when the door was opened.

Libby Wiseman was a heavy-set woman of about sixty. Her dark hair was streaked with grey and hung loose down to her shoulders. She was dressed in a long denim skirt and a baggy green sweatshirt. She was expecting him: he had called earlier that morning. She smiled as she led him into a large kitchen smelling of damp and gas.

'Interesting neighbourhood,' Calder said.

'It's a war zone,' Libby said.

'Ah.'

'Yeoville used to be the radical capital of South Africa,' Libby said. 'My grandparents came here from Lithuania a hundred years ago. Good Bolsheviks, they were. The tradition lived on: in the early nineties, when the ANC exiles began to return to South Africa, they set up home here. I was born here and after my divorce in 1991 I left Cape Town to come back. I even had a brief stint in politics myself.'

She picked out a cigarette from a packet on the kitchen table and lit up. 'Sorry, do you want one?' she said, waving the packet vaguely at him. He shook his head. 'Thought not.'

'Then the whole world wanted to move here,' she continued. 'South Africans, Nigerians, Congolese, Kenyans, everybody. The area became very cosmopolitan. Too cosmopolitan for all those radicals. They hightailed it for the white suburbs, leaving a couple of old crones like me behind them.'

'Why do you stay?' Calder asked.

'I spent the first half of my life fighting segregation. I'm not going to spend the second half running away from the consequences.'

'You said you were a politician for a while?'

Libby laughed. 'That only lasted a year. I soon realized my mistake.'

'Didn't you like Mandela?'

'Oh, everyone loves Mandela, even me. No, it wasn't that. The ANC was supposed to be a socialist organization. I was a member of the Communist Party. We were going to nationalize the means of production, feed the poor, give them schools and hospitals and houses and land. I know it sounds incredibly old-fashioned these days, but I really believed that stuff; still do, as a matter of fact. As soon as the ANC comes to power, what does it do? *Privatizes* everything in sight. A government like that wasn't for me, so I quit.' She stared at Calder's face. 'What did you do to your cheek?'

Calder touched the scab. The damage from the plaster on Visser's study wall had only been superficial, but the memory of that rifle shot distracted him. He didn't answer.

'Do I take it you have already experienced the warmth of sunny South Africa's hospitality?' Libby said.

'Er . . . yes. You could say that.'

'Sorry, I'm getting cynical, I suppose. I just hoped that when apartheid disappeared, so would the violence in this country. It hasn't.'

'It's violence I wanted to talk to you about. Murder, specifically.'

'Yes. George Field called me and said you were trying to find out what happened to Martha van Zyl. He said I should trust you and give you all the help I can, by the way. I don't know George well, but he was a brave man in his time, and I'm inclined to do what he asks.'

'Thank you. I understand you and Martha were friends. You were both on the board of a charity?'

'Yes. A literacy project in Guguletu. We weren't *great* friends, I'm not sure Martha had many true friends in South Africa, but we liked each other. She was a little naïve, but her heart was in the right place. Her husband sold out, though, and I don't think she was very happy with that.'

'Sold out?'

'Yes. Literally in his case. I was never convinced by those businessmen who raked in profits off the backs of the black labour they were exploiting and then wrung their hands in anguish over apartheid. But in his case he gave up, demolished the *Cape Daily Mail* and disappeared to America to make his millions. He must be seriously rich by now, isn't he?'

'I think so,' Calder said.

'Well, Martha didn't like his plan, and I don't blame her.'

'Do you have any idea why she was killed? Do you believe it was the ANC?'

'It may have been. Or it may have been someone else.' Libby smiled conspiratorially. 'I know one thing that the official account missed out. She didn't travel to Kupugani alone.'

'What do you mean?'

'She went with a man.'

'What!'

Libby smiled. 'Cornelius had found himself a lover. So Martha did the same. He was quite a bit younger than her, but she was nuts about him. I think it was as much the excitement of conducting an illicit affair as anything else, and this one was *very* illicit. I was all in favour of it, by the way. In fact, I was jealous; my own marriage was on the rocks and I could have used a toyboy to cheer me up.'

'So that's why she went up to Kupugani?'

'That's right. It was me who suggested it. I went to school with the owner, Phyllis Delahay. She's an old friend. Kupugani is a beautiful place. Very discreet. And Martha needed somewhere discreet. Somewhere where her lover wouldn't attract attention.'

'Why would he attract attention?'

'He was black. A black American.'

Benton! Benton bloody Davis. No wonder Martha wanted her mother to talk to him if anything happened to her. And what had Benton said? That he knew nothing, when in fact he knew everything.

'You don't look very happy with that information,' Libby said. 'I take it you know the man in question?'

'I do. I used to work with him.'

'Well, she never told me his name, but she did say he was a banker working with Cornelius.'

'And you never told anyone else about him?'

'No,' Libby said. 'There was no way I was going to talk to the police about it, especially since they almost certainly knew already, and her husband was out of the question.'

'So why tell me now?'

Libby examined Calder's face. 'I trust you. God knows why, but I do. I've thought for a while now that it would be wrong to keep silent for ever. Someone has to know. Someone probably should tell Martha's children; I'm not sure about that, I'll leave that up to you. And someone needs to find out what really happened to her. Perhaps that person is you.'

'Did Cornelius know about him?'

'That's the big question, isn't it?' Libby took a last drag

on her cigarette and stubbed it out. 'It seems to *me* that in these circumstances the husband is the most likely suspect. He was rich enough and powerful enough to ensure the police stayed quiet. Martha told me she was scared of him, especially when he was angry. He had a motive: men like that do not enjoy being cheated on, whatever their own record of fidelity. He probably didn't do it himself: perhaps he paid someone. Who knows? But it would explain why no one has come to talk to me about her death until you show up on my doorstep eighteen years later.'

24

August 22, 1988

He's coming to Cape Town! Tomorrow. I can't believe it. Neels told me this morning. It was one of the few things we actually said to each other all day. Apparently he asks about me quite often. Apparently I made quite a hit with him, baking those cookies. I asked innocently whether he would be coming to dinner again. Neels said no. But I'll see him. I'll figure out a way of seeing him.

August 23

I called him! He really is back in South Africa already. He has wall-to-wall meetings with Zyl News people, but there's a hole in his schedule tomorrow around one-thirty. I'm meeting him for lunch at his hotel. This is stupid, but I really can't wait. I feel like a schoolgirl on her first date. No, her second date.

Talked to Todd last night. He's looking forward to coming home. It's only ten days away now. He sounds quite taken with this Francesca girl.

Boy, what a great day! We shouldn't have done that, but I'm so glad we did. I want to tell the whole world how happy I am, if only for a few hours. But I can't do that so I'll just write it down here.

It's obvious who I'm talking about from the last couple of days' entries, isn't it? It's Benton. It's so good to be with him. Physically, he's young and strong and he has a great body. I like my men big, and he's bigger than Neels. Oops – I didn't mean that quite as it looks on the page. He's tall and he has broad shoulders and he's . . . Yeah. Well. Maybe I did mean that.

But he's intelligent and he's well educated and well read and yes he is black and yes there is something illicit about that which I find exciting and yes in this country black is the forbidden fruit and yes there is something exhilarating about showing these Nazis that a blonde white woman can want to have sex with a black man, can enjoy it, that it's natural, healthy and right. It just feels right. I know it's so wrong but it feels right.

We were oh, so restrained at lunch. I didn't touch him apart from a quick kiss on the cheek when we met. People turned and stared, I mean Benton is a very tall man and he dresses very well, and I recognized one of Neels's business acquaintances. Although we didn't tell Neels we were meeting, we will tell him we had lunch afterwards. It will be natural, innocent.

Then we blew it. We only had an hour and a half for lunch before Benton had to go to his next meeting and time was nearly up when he grinned and said he needed to make a call. He was back a minute later to say that something had come up on another deal he was working on and he would have to go up to his room and sort it out. It would mean he would miss his next meeting at Zyl News. We left the restaurant, he went upstairs to his room, I spent five heart-thumping minutes in the bathroom, it seemed such a long time, and then I took the elevator up and joined him.

It was fantastic!

I told Benton about Operation Drommedaris. I made him promise not to discuss it with anyone, no one at Bloomfield Weiss and certainly not Neels. I had to tell someone about it, and he's the one person I know who I trust and couldn't possibly have links to the Laagerbond. I didn't tell him about the man Moolman, but he could see I was scared.

It sounds like my suspicions are well founded. The people at Bloomfield Weiss and Zyl News have been trying to figure out how they can raise their bid for the *Herald*. They are all desperate. Zyl News is bust if they don't do a deal, but if they overpay it's bust too. Then last week Neels announced to Benton and his boss that he had a possible new source of funds. He was very cagey about where these funds came from and Benton is suspicious. Even though the origin appears to be South African, Neels assured them that there would be no exchange-control issues. Money is money and Bloomfield Weiss aren't about to ask difficult questions.

Benton says that Beatrice Pienaar goes everywhere with Neels. She's in South Africa right now. But this time, in Benton's arms, I don't mind so much. In fact, it makes me feel less guilty.

I told him I *have* to see him again soon. He's flying up to Jo'burg tomorrow to do some more due diligence on the Zyl News papers there, and he says he can stay on for the weekend. Neels is flying back to Philadelphia tonight, so it might work. We'll have to be much more careful. I said I would find somewhere discreet for us to go, somewhere outside the city. I'm not sure where, but I will think of something.

I still feel scared about all that Laagerbond stuff, but I'm scared and excited at the same time.

God, I can't wait till the weekend!

August 25

We had a board meeting of the Guguletu Project today. Libby and I went for a walk in the Kirstenbosch Gardens afterwards. I love that place: it's halfway up the eastern side of Table Mountain and you get a view of the huge sprawl of townships on Cape Flats, including Guguletu. All the plants in the gardens are native to South Africa. It's where I got most of the ideas for the fynbos beds at Hondehoek.

I told Libby about Benton; I couldn't help it. She was encouraging almost to the point of jealousy. I really don't give her marriage to Dennis much more time. She was also amazed by how young he is. It's true that he is ten years younger than me, but he doesn't seem that way to me. God knows what he sees in me. Libby said something bitchy about the boss's wife. Maybe there is something in that. Maybe I'm his forbidden fruit.

We discussed the problem of where to take him. I told her I'd like to show Benton the bush, the real Africa. I had thought about Mala Mala, but that place is so popular now. Then she suggested a game farm that an old friend of hers from school owns. It's very private, very discreet, and there are plenty of lions. I love watching lions. It's called Kupugani, which means "raise yourself" in Zulu. It's named for that big campaign in the sixties to give away the surplus milk produced by white dairy farmers to starving Africans. It was quite subversive in its time. Phyllis, the owner, is a widow and shares Libby's liberal views. Libby's quite sure that Phyllis wouldn't mind a mixed-race couple, in fact Libby thought she would get a kick out of it.

The idea appeals. Libby said she'd call her friend. I'll need to come up with a good excuse. Or will I? Neels jets around the world at will with his girlfriend without asking my permission. Why should I ask his? I'll just say I need to go away for a couple of days.

I think that Moolman has gotten the message that I have stopped asking questions about the Laagerbond. I haven't seen any sign of him for almost two weeks now since I caught him hanging around outside Caroline's school. But you never know, I'm still scared. I decided to write a letter to Mom in case something happens to me. I know it will freak her out, but at least I can trust my own family to do the right thing.

25

Calder kept a careful watch in his rear-view mirror all the way from Yeoville back to Sandton. The traffic was heavy and he was no expert at counter-surveillance so he couldn't be certain whether there was anyone on his tail. As he approached the northern suburb, he took a diversion through a white residential neighbourhood, driving around two or three blocks and then back on the main street to Sandton. Nothing followed him.

The wealth of Sandton amazed him anew after the dilapidation of Yeoville. The whites had abandoned the centre of Johannesburg to create their own fortress of privilege, comforting to the well off, threatening to the dispossessed. They were behaving just like rich white people did all over the world. Libby had a point, Calder thought.

He parked the car in a well-secured underground bunker and took a lift up to the hotel forecourt and walked inside. Someone was waiting for him in an armchair facing the entrance.

Cornelius.

Calder checked the rest of the lobby. Empty apart from the hotel staff. He looked behind him. Two middle-aged women with cases were climbing into a cab.

'I'm alone,' said Cornelius, getting to his feet.

'What are you doing here?'

'I came to see you.'

'From London?'

'You've done an awful lot for my family over the last few

weeks,' Cornelius said. 'I thought you deserved an explanation. In person.'

'Todd talked to you?'

'He did. Come on. Let's get out of here.'

Calder followed Cornelius out of the hotel and through a series of walkways, constantly looking over his shoulder as he did so. In a few minutes they came to a kind of modern piazza, presided over by a thirty-foot bronze statue of Nelson Mandela and with a fountain in the middle. Around the piazza were a series of cafés and restaurants under awnings. It was cool, and very few people were sitting outside. Cornelius had no problem finding a quiet table.

'Todd's doing well,' Cornelius said.

'He shouldn't have spoken to you. I didn't want him to.'

'I'm sorry about your sister,' Cornelius went on. 'And very grateful for all you have done for Todd and Kim. I realize you nearly got yourself killed on two occasions for them.'

'Three,' said Calder, remembering Visser's bullet. 'And I'm doing this for *me* now. How did you find out where I was?'

'Kim told me.'

Calder remembered the voicemail message he had left for her. But why had she disclosed his location to Cornelius, of all people?'

Cornelius ordered coffee. Shoppers strolled through the square. A gaggle of white teenage girls paused in front of them, giggling and shrieking. One of them pulled out a dinky mobile phone and started flicking her thumbs while the others looked on.

'It's true that Daniel Havenga came to see me at Hondehoek with a friend, Andries Visser. It's also true that they offered to finance the bid for the *Herald*. And not just that.

They wanted to provide funding for a string of newspaper and magazine acquisitions afterwards.'

'Did they say where the money was coming from?'

'Yes. Something called the Laagerbond. They said it was a highly secret group that existed to promote the interests of the Afrikaner nation. They didn't believe in violence or even in the continuation of apartheid, which they recognized was an obsolete ideology, but they did believe in the power of public opinion. They had access to substantial funds which were lodged in Switzerland. Daniel said the group wasn't part of the government and it would continue to exist if the government fell. They wanted to fund someone, a man with influence in the world's media, who could build an international stable of newspapers and magazines which would put the Afrikaner point of view in the future. Daniel felt that the main threat to Afrikaners was international public opinion. He had seen what had happened to Nazis after the fall of Germany and he didn't want something similar to happen here. He said he believed that Afrikaners were not evil, but someone had to persuade the rest of the world of that. Me.'

'What about the *Cape Daily Mail*?'

'They were happy to see that closed. They wanted me to keep hold of the other South African papers, although in the climate of US hostility to investment in South Africa at that time, I think that would have been difficult. Their idea was that my papers would gradually take on a more favourable editorial slant, not necessarily pro-government, but pro-Afrikaner.'

'Did they want you to become a member of this Laagerbond?'

'They didn't say so specifically, but I got that impression.'

'And you said yes?'

'I said I'd consider it. And I did.'

'But why? After all you had done to fight apartheid?'

Cornelius sighed. His eyes moved over to the giant statue. Nelson Mandela was laughing. It said a lot for a country that it would build a monument to its founder not looking grim and statesmanlike but having a good time. 'By then I could see that apartheid was finished. What scared me was what would come later. South Africa was in the middle of a violent revolution. The townships were in flames, people were killing each other, my brother was blown up by guerrillas, the communists had an execution list with my name on it. I was torn. Part of me wanted to flee the country, go to America and start a new life. But part of me was reluctant to abandon my roots. My Afrikaner roots. Three hundred years of family history. Generations of hard-working, honest, decent people who suffered terrible hardship and survived through prayer and strength of character. I had denied them for most of my adult life, I had married two English-speaking women, but I knew that much of the Afrikaner way of life was good, and I didn't want to see it disappear in flames.'

'Did Beatrice Pienaar influence you?'

Cornelius glanced quickly at Calder. 'You know about her?' Calder didn't answer. 'Yes. Yes, she did. She was a perceptive woman: she felt that the Afrikaner nation was facing its biggest challenge. The answer wasn't in preserving the past, it was the duty of her generation to find a position for Afrikaners in the world of the future.' Cornelius smiled. 'She sounded like Daniel Havenga's pupil. And yes, she made me think that perhaps I had a duty as well.'

'So. Are the Laagerbond funding your bid for *The Times*?

Cornelius laughed. He and Nelson shared the joke.

'What's so funny?' said Calder.

'I said no. After Martha died, I said no. Then I really did want to quit the country as soon as possible. I told Daniel and his friends I wasn't interested, sold my newspapers here, and went to the States.'

'But you bought the *Herald*?'

'Yes. For some reason that I have never been able to fathom, Lord Scotton ignored Evelyn Gill's bid and went for mine. We bought the *Herald*, we turned it around, we battled through the recession of the early nineties and came out the other side all guns blazing. Zyl News never looked back. And we never took a cent of the Laagerbond's money.'

'Do you expect me to believe that?'

Cornelius looked at Calder levelly. 'Yes. That's why I came down here.'

Cornelius looked like a man who was used to getting his way. But he also looked honest.

'Hold on,' Calder said. He pulled out his mobile phone and called Tarek's home number. It was a Saturday and Tarek's small daughter answered with a disconcerting Home Counties accent. A moment later, Tarek was on the line.

'Hi, it's me,' said Calder. 'Any luck?'

'Actually, yes. I spoke to our media analyst in New York. He's been covering Zyl News for fifteen years and knows the company very well. When the first US acquisitions were made in the early eighties Bloomfield Weiss did some fancy stuff with parallel loans to get around South African exchange controls. But since then all their acquisitions have been made with either internally generated funds, the syndicated loan market, or high-yield bonds. The accounts are all public and they add up. Our guy is sure that there is no major South African financing.'

Calder glanced at Cornelius. 'Thanks, Tarek.'

'Wait,' said Tarek. 'We were discussing *The Times* takeover.

My analyst said that the more interesting question is where Evelyn Gill's funding comes from. We know he has relationships with Swiss private banks. Three years ago a Sunday newspaper in London ran a story that the money had ultimately come from Islamic sources, but Gill denied this and sued the paper successfully. My man believes that South Africa is a more likely possibility.'

'Really?'

'As it happens, I went to school with a guy called Jeff Tidwell, who was FD of Beckwith Communications until a couple of years ago.' Calder knew that Tarek's expensive education had included a stint at an English public school, before university in the States. 'I called him yesterday. He said he had no idea what I was talking about, he said Gill had used his own funds all along, he'd never taken a penny from outside investors.'

'That can't be right, can it?'

'Actually, no. According to my analyst there are tens if not hundreds of millions that must have come from somewhere outside Beckwith Communications, and Gill never made that much from his metal-trading business. I think Jeff was lying to me. Which shouldn't surprise me, I never really trusted him at school.'

'All very interesting. Thanks again, Tarek.'

'Any time, my friend.'

Cornelius's eyes had never shifted from Calder. 'Well?' he said.

'I believe you,' said Calder, putting away his phone. He then told Cornelius about Tarek's suspicions of Gill.

'Of course!' said Cornelius. 'How stupid of me.' He drummed the table with his fingers, his brain firing. 'After I said no, the Laagerbond looked for someone else to back. And they found a right-wing bigot who would do anything for money and power. It makes sense. I've noticed that his papers have an anti-ANC bias whenever they report on South Africa. I thought it was personal: he was so angry with me for beating him on the *Herald* deal that he took it out on my country. But that never made much sense. Laagerbond backing does. Plus he now owns a couple of major titles in this country.'

Calder watched the older man. 'What about Martha?'

'I didn't kill her.'

Calder sipped his coffee, considering Cornelius's response.

'I want to help you,' Cornelius continued. 'This isn't just about Martha. When it was I could try to put everything behind me, forget about it. But this is about Todd and your sister and Caroline and Kim and you.' Cornelius leaned forward, brushing a salt cellar out of the way. 'For the last eighteen years I have been in denial. I didn't want Martha's death dragged up and picked over, nor did I want my connections with the Laagerbond dogging me for the rest of my career, even though they didn't come to anything. So when Martha's mother asked me questions about the Laagerbond and urged me to go to the Truth and Reconciliation Commission, I ignored her. Just like I ignored Todd later. I never considered whether the Laagerbond had anything to do with Martha's death, I did my best not to consider her death at all. The police said it was a random guerrilla killing and that fit with my view of what was happening in South Africa at the time. It was buried and I wanted it to stay buried. It was only when Todd spoke to me yesterday that I realized I had to face the truth.' Cornelius stared hard at Calder. 'I want to help.'

'OK.' Calder took a deep breath. 'There are a couple of things you need to know, if you don't know them already. I warn you, they will make unpleasant listening.'

'Tell me,' said Cornelius.

'Did you know Beatrice Pienaar was a spy?'

'George Field claimed that, but it was paranoia,' Cornelius said. 'He could never prove it.'

'He can now,' Calder said. 'It came out during the Truth and Reconciliation Commission hearings. She was a lieutenant in the security police.'

'No!' said Cornelius. 'No one ever told me.'

'Did you ask?'

'No,' Cornelius admitted.

'What happened to her?'

'I don't know. After Martha died we became . . . less close. She quit Zyl News.'

'The second thing is . . .' Calder hesitated. He wasn't sure that Cornelius deserved to hear the next bit.

'What?' Cornelius said.

Calder ploughed on. As Cornelius himself had said, this was about much more than him. Calder needed to find the truth. 'Did you know your wife had a lover?'

'No!' Cornelius looked truly shocked. 'Oh, God.' He put his head in his hands. 'And I was just worried about what she thought about Beatrice. This was at the end, wasn't it? Just before she died.'

'Yes.'

'Who was it? Not George Field? Or Havenga? He was a randy old bastard but I can't imagine him and Martha. I can't imagine anyone and Martha.'

'Benton Davis.'

'What!' Calder kept quiet as he let the idea sink in. Cornelius's shoulders slumped. 'I suppose it was because of Beatrice.'

'I think she did suspect something.'

'You know the stupid thing is, Beatrice and I didn't even

sleep together,' Cornelius said. 'Oh, I was besotted with her all right. And she did have a big influence on my attitude then, I was so confused about everything. But I never slept with her. I had never been unfaithful to Martha and some part of me wanted to try to preserve that, even though things were going so badly between us. Damn!' He slammed his hand on the table so the coffee cups clattered. 'Damn!'

'That's why Martha went to Kupugani. To meet Benton. He spent a couple of days in Johannesburg and sneaked up there to meet her. The authorities covered it up. That's why Martha mentioned Benton in the letter to her mother that Todd found. And that's also why Benton lied to me.'

'Benton Davis, the two-faced, slimy bastard! All those years we worked together, all that arse-kissing he went in for, and all that time he knew he'd screwed my wife.' He shook his head. 'I guess it was my fault.' The anger subsided a notch. 'OK. So who did kill her, then? You've found out so much about my family so far, but can you answer that question?'

'No,' Calder said. 'It could be the Laagerbond. I had a nasty experience with Andries Visser which suggests that they are capable of violence. Or it could have been the police. Or, well . . .'

'Yes?'

'Well, it's just a suspicion.'

'Edwin?'

Calder shrugged. 'Maybe. I don't know. I do know he tried to blackmail someone into stopping me asking awkward questions.'

'Blackmail who? You?'

'It's not me. In fact I'd rather not say who it is, or what he's got on them. Although if Edwin has his way, you'll find out soon enough.'

Cornelius frowned. 'Don't tell me.' His face was grim. 'I'm not altogether surprised. I've always suspected him of blackmailing Lord Scotton somehow when we took over the *Herald*; the way Scotton sold out to me instead of Gill never made any sense.' He shook his head. 'I've put far too much trust in Edwin over the years.'

'One thing's for sure,' Calder said. 'Benton knows a lot more about all this than he has told me.'

'You're dead right, the bastard.' Cornelius's fingers drummed the table. 'Let's find out what he does know.' He pulled out his own mobile phone and pressed some buttons. 'Benton? ... Sorry to interrupt your weekend ... That's right, I'm in Johannesburg. Look, I really need you down here as soon as possible ... I can't talk about it over the phone. It's delicate ... No, just you ... I'm staying at the Intercontinental in Sandton ... Good, we'll have breakfast together tomorrow morning.'

Cornelius put his phone down and grinned. 'I love the way when you tell an investment banker to jump all they want to know is how high.'

'That's bloody marvellous! Good on yer.' The Yorkshire accent echoed around the room from half a world away. 'There's one decision you won't regret.' A heavy chuckle boomed down the line. 'I know some people as will *hate* the idea of *The Times* being owned by a lad from Sheffield. Someone who had to make his own brass.'

'I'm sure they will, Evelyn,' Visser said, leaning forward towards the speaker phone. He decided not to point out that Gill had received most of his funds from the Laagerbond. Visser was in Dirk du Toit's office at the headquarters of the United Farmers Bank near Church Square in the centre of Pretoria. There were few people working in the bank on a Saturday; it was an ideal time for du Toit to focus on Laagerbond business.

Du Toit was smiling. They had just told Sir Evelyn Gill that the Laagerbond agreed to go up to a price of nine hundred and twenty million for *The Times*. It was a high price, but it was worth it. And as Gill never tired of telling them, they had made a handsome profit on all the publications they had backed him to buy so far. 'If you call Hans in Zurich, everything should be in order,' he said.

'And get *The Times* on to the AIDS campaign right away,' Visser added. 'We're becoming increasingly worried about our president. If he carries on the way he's going, this country will be a one-party state run for the benefit of the blacks.'

'Government by the Kaffirs for the Kaffirs.' Gill's laughter boomed around the room. Visser caught du Toit's eye and winced. But by now he knew it was just a show of Yorkshire bluntness. Evelyn Gill was a very effective manipulator of his editors: forceful at some times, subtle at others. 'Don't worry,' Gill went on. 'Half the world knows your president's barking mad because he thinks there's no link between HIV and AIDS. Once we've got hold of *The Times*, we'll point it out to the other half.'

'I know we can rely on you, Evelyn.'

'Bloody right you can. Oh, by the way. I got a call from a lad who used to work for me as my finance director. Jeff Tidwell, you remember him. I had to get rid of the bugger in the end, he was a lazy sod. But he did tell me that someone at Bloomfield Weiss had been on the phone asking where we got our funding from.'

Visser sat up straight. 'What did he say?'

Gill chuckled. 'Don't worry. Jeff's a bit dozy, but he's not that dozy. He knows not to let me down. He told the merchant wanker it were all me own cash. Now, I must get on to Zurich.'

Du Toit leaned forward and switched off the phone. 'I don't like the sound of that, do you?'

'No,' said Visser. He closed his eyes. Once the van Zyls got hold of the link between the Laagerbond and Gill, it was all over. The bid for *The Times* would crumble. It wouldn't take long before Operation Drommedaris would come to light and then the whole Laagerbond would unravel. Under *his* watch as chairman.

He regretted now not shooting Calder when he had had the chance. Although he had ordered the execution of a number of people in his time, he had never actually killed anyone himself. Despite what he had said, the local police would have taken an interest and it would have been awkward to sort that out. He could see that he had scared the hell out of Calder, scared him enough to make him leave the country, but the man was still causing trouble.

Freddie Steenkamp had been right all along.

He glanced at du Toit. 'Do you mind?' he said, picking up the phone. He dialled Freddie's number and explained what was going on.

'We've got to act,' the former head of military intelligence said.

Visser sighed. 'You're right. We know Alex Calder is back in London. Send Moolman over there to deal with him.'

'And Cornelius van Zyl?' Steenkamp asked.

'Yes,' said Visser.

'What about the woman?'

Visser glanced at du Toit, who could hear only Visser's side of the conversation. 'Is that necessary?'

'We know how much trouble she can cause. We should have dealt with her years ago, I've always said that.'

329

'I know you have, Freddie. All right.'

'I'll get Kobus on to the woman right away. Then he can go to London and finish the job.'

'Good. But no fuck-ups this time.'

'It's not me who fucked up,' said Freddie Steenkamp.

Visser put down the phone. He saw du Toit staring at him.

Visser broke out in the explosion of coughs he had been restraining as he was speaking to Steenkamp.

'That's not just a cold, is it?' du Toit said.

Visser shook his head. 'Cancer. The lung.'

Du Toit winced. 'I'm sorry.'

'At least I will have seen the Laagerbond buy *The Times*,' Visser said. He knew now he was a dying man. He wanted du Toit to know it too.

'You've done a lot for the Bond, Andries.'

Du Toit's concern was touching. Despite the slicked-back red hair and the fancy office Dirk du Toit still had an air of youth, energy and innocence. He was a big, strong, honest man with an open, honest face. The kind of man who went to *kerk* every Sunday, who read to his children every night, who helped out his neighbours when they were in difficulty. The kind of man who had built the Afrikaner nation. The kind of man Visser had always wanted to be.

'When I go, I don't know who will take over from me. I'd like it to be a younger man. Even if Freddie Steenkamp does succeed me, I would be happy knowing that you had a senior role in the Bond.'

Du Toit smiled gravely. 'It would be an honour.'

'There's something you should be aware of,' said Visser. 'Something that until now has been handled by myself, Daniel Havenga and Freddie.'

'Yes?'

'You remember when Martha van Zyl was murdered back in 1988?' Visser said.

'Yes. That wasn't us, though, was it?'

Visser tried to smile, but coughed instead. 'No. As you know, I'm against the use of violence except when it's necessary. But you also know that occasionally Freddie Steenkamp is right, it *is* necessary.'

'Perhaps,' du Toit said. 'Although was it really necessary to kill Cornelius van Zyl's brother?'

'From what Impala told us, it had a major effect on van Zyl's psychology. Together with his name on the phoney SACP hit list we planted. Impala was confident that he would have gone along with Drommedaris if it hadn't been for the death of his wife.'

'Perhaps.'

Visser could see du Toit looked unhappy. But if he were to enter the inner sanctum of power of the Laagerbond, he would have to know everything. 'Well, after nearly twenty years her son has stirred up a lot of people running around trying to find out what happened. I've scared one of these people back to London, but if we are to retain control of the situation we are going to have to use violence again. There is no other way. Kobus Moolman is seeing to it as we speak.'

'Who are the targets?'

'Cornelius van Zyl. A man called Alex Calder. And –' Visser's chest rasped again. He knew du Toit would not like the answer, which was why it was important he be informed early, rather than find out later. 'And Zan van Zyl.'

26

Benton couldn't sleep. For a man of his height it was difficult, even in the first-class cabin. He had no compunctions about charging Zyl News for the upgrade, even though most Bloomfield Weiss trips these days were business class. But he was apprehensive about going to South Africa again.

He hadn't been since that awful time so long ago when Martha van Zyl had been brutally murdered in front of him and he had been lucky to escape with his life. He still had nightmares about that. They had morphed over the years, until they settled into a disturbing slow-motion scene where, naked, Martha stretched out her arms towards him and he slowly raised a heavy gun and shot her several times. As she died, she mouthed, 'Stay with me, Benton.' Now he did not want to go to sleep. He did not want to conjure up that dream.

The police custody had been a nightmare of its own. Although it should have been evident that he had only just escaped being shot himself, the cops had arrested him. They left him alone for an hour or so, and then they asked him whether he had murdered Martha. They seemed strangely pleased when he refused to admit to anything. With unmistakable relish they began to persuade him to confess. They stripped him naked and one of them beat him with a weighted hosepipe. It hurt like hell. The pain was so bad that he passed out. When he came to they had manacled his hands and suspended him from a beam along the ceiling of the cell. His muscles, still sore from the beating, burned with pain as they bore his weight. His left arm felt broken. Still he refused to speak, apart from cursing his captors and demanding to see someone from the US embassy. It was his anger that made him hold out. He was angry that they were treating him like an animal because he was black and he was angry that they were doing nothing to find the people who really had shot Martha.

They left him there for a couple of hours in his own private hell. There was the physical pain and there was the memory, still very fresh, of watching Martha die. Then a new man came into the cell. He looked tougher and even meaner than the others. Benton had had enough. He was ready to confess to just about anything and everything. Then the man smiled. He ordered Benton to be lowered from the beam and his clothes were returned to him. Dressed, Benton sat opposite the man at a bare table.

'Your name is Benton Davis?' he said, leafing through his blue United States passport. Benton noticed that his wallet and his other possessions were in a clear plastic bag.

Benton nodded.

'And you're an investment banker?'

Benton nodded again.

'How does that work?' the policeman said, looking up with a thin smile. 'I didn't know apes could add up.'

Benton sat there, impassive. He could put up with insults all day as long as they didn't hit him any more with that hosepipe.

'You can go now,' the man said, tossing the passport and the plastic bag to him. 'We know you weren't responsible for Martha van Zyl's death. We apologize for any inconvenience we may have caused.'

'The way you have treated me is outrageous —'

'Let me stop you there, Mr Davis,' said the man, leaning

forward. 'My name is Moolman. Colonel Moolman. The men who interrogated you here are amateurs. I'm a professional.' Moolman smiled again. He had a thick neck, a pillar of muscle. Benton kept quiet.

'We will never see each other again, provided you remember one thing. You were never here in this police station. You were never even at Kupugani. We'll take you to Johannesburg and throw you in the street. You can tell everyone you were attacked and robbed.' Moolman chuckled. 'If we dump you in the right place, you may even be attacked and robbed for real.' He leaned forward, his hard grey eyes looking directly into Benton's. 'Do you understand?'

Benton didn't answer.

'You see if you do mention any of this to anyone, I will find you and kill you. And believe me it will be a more painful death than you could possibly imagine. And don't think that just because you live outside South Africa you will be safe. Our enemies come to unfortunate ends all over the world. Remember Olof Palme, the prime minister of Sweden, who was shot two years ago in Stockholm? If we can get him, we can get you.'

Benton had agreed to Moolman's terms. He had never mentioned that awful day to anyone. And, given what had happened to Todd and then Alex Calder's sister, he was glad. He hadn't needed the message Moolman had left him at Bloomfield Weiss to be reminded of the ex-policeman's existence. He knew he was out there somewhere.

Benton had never been back to South Africa. He wondered what the hell Cornelius wanted to see him about now. It had seemed odd that the old man had suddenly decided to fly down to Johannesburg. Perhaps he had uncovered a new source of equity that would allow Zyl News to support a higher bid for *The Times*. Cornelius had told Dower he didn't have a secret fund stashed away somewhere, but perhaps he had lied. Benton remembered the mysterious Laagerbond that Martha had told him about just before she died. Whatever it was, Benton hoped it would strengthen the deal. He had cashed in all the chips he had to persuade the Underwriting Committee to back his pledge to Cornelius to raise the money. But his career was on the line. The deal was risky, possibly too risky even for the junk-bond market, and Benton knew that if Bloomfield Weiss couldn't find buyers for most of the junk-bond issue, it would all be over for him. If Cornelius had access to even a hundred million pounds of equity investment, that would reduce the amount of debt that had to be raised and would make the deal a lot less risky.

At least Cornelius wanted to talk to Benton alone. No Dower. No flunkies. If the deal worked, Benton would take the credit. All the credit. For the first time in a long time he would earn himself a decent bonus.

And when you really got down to it, that was what it was all about.

The Intercontinental Hotel took up one of the towers that clustered around the indoor shopping complex that was the heart of Sandton. The dining room was quiet, early on a Sunday morning, all black, gold and mirrors. Calder and Cornelius ordered some orange juice and coffee while they waited.

Benton looked cool and confident as he strode into the room, well dressed as always, white shirt bright and unwrinkled, tie knotted just so, suit hanging perfectly from his tall frame, cufflinks flashing. He smiled when he saw Cornelius and held out his hand. Cornelius returned his smile. Then Benton saw Calder.

The surprise registered on his face, but only for a moment. 'Alex? A pleasure as always. You do pop up at the most unlikely breakfast tables.'

'Benton.'

'OK,' Benton said, taking a seat. 'I'm not going to even try to pretend there's nothing weird going on here.'

Cornelius was silent. The smile had left his face. He looked serious. Deadly serious. Benton flicked his glance from Cornelius to Calder and back again. It dawned on him. He knew Calder had been asking questions about Martha's death. Now he realized Cornelius had some of the answers.

Benton's shoulders slumped. No one said anything. Then Benton straightened. His eyes met Cornelius's. 'I guess this is the opportunity I've been hiding from for the last, whatever it is, eighteen years. I'm sorry, Cornelius. I'm truly sorry. What I did was wrong, and I regret it. It would have been wrong in any case, but given what happened to Martha . . .' Benton shook his head. 'I'm sorry.'

'You're *fokkol*, Benton,' Cornelius said levelly. The waiter, who had been hovering to take a breakfast order, backed off.

'I can guess what that means,' said Benton. 'And you are probably right.'

Cornelius shook his head. 'We are both *fokkol*. She suspected something was going on with Beatrice, didn't she?'

Benton nodded.

'I didn't sleep with her, you know.'

Benton didn't reply.

Cornelius looked around the dining room in exasperation, as if there were someone, somewhere, who could undo everything, who could absolve him of what he had done. 'I can't bear to think that she died hating me,' he said.

'She loved you,' Benton said quietly. 'She always loved

336

you. That's why she was so angry with you. In a twisted way, that's why she went with me. I guess I knew that.'

Cornelius took a deep breath. 'You were there at the time. When she died?'

Benton nodded.

'What happened?'

Benton closed his eyes. He owed it to Cornelius to tell him. For nearly twenty years he had been carrying the guilt of his affair with Martha. Perhaps this was his chance to atone for what he had done. To hell with Moolman.

'We were at Kupugani, in an isolated cottage a few hundred feet from the main camp. They wanted to keep us away from the other tourists; in those days a white woman and a black man together could cause all sorts of problems, even way out in the bush. It was the morning, we were just getting up. I was in the bathroom shaving. She was lying on her bed, writing in her diary. The bathroom door was open.'

He opened his eyes. A film of sweat had appeared on his forehead. He looked down at his hands. 'There was a shot, and the window shattered. Martha screamed. I turned and looked. There was another shot.' Benton swallowed. 'She stopped screaming. She stopped screaming.' He blinked at Cornelius. 'She died instantly. I started to move toward her and then I dived for the ground as a third shot rang out. There was a lot of blood. The diary had fallen on to the rug at the foot of the bed. I grabbed it and slid along the floor back to the bathroom. I slammed the door shut, broke the window at the back of the cottage, climbed out and ran.'

'Did you see who fired the shots?' Calder asked.

'No,' said Benton. 'I ran down the path and then ducked into a maintenance shed. I hid behind some metal roofing material. I heard someone run past, and then a few seconds later I heard him run back. He checked the shed, but didn't

337

look behind the metal. I waited for about ten minutes and then crept back to the main camp.

'I never saw her again. I mean her body. The police came and arrested me. They beat me up, tried to get me to confess. Then some big shot showed up and let me go. He said he'd have me killed if I told anyone I had been there.' He glanced at Cornelius. 'He meant it.'

Cornelius grunted.

'Martha's mother came to see me as soon as I got back to New York,' Benton continued. 'I wanted to tell her everything, but, well, I was scared. Scared of the South African police, and scared of you.'

'I can understand that,' muttered Cornelius.

'Surely when you were back in New York you were safe from the South Africans?' Calder said.

Benton shook his head. 'The policeman's name was Colonel Moolman. I will always remember him. He was very convincing. He said that they would get me wherever I was in the world, and I believed him. Especially when Todd was nearly killed after he started asking questions. So when Alex wanted to know about Martha's letter to her mother and the diary, I wasn't about to say anything.'

'Can you tell us about the Laagerbond?' Calder asked. 'About Operation Drommedaris?'

'A bit, but I guess I don't know much more than you, Cornelius. Martha told me how she had read some papers about the group in a briefcase left in a car by two members who came to see you at Hondehoek. She copied down some details. She thought the Laagerbond were going to fund your bid for the *Herald*. That fitted with what you had told us at Bloomfield Weiss: that you were considering a new source of funds.'

Cornelius nodded.

'Martha was very angry. She said she had wanted to do something about it, but she was too scared. I'm not sure why. I assumed it was you she was afraid of.' Benton glanced at Cornelius, who was listening impassively. 'I think she wanted to talk to me some more that weekend, but she never got the chance.'

'Did the Laagerbond fund Zyl News?' Calder asked. He wanted to make sure.

'No,' said Benton. 'Bloomfield Weiss arranged all the funding from the banks and the high-yield bond market. It was tough, but we did it. As far as I'm aware, the Laagerbond never did finance Zyl News. Although it did cross my mind that that might be why you called me down here.'

'When I turned them down, they went to Evelyn Gill,' Cornelius muttered.

'No!' Benton's eyes widened. 'So that's where he gets his funding?'

'We don't know for sure,' said Calder. 'But it fits.'

'I guess it does,' said Benton.

'What about the diary?' said Calder.

'It was very important to her. She said it was like her confidante, her friend.' Benton smiled. 'In fact, as I was shaving, she said it was the first time she had written in it in the presence of someone else. She said it felt good to be able to trust someone enough not to be secretive about it.' The smile disappeared as Benton glanced at Cornelius. 'Sorry.'

'I knew nothing about any diary until Martha's mother mentioned it,' Cornelius said. 'But I guess that was the point.'

'Did you read it?' Calder asked Benton.

'No, no I never did. I know there was some important

stuff in it about the Laagerbond and Operation, what was it, Dromedary?'

'Drommedaris,' said Calder.

'Whatever. And I guess there was a lot about me and about you, Cornelius, and the rest of your family. Besides, I was never going to read it while she was alive.'

'But after she died?' Calder asked.

'I couldn't.'

'Why not?'

'Because I didn't have it.'

'I'm sorry. I thought you said you picked it up off the floor and took it with you?'

'Yes, I did. It was an instinct, I guess. I knew it was important and something told me that the shooting had just made it more important. But I didn't want to take it with me back to the main camp, and so I hid it. And then, after Moolman's warnings, I decided to leave it.'

'Why didn't you just stuff it in your pocket?'

'I wasn't wearing pants. In fact, I wasn't wearing anything. I think I gave the camp owner quite a fright.'

'Ah.' Calder could feel the tension around the table. Benton's nakedness was a reminder of why he and Martha were at Kupugani in the first place.

'Where did you hide it?' growled Cornelius.

'In the maintenance shed. On a beam under a brick.'

'Could it still be there?' Calder asked.

'I have no idea.' Benton thought it over. 'It might be. The shed was full of junk. I had to stand on something to reach the beams, and you can see how tall I am. It's not the kind of place that got an annual spring clean, and even if it did I doubt anyone would go up into the beams. My guess is, as long as the shed hasn't been torn down or converted into something else, the diary could still be there.'

Calder and Cornelius exchanged glances.

'In that case, Benton,' Cornelius said. 'You're coming with us to Kupugani to show us where it is.'

Benton was opening his mouth in protest when a mobile phone rang. Calder knew he had his switched off. It was Cornelius's.

'Yes, Edwin . . . Yes . . . Yes, I've got Benton here with me now . . . how much? . . . Nine twenty? . . . We'll get back to you.'

He put his phone down, a scowl on his face.

'Bad news?' Benton said.

'Evelyn Gill has just come up with a new offer. Nine hundred and twenty million. Laxton are going to make the announcement at seven tomorrow morning.'

'Shit,' said Benton.

Cornelius and Benton shared looks of resignation. 'There's no way we can match that, is there?' Cornelius said.

Benton shook his head. Gloom descended on the table.

Calder broke the silence. 'Gill's getting his money from the Laagerbond. If we expose that, his bid crumbles. You win *The Times*.'

'He's right,' said Benton.

Cornelius glared at Benton. 'We definitely go to Kupugani this afternoon.'

Cornelius and Benton went up to Cornelius's suite to make arrangements. Calder returned to his own more modest hotel near by. In his room he switched on his mobile phone. There was a message from Zan asking him to call her, but first he called Anne's house in Highgate.

Kim answered. Anne was now definitely out of danger, and recovering well. Todd was doing well too, although they still wanted to keep him in hospital under observation. Dr Calder had just taken the kids out to the park.

'Have you heard any more from Edwin?' Calder asked.

'No. But I decided to call his bluff. I phoned Inspector Banks and told her about Donna Snyder visiting Todd. I also told her that Edwin had tried to use the information to blackmail me.'

'Is she suspicious of you?'

'I don't think so. I asked her if she was going to interview Edwin again, and she said probably not, but she sounded frustrated. I told her a little bit about what you had discovered and she told me to wish you luck.'

'Really?'

'My guess is that she's been warned off the van Zyl family and I think she's pissed off about it.'

Calder told Kim all about Benton and Cornelius and the diary hidden in the game reserve. She sounded pleased, although she wasn't entirely convinced of Cornelius's innocence. Calder promised to keep her informed.

Then Calder returned Zan's call. 'Zan, it's Alex.'

'Oh, hi.' It sounded as if she were in a car. 'I'm glad you called back. My contacts in the NIA have struck gold. I'd like to talk it over with you. Where are you?'

'I'm in Johannesburg with your father. We're going to Kupugani this afternoon.'

'Where Martha was killed?'

'That's right. We think her diary was hidden there. We're going to see if it's still hidden.'

'After all these years? There's no chance of that, is there?'

'It's a long story.'

'You must tell me.' Zan paused. Calder could hear a change in pitch in the background engine noise as she shifted gears. 'Look, can I meet you up there?' she said. 'I'd like to discuss this Laagerbond stuff with you face-to-face. And I'd like to help.'

'I suppose you can,' said Calder. 'Can you get there in time?'

'Are you flying from Johannesburg airport?'

'I don't know. Cornelius is arranging it.'

'You probably will be, it's the quickest way. I'll see if I can get there this afternoon. I'm not too far from Cape Town airport now. I'm just about to meet someone and then I'll go straight back to the airport and catch a flight to Jo'burg.'

'Is this meeting something to do with the Laagerbond?' Calder asked.

'Yes,' said Zan. 'I'll tell you about it when I see you.'

'Be careful,' Calder said. 'My last encounter with a Laagerbond member was a little disconcerting.'

'Don't worry,' Zan laughed, but Calder thought he detected a hint of nervousness. 'I can look after myself.'

Calder hoped she could.

The rain was beating down on the surface of the Thames outside Madeira Quay, and Edwin couldn't even see the top half of the Canary Wharf tower, enveloped as it was in angry grey cloud. He put his head in his hands. He had fought so hard for so long to try to maintain control of events, to stay one step ahead of the next disaster, but he had a horrible feeling he was losing it, losing everything.

He had just put the phone down to Detective Inspector Banks. After not hearing anything from Kim he had had no hesitation in carrying out his threat. Anything to muddy the waters of the police investigation. But Banks had said that she already knew about Donna Snyder, and she had been contemptuous of Edwin's suggestion of an affair between

Kim and Calder. The hostility was obvious: Banks had been warned off pursuing Edwin and Cornelius and she didn't like it. Edwin decided to get off the phone quick.

He didn't know exactly what Calder had discovered in South Africa, but Cornelius's decision to rush down there worried him. And then there had come the higher offer from Evelyn Gill for *The Times*.

There was no way that Zyl News could match that. And there was no opportunity to repeat the strategy he had used so successfully with Lord Scotton. Peter Laxton was a different kind of man entirely. He might have skeletons in his closet, but, like Kim, he wouldn't be easily intimidated. Besides, Laxton Media was a public company owing a lot of money to at least a dozen banks. It would be hard – no, impossible – for Peter Laxton to reject a higher bid promising hard cash.

Edwin had suggested once that Cornelius ask Caroline's billionaire husband to come in with him as an equity partner, but Cornelius hadn't even dignified the idea with a reply. He was far too proud, Edwin knew. And, as Cornelius had said, there were no nest eggs hidden anywhere.

Losing *The Times* was disappointing, but Edwin had a powerful feeling that worse was to follow, that the questions Kim and Calder were asking would set in train a series of events that would end badly for him. His father would have to retire some time in the next few years and Edwin was set to succeed him. But he was under no illusions that Cornelius was happy with that idea. It wouldn't take much for him to change his mind.

Edwin stared out of the window again. What could he do?

He picked up the phone and dialled a number in South Africa.

*

Visser was pacing up and down in his study at the farm when the phone rang. He picked it up.

'Andries, it's Freddie.'

'Have you heard from Kobus?' Visser asked.

'He flew down to the Cape this morning,' Steenkamp said. 'He should be finished by this afternoon.'

'Good. The sooner we get him on a plane to London, the better.'

'Not necessarily,' said Steenkamp. 'Paul Strydom just told me that Cornelius van Zyl is in South Africa. With two other men: one of whom sounds like Alex Calder, the other is tall, black and American and could very well be Benton Davis.'

'Where are they?'

'Cornelius is staying at the Intercontinental in Sandton.'

'Get Kobus up there as soon as he has finished his business in the Cape.'

'I was going to do just that,' said Steenkamp.

Visser slammed down the phone. If only he had been more decisive earlier! He slumped into his chair. Suddenly he felt very tired. His chest hurt: it never stopped hurting, nor would it stop until the end. And he felt the end was rushing towards him like an express train out of a tunnel. At that moment he felt like lying down on the tracks in front of it.

Zan was driving through the broad Franschhoek valley. The landscape was green and lush, dotted with farmhouses and vineyards, enclosed on three sides by high rock walls. She was heading for the pass at the top of the valley.

She thought about her conversation with Alex Calder. It looked as if he was getting somewhere. She definitely wanted to be there when he found the diary, if he did. She picked up her cell phone and called her husband, saying that she was going up to Johannesburg for the night. It was an interesting new property that she would have to move fast on: she'd explain later. Piet had learned to tolerate her erratic movements. Florence, the maid, would be there to take care of the kids until Piet got back from the office.

It would be strange to see her father again after all this time. She had followed his career in the press and seen countless photos of him, but she hadn't actually spoken to him for over ten years. At times in her youth they had fallen out, but she had always admired him: his strength, his power, his integrity. She still hadn't got over her disappointment at the way he had left the country after Martha died. Since then she had never really felt she could trust him. She wondered what his reaction to her would be.

She passed through the town of Franschhoek with its bijoux galleries and shops and its monument to the Huguenots who had settled there three hundred years before. She followed the road sharply upwards. As she crossed over the pass, the landscape changed. Before her was a bleak expanse of fynbos, punctuated by outcrops of grey rock, sloping down to a plain and a lake shimmering light blue in the distant sunshine. No signs of cultivation, or even habitation. It certainly was a lonely spot, and presumably that was why it had been chosen for the meet.

A couple of kilometres down the slope from the pass Zan reached a dirt track. She followed this as instructed for a further four kilometres and came to a halt at a turn-off. She checked her watch: twelve minutes early. The spot was out of sight of the main road, out of sight of anything but fynbos and bare rock.

She settled back to wait. She was nervous. She knew it was dangerous to meet here, in the middle of nowhere, but she was thoroughly prepared. It seemed worth the risk.

She heard a car behind her, a dirty blue Toyota, not the mode of transport of the man she was expecting. The car pulled up twenty metres away.

She got out of her own vehicle.

The man in the Toyota got out too. He was heavy set with close-cropped hair, a moustache and a thick neck, wearing an open-necked shirt and a coat. He began to walk towards her.

'Stop!' she said.

The man continued. Zan tensed. She hoped her preparations and the training she had received all those years ago in the ANC camps in Mozambique would be effective.

'Where's Dirk du Toit?' she called out in Afrikaans.

'He couldn't make it,' the man said.

Zan reached behind her for the pistol shoved in the waistband at the small of her back. The other man was quick. Before she could aim, he had whipped his own weapon out from a shoulder holster and was pointing it at her. He fired and she felt a thud in her chest as the round hit her body armour. She fell backwards, twisting as she hit the ground so that her own gun was pointed straight at the man who was lumbering towards her. She fired twice, hitting him in his unprotected chest. He slumped to the ground.

She scrambled to her feet and ran over to him. He was still breathing. His gun was an inch from his hand and she kicked it away. She pointed her pistol at the man's head.

'What's your name?'

He shook his head.

She kicked him in the ribs, a few inches below one of the entry wounds. The man screamed in pain.

'I said, what's your name?'

'Moolman,' the man whispered.

'Kobus Moolman? Colonel Kobus Moolman?'

The man nodded.

Zan remembered the name. He had been a leading member of the Vlakplaas death squad that had killed so many comrades in the struggle. And a minute ago he had tried to kill her; her breast still ached from the impact of the round on the Kevlar.

She glanced at his wounds. It was just possible that, if she called an ambulance, he might survive.

She pulled the trigger twice more.

27

'If she's going to come, she'd better hurry up,' Cornelius said checking his watch. 'The plane leaves in fifteen minutes.'

Calder, Cornelius and Benton were at Johannesburg airport waiting in the small but comfortable lounge of the charter company that was going to fly them to Kupugani. A group of four young German tourists were drinking beer at a nearby table: they were due to be dropped off at a game reserve eighty kilometres further on. The tension between Benton and Cornelius was unmistakable, but they had come to a kind of truce, burying their mutual suspicion in their joint desire to find the diary and the cause of Martha's death.

'Shall we hold the plane?' Benton said.

'No,' said Cornelius sharply. 'We want to make sure we have a chance to take a good look round before it gets dark.'

'You haven't seen much of Zan, have you?' Calder said to Cornelius.

'Not much, if anything at all. After Martha died I got the strong impression she was judging me for quitting South Africa. She's a strong-willed woman,' he smiled, 'like her father, I suppose. We were both too stubborn to give the other a chance. That can happen in families.'

It certainly could happen in the van Zyl family, Calder thought. Outside on the apron he saw two young pilots, a man and a woman, climb into the Cessna Caravan and begin their pre start-up checks. It was a twin-engined aircraft which could carry ten passengers and was ideal for short runways.

Benton disappeared to the bathroom. Cornelius was leafing through a copy of one of the national newspapers. 'It's good to be back in this country, you know. I've hardly been here at all since Martha died.'

'It's a beautiful place . . .' Calder said.

'But? There was a "but" in there that you didn't say.'

'But it's still screwed up, ten years after apartheid.'

'I wonder what Martha would have thought of it today?'

'She would have been pleased, wouldn't she?'

'Oh, yes, yes she would.' Cornelius considered the question. 'I guess she was right and I was wrong. South Africa's still a violent place, but there hasn't been the anarchy I expected.'

'Do you regret leaving?'

'Oh, no,' Cornelius said. 'I'm proud of Zyl News and what it's done. But . . .'

'But what?'

Cornelius glanced at Calder. 'You know all our family secrets. You know about Todd and about Edwin. If I do win *The Times*, what will I do with it? I'm seventy-two. I might stay on a couple of years to turn the paper around, but then who runs Zyl News? Todd won't have it and I'll make damn sure Edwin doesn't get his hands on it.' Calder smiled and Cornelius noticed. 'I've turned a blind eye to Edwin's activities for too long.'

'There must be some managers within the company you could rely on to carry on after you. Or you could hire someone.'

'Yes, I could do that. I probably will do that. Want a job?'

Calder grinned. 'I used to have a paper round when I was sixteen. I gave it up after a couple of months. I'm not a natural newspaperman.'

Cornelius smiled. 'I wonder what Martha would want me to do.'

Calder fished a card out of his pocket and handed it to Cornelius. 'You know what? When all this is over, give George Field a call.'

'George? He'd never talk to me now.'

Calder shrugged. 'He might.'

Cornelius put the card in his pocket.

Benton returned from the bathroom and the ground staff announced that the aircraft was ready for boarding. As they filed out on to the apron, Zan joined them, out of breath.

'You made it,' said Calder.

'Only just.'

Cornelius turned to face her. The aircraft engines roared a few feet away.

Zan hesitated and then drew near to him. 'Hello, Pa,' she said, and kissed him on the cheek.

He smiled and they embraced. 'I'm glad you could come,' he shouted above the engine noise.

'You look good, Pa,' she smiled. 'Better than you do in your pictures in the paper.'

Cornelius grinned. 'So do you.'

They climbed on to the aircraft and took up their seats towards the front. Zan paused next to the open seat by her father, and then decided to sit next to Calder. They strapped themselves in and the plane taxied to the hold.

'We didn't think you were going to make it,' Calder said.

'I almost didn't.'

'You said you were meeting someone about the Laagerbond this morning. Did you find anything out?'

'Yes. Don't trust the bastards.' Zan explained how she had received a call that she should meet Dirk du Toit, a senior banker and presumably a Laagerbond member, at a deserted spot near Franschhoek. She described her rendezvous with Colonel Moolman, how she had had the foresight to wear a bullet-proof vest and how she shot him after he had tried to kill her. She omitted to mention how she had finished him off.

Calder was shocked by how coolly she described it all. 'Is he dead?'

'I'm afraid so,' she replied.

'And you still flew up here? What about the police?'

'I'm sure they can sort it all out by themselves. I'll speak to them when we've finished here. I'm not that easily put off.'

'You certainly know how to handle yourself.'

'The ANC taught me well in Mozambique,' Zan replied. 'Moolman was complacent, probably because I'm a woman. His mistake.'

At least the Laagerbond had lost one of their killers, Calder thought. But there were almost certainly plenty more where he came from, and the attempt to kill Zan showed that they were becoming more desperate. It wouldn't be long before they discovered that Calder and Cornelius were together in South Africa, if they hadn't already.

'So what did your NIA contacts tell you about the Laagerbond?' Calder asked.

'I've got some names. Eight.'

'Great. Anyone important?'

'Two former cabinet ministers and a general. But they're dead now. Then there's Dirk du Toit, Andries Visser, Daniel Havenga and two others I haven't heard of. Maybe Moolman makes nine. I've made some notes, they're in my bag.'

'Well done,' Calder said, although he was actually a little disappointed. The dead people weren't of much value, and he knew about Visser and Havenga. Du Toit might be a useful lead.

'So,' said Zan. 'How do you know the diary is hidden at Kupugani?'

Calder explained.

They flew east over the wide brown plain of the high veld, over the peaks and gorges of the Drakensberg mountains to the bush veld on the other side. Trees and scrub stretched from the high escarpment behind them as far as the eye could see, like a sparsely planted forest. Soon the aircraft descended and joined the circuit above a clearing with a stripe of tarmac at its centre. Calder could see a cluster of buildings that was the main camp about a mile to the south. On final approach the pilot pointed out a small herd of five elephants grazing on the trees and then the aircraft was on the ground. They disembarked, and the aircraft taxied back to the runway threshold and took off, taking the group of German tourists on to their destination.

A Land Rover approached them driven by a young ranger who introduced himself as Darren. They piled on board and he drove them off to the main camp.

'Whose are those?' Zan asked, pointing towards three single-engined aircraft parked under a makeshift hangar. There were two Piper Warriors and a Cessna 172.

'They belong to some of the guests,' the ranger replied.

'You could have flown up yourself, Zan,' Cornelius said.

'I would have if I'd had time.'

'Do you fly?' Calder asked.

'Yes, every now and then,' she said. 'I own a Saratoga, which I keep at Stellenbosch. It would take a couple of days to fly from Cape Town to here, though.'

The Land Rover lurched along a rough track, surprising a warthog on its way. They soon approached the camp, which comprised half a dozen thatched wooden cottages clustered around an old farmhouse. As they climbed out of the Land Rover a thin woman with short grey hair and a tanned, weatherbeaten face emerged from a door marked

'Office' to greet them. She was wearing a khaki tunic and trousers, just like the ranger.

She approached Cornelius first, holding out her hand. 'Welcome to Kupugani,' she said. 'I'm Phyllis Delahay. You must be Mr van Zyl.'

'That's right. Thank you for seeing us at such short notice,' Cornelius said.

'Not at all. I must admit I was surprised I didn't see you eighteen years ago. Now, introduce me to your companions.'

Cornelius was a little taken aback to be put so firmly in his place, but he introduced Zan, Calder and Benton.

'Yes, I remember you, of course,' Phyllis said to Benton. 'I do hope the police weren't too hard on you?'

Benton smiled. 'They were pretty rough, Mrs Delahay. But they let me go in the end. This is the first time I have been back to South Africa since then.'

'It's changed. For the better. And you?' The woman turned her eyes on to Calder. They were searching; hers wasn't just a polite enquiry, she wanted to know what he was doing there.

'I'm an old friend of Todd van Zyl's wife,' he said. 'Todd is Martha's son.'

'This is the man who has been asking the awkward questions about her death,' Cornelius said.

Phyllis smiled quickly. 'Ah, yes, Libby mentioned she had met you. And you're Martha's daughter?' she said, turning to Zan.

'Stepdaughter,' Zan said.

'I see.' Phyllis seemed to disapprove. 'Will you have some tea?' she asked.

She indicated some rattan chairs on a verandah overlooking a small watering hole. Monkeys played in the trees above. The chairs caught the afternoon sun, which was warm without being hot. Strange bird calls, unfamiliar squawks, whoops and trills, emanated from the bush surrounding the camp on all sides. Calder wondered how far away the elephants were that they had spotted from their aeroplane. A uniformed waiter appeared with a teapot, followed by a waitress with some cake.

'A nice place you have here, Mrs Delahay,' Cornelius said.

'Thank you. My father bought it in the 1930s. We used to use the farm just for ourselves and our guests. As time went on we began to take in tourists. Now Kupugani has become big business. Financially that's good, of course, but I sometimes think it's unfortunate.' She sipped her tea. 'All the guests have just left for the afternoon game drive. They won't be back until after dark.'

'As I told you over the telephone,' Cornelius said, 'we've come here to try to find out more about how my wife died.'

'Yes, I understand,' Phyllis said. 'But frankly I'm a bit surprised you've all come together.' She raised an eyebrow at Benton.

'Martha's death upset all of us,' he said. 'Cornelius and I have been talking; he knows why Martha and I were here. I'd like to help him.'

'Do you have any idea who shot her?' Zan asked.

Phyllis shook her head. 'No. I know it wasn't guerrillas as the police claimed. My trackers found footprints from a single man, wearing expensive boots. From the size of his feet they guessed he was of below-average height. I told the police this, of course, but they ignored me. I decided to let it drop. I knew that you were a powerful man, Mr van Zyl, and I expected to be hearing from you. When I didn't, well, I assumed that you had colluded in the police's cover-up.'

'An understandable assumption, but mistaken,' Cornelius said.

Benton cleared his throat. 'Martha had a diary. It was a black notebook about this big.' He indicated the size with his hands. 'We are pretty sure that it contains some important clues as to who killed her. I grabbed it when I ran away, and hid it. We'd like to look and see if it's still where I put it.'

'Heavens,' said Phyllis. 'And where was that?'

'In a maintenance shed near the cottage.'

'Is the shed still there?' asked Cornelius.

'Yes, it is,' Phyllis said.

'Has it been cleared out over the last twenty years?'

'No,' Phyllis replied, after a moment's thought. 'Things will have been brought in and taken out. But it hasn't been repainted, or even repaired that I can remember.'

Cornelius exchanged glances with Calder. This was looking good. 'Can we see it?'

'I don't see why not.' Phyllis put down her tea cup and went over to a wall where three bolt-action rifles rested in racks. She took one, loaded it with five rounds, picked up a small backpack and headed off into the bush. 'Follow me.'

She led them along a sandy trail into the scrub. On either side termite mounds rose precariously, some of them ten feet high. Despite her age and size, Phyllis seemed supremely confident in the bush.

'Do you really need the gun?' Calder asked.

'This camp is unfenced,' she said. 'You never know what you'll run into. See that?' She paused and pointed to some marks in the sandy track. 'That's leopard.' She studied the print for a couple of seconds. 'Probably came through here last night. We'll be fine during daylight, but you do have to be careful when it's dark.'

'Would you shoot? If we did run into something?'

'Oh, no,' Phyllis said. 'Only as a very last resort. The important thing to remember is not to run. If you hold your ground, you'll be OK. Mind you, this is a powerful rifle. They tell me it will drop a charging elephant, although I'd rather not test that one out.'

They walked through the trees for a couple of minutes before they came to a cottage, much like the others in the camp. It stood by itself, overlooking a dry river bed. As they approached a pair of hornbills flew from a tree, kicking up a fuss as they went, their flared tail feathers balancing their large beaks in ungainly flight. To the west it was just possible to see the peaks of the Drakensberg mountains in the distance.

'This is where we stayed,' Benton said.

'It's a lovely spot,' said Calder.

'You can see it's very discreet,' Phyllis said. 'And a lot of game passes along the stream bed.' She pointed to the dry sand which was crisscrossed with animal and bird tracks of all kinds. 'The killer fired his shots from over there.' She pointed to the other bank. 'Just behind that mopane tree.' It was a distance of about sixty yards, no problem for a good shot.

Calder glanced at Benton. He was standing still, a faraway look in his eyes. Everyone was quiet, watching him.

He smiled grimly. 'Sorry. Just that being here, it brings it back.' He took a deep breath. 'Anyway, I broke the bathroom window and climbed out the back. Here, I'll show you.'

He strode rapidly round to the back of the cottage, his long legs leaving the others behind. The bathroom window was out of sight of the spot where the killer had stood. 'Then I ran along the path, but I ducked to the right here.' There was a turn-off where a narrower path headed into the trees. After twenty yards or so it passed a small shed. 'And this is where I hid.'

357

'Can we look inside?' Calder asked Phyllis.

'Certainly.' She pulled out a key. 'It's locked now, but it wasn't then. Let me show you.'

She switched on the light from a single electric bulb. The shed was small, about the size of a garage. It was full of old equipment: gardening tools, an axe, oil lamps, pieces of wood, a broken table, some cans of paraffin, and an insect screen for a window. 'When I hid in here there was some metal roofing material over there,' Benton said pointing to one wall. 'I squeezed myself behind that.'

Cornelius looked up at the roof. There were beams running the length of the shed, about eight or nine feet off the ground. 'And where did you hide the diary?'

'Up there.'

The beams were old and unpainted. And lying lengthways on one of them Calder could see the edge of a brick.

'Is that it?' asked Calder.

'I think so,' said Benton. He looked around for something suitable to stand on, and found an old tea chest. It creaked under his weight as he climbed up on to it. He reached up, lifted the brick with one hand, and ran his fingers along the beam with the other. 'It's not there.'

'Check further along,' said Cornelius.

With help from the others, who cleared a path along the floor, Benton slid the tea chest under the beam the length of the building, and reached upwards. Nothing.

'Are you sure no one has found a diary?' Cornelius snapped at Phyllis, unable to keep the frustration out of his voice.

Phyllis shook her head. 'I'm sorry, Mr van Zyl,' she replied primly. 'I'm afraid your trip has been a waste of time.'

A wave of disappointment washed over Calder. Vague hope had somehow turned into near certainty that they would find the diary after such a long time, certainty that he now realized had always been groundless. He could see that Cornelius and Benton felt equally crushed. Only Zan seemed to take their failure with equanimity, but of course she had less at stake than they did.

'Can we go back and see where the killer stood?' Cornelius said.

'All right,' Phyllis said, and led them back to the cottage and down into the river bed. Phyllis was talking to Benton in murmured tones, no doubt commiserating with him for all those years ago. As they reached the far bank she paused. 'It's just by that mopane tree I showed you earlier,' she said. 'Benton wants to spend a couple of moments alone in the cottage. I'll take him back there.'

Calder and Cornelius climbed the bank and pushed through the scrub to the tree. There was a good view of the cottage on the other side of the bank. They could see Benton and Phyllis inside. And Zan hurrying back across the stream bed towards them.

'What's Zan up to?' Calder asked. 'Do you think she's scared?' He did suddenly feel vulnerable out in the bush without the protection of the rifle, which Phyllis had taken with her.

'Zan, scared?' Cornelius said. 'Never.'

The urgency with which Zan was moving worried Calder. He hurried after her, followed by Cornelius. They scrambled down the bank and back to the cottage. The door was open. They walked in together to see Phyllis and Benton standing side by side next to a bed, on which lay Phyllis's open backpack. In Benton's hand was a black notebook. They were both staring at something over Calder's shoulder.

He turned round.

'Get in!' said Zan. She was standing in the corner of the

room, holding Phyllis's rifle, which she was pointing at Calder and Cornelius. She waved them over to where Phyllis and Benton were standing and kicked the door shut. 'Now . . . very slowly, Benton . . . hand me the diary.'

28

God, it's all getting out of control. I can't trust anyone. No one!

Perhaps if I write it all down calmly it will seem clearer to me.

Zan's flying to London today. In fact she'll be taking off in six hours from now, thank God. I told her this morning that I would spend the day in Guguletu with Miriam Masote and a bunch of visitors from the American Council of Churches, but I'd be back late afternoon so I could take her to the airport. Well, I got a call from Miriam just before I left home that there had been some kind of riot in Guguletu last night and she had decided to postpone the visit till tomorrow. So I went into Stellenbosch to do a little shopping.

I was on my way back to the car from Oom Samie's, walking along Church Street, when I spotted Zan at a table by the window of a coffee shop. I was crossing the road to say hi, when I saw who she was with. Three men. I recognized Daniel Havenga first, and I thought it was odd that she should be seeing him: I didn't realize she knew him. Then I noticed that someone was holding her hand across the table, a big red-haired man in his mid-twenties, quite cute. So Zan does have a boyfriend after all, I thought, she's kept that very quiet, I wonder who he is. Then I saw the third man: Andries Visser. None of this made any sense. I took an instant decision, turned around in the middle of the road and hurried off. I didn't look back so I wasn't sure whether they had seen me or not.

I drove back home trying to figure out what was going on. It didn't add up at first. Havenga and a young woman by herself meant philandering. Havenga and Visser together meant Laagerbond. Why would someone like Zan, a fully paid-up radical opponent of apartheid, be talking to the Laagerbond, her bitter enemy?

Perhaps she was acting as some kind of agent for Cornelius? Yes, that made sense, I thought. I could imagine Cornelius trusting her and neither of them telling me about it. Yes that must be it.

I arrived back at Hondehoek, made myself a cup of coffee and took it out into the garden. It rained last night, but it was a bright clear morning. As I felt the gentle sunshine on my face I knew that wasn't the right explanation, however much I wanted it to be.

The three men and Zan were not in the midst of a tense negotiating session. They were relaxed in each other's company. Visser was smoking a cigarette, Havenga was chattering away and laughing, Zan was smiling too. They were *conspiratorial*. That was it, conspiratorial.

And what about the red-haired man? He was holding Zan's hand in a familiar way, the way you would hold the hand of someone you knew for a long time, a long-standing girlfriend. Yet there was also something illicit about it. His eyes were on Zan. He was happy in her company, enjoying their brief time together. And he was with Visser and Havenga.

He looked intelligent, clean cut, a young professional.

It's obvious. She is his girlfriend. Both of them were conspiring with the Laagerbond.

Okay, but how could Zan, the activist member of the Black Sash and the End Conscription Campaign, talk to these people in such a familiar way? The old Zan maybe, the Zan who enrolled in the Rand Afrikaans University to spite her father perhaps, but not the new Zan, the Zan who transferred to Wits, joined marches and protested against apartheid in all its forms.

Unless the old Zan has never changed.

Everyone knows that over the last ten years the security forces have infiltrated the main opposition groups, the SACP, the UDF, the ANC. They've done it with spies; often white spies, which is why so many black opponents of the regime have become wary of dealing with whites over the years. Well, one of those spies is Zan.

She probably met her red-haired boyfriend at the Rand Afrikaans University. The security police would think she's a perfect candidate, the pro-Afrikaner daughter of a prominent English-speaking liberal family. All they had to do was to get her to deny her opinions and bury them. Which she has done very effectively.

And that's why she has suddenly reappeared in our lives. She is working with the Laagerbond to warm up Cornelius, observe him and ultimately help persuade him to join forces with them. Just like Beatrice Pienaar.

The Operation Drommedaris paper I read in Daniel Havenga's briefcase mentioned Impala's opinion of Cornelius. I assume Impala is Beatrice Pienaar. It said this opinion was confirmed by Eland. Is Zan Eland?

It would be wrong to say that I never believed in Zan's change of heart. I *did* believe in her radicalism, her return to the family, because I wanted to believe in it. I always hated the way she turned against Cornelius and me, and there was nothing I wanted to do more than accept her back.

But the prodigal daughter is a spy.

Here comes her car now. What the hell am I going to say to her?

Later . . .

Zan's gone. Finneas is driving her to the airport; I couldn't.

She sat in the kitchen while I made us some coffee. She seemed cool, relaxed. "You didn't go to the Project today, did you?" she said.

"There was a riot last night. The visit was postponed."

"I see. Was that you I saw in Church Street?" she asked casually.

She had obviously seen me. She was fishing to find out whether I had seen her. I smiled. "Yes, I ran some errands." I turned away from her and fiddled with the kettle. "Where were you? I didn't see you." I could hear my voice was strained. Hoarse.

"Yes you did," Zan said slowly. Matter-of-factly.

I turned to face her. "What the hell were you doing with those men?" I demanded, giving up all pretense of innocence.

Zan smiled. "They're friends of mine."

"You're a spy, aren't you?" I said. "A spy for the Laagerbond. You're trying to lure your father into joining them."

"I don't know what you're talking about," said Zan. "What's the Laagerbond?"

"Who was that boy whose hand you were holding so sweetly?" I asked.

"Just an old friend from university," Zan said.

"University? Which one."

Zan didn't answer immediately. She seemed to be thinking. "Those friends I was with," she said at last. "They are

364

very powerful people. I like them, but they can be dangerous. They can even get people killed."

"Are you threatening me?"

"I'm just suggesting that it would be a good idea if you didn't tell anyone who you saw me with today. And I wouldn't share your wild ideas about me being a spy with anyone else either. Especially Pa."

"You *are* threatening me! Get your stuff and get out of my house now!"

Zan smiled again. "All right," she said, slowly pulling herself to her feet. And then, as she was at the kitchen door: "Enjoy your weekend with Benton."

I rushed into the garden to give her time to pack. She was quick. Thank God she's going to London. But what the hell do I do now?

I can't believe what she's done. That she was betraying us, her family, the whole time. She's eaten with us, talked to us, laughed with us. And who else has she betrayed? How many people who work for the cause are in jail because of her? I thought that hatred that she showed me when she was a teenager had disappeared, but it hasn't. It has grown and festered under her skin. I suppose I can imagine her betraying me, but her own father? Except in her twisted mind she probably believes she's helping him to see the light.

I've no doubt her threat is real. Perhaps I should just keep quiet as she suggested. But how can I do that when it will mean that Cornelius will sell out to the Laagerbond? I can't go through the rest of my life pretending that Zan is my sweet little radical stepdaughter. God knows what damage she will do to the ANC once she gets to London.

Plus she's read this diary. And recently as well. How else would she know about Benton? Of course that's the other part of the threat. She's going to tell Cornelius about him.

I don't know what to do. I need to talk to someone about it. Talk to Benton. He's the one person who can give me a sensible, objective view.

I'm glad I wrote that letter to Mom yesterday. Next time I hear from Zan, as I surely will, I'll tell her that if anything happens to me it will all come out.

I'd like to talk to Cornelius. He's in Philadelphia at the moment and won't be back here for a couple of weeks. I'm worried about using the phone; after my run-in with the security police I wouldn't be surprised if it was tapped. And I don't know whether I can trust him. I don't know how deep Zan and Beatrice and the Laagerbond have gotten their claws into him.

Oh, God, I'm so scared. How did I get myself into this mess?

At least I'm seeing Benton tomorrow night. I can't wait.

29

'Put the gun down, Zan.' Cornelius's voice was strong, authoritative.

'No,' said Zan.

Cornelius took a step forward. 'I said, put it down.'

'I'll shoot you, Pa,' Zan said. 'I don't want to, but I will if I have to. I've killed a lot of people, believe me.'

Cornelius halted.

'Take three steps back,' Zan commanded.

Cornelius slowly did as he was told. 'When you said you'd killed people, did you mean Martha?'

'Yes,' Zan said.

'And you tried to kill Todd?'

'No, that was the Laagerbond. Edwin told me Todd had been asking questions. He also told me about the joy ride in the Yak he had planned. It seemed like a good opportunity for them to shut him up.'

'But how could you do that to Todd?' Cornelius asked. 'He's your brother.'

'Half-brother. I hate him, Pa. I always have, ever since I was fourteen. That's when I realized that he and Martha had stolen you. I tried to win you back, but you left me. You left me and you left your people and you ran away.'

'My people?'

'The Afrikaner people. Our people.'

'But you were a supporter of the struggle against apartheid!'

'Not me, Pa,' said Zan, smiling. 'How could you ever

believe that? I was always working for our people. It was me who first suggested that the Laagerbond approach you. We had it all planned perfectly. The SACP hit-list; Beatrice.'

'And Hennie?' said Cornelius. 'Did you kill Hennie?'

'No,' said Zan, frowning. 'No, guerrillas did that.' But there was doubt in her voice.

'Just like they killed Martha, I suppose,' Cornelius said, his voice laced with scorn.

'You ran away! Why did you run away, Pa? Operation Drommedaris was perfect for you. It would have brought us together, doing something for our people, father and daughter. But when *she* died, you left. Left your country, left your people, left *me*. You went to America and married another American woman and forgot all about your home-land. How could you do that to me after everything I had done for you?'

Cornelius's face was a mixture of disbelief and revulsion. 'But why kill Martha?'

'I had to. She had figured out what I was up to. She knew about the Laagerbond and she knew I was working for the security police. And she was sleeping with *him*,' she jerked the rifle towards Benton. 'I read all about it in this.' Zan nodded at the diary which she had placed on the small table beside her. 'I bet the last entries are all about me.'

'So the Laagerbond told you to kill her?' Calder said.

'Oh, no. I told them they should do it, but they refused. They didn't want to scare you off, they said. I decided not to fly to London, but to Johannesburg instead. I got hold of a rifle and drove over to Kupugani. After all those trips hunting springbok with Uncle Hennie I knew how to use one, even then. And when I saw Martha with Benton it wasn't difficult to pull the trigger. I'm just sorry I didn't get you as well.'

She glared at Benton. He scowled back.

'The police caught me driving out of Kupugani. I called the Laagerbond. They were unhappy, but they had to help me cover everything up, and so the police let me go. It would have stayed covered up if Alex Calder hadn't asked so many damned questions.' Anger burned in her eyes as she glared at Calder. 'Phyllis knew,' she said. 'That was why she tried to sneak the diary to Benton without me seeing. You found it and you read it, didn't you?'

'Yes,' said Phyllis, her voice strong. 'We discovered it about five years ago. When I'd read it I decided to keep quiet about it. I was afraid something like this might happen.'

'Did someone from the Laagerbond really try to kill you this morning?' Calder said.

'Oh, yes. After the Laagerbond had failed to stop you I told them I would take care of things myself. Like I did with Martha. I thought I was going to meet an old friend who is a member to talk it over, but it was a trap. For some reason they must think I'm more of a danger to them than you are.'

'I'm not surprised,' muttered Cornelius.

'But you don't really have an NIA contact?' Calder said.

'Of course not. I wanted to give you just enough information about the Laagerbond to make you believe I was on your side, but not enough to actually be useful.'

'Is your brother in on this with you?' asked Cornelius.

'Edwin?' Zan snorted. 'I wouldn't trust Edwin any more than you would. But he has kept me well informed the whole time, in fact he called me this morning. He knew I was interested in your activities, but he didn't know why, although he may have guessed. It was Edwin who told me that you and Kim were so eager to find out about Martha, and I passed that on to the Laagerbond. Except they screwed up again.'

369

'And so they blew up my sister. Crippled her.' Scorn and anger mixed in equal measure in Calder's voice. 'An innocent woman. A mother.'

'As I said, they screwed up,' said Zan. She turned to Phyllis. 'Where are the keys to the aircraft?'

'They're locked in a cupboard in the hut at the airstrip.'

'And where's the key to that?'

Phyllis didn't move. Zan was still pointing the rifle at Calder. 'You're a brave woman,' said Zan. 'Give me the key or I'll shoot him.'

Phyllis blinked. Then she slowly pulled a set of keys out of her pocket, and began to select one.

'Throw me all of them,' Zan said. 'By my feet.'

Phyllis tossed the keys on to the floor, and Zan crouched down to pick them up.

'Good. Now, put your hands on your heads and come out of the cottage one at a time.'

She placed the diary in Phyllis's small backpack, which she slung over her shoulder. Then she opened the door and backed out. Phyllis came first, followed by Calder and Cornelius. Benton came last. As Zan was backing away, he paused before the threshold and slammed the door shut. Zan lowered her rifle and pressed the trigger. It was a giant round. It rammed into the door, shattering it, and on the other side Benton let out a cry. The door swung open to reveal him lying on the ground, clutching his shoulder.

'Up!' Zan shouted. Benton didn't move. 'I said get up!'

Benton sat on his haunches, his face crumpled in agony. He was trying not to scream and barely succeeding.

'Get him, Alex,' Zan said.

Calder slowly went over to Benton and picked him up.

'Now move! Over to the shed. And take it slowly.'

They walked in single file, Zan's gun raised behind them.

Calder staggered under Benton's weight. He was losing a lot of blood.

'Get in!' barked Zan as they reached the hut. 'In!'

They did as they were told. 'Back! Back as far as you can!' They moved to a pile of junk along the back wall, as Zan stood in the doorway. She raised the rifle, aimed at the light bulb and fired, all in one movement. The report of the powerful weapon sounded like an explosion in the confined space and the bulb shattered. She was a good shot. Calder saw his opportunity to lunge forward, but in an instant the gun was lowered and pointed at his chest.

'I said, back!'

Calder stepped back.

Zan's eyes fell on Cornelius. She hesitated, unsure what to do with him. 'Pa? Pa. Won't you come with me?'

'Come with you? Where? You have nowhere to hide. The only place you'll be going is jail!'

'Don't you see that I did all this for you? For you and for our people? Martha was an evil woman. She had just had sex with this man when I shot her. You're a powerful man, Pa. You can fix this. You can make things all right again. Come with me.'

'Zan, you are the evil one,' Cornelius said. His voice was hard and cold and laced with contempt. 'God damn you, you're no daughter of mine!'

A tear ran down Zan's cheek, then another. She bit her lip. All her strength and bluster seemed to be slipping away. For a moment Calder thought she was going to put down the rifle and slump to the ground. Then she blinked back the tears and her face hardened as she made up her mind. She moved with manic energy. With one hand she grabbed a small can of paraffin and threw it outside, the rifle pointing steadily at her captives. She snatched a box of matches by the oil lamps and backed out of the hut. She slammed the door shut.

There was no window, it was pitch black. Calder threw himself at where he remembered the door was but it held. His hands fumbled for the latch, but he heard a key turning in the lock. He felt Cornelius beside him. Also scrabbling for the latch. 'She's locked it,' Calder said.

'What's that?' said Phyllis.

They could hear the trickle of liquid, then they could smell paraffin.

'Oh, God,' said Cornelius. 'Zan! Zan!' he yelled. 'Let us out! Zan!'

Calder stepped back and trod on something. Benton screamed in pain. Then Calder charged at the door. It held.

Sounds outside. A gentle *whump*. Then crackling as the wood caught light. As Calder hit the door again, he could feel its warmth. He paused. In the confined black space the noises were loud, so loud. Benton's whimpering. His own heavy breathing. The sound of Cornelius banging against the wall. The darkness was already getting warmer. He felt a rising tide of panic within him, a desire to lash out, to beat the walls with his fists, to do anything to get out of there.

'There's a pickaxe,' Phyllis said calmly, her disembodied voice a couple of feet behind him. 'There's a pickaxe over by the far wall. I'll get it.' Calder could hear her moving, bumping into things. 'Stay calm. Stay by the door. It's the weakest part of the structure, the walls are solid log.'

Calder remained still, taking deep breaths to try to stay calm. The door was warm. The hut was growing warmer. The crackling was growing louder. Panic seeped through the darkness: Cornelius and Benton managed to remain silent, but he could feel their fear. He couldn't yet see the flames or smell the smoke; when he could it would probably be too late. Phyllis was taking for ever. He wanted to tell her to hurry up but he knew that wouldn't help.

'Got it!' said Phyllis. 'Where are you Alex?'

'Here!' Calder shouted.

Phyllis bumped into something and gave a little cry. Then there was a scream of pain as she stepped on Benton. 'Where?'

'Here!' repeated Calder urgently. He held out his hand and felt Phyllis's. A moment later the pickaxe handle was in his grasp.

'Stand clear!' he said. He stepped back and swung. The pickaxe bounced off hard wood. The wall. He could smell smoke. It stung his eyes in the blackness. He saw a flicker of light at the bottom corner of the door. The flames would be in the hut in a moment. He swung again, above and to the right of the flicker. Wood splintered. Another swing. More splinters, the flicker of flames, smoke, a sliver of daylight. Another swing. More daylight now. Smoke tickled his throat. If he coughed it would all be over. He held his breath, aimed for the door lock which he could now see, and swung again.

The lock shattered and the door swung open, letting in a ferocious wall of heat. Flames licked into the hut, running almost instantaneously over the beams and along the roof. Cornelius charged through the flames out into the open. Calder turned and grabbed hold of Phyllis. 'Go!' he yelled and pushed her into and through the flames.

He breathed in smoke. Coughed. Bent down, grabbed Benton's leg. Pulled. Benton yelled and began to scrabble along the floor. God, the bastard was heavy. Calder coughed again. Benton's screams were smothered in his own spluttering. Calder charged at the flames in the door, keeping his head down, dragging Benton behind him. It was searing hot, he felt his hair ignite, his skin burn and then he was through into the delicious open air.

Cornelius grabbed Benton's other leg and dragged him out. Benton's clothes were on fire. Cornelius ripped off his shirt and smothered the flames. Benton gasped for air.

'Which direction is the airstrip?' panted Calder.

Phyllis pointed towards the bush.

'You stay with Benton,' Calder said to her. 'Cornelius, you go back to the camp and get some help.'

Cornelius nodded and started along the track. Calder set off into the bush after Zan.

30

The ground was rough and bumpy, with stones and holes hidden under the yellow grass. It was possible to make a path through the scattered trees, bushes and termite mounds, but Calder soon realized he wasn't moving in a straight line. He had only gone a few yards, but he could no longer see Benton and Phyllis. He glanced up at the sun and decided he needed to aim just to the right of it. He estimated the airstrip was less than a mile away. Zan ran marathons; it wouldn't take her long.

It was hard running on that terrain, and his chest was soon rasping for breath. He wasn't sure what he would do if he caught up with Zan, but he knew that after what she had done to his sister he couldn't let her get away. He dodged round a thorn bush and caught his sleeve in one of the branches, which pulled him up short. He tugged, but the thorns were barbed and wouldn't let go. He brushed his left hand on one and it scratched him badly.

He stopped and carefully ripped at his shirt, making sure that he kept the rest of his body away from the bush. It took him a full minute, but eventually he broke free, leaving a strip of cloth attached to the thorns.

He checked the sun for his bearings and saw, right in front of him, an elephant watching him. It was only a baby, about five foot high. It turned and moved rapidly away from him towards some trees twenty yards away.

He didn't move.

Behind one of the trees was what looked at first like a

375

huge grey wall. There was an explosive trumpeting sound, and a crashing of leaves and snapping wood as the tree was brushed aside and a massive elephant erupted towards him, ears flapping wide. Don't run, Phyllis had said. Calder planted his feet apart and raised his arms. The elephant kept coming. Calder kept his eyes open and focused on the tusks, which must have been more than six feet long and sharp. The elephant was close, too close, such a heavy beast moving at such a speed couldn't possibly stop in time.

He closed his eyes. Then opened them. Somehow the elephant had halted. It was only ten yards away, a huge tower of grey muscle. Calder's arms were still outstretched. He didn't move. For a moment he looked up and caught the elephant's eyes. Angry, threatening: don't mess with my kid.

He lowered his gaze, fearing that he might antagonize her. The calf had trotted to a safe distance behind its mother, together with three other elephants that had stopped and were watching.

It was difficult, but he stood his ground. The elephant continued to stare at him, ears flapping, for a minute, maybe two. Then she turned and moved halfway back towards the calf.

Calder shifted sideways, always facing the animal. The elephant reached up to some branches with her trunk and snapped them angrily. They were thick branches: her strength was extraordinary.

It took him another minute to move into the cover of the nearest trees, and even then he walked slowly backwards for fifty yards or so, listening to the snap of branches, and the occasional angry trumpet.

Behind him an aircraft engine sputtered into life. It was close. He was now what he judged to be a safe distance away from the elephant, so he turned and ran towards the noise. He broke into the clearing to see one of the Piper Warriors lining up on the runway. A small herd of antelope were scattering in front of it, leaping in all directions to confuse this strange predator. As the aircraft began its take-off roll, Calder sprinted to the small hut near the remaining parked aeroplanes. Sure enough, the door was open, and inside was a metal cupboard, also open. Calder grabbed the two sets of keys and ran over to the Cessna 172. He looked up and saw Zan's plane clearing the trees to the west, towards the mountains.

He climbed up on to the fuselage and quickly checked the tanks for fuel. He could barely see any, but it was notoriously difficult to assess visually how full a Cessna's tanks were. He heard the sound of a vehicle and saw a Land Rover speeding towards him, driven by Darren, the ranger, with a bare-chested Cornelius in the passenger seat. Calder started up the engine. Cornelius jumped out of the Land Rover carrying one of the game reserve's rifles and ran towards the aircraft. Calder opened the passenger door for him and he climbed in.

'Let's go,' he said.

Calder did as many of the take-off checks as he could while taxiing to the threshold of the runway, lined up, and opened the throttle for full power. As the aircraft began its take-off roll, he glanced at the fuel gauges. Half full.

'How's Benton?'

'We got him back to the main lodge. Phyllis is binding up his shoulder, she seems to know her first aid. An ambulance is coming, and the police, but they'll take a while to get here.'

The wheels left the runway and Calder entered a low climb at full power. Zan had about five minutes on them, which in a Warrior equated to about eight miles. But she would not necessarily be flying at maximum speed. He hoped to be able to catch her before she realized he was on her tail.

As they climbed, he and Cornelius scanned the horizon ahead of them. It was hot in the small cockpit and there was a strong smell of Calder's burnt hair, mixed with sweat. He opened up all the vents. The sky was mostly clear, with a few white puffy clouds about 6,000 feet up. Calder had been trained to scan the sky for small dots, but it was Cornelius who spotted Zan, about seven miles ahead and 1,000 feet above them. They were gaining on her. She was climbing; in a few minutes she would reach the Drakensberg escarpment.

'Where's she going?' Cornelius asked.

'I don't know. Maybe she's looking for a quiet airfield somewhere a long way from here where she can land and disappear. Has she much flying experience?'

'Oh, yes,' said Cornelius. 'She's flown all over the country.'

'Let's follow her and see where she lands. Then at least we can tell the police. Here, pass me that.' Calder pointed to a map on the coaming in front of Cornelius. He handed it over.

Calder glanced at it. South Africa was a huge country, covered in small landing strips. She could be going anywhere.

'I'll see if we can get some help,' he said, pressing the mic button on his radio. He had no idea of the local channels: the radio was tuned to 119.0. 'Mayday Mayday Mayday. This is . . .' He glanced at the aircraft registration taped to the instrument panel '. . . Zulu Sierra Romeo Tango Oscar.'

'Mayday, Zulu Sierra Romeo Tango Oscar, Lowveld Information, go ahead.'

'Lowveld Information, I'm a Cessna 172 about fifteen miles west of the Kupugani game reserve. I'm pursuing a

Piper Warrior about five miles ahead of me. The pilot was involved in an attempted murder at Kupugani. The local police have been informed. My intention is to track her and watch where she lands.'

There was a brief silence as the controller digested what must have been a very odd radio call.

'Tango Oscar, squawk two-one-zero-seven for identification. We'll contact the police now.'

Calder twiddled the knob on his transponder to 2107. The transponder would send out a signal that Lowveld Information could monitor to find his position.

'Tango Oscar, we have you identified.'

'Can you see the aircraft in front of me?' Calder asked.

'Negative, we have secondary radar only.' That meant they wouldn't pick up a signal from Zan's aircraft unless her own transponder was switched on, which was highly unlikely.

'Have you contacted the police yet?'

'Tango Oscar, stand by.'

'She's changing direction!' Cornelius was pointing up towards Zan's Warrior. It had indeed altered course about thirty degrees to the north.

'She must have heard our radio transmission,' Calder said. 'She's looking for us.'

While they were directly astern and below Zan, it was impossible for her to see them, and they had been able to catch her on full power setting. Now they were no longer gaining as Zan, too, put on full power.

'Damn. She's heading for that cloud!' They were climbing past 6,000 feet, the level of the white puffs of cloud. Zan's aircraft was heading for the largest of these. Within a minute it had plunged inside. Calder throttled back and stayed beneath the cloud, craning his neck from side to side. No sign of Zan. They passed the length of the cloud, but the Warrior hadn't emerged.

'She must be circling in there,' said Calder.

'There she is!' said Cornelius.

She was now heading south-west, climbing towards a larger cloud bank that was forming just above the Drakensberg escarpment. Calder turned tightly to follow her. Once again she entered the cloud. The mountains were too close below, so Calder climbed to try to get above the layer. A thousand feet higher he set up a wide circle pattern.

He couldn't see her.

She'd got away.

'Tango Oscar, this is Lowveld Information. We've spoken to the police and they have confirmed your story. Do you still have visual with the Warrior?'

'Negative,' said Calder. 'I'm still looking but we lost her in cloud. She was heading south-west on two-three-zero, but God knows where she is now.'

'I'll see if Hoedspruit can help,' said the controller.

'Hoedspruit?'

'It's an air-force base with primary radar. Stand by.'

Thirty seconds' more circling and then the radio crackled into life. 'Tango Oscar, Hoedspruit has identified the other aircraft on their radar. It's heading zero-four-zero about fifteen miles away from you, descending.'

'Zero-four-zero!' said Calder, examining the map. 'That's, towards Zimbabwe.'

'Affirm,' said the controller.

'We're going after her,' Calder said, and turned his aircraft to the north-east. 'Can you scramble a jet or something to intercept her?'

'I'll see what I can do,' said the controller. 'But scrambling fighters is a big deal.'

380

They were once more over the low bush, miles and miles of it stretching forward as far as the horizon. Although they couldn't see Zan's aircraft, the controller gave them bearings. She had descended to 300 feet, which would make her more difficult to spot, but it did slow her down. Calder stayed at 2,000, where the air was that little bit thinner, hence providing less resistance and better fuel consumption. The Cessna and the Piper had broadly similar cruising speeds, but they had a weight disadvantage in the shape of Cornelius, two hundred and something pounds of him.

Calder pulled back on the throttle a little. Maximum power meant maximum fuel usage. They could continue to follow Zan only if they had enough fuel to keep them up in the sky. Of course, Calder had no idea how much Zan had left.

'You know, it's a terrible day when you realize your daughter's a monster,' Cornelius said.

'Don't blame yourself,' Calder said. Cornelius might not have been the perfect father, but he hadn't deserved what his daughter had visited on him.

'She had me completely fooled,' Cornelius said bitterly. 'I thought she loathed apartheid. I never realized she was manipulating me; they were manipulating me. And I thought all these years she was angry with me for not supporting the struggle.'

'She was certainly angry,' Calder said.

'You know, I'm sure the Laagerbond did kill Hennie, despite what she says,' Cornelius said. 'They just didn't tell her they'd done it because they knew she was so fond of him.'

'Too many people have died, one way or another.'

'I'm sorry about your sister, Alex. After all you have done for us.'

'Don't worry,' Calder said through gritted teeth. 'Zan will pay. I'll make sure of that.'

'I think she's lost touch with reality,' Cornelius said. 'The way she was talking back there. The idea that I would go with her.'

'You could have humoured her on that one.'

'I didn't think she was going to try to kill us!'

'She's desperate and she's dangerous,' said Calder. 'At this stage I don't think she cares who she kills.'

They continued northwards, passing over a river, the Olifants according to Calder's map. The landscape beneath them changed, the trees became sparser and their trunks became thicker, squat baobabs. Between them were the black specks of game: elephant, antelope, wildebeest and the odd giraffe, recognizable even from that height.

Then Calder saw a shadow skimming the grass in the distance. Next to it was a white speck.

'Lowveld Information, we have visual contact,' he said.

'Good,' replied the controller. 'She's flying too low; Hoedspruit are losing radar coverage. She'll reach the Zimbabwe border in ten minutes. There is a police helicopter on its way to intercept her, but it won't make it before then.'

'Can you get us clearance to enter Zimbabwean airspace?' Calder asked.

'I can try, but I don't hold out much hope. Stand by.'

Minutes ticked by. The fuel gauges were low. The trouble with any light aircraft's fuel tank is that there is no way of being sure exactly how much fuel is left in it. The gauges are only a rough indicator. The calculation is usually made by considering time flown and hourly rate of fuel consumption. But since Calder had no idea how long the Cessna had been in the air during its flight to Kupugani, that wasn't a calculation he could do with any accuracy. He ran through some figures in his head. Assuming the aircraft was half full when they took off and assuming a high level of fuel consumption at maximum power for the flight so far, they might have a couple of hours' flying time, give or take half an hour. They had been in the air for an hour and forty minutes.

Calder thinned the fuel mixture some more. He did not want the engine to cut out here. He didn't fancy a forced landing into a baobab, especially now the sun was plunging towards the western horizon.

The radio crackled into life. 'Tango Oscar, you have been refused permission to enter Zimbabwean airspace. Estimate the Zimbabwe border in three minutes. What are your intentions?'

Calder glanced at Cornelius. Crossing international boundaries without a flight plan was a major sin as far as air-traffic controllers were concerned, however generally helpful they were. He decided it was best to be vague. 'Lowveld Information, this is Tango Oscar leaving your frequency. Thanks for all your help.' With that he turned the radio off.

They were still at 2,000 feet. Zan remained at 300 and was pulling away. She was very hard to see. Calder checked his map. She was making a direct line for a small airport at a place called Chiredzi. That was where she probably hoped to refuel and stay the night. Calder did not warm to the prospect of chasing her over the African bush in the dark.

Ahead, her plane skimmed across a lake, sending up a swarm of hundreds if not thousands of large white birds, cranes of some kind. Calder and Cornelius lost her. By the time the flock had peeled off to the west her aircraft was too low and too far away to be seen.

Time passed. Two hours. Two hours five minutes. Two hours ten minutes. Any moment Calder expected to hear the cough of the engine cutting out. He kept his eye on the ground looking for clearings where he could make an emergency landing without doing too much damage. The sun was glowing red in the west and the light was going.

Two hours fifteen minutes. On the horizon they spotted smoke, chimney stacks, some kind of large processing plant. Then they made out the shape of a runway in the twilight. Calder had no idea whether Zan was there or not, at this point he just wanted to get on to the ground before his fuel ran out. He decided not to call up the airfield on the radio, in case they refused him permission to land.

Two hours twenty minutes. The fuel gauges of both tanks were on empty. The engine coughed. Calder switched the tank selector to the right and the engine restarted. The left tank was finished. It wouldn't be long before the right failed too.

They were nearing the runway. Ideally he should join the circuit overhead to inspect it first, but he had no time for that, and he lined up the aircraft for a straight-in approach, keeping high. The engine coughed again, sputtered and died.

Everything went very quiet. Below him were fields of sugar cane, not comfortable if he landed short.

He trimmed the aeroplane to its best rate of descent and glided towards the runway. The numbers on the threshold drifted up in the windshield, a sign that he was sinking. He resisted the temptation to raise the nose; that would just cause the aircraft to lose speed and sink even faster.

They weren't going to make the runway, but there was a stretch of brown grass a hundred yards before it. In front of that was the airfield perimeter and the sugar-cane field.

'There she is,' said Cornelius. Calder could just see the Warrior on a taxiway a few yards from the runway, but he was focusing on getting the aircraft down in one piece.

They skimmed over the perimeter fence and he flared the aeroplane for a bumpy landing on rough grass. At least they were down. They rolled to a halt on the runway threshold.

Silence from the aircraft, but they could hear excited chattering thirty yards to their left. Zan was standing by her aircraft in front of a group of three angry Africans, shadowy figures in the gathering darkness. She was screaming at them and waving her rifle. A uniformed policeman was marching towards her from the control tower, shouting. He seemed to be unarmed.

Zan turned towards their Cessna and raised her rifle. Calder and Cornelius ducked. There was a crack followed by the explosion of the windshield shattering.

'Jesus!' muttered Cornelius. He reached behind him for the rifle which was lying on the back seat.

They raised their heads gingerly over the coaming. The policeman had stopped, but he was still shouting at Zan. The other Africans, one in shirtsleeves and two in overalls, were backing off.

Zan screamed something at the policeman and raised the rifle to her shoulder, pointing it directly at him. He shut up.

She pressed the trigger. The round sent the policeman flying backwards.

'Here!' said Cornelius, handing the rifle to Calder. 'You've got to stop her. I can't.'

Calder hesitated. He had never killed anyone before, let alone a woman.

'Quick, man, before she shoots someone else!' Cornelius's eyes were full of pain – pain and desperation.

Calder took the rifle, unlatched the aircraft door and pushed it open. On the taxiway the Africans were running away. Zan lifted the rifle to her shoulder again, aiming at their backs.

Calder chambered a round, flicked off the safety, threw himself on to the tarmac and rolled once. He stared down the sight of the rifle and moved it downwards and to the right, so that it covered Zan's upper body. She had seen the movement from the aeroplane and was swinging her own weapon round towards him.

He pressed the trigger. A gaping hole appeared in Zan's chest as she staggered backwards, an expression of total surprise on her face.

By the time Calder and Cornelius had run over to her felled body, she was dead.

31

Calder looked down on the familiar countryside to the west of Heathrow, landscape he had flown over many times at weekends when he was still working in the City. He recognized the airfields of White Waltham and Blackbushe and the scattering of wealthy towns and villages hugging the Thames. It was seven hours to New York. He had no idea what would happen in the next few days, but he was optimistic.

He had received a short, simple e-mail from Sandy.

Got three days off next week. Can you come? We can talk when you get here.

Sandy

PS – Tell Kim van Zyl I'm sorry I was so hard on her. She's a good friend of yours and I admire her courage for talking to me.

PPS – I promise I'll be here when you arrive!

PPPS – Please come.

He had spoken to Kim, who admitted to her attempt to see Sandy on his behalf. She urged him to go, and he was surprised how much he wanted to. There were all kinds of difficulties and problems with the relationship, past and future, but at that moment he realized it was only the present he was interested in. So he had booked the flight.

Kim and Todd had flown back to the US a couple of

days before. Todd was still improving and was planning to return to his teaching job for the new school year, although the doctors thought that might be a little optimistic. Kim had told Calder she was pregnant. She was overjoyed, and to Calder's immense relief, she was sure the baby was her husband's, not his.

Anne was due to leave hospital soon. She would be in a wheelchair at first, but she would be fitted up with a prosthetic leg in time. Against William's strongly expressed wishes, Calder had visited her. She had been polite initially, asking what happened in South Africa in a dispassionate voice, but Calder could see she was hiding her anger with him. Then a tear had emerged in one eye and she had turned away from him. He tried to talk to her but she wouldn't reply. He couldn't blame her, but he could blame himself. He thought bleakly of her struggling to raise her children from a wheelchair, hobbling after them on a false leg in the school playground. His relationship with his sister had been perhaps the most stable thing in his life since his mother had died. As so often before he had put himself in danger, but this time it was she who had got hurt.

His father was much more supportive, congratulating Calder on finding who had crippled his daughter. He didn't actually say it, but he was clearly glad that Calder had shot Zan, and that Moolman was dead.

Calder felt no such warm glow of revenge. He knew he had had no choice but to shoot Zan, otherwise yet another innocent man would have died. He also knew she was an evil woman. But he recognized that she was a product of a screwed-up family in a screwed-up country. It would take many years for the wounds of apartheid to heal; brutality like that couldn't just be buried and forgotten, as Cornelius had discovered.

It was fortunate Cornelius had been with him. The Zimbabweans were not sympathetic to strange white men arriving in their country and shooting people, but Zyl News, and in particular Cornelius's wife Jessica, had swiftly brought the full force of his network of contacts and influence to bear on the Zimbabwean government. In the end, they had spent only two days in custody, although two days in a Zimbabwean jail was more than enough for Calder.

The revelation of the Laagerbond's connections with Sir Evelyn Gill had led to the collapse of his bid for *The Times*. Cornelius's own bid had expired and he decided not to renew it, much to the relief of the Bloomfield Weiss Underwriting Committee. It looked highly likely that one of the original bidders, the Irish entrepreneur, would buy the newspaper at the lower price of eight hundred and twenty million pounds. Laxton Media jumped at it; their need for cash was becoming desperate.

Benton's arm was still in a sling, the bullet from Zan's rifle had torn a nasty hole in his shoulder which was taking a while to heal. Tarek had told Calder that it was common knowledge within Bloomfield Weiss that Simon Bibby had his own sights firmly trained on Benton. The smart money was on head of Global Diversity or possibly head of the Moscow office, if Benton survived in the firm at all. Much to his surprise, Calder found himself hoping that he would.

Cornelius had fired Edwin and announced that an up-and-coming American executive from the Philadelphia office would take over from him as CEO of Zyl News in six months. In the meantime he had already visited Cape Town to talk to George Field about funding the *Rainbow*. Just a minority stake, no editorial influence. At least that's what he said his intention was.

The details of the Laagerbond in Martha's diary were

passed to the authorities in South Africa and Britain. The big breakthrough was that Dirk du Toit and Daniel Havenga promised to cooperate. According to du Toit's records the Laagerbond had investments valued at four billion dollars around the world, although a significant chunk of it comprised its stake in Evelyn Gill's collapsing Beckwith Communications. Andries Visser was in hospital undergoing intensive chemotherapy. The doctors thought it unlikely that he would live to face his trial.

The plane flew into cloud and Calder returned to the newspaper on his lap. He finished an article about more oil supplies coming on stream in Russia, which would help the spread bet he had hastily taken before he left England on a fall in oil prices. That was a relief; he had probably put too much on that one. Since he had returned from South Africa he had made a number of large financial spread bets, with mixed success. It distracted him from Kim and Anne and Zan, gave him something else to focus on.

He shoved the paper into the pocket on the seat in front of him, and reached into his hand luggage for a folder containing a sheaf of A4. Martha's original diary was in the South African authorities' possession to be used as evidence, but Cornelius had given him a photocopy. Her handwriting was flowing, assured, easily legible. He began to read.

It was an odd feeling. He had spent so much time thinking about her, trying to decipher her actions and motivations over a distance of eighteen years, it was strange to read her words, immediate, in the present tense. He liked her, he realized. She had not deserved to be forgotten by her family. He was glad that he had played a part in throwing some light on her death.

The aeroplane was well to the west of the coast of Ireland when he turned to the last entry.

We're here at Kupugani and it's a fantastic place. Libby's friend Phyllis was really friendly, not at all freaked out by Benton, and she's put us in a cottage a ways away from the main camp. Yesterday evening we were sitting out on our porch and we saw a leopard walk along the stream bed right by us as cool as you please. And last night we were woken by the lions grunting and groaning. We didn't make it up early enough this morning for the game drive. In fact, the way we are going we'll be lucky if we ever leave this cottage at all!

Benton's in the shower now. I can see him as I write this. He's heavenly. It's wonderful to be with him. But time goes so fast! We only have twenty-four more hours together and then we go our separate ways.

It's good to be able to write this in front of him, without being worried about what he reads. It's good to be able to trust someone at last. I haven't spoken to him yet about Zan and the Laagerbond. I didn't want to spoil our time together, but I'm going to have to.

I'm trying not to think about that. Because when I do I'm really scared. Zan might have gone to London, but she's left her nasty friends behind. She knows she can't trust me to keep quiet, so what's she going to do? What are her friends going to do? Arresting me would be very messy: I'm an American citizen and Cornelius's wife. But they could just kill me.

If they're going to kill me, they'll do it soon. They might not know where I am here, but once I get back to Hondehoek I'll be an easy target.

If I died, what about the children? Who'd look after Caroline? Todd doesn't need much looking after these days, but he'd miss me. I can't stand the thought of not seeing him grow up to be a man. My mother's a strong woman, but it will kill my father.

If my life ends now, what will I have achieved? I've always felt American, but my life, certainly my adult life, has been all about South Africa. A country I hate and I guess I love at the same time. About South Africa and about Cornelius.

Cornelius. He's the man who has dominated my life. Until this past year I've loved him, respected him, admired him, believed in him. But if it all ended now . . .

He's as scared as I am. And we've both done the same thing. He's run off to his beautiful blonde woman, me to my beautiful black man. But what is Benton? Oh, he's more than just a good body. I like him, he's intelligent, I like the way he's so well read, but in ten years' time, when I'm fifty-four, I can't really kid myself that we will still be together.

He's shaving now. He just smiled at me. Oh, God, I hope he never reads this. So much for being able to write in front of him.

There's only one thing for me to do, I have to go see Cornelius. Grab Caroline and get on a plane to America before those evil bastards get me. Go to Philadelphia and talk to him about everything. If South Africa goes up in flames, if his business goes bust, we still have each other and Todd and Caroline. After all we've been through together, it would be wrong to die apart. So wrong.

Yes. That's what I'll do. I've made up my mind. But I'm going to have to tell Benton. He's already noticed something's up, he just asked me what the matter is. I lied – I told him I was fine. It will ruin everything, but I must tell him my decision today, this aftern

*

392

The handwriting finished halfway down the page. But in the bottom right-hand quarter, Calder could make out an arc of tiny black splashes on his photocopy. Blood. Martha van Zyl's final signature.

Author's Note

When writing about businessmen it is always difficult to stay on the right side of the line between fiction and fact and still maintain a feel of authenticity. This is especially true in the world of international newspapers. Although Cornelius van Zyl shares the characteristics of a number of media magnates, he does not represent any one of them. Nor do any other characters in the book represent real people. The companies too are fictitious. The Broederbond was real, as was Muldergate. What the white South African government did with the millions it funnelled through its defence special accounts during the 1980s remains a mystery

I have drawn on the help and advice of a number of people: the South African thriller writer Deon Meyer, Alice Harrison and her family, Isobel Dixon and her family, Jonathan Braack and Darren Green at Ngala game reserve, Troy Reiser of Federal Aviation in Johannesburg, Allan and Stephanie Walker, Mark Aitken, Susan Griggs, Lynn Gluckman, Neil Klein, Adam Buchan, my agent Carole Blake and my editor Beverley Cousins. I would like to thank them all. Where there are mistakes, they are mine.

CIRCULATING STOCK ▮▮▮▮ PUBLIC LIBRARIES

BLOCK LOAN

MOBILE NORTH
MOBILE SOUTH